IAIN BANKS

'Brilliant' *Daily Telegraph*

'A mighty imagination' *Mail on Sunday*

'Outstanding' *Financial Times*

'Masterful' *New Musical Express*

'Best British writer of his generation' *Vector*

'Serious but playful' *City Limits*

'The great white hope of contemporary British literature'
Fay Weldon

'Stunning verbal display' *London Review of Books*

'Curdling power and imagination' *Cosmopolitan*

'Great artistry, great virtuosity, great exuberance'
New Statesman

'Amazing' *Punch*

'Brilliantly effective' *Books and Bookmen*

Also by Iain Banks and published in Futura

THE WASP FACTORY
WALKING ON GLASS
CONSIDER PHLEBAS

ESPEDAIR STREET

IAIN BANKS

Futura

A *Futura* Book

ISBN 0 7088 3997 5

Reproduced, printed and bound in Great Britain by
Hazell Watson & Viney Limited
Member of BPCC plc
Aylesbury, Bucks, England

Futura Publications
A Division of
Macdonald & Co (Publishers) Ltd
Greater London House
Hampstead Road
London NW1 7QX
A member of Maxwell Pergamon Publishing Corporation plc

For Les,
and all the People's
Republic of Glenfinnan

ONE

Two days ago I decided to kill myself. I would walk and hitch and sail away from this dark city to the bright spaces of the wet west coast, and there throw myself into the tall, glittering seas beyond Iona (with its cargo of mouldering kings) to let the gulls and seals and tides have their way with my remains, and in my dying moments look forward to an encounter with Staffa's six-sided columns and Fingal's cave; or I might head south to Corry-vrecken, to be spun inside the whirlpool and listen with my waterlogged deaf ears to its mile-wide voice ringing over the wave-race; or be borne north, to where the white sands sing and coral hides, pink-fingered and hard-soft, beneath the ocean swell, and the rampart cliffs climb thousand-foot above the seething acres of milky foam, rainbow-buttressed.

Last night I changed my mind and decided to stay alive. Everything that follows is . . . just to try and explain.

Memories first. It all begins with memories, the way most things do. First: making a cloud.

Inez and I made a cloud once. Seriously; a cloud, a real honest-to-goodness cloud up in the big blue sky. I was happy then, and doing something like creating a cloud just filled me with delight and awe and a delicious, frightening feeling of power and tininess together; after it happened I laughed and hugged Inez and we danced in the cinders and kicked up the black smoking debris which scorched our ankles while we jigged and swirled, choking, eyes watering, laughing and pointing at the vast thing we'd made,

1

as it gradually drifted away from us.

The sooty lengths of straw smudged our jeans and shirts and faces; we made each other up as commandos, painting dry streaks on the other's brows and cheeks and nose. The smell clung to our hair and stayed under our nails and up our noses after we changed and only washed quickly, did not shower, and at dinner with her parents we kept glancing and remembering and grinning at each other, and when as usual I crept along to her room that night – just as usually feeling foolish; *if my fans could see me now; tiptoeing like some scared kid* – the smoke smell was in her hair and on her pillow and the taste of it on her skin.

Now, making a cloud would doubtless depress me. Something to block the sun, cast a pall, rain soot, rain rain, and cast a shadow . . .

That was . . . long ago. We'd just finished working on *Night Shines Darkly*, or maybe it was *Gauche*; I can't remember. Inez always kept a diary and I used to ask her things about the past sometimes, but I grew too used to that, and now . . . now I'm sort of lost without her to tell me what happened when. Maybe it was '76. Whenever. I was there that summer. End of summer . . . September? Is that when they harvest? I'm a city boy so I'm not sure; a country lad would know.

Her parents were farmers, in Hampshire; Winchester was the nearest big town. I only remember that because I kept humming 'Winchester Cathedral' all the time, which was pretty ancient even then, and annoyed me almost as much as it annoyed Inez. The harvest had just been gathered and the fields shorn and the stubble lay about in long raggedy lines (*Blonde on Blonde*, I remember thinking), and crows flew about, twirling and dipping and bouncing when they landed, and strutting and jabbing at the hard dry ground. Inez' dad usually burned off the stubble by dragging a petrol-soaked rag behind his tractor, but Inez asked if she and I could do it that day, on the top field, because the wind was right and anyway it wasn't near a road.

So we walked sweating through the fields on a beautiful bright day; the fields were either crew-cut, still waiting to be set alight, or burned black-flat, so that from above the whole countryside must have looked like some haphazard, anarchic chessboard. We sweated up the hill with rags and jerrican, past a rusty old half-fallen building, all corrugated decrepitude, through a copse of tall trees (for the shade) and then to the field, where the passing shadows of small clouds moved slowly.

And we set fire to the stubble. Soaked the rags with gasoline and then dragged them on lengths of rope and chain down two sides of the huge square field, until the fire had caught in a pair of long crackling lines, and the bright orange flames surged through the dry straw, rolling yellow-red inside the dark grey bank of smoke while we stood, breathless, wiping sweat from our brows, kicking dust-dry clods of earth over the guttering flames of the rags we'd towed.

The blaze moved over the field, leaping down the rows of desiccated stalks and flinging them burned or burning to the sky; flames flicked curling against the wall of grey smoke like broad whips, leaving the scorched ground smoking greyly, tiny clumps still burning, miniature whirlwinds dancing madly while the wall of fire crackled and flowed and leapt beyond. Smoke flooded the sky, brown against the blue; it made a shining copper coin of the sun. I remember shouting, running down the side of the field, to keep pace, to see, to be part of it. Inez followed, striding down that smoky margin, arms crossed, face gleaming, watching me.

The piled stubble burned quickly, and the fierceness of the blaze made me squint; the heat of the flames hurt my eyes, and the smoke when it swirled, backing up momentarily, filled my nose and mouth and made me cough. Rabbits ran away from the wave of fire, white tails bobbing into the wood; fieldmice scampered for ditches, and the crows circled away and swooped for the tree tops, croaking distantly over the sizzling voice of the fire.

When the flames began to die, reaching the barren edges of the field, Inez looked up, and there was our cloud; a thunderhead of white crowned the vast fist of grey-brown smoke we'd sent up. It towered over us, slowly drifting away with the rest of the puffy white clouds, its white-capped head plain and perfect above the lumpy stalk of swirling brown smoke. I was amazed; I just stood and stared, mouth open.

I thought even then it looked like a mushroom; it was an apt description, and as the cloud and the last of the smoke drifted off, casting its shadow over a village in the next valley, you couldn't help but make the obvious comparisons . . . but it was *beautiful*; and it hadn't hurt anybody, it was part of the way country life was run, part of the seasons' cycle, glorious and sublime.

Normally, I'm sure I'd have thought there must be some way of *using* the experience; there had to be an idea, a song in there somewhere . . . but I didn't, maybe because we'd just finished the album and I was sick of songs, especially my own, and this whole rustic thing was supposed to be a complete holiday from work. Can't fool the old subconscious, though; if it sees a fast buck to be made out of something that's happened, it'll use it, whether you like it or not, and – much later – I realised that that was just what had happened.

One of the ideas for the 1980 world tour came from that sight, that day, I'm sure. We called it the Great Contra-flow Smoke Curtain. It cost a fortune to get right and ages to set up, and it was only because I was so insistent that we persevered with it; nobody else thought it was worth the trouble. Big Sam, our manager (and, for a manager, remarkably close to being human), couldn't see past the columns of figures, never mind the columns of smoke; total apoplexy; just couldn't understand my reasoning, but there was nothing he could do except shout, and I have a gift for listening quietly regardless of the incoming decibels. Listening quietly, but not at the right time.

Story of my life, or a sub-plot at least. Either I know I ought to do something but I just don't get round to it, or I keep hammering away furiously at something I end up profoundly regretting later. The Great Contra-flow Smoke Curtain was an instance of the latter. We got the damn thing to work eventually, but I wish we hadn't. I wish I'd listened, and I'll blame myself to the end of my days for being so determined to impose my own will on the others. I didn't know what was going to happen, I couldn't have guessed the eventual, awful, result of my expensive pig-headedness, and nobody ever said they held me responsible, but . . . The point here is, however, that the cloud Inez and I made *was* used; money was made out of it. Exploitation will out. It has its own survival instinct.

Now that's something Big Sam *would* have understood.

There you are, though; story of a day in the country. If anything like that happened now, the comparison, the accidental

4

creation of the image of our deathcap threat, would upset me, plunge me into some crushed state of absolute dejection, reflecting that no matter what I did, regardless of my actions and whatever good intent lay behind them, emblems of chaos and destruction dogged me; my personal shades.

But not then. It was different then. Everything was different then. I was happy.

And, God almighty, it all seemed so easy; the living, the playing, the songs:

Why do you bite me on the shoulder,
Why do you scratch me on my back?
Why do you always have to make love
Like you're making an attack?

Liza-bet, do you love me?
I asked her one fine morning
Yes indeed I do said she
And loved me without warning

I am old, my thoughts get blown like ash
By the winds of grief and pain,
Young minds only do not fear such blasts,
Which but serve to fan the flame.

Three of the better examples there. Bits I'm almost proud of. I could have chosen . . . but no, I'm too embarrassed. I still have some pride left.

And now there's a new song, anyway. Something else to work on, after so long. I need a few new words, but the beat and the music are already there, a framework; a skeleton.

A new song. Is this a good sign or a bad one? Wish I knew. Never mind the consequences, just get on with the work. Try not to think about the past twenty-four hours or the last week, because they've been too fraught and traumatic and ridiculous; pay attention to the song, instead, play to your strengths, such as they are.

I thought this must be the end . . . Well, it's not.

Jeez, what a day. From the brink of likely death to genuine financial suicide; not to mention an insane and doubtless doomed new scheme, a last crazy chance to grasp whatever the hell it is I really want; happiness maybe, absolution certainly.

I'd love to put everything into the one song, to sing a song of birds and dogs and mermaids, hammerheaded friends and bad news from far away (again, like confirmation, like a lesson, like vengeance), a song of supermarket trolleys and seaplanes, falling leaves and power stations, fatal connections and live performances, fans that spin and fans that crush . . . but I know too well I can't. Stick to the one song, verse and chorus, sing the music, tap the beat, fit the words in . . . and call it 'Espedair Street'.

That's what it's called. I know what the ending of the song is but I don't know how this ends. I know (I think) what the song means . . . but I still don't know what this means. Maybe nothing. Maybe neither is meant to mean anything; this is always a possibility. Nothing always is.

Three-twenty in the morning according to the watch I bought this afternoon. My eyes are sore and gritty-feeling. The city sleeps on. Maybe I should make more coffee. Funny how quiet Glasgow gets at this time in the morning. I can hear, quite distinctly, the engine of a truck on the motorway, its engine echoing in the concrete trench, then fading under the bridges and tunnels, finally sounding distant and small as it reaches the Kingston Bridge and arcs over the Clyde, heading south and west.

Three twenty-one, if the watch is right. That means two and a half hours to wait. Can I bear that? I suppose I have to. I've borne the waiting so far. Two and a half hours . . . five minutes to get ready, then . . . how long to the station? Can't be more than fifteen minutes. Total of twenty minutes. Call it half an hour. That leaves only two hours to wait. Or I could leave even earlier and spend more time in the station. Might be a café open, or a hamburger van in George Square (though I'm still too nervous to be hungry). I could just go for a walk, waste time wandering through the cold streets kicking at the litter, but I don't feel like that. I want to sit here in my preposterous stone tower looking over the city, thinking about the past twelve years and the last week and the day just gone, then I want to get up and go and maybe never come back. Three twenty-two and a bit. Doesn't time go quickly when you're having fun?

Where is that train now? Two and a half hours away; or less . . . yes, less. Two hours and a bit; Carlisle? A bit further south maybe; still in England definitely. Perhaps hauling itself up to Shap Summit, through the thin drifts of starlit snow, hauling its load of rocking, sleeping passengers northwards. If it comes that way; I didn't ask about that when I went to the station. Maybe it comes up the east coast route, stopping at Edinburgh before heading west. Damn, I should have checked; it seems very important to know now. I need something to keep me occupied.

Three twenty-three! Is that all? Doesn't time – no, I've already said that, thought that. I sit and watch the seconds change on the watch. I used to have a limited edition Rolex worth the price of a new car but I lost it. It was a present from . . . Christine? No, Inez. She got fed up with me always having to ask other people what the time was; embarrassed on my behalf.

I grew up – I ended *grown*-up lacking so many of the standard props; a watch, a wallet, a diary, a driving licence, a chequebook . . . and not just the props, not just the hardware, but the brain-implanted software to make use of them, so that even when I did end up with all that gear I never really felt it was part of me. Even after Inez bought me the Rolex I'd wander up to roadies and ask them how long we had to the start of the gig. The record company gave me a Gucci wallet, but I'd still stuff pounds and fivers into various pockets – I'd even cram them into the pocket where I'd put my wallet, absently wondering why it was so difficult to squeeze the crumpled bits of paper in there.

Hopeless. Just a hopeless case; always have been.

Inez kept a diary for me because I never could; I always started faithfully every second of January (I think Scots require some sort of special dispensation to admit to doing anything organised on the *first* of January), but by the second week I always found that – somehow, quite unaccountably – I'd already missed out several days. Those blank spaces, accusatory, filled me with a nervous dread; my memory instantly locked up; I could never remember what had happened during the missing days, and felt too ashamed to ask anybody else. The easiest thing was to throw the embarrassing diary away. I still don't have a driving licence, and I kept losing chequebooks . . . nowadays I stick to cash and plastic money which, if you're sufficiently well off, is wonderful.

7

Always hated telephones, too. Don't have one in the house (not that you'd call *this* a house, but never mind). If I had a phone I could call up Queen Street station, to find out what route the train takes, and where it is now. But I don't have a telephone and I can't be bothered looking for an undamaged public phonebox. No television either. I am screenless. They have that Ceefax or Prestel or whatever they call it, these days. I might be able to find out from that where the sleeper train from Euston is now.

Oh, God, what am I doing? Do I know what I'm doing? I don't think I do. I don't think I'd be asking myself this now if I did know what I'm doing. Not that this confusion is my fault, really it isn't; just a troubadour with a very limited attention span; a technician in the machine where the industry standard is the three or four minute single (*single*, you'll notice; as in *track*, as in *mind*. Of course, if you'd prefer a three record set concept album . . .). Hell, I never claimed to be an intellectual, I never even thought I was clever. Not for long, anyway. I just knew what I was good at and how good I was compared to everybody else, and that I was going to *make it*. Oh, the ambition was there, but it was a helpless, stupid sort of ambition; blinkered.

Talent. That's what I had, all I had; some talent . . . And even a small amount of talent can go an appallingly long way, these days. I'd love to claim there was more to it, but I can't. Being honest with myself, I know I was never . . . driven enough to be more than just talented and lucky. I didn't *have* to do what I did, I just wanted to, a lot. If they'd said I couldn't ever write a note of music or a word of lyric for the rest of my life, but there was a secure job waiting for me in computing, or (to be more realistic) a distillery, then I wouldn't have minded that much. And everything would have been a hell of a lot simpler.

So I tell myself, now.

Three twenty-five and a quarter. Dear God, it's slowing down. Check out the surroundings. A mostly clear sky; sharp little stars and a sliver of moon.

Silence in the city and no one to talk to.

A car drones down St Vincent Street, stops at the Newton Street traffic lights, idling in the mixture of darkness and yellow sodium-vapour light. Its exhaust curls, the left indicator winks. The trough of the buried motorway, cut through the city like a

8

deep scar, lies beyond, on the far side of the lights, beneath the St Vincent Street flyover. No traffic on the motorway. Little green men become little red men; the main lights change, the car moves off, quiet and alone.

Wish I could drive. I always meant to learn but – like a lot of things in my life – I never got round to it, and went too quickly from not being able to afford a car at all to having a chauffeuse for my Panther de Ville, and seriously thinking about going straight from pedestrianism to learning how to fly (a helicopter). Well, I never got around to that either.

Crazy Davey; he did all that. He had the fast cars and big bikes and the planes, and the mansion. And he *was* crazy.

I may be stupid but I'm not – I never was – crazy.

I left that to Balfour. Our Davey *collected* dangerously insane things to do. Like the Three Chimneys tour; a case in point. Mad bastard nearly killed me, and not for the first time. That was one of his more dramatic escapades. Made what eventually happened even more ironic. And hard to bear.

But then a lot of it seems hard to bear, at the time. You get good at it, though, with sufficient practice and the right attitude.

And Christine, shall I probe that wound? *Angel*, I thought when I first saw you, heard you. That mouth, those lips, the voice of silk and gold; I lost you too, I threw you away, turned my back and condemned you, worshipper from the first, Judas to the last.

I always knew it would amount to nothing. Somehow I expected that. Right from the start I accepted I was a misfit and I'd never really be comfortable anywhere, with anyone. I just decided that if that was the case then I might as well try to be as successful a misfit as possible, make as big a noise about it as I could; give the bastards a run for their money. I suppose every society has its escape routes, ways the not-normal can be themselves without hurting those around them, and (more importantly) without harming the fabric of that society. I was lucky that the time I was born into actually heaped riches on misfits who could more or less behave themselves . . . providing they had something to offer in return, of course.

Ah, Jesus . . . Davey, Christine, Inez, Jean . . . all of you; what did you see when you looked at me? Did I look as stupid and awkward to you as I looked to myself? Worse, maybe. Deep down I never did give a damn what other people thought of me, but somehow I still worried like hell about it. I never expected to be loved, but I never wanted to hurt anybody either and that meant trying to be nice and generous and kind and supportive and generally behaving as though I was desperate to be loved, and for myself, not for my work.

Here I am, one of the few people awake in Glasgow, sitting in Mr Wykes' absurd, blasphemous tower, looking out over a churchyard that is not a churchyard, full of gravestones that are not gravestones, staring at the sky and the ever-changing traffic lights that tick and change and cycle through their simple programme regardless of an audience or cars or anything else short of a power failure, and I'm waiting for a certain train and thinking about – very possibly – doing something really stupid.

Anna Karenina?

No. Though I may well go west.

My hands are shaking. I'd kill for a cigarette. Not a person, of course; I wouldn't kill a human for a cigarette. I'd kill . . . a minor plant maybe, or a flatworm perhaps; nothing with a proper central nervous system . . . no, come to think of it, I'd kill a woodlouse for a cigarette (not that many woodlice carry fags), but that's only because I hate the horrible little crawling bastards. Inez said that she always used to stamp on them too, but then one day she started to think of them as baby armadillos and found she could suffer them to live.

Baby armadillos; good grief.

Gave up smoking years ago but I'd love a fag now; maybe I should go out; find an all night petrol station and buy a packet of straights.

No; this is just nervousness. I suffer terrible guilt pangs after smoking. Better not to. God, I'd like a drink, though. That's a lot more tricky. Drink. Drink drink drink. Trying to keep my mind off it, trying to keep my hands off it. I have the continual temptation of knowing there are several dozen large wooden crates stacked on the ground floor here and crammed with drink; red and blue label Stolichnaya, Polish vodka, Hungarian brandy, white and red Georgian sparkling wine (méthode champenoise), real Budweiser and East German schnapps. Cases of the stuff; gallons and gallons of commie booze; sufficient alcohol to provide a lethal dose for every stockbroker, judge and priest in Glasgow; a small swimming pool's worth of genuine Red Death. The ground floor of Mr Wykes' Folly – my home – also holds a Yugoslavian dumper truck, a Russian tractor and a Czechoslovak bulldozer, not to mention a quantity of other Eastern Bloc products sufficient to fill a small and probably rather unexciting department store.

There is a perfectly logical reason for me having all this.

. . . More words for the song. I scribble them down on the back of another man's card, like a thank you for information received. Just please let that news be true, let it not be false or wrong or incomplete. Let it be right if the song is right, and I'll try my hardest, honest.

Scribble scribble. There.

Another time-check. Three-thirty; thank goodness. An hour and fifty minutes left. Time to think clearly, time to review, reconsider.

Let's try and get all this into some sort of perspective; let's put it in context, shall we? Order it.

My name is WEIRD, my name is Dan or Danny or Daniel, my name is Frank X, Gerald Hlasgow, James Hay. I am thirty-one years old and old before my time and still just a daft wee boay; I am a brilliant failure and a dull success, I could buy a nearly-new Boeing 747 *for cash* if I wanted to but I don't own an intact pair of socks. I've made a lot of mistakes that paid off and a lot of smart moves that I'll regret forever. My friends all seem to be dead, fed up with me or just disgusted and on the whole I can't blame them; I'm an unholy innocent and wholly guilty.

So come on down, roll up, come along, come in, sit down and shut up, calm down and listen up . . . join me now (hey gang, let's do the show right here!) . . . join me now as we journey into the past down the teeming thoroughfare that is . . . (you guessed)

TWO

Frozen Gold: I hated that name right from the start, but I was so damn sure of myself I was perfectly confident I'd persuade them to change it.

Wrong.

A wet Tuesday in November, in Paisley, in 1973. I was seventeen; I'd left school a year earlier and started work at Dinwoodie and Sons, a light engineering works carrying out component work for the big Chrysler car plant at Linwood (the Chrysler factory had been a Rootes factory, would later become a Talbot factory, and finally end up a Closed factory; a car plant that withered).

I spent most of my time collecting swarf from around the lathes, making up songs in my head and going to the toilet. In the toilet I smoked, read the papers and wanked. I was bursting with youth then; seething with semen and pus and ideas; bursting spots, pulling myself off, scribbling down tunes and words and bad poetry, trying every form of dandruff control known to Man save cutting all my hair off, and wondering what it was like to get laid.

And feeling guilty. Never forget the feeling guilty; the constant bass line to my life. It was one of the first things I was ever aware of (I don't know what I'd done; peed on the carpet, thrown up over my da, hit one of my sisters, sworn . . . doesn't matter. The crime, the misdeed, is the least important part of it; what counts is the guilt). 'You bad, *bad* boy!' 'You *wicked* child!' '*Ye wee bugger ye!*' (*skelp*) . . . Jesus, I took it all in, it was my most formative experience; it was part of the fabric of reality; it was the most natural thing in the world, the principal example of cause and effect; you did something, you felt guilty. Simple as that. To live was to feel, 'Oh, God! What have I *done*?' . . .

Guilt. The big G, the Catholic faith's greatest gift to human-kind and its subspecies, psychiatrists . . . well, I guess that's putting it a little too harshly; I've met a lot of Jews and they seem to have just as hard a time of it as we do, and they've been around longer, so maybe it wasn't the Church's invention . . . but I maintain it *developed* the concept more fully than anybody else; it was the Japan of guilt, taking somebody else's crude, unsophisticated, unreliable product and mass-producing it, refining it, fine-tuning it, optimising its performance and giving it a life-time guarantee.

Some people get away from it; they honestly seem to just shuck guilt off like a backpack as soon as they leave home; I couldn't. I took it all too seriously, from the start. I believed. I knew they were right; my ma, the priest, my teachers; I *was* a sinner, I was dirty and soiled and horrible and it was going to be a full time job saving me from the fires and the torment; real professional work was going to be needed to rescue me from the eternal damnation I felt forced to agree I so thoroughly deserved.

Original sin was a revelation to me, once I understood it properly. At last, I realised, it wasn't necessary to have actually done something to feel guilty; this dreadful, constant, nagging sensation of wracked responsibility could be accounted for just by being *alive*. There was a logical explanation! Hot damn. It was a relief, I can tell you.

So I felt guilty, even after I'd left school, even after I'd stopped going to church (oh, Jesus, *especially* just after stopping going to church), and even after I'd left home and started sharing a flat with three atheist prod students. I felt guilty about having left school and not going to university or college, guilty about not going to church, guilty about leaving home and leaving my ma to cope with the others alone, guilty about smoking, guilty about wanking, guilty about skidging off to the bog all the time and reading my newspaper. I felt guilty about not believing in guilt any more.

That Tuesday evening I'd called in to see my ma and whatever brothers and sisters happened to be in the house. Our flat was on

13

Tennant Road, in the Paisley suburb of Ferguslie Park, the roughest area in Paisley at the time, a wasteland of bad architecture and 'problem' families. It was a toss-up which were the most broken; the families or the houses.

Ferguslie Park lay in a triangle of land formed by three railway lines, so no matter what direction you approached it from, it was always on the wrong side of the tracks. The streets were full of glass and the ground-floor windows were full of hardboard panelling. The only thing holding up the walls was the graffiti.

Spray paint was something of a status symbol amongst the local gangs then, like owning a Parker pen; a sign you'd *arrived* as a menace to society and could afford to devote some of your valuable time to the theory and practice of artistic despoliation as well as the more strategically effective but less aesthetically satisfying forms such as smashing holes in walls, wrecking cars, and carrying out al fresco, enthusiastic, but usually non-improving amateur plastic surgery on the faces and bodies of rival gang members.

The closes in the squat, ugly, buildings silted up overnight with empty bottles of fortified wine and drained cans of strong lager; it was as though people put out wine bottles instead of milk bottles, waiting for a morning delivery that never came.

I didn't stay long at my ma's; the place depressed me. That made me feel guilty too, because I felt I ought to love her so much it would outweigh the bad memories the place held for me. Our flat always smelled of cheap cooking; that's the only way I can describe it. It was the smell of old chip fat, reheated cans of cheap Irish Stew, too many cans of baked beans and burned slices of white sliced bread, and the greasily solidified remains of fish suppers, take-away Chinese meals and curries; all overlaid by the smell of cigarette smoke. At least my youngest brothers and sisters were past the age of regular vomiting.

My ma, as usual, started trying to persuade me to go to church; at least to go to confession. I wanted to talk about how she was, how the kids were, whether she'd heard anything from da . . . anything but the one thing she wanted to talk about. So we didn't talk together; we talked apart.

It washed over me, I felt guilty and inadequate and hopeless and nervously out of place. I just sat nodding or shrugging or very occasionally shaking my head, and concentrated on trying to put one of wee Andrew's toy cars back together for him (he was crying). It was cold in the flat, and damp, but I was sweating. My ma was smoking her usual number of fags and I had always promised not to smoke so I couldn't take out my own packet. I sat there, scanting for a cigarette and trying clumsily to mend my wee brother's toy car and wanting to get away . . .

I got away. Left a fiver on the ledge beside the little container of holy water by the front door, and got out, but not without promising that I'd come back after the pubs were shut with some fish suppers, also not without promising to think about going to chapel again or at least to go and see Father McNaught to have a talk, and to be good generally and work hard . . . the faint smell of urine in the close was almost a relief; it was like I'd just started breathing again.

It was raining; I turned my collar up and tramped across the street, feet crunching on the broken glass that was Ferguslie's equivalent of a gravel drive, then marched over the muddy grass, past half-burned sheets of hardboard and sodden chip pokes and half-crumpled aluminium take-away containers holding little greasy puddles of rainwater, until I was out of sight of the flat. I ducked into a close on Bankfoot Drive, and lit up, sucking at the smoke like life itself. The close stank, there was illiterate graffiti carved into the tiled wall opposite, and I could hear a man shouting in one of the upstairs flats. The flat nearest to me turned their telly up, presumably to drown out the noise from upstairs. I smoked my sawn-off Embassy and looked out at the damp dreariness of Ferguslie Park, shivering a little as some water ran down my neck.

Dear Ferguslie; my cradle, my adventure playground. I'd moved away from it, but only a mile away. It still held me. Christ, what a dump, what a sorry mess it was. They should make a documentary about it; it was ideal material. Urban deprivation? The failure of post-war town planning? An indictment of the ghettoisation of problem families? It was all here. Bring lots of film and fashionable theories, chaps, but don't forget the lockable petrol cap and theft-proof wheelnuts for the Range-Rover. And maybe a riot gun or two.

I wanted out of this. I wanted away.

I reached into my jacket's inside pocket and took out some folded sheets of paper. One of my flatmates had let me use his typewriter to print out a few of my songs. I'd bought real stave paper from a music shop, carefully transcribed all the quavers and hemi-demi-semiquavers from my old exercise jotters, and then typed in the words underneath.

I knew I'd never make it as a singer–songwriter, so I was currently looking for a band to make rich and famous. I had a third or fourth-hand bass guitar I'd almost learned to play, and knew the most basic rudiments of writing music. I'd started out with my own system of musical notation; at the age of eight I'd invented a way of writing down music based on the use of graph paper and twenty coloured pens I'd been given for Christmas. Curiously enough this system, though complicated, did work. It became a sort of personal institution, something I was proud of, and I'd spent the last eight years stubbornly resisting the inevitable, refusing to learn the system everybody else used and trying to persuade anybody who'd listen that my way was better. I honestly, fervently believed that the musical world would see that my system was superior, and change over. It would be like going metric, it would be like decimalisation . . .

Insane.

Anyway, I had, with much ill grace, finally bought myself a teach-yourself music book, and grudgingly learned about the basic arithmetic of staves and time signatures, even if diminished minor sevenths and chord progressions still seemed like higher mathematics (I wasn't worried; I knew what the songs sounded like in my head, and they were brilliant. It would be a minor matter to transfer them into the real world. Any fool could play a guitar or a keyboard and notate; the real talent lay in thinking up the tunes).

And tonight I was off to the Union of the Paisley College of Technology, where a band called Frozen Gold were playing. A lad I'd known at school, who now worked as an assistant on one of the lathes in Dinwoodie's, had seen the group play in some pub in Glasgow and recommended them. I was sceptical in the extreme. *Frozen Gold*? Pathetic. I had lots of far better names. In the unlikely event this lot turned out to be the ones to go with, I'd let them choose from those I'd come up with.

I tramped through the rain, shoulders hunched, hands as deep in the shallow pockets of my corduroy bomber jacket as they would go. I kept the Embassy Regal between my lips and smoked it down to the filter, staring down at the sodden ground, protecting the fag from the rain with my head. I spat the dog-end into the gutter as I walked under the railway line and out of Ferguslie Park.

The Union was warm and noisy. The beer cost twenty pence a pint and it was only fifty pence to see the band. I knew a few people in the bar, and nodded, grinned, said a couple of hellos, but really I was there on business, so I was trying to look serious and distracted and generally as much as possible like a man with more serious things on his mind than standing around talking and drinking and enjoying himself. I would probably have been like that even if there hadn't been any women there, but to be honest it was mostly for the chicks. I was a man with a mission, a young fellow with the future history of the popular song resting next to his breast. I was going places; I was important . . . or at least I was very obviously going to be important, and soon.

I took my pint of lager down to the Union's modestly proportioned lower hall, usually used as its snooker room. The Union building, an off-grey edifice on the side of a hill facing the Gourock–Glasgow railway line, was Paisley's old Social Security office, and had – consequently, apparently – been designed in an appropriately depressing blind-cubist-with-a-hangover style. The low-ceilinged room where Frozen Gold would have their unwitting appointment or near-miss with Destiny was already smoky and warm. I could almost feel the steam coming off my wet clothes; I could smell my own body, too. Nothing too offensive, quite comforting in fact, but I was standing beside a couple of girls for the set and I wished I'd gone home first and put on some aftershave.

Frozen Gold were a five-piece band. Lead, rhythm and bass guitars, drums and Hammond organ. Three mikes, including the one for the drummer. The equipment looked surprisingly new; the amps and speakers were hardly battered at all, and the Hammond was in mint condition. They even seemed to have their own two roadies, who were finishing the setting up. No sign of the

17

band themselves yet. It puzzled me that a fairly well-off band should be playing this small, hardly publicised gig. Somehow it made it even less likely they'd be what I was looking for. If I hadn't just started my pint I'd have left then, drained the glass and swept importantly out of the building, into the rain and back to the flat. Another evening in, sitting in front of the one-bar electric fire, watching the black and white telly with the lads, or reading my library books, or messing about with Ken's acoustic guitar, or playing poker for pennies, and maybe a pint or two in Bisland's before ten . . . but instead I stayed, though I felt a sense of incipient hopelessness.

The band; four guys, one chick. The two girls standing nearby clapped enthusiastically and shouted; the band smiled and waved; the girls seemed to know them by name. 'Ayyy, Davey . . .!' they yelled; a young blond guy, about my own age and carrying a Les Paul, winked at them, then plugged the Gibson in. He looked like a male model; perfect hair and teeth and skin, broad shoulders, narrow hips. He took off a black leather jacket that looked too soft to be real leather and too expensive to be anything else and revealed a white shirt. Silk, my brain told me, though I didn't remember ever seeing a silk shirt in my life before, not in the flesh. Faded Levis. He adjusted the mike. He was a little smaller than I'd thought at first. He grinned out at the gradually gathering audience. I caught a glimpse of a guy's watch in front of me; good grief, they were starting on time!

I didn't notice the other three men; by then I was looking at the chick. Blonde too, quite small, semi-acoustic guitar, dressed very similarly to the bloke; white and faded blue, reading from the top. Again, about the same age as me, maybe a little older. A looker, I thought. Bet she can't sing and the guitar's not even wired up properly. What a face though. Just on the plump side of beautiful, if you were clutching at straws to find something to criticise. Nobody could look that good and have a voice too.

Jesus . . . and what a smile . . . I was left metaphorless before the warmth of a small, shy grin. She looked from the audience to the Les Paul Adonis and gave him a smile I'd have killed a higher vertebrate for.

I didn't know what this lot were doing here, but they weren't for me. They hadn't played a note but they just *looked* together,

18

already set up. They gave the impression they already had a recording contract (though I'd been told they hadn't). I was looking for some hardly formed, rough-edged squad of rockers who could more-or-less play, didn't have any original material, and would do as they were told, musically at least; play the goddamn songs and the absolute minimum of flash solos.

I was wrong about the girl. She and the Greek god led off together; lead and rhythm, both singing. 'Jean Genie'; recent Bowie. She could sing and he could play. In fact, she could play too; perfectly decent rhythm guitar, steady and energetic at the same time, like another storey on top of the bass line. The bass was a factory; big, regular, efficient . . . the chick's rhythm guitar was an award-winning office block, glossy but human. The blond guy's lead was . . . Jesus, a cathedral. Gothic and Gaudí; by the Late Perpendicular out of the NASA assembly building. It wasn't just speed; he didn't just play fast, like there was some sort of world lead-guitar-playing sprint record waiting to be broken; it was fluid, it just flowed, effortless, natural, perfect. He made all the local board merchants sound like lumbering Jumbos, and this guy was an F1-11 doing aerobatics.

They didn't stop at the end of Bowie's song; they launched straight into the Stones' 'Rock This Joint', then Led Zep's 'Communication Breakdown' . . . played a little faster, if anything, than the original.

I came to be cynical, and for the first thirty seconds of the Bowie song I was, just because I was a hopeless musical snob and Bowie was too 'commercial' for my taste; they were on more credible ground for me with the Stones and the Zeps . . . but that feeling didn't last long. I ended up stunned. They were doing just by playing what I wanted to do by writing. There were rough edges, sure enough; they weren't all that tight, the drummer was more enthusiastic than his skills would let him get away with, the guy with the Hammond seemed to want to show it off rather than play with the rest of the band, and the chick's voice, though it was technically good, and powerful, sounded too polite. Classical training, I decided immediately, trying hard to find something analytical to hold onto.

Even the lead guitarist occasionally tried riffs he wasn't quite capable of, but watching his face as he twisted and screwed the notes out of the Les Paul, I got the impression he'd get there one day, before too long. He would give a little grimace, even a small smile and a shake of the head as he lost his way in a torrent of notes heading for a climax and had to back off, settling for something a little more conventional, as though these were partly scripted little exercises he'd worked on and could play in rehearsal and get right most or some of the time but hadn't quite managed tonight.

In short, they were good. Their choice of material was about the only thing I really took issue with. They didn't seem to know where they were going; the first half of their set was a mish-mash of stuff from sources as far apart as Slade and Quintessence, some of it obviously chosen to let the lead player show off (including a couple of Hendrix tracks he did no injustice to, just followed The Man's line a little too closely), and some chosen just as your average stomping good-time dance music.

Messy, but good fun. Rather like sex had been described to me by my older brother. By the end of the first half I was sweaty, my feet were sore and my ears were ringing. My lager was warm and I hadn't drunk more than another two mouthfuls since I'd entered the room. A fag I'd started during the first song had burned right down and singed my fingers; my head was throbbing and my brain was vibrating with crazy possibilities. These people were all wrong, not at all what I wanted, not really . . . but; but but but but . . .

I don't know what my face must have looked like, but one of the two girls I was standing beside looked up at me and was obviously so carried away with the band her enthusiasm overcame her natural and understandable reluctance to have anything to do with the tall, ugly, staring-eyed loony at her side. 'Magic, aren't they?' she said. Both girls were looking at me now. 'Whadjey think, eh? Good eh?' The second one said. I was so knocked out by the band I didn't even register that I was in conversation with two quite attractive chicks, and *they* had started talking to *me*. I nodded rapidly, swallowing on a dry throat.

'V-v-very good.' Even my stutter didn't put them off.

'Ah think they're fuckin brilliant,' the first one said. 'Abslutely fuckin brilliant. See them? They'll be bigger than . . .' she stopped, searching for an adequate comparison. 'Slade.'

'Or T Rex,' her friend said. They were both small and had long dark hair. Long skirts. 'Bigger than T Rex.' She nodded vehemently, and the other one agreed, nodding too.

'Bigger than T Rex, or Slade.'

'Or Rod Stewart,' the second one said.

'He's no a band, he's one guy,' the other said.

'But he's goat a band; the Faces; ah saw themm at the Apollo an . . .'

'Aye, but . . .'

'D-d-d-' I began.

'Bigger than Rod Stewart, defnitly,' the second girl announced.

'B-b-b-' I said, changing tack.

'Well bigger than hum *an* the Faces then, okay?'

'B-but d-d-don't they have any original m-m-m-m-material?' I managed.

They looked at each other. 'What, their own songs, like?'

'Mmm,' I said, drinking my warm lager.

'Don't think so,' the first one said. She was wearing an ankh on a leather thong and lots of cheap Indian jewellery.

'Na,' the other said (tie-dye vest under a heavy fake fur jacket). She shook her head. 'But ah think they're working on some. Defnitly.' She looked at me in a sort of assessing way; the other one looked at the small stage, where one of the roadies and the drummer were adjusting the bass drum pedal. I got the impression I'd said something wrong.

'Cumin' fur a drink?' the first one said to her friend, tapping one empty glass against another. They drifted off while I was still stuttering over 'Can I buy you both a drink?' Awful lot of hard consonants in that short sentence.

The second half wasn't so good. They had problems with the equipment, and broke a total of four strings, but it wasn't just that. The material was the same mix as in the first part of the set, which I found a disappointment in itself, but the songs were less well put across anyway, as though the first half was all stuff they'd learned fairly thoroughly and the second made up of songs they were still learning. There were too many bum notes, and too many times when the drummer and the rest of the group were out of synch. The crowd didn't seem to mind though, and stamped and clapped even more noisily than before, and I knew I was being very critical; Frozen Gold were still streets ahead of anybody else I'd heard on the local circuit . . . Jesus, they weren't just streets ahead, they were in another town, heading for the city and the bright lights.

They finished with 'Love Me Do', encored with 'Jumping Jack Flash', and wound up finally – with the Union janitor making pointed signs at his watch from the doorway, and the roadies already starting to disconnect the equipment – with an acoustic version of 'My Friend The Sun', by Family. That was just Adonis and the chick together with one guitar. They were as near perfect as makes no difference to anybody but the most bitter rock journalist. The crowd wanted more, but the janny was turning the lights on and had already switched their power off. I joined the fans clustering round the front of the low stage.

The two girls who'd talked to me earlier were talking to the guy; a couple of drunken students were telling the blonde girl she was the most incredibly beautiful female they had ever seen in their lives and would she like to come out for a drink some time? while she smiled and shook her head and dismantled the mike stand. I could see the blond lead guitarist watching this from the corner of his eye while he talked to the two lassies.

I sidled up to the girls and tried to look serious but interested, like a man who has important things to discuss and doesn't just want to say 'Great, man,' or whatever, while still making it obvious how impressed – though with certain criticisms – I nevertheless was. What my resulting expression actually looked like I'd prefer not to think about; probably the message that came across was more like 'I am at best a dangerously drunk sycophant, but more likely a clinical psychopath with an obsession about musicians'. The guy glanced at me a couple of times, but I wasn't able to catch his eye until the two girls had found out where the band were playing next and one had secured a ballpen autograph on her forearm. They left happy.

'Aye,' the guy said, nodding at me, giving me a little smile.

'You're v-v-very good,' I said.

'Ta.' He started winding up some cable, then accepted an open guitar case from one of the roadies and put the Les Paul into it. He turned away.

I cleared my throat and said, 'Emm . . .'

'Yeah?' he looked back, just as the girl came over and hugged him round the neck, kissed him on the cheek, then stood beside him, arm round his waist, looking frowning down at me.

'I was w-w-w-wondering . . .'

'What?' he said. I watched as the girl's hand stroked his waist slowly through the silk shirt; an absent, unthinking gesture.

My nerve failed. They looked so good, they looked so together and happy and beautiful and talented, so clean and well groomed, even after that energetic set; I could smell some expensive scent off one or other of them and I just knew I couldn't say any of the things I wanted to say. It was hopeless. I was me; big ugly stupit Danny Weir, the mutant of the household, the big lanky dingbat with the acne and the lank hair and the bad breath . . . I was some cheap pulp magazine, yellow and dog-eared, and these people were parchment and leather covers; I was some cheap warped EP made from recycled vinyl and these people were gold discs . . . they lived in another world, and they were heading for the big time; I knew it. I was doomed to Paisley and grey walls and chip suppers. I tried to speak but couldn't even stutter.

Suddenly the girl's frown deepened and she said, nodding at me, 'You're Weird, aren't you?'

The guy looked at her then, a little shocked, certainly surprised; his brows and mouth trembled somewhere between a frown and a smile; he looked quickly from her to me while I stumbled out 'Y-yes, yes, that's m-m-me.'

'What?' the guy said, to me. I held out my hand but he'd turned to her again. 'What?'

'Weird,' the girl told him, 'Danny Weir; D. Weir . . . Weir, comma, D, in the school registration book, so, "Weird". It's his nickname.'

The guy nodded, understanding.

'That's me,' I grinned, suddenly jubilant. I gave a sort of stupid half-assed wave with one hand and then fumbled for my cigarettes.

'Remember me?' she said. I shook my head, offered them both a fag; she took one. 'Christine Brice. I was in the year above you.'

'Ohh,' I said, 'yeah; of course. Yeah; Christine. Aw yeah, of course; Christine. Yeah. Yeah; how are ye then, emm . . . how's things?' I couldn't remember her at all; I was ransacking my brains for the vaguest recollection of this blonde angel.

'All right,' she said. 'This is Dave Balfour,' she added, indicating the guy she had her arm around. We nodded to each other. 'Hi.' 'Hello.' There was a pause, then Christine Brice shrugged at me. 'What'd you think?'

'Of the b-band? The gig?' I said. She nodded. 'Aww . . . great . . . aye; great.'

'Goo . . .'

'B-but you need your own m-m-material, and the second half stuff needs more practice, and you could be a lot t-tighter, and the organ could make more of a c-c-c-c-contribbb . . . ution, and the drums need to be a lot more disciplined . . . and of course the name just w-w-won't . . . umm . . .' The expressions on their faces told me this wasn't going down too well. I buried my mouth and nose in the plastic pint glass to pretend I was taking a drink, and received a warm dribble of totally flat lager.

Jesus God Almighty, what was I saying? It sounded like I hated everything they'd done. What was I thinking of? I ought to be courting these people, not kicking them in the teeth. Here they were, nicely turned out middle-class kiddies having good fun with their wee band, turning out the best music in town and probably all set for greater things if that was what they really wanted, and no doubt used to praise and plaudits and each other's glamorous company, and here was this huge, shambling, babbling maniac telling them they were doing it all wrong.

What must I have looked like to them? I was six foot six in my (holed) stocking soles, but hunched over, head almost buried between my shoulders ('Vulture' was just one of my many school nicknames. I had dozens, but the one that stuck was the best). My eyes bulged, my nose was huge and hooked, and my hair was long and thin and slick with its own grease. I have long arms and huge mis-matched feet, one size eleven, one size twelve; I have big, clumsy strangler's hands with fingers which are too thick to let me play the guitar properly, no matter how hard I try; I had no real choice about taking up the bass; its strings are further apart.

I'm a monster, a mutant; a gangling ape; I scare children. I even scare some adults, come to that, though the rest just laugh or look away, disgusted. I'd been a funny looking kid and I'd blossomed into an ugly young man who didn't even have the common courtesy to be ugly on a small scale; I was *imposingly* bad-looking. I was exactly the last thing these beautiful, exquisitely paired, *nice* young people needed to see. I felt guilty about just being in the same room as them. What had I *said*?

The keyboard player passed behind just then, pushing the Hammond in front of him; he must have heard some of what I'd said because he muttered, 'Fuckin music critic, eh?'

Dave looked at me like I was some very low form of life, then gave a sort of hissing laugh through his nose. 'Apart from that though, all right, aye?'

'Awww . . . *yeah*,' I said quickly. 'Brilliant. I . . . I . . . I think you c-c-could go . . . you know . . .' I wanted to say 'to the top', but that sounded silly. '. . . you could do whatever, emm . . . you know . . .' I was not, it occurred to me, at my most articulate just then. And my most was the average punter's least at the best of times. 'Oh f-f-f . . .' I almost swore. 'Look, I'd like to b-b-buy you all a drink sometime, and talk b-b-business.'

'Business?' Dave Balfour looked dubious.

'Yeah. I think I've got the songs you need.'

'Oh, aye, have you?' Dave Balfour said, and looked like he was choosing between just walking away or cracking a mike stand over my head. I nodded, drew on my cigarette as though it contained some self-confidence drug. Christine Brice was smiling humanely at me.

'Ssseriously,' I said. 'Just let me have a t-t-talk with you. I've got the tunes and the words; everything. Just needs somebody to . . . g-get interested. You'd like them, honest. They'd be just right for you.'

'Well,' he began, then the janitor started hassling them. The roadies had opened a side door to the rain-filled night and the cold wind and were lugging the gear out. I picked up one end of a speaker and helped a roadie carry it out and down some steps to where a Transit van sat waiting in Hunter Street. My normal clumsiness deserted me momentarily and we made it down the steps without me dropping it. Dave Balfour was putting his guitar case into the back of an old Hillman Hunter standing just behind the Transit. Christine sat in the passenger seat. I went up to

Balfour, my shoulders hunched against the rain and the fresh cold of the open air. 'You really got some material?' Balfour said, pulling his glove-leather collar up.

I nodded. 'No shit.'

'Is it any good, though?'

I let a few seconds pass, then said, 'It's so good it's even better than you're going to b-b-be.' Shit! Fluffed it on the home stretch! That was a question I'd been waiting for somebody to ask, and a line I'd been waiting to deliver, for the past two years. The line didn't sound half as serious and intriguing and encouragingly ambitious as it always had when I rehearsed lying in bed at night, fantasising, but at least it was out. Dave Balfour took a second to digest it, then laughed.

'Aye, okay then; you buy us that drink then.'

'When?'

'Well, we're practising tomorrow night; come along then if you want; have a pint afterwards. Okay?'

'Fine. Whereabouts?'

'A hundred and seventeen St Ninian's Terrace. We'll be in the garage. 'Bout eight.'

'See you there,' I said. He got into the car as the roadies slammed the door on the Transit. I could see a couple of pale faces inside, staring out.

I started walking down the slope of Hunter Street, heading for a chip shop and then ma's. The Transit coughed and bounced past me, then the Hillman. It stopped, and Christine Brice stuck her head out.

'Want a lift?'

'Ferguslie Park for me,' I laughed, shaking my head. 'Yer t-t-tyres would never get out alive.' She turned back to Dave Balfour and they talked. I got the impression stopping had not been Dave's idea.

'We'll drop you nearby.'

'Ah . . .' I shrugged. 'Ah've got tae p-pick up some chips first, like; you'd . . .'

'Aw, get in.' She opened the rear door. 'I'll have some chips too.'

We stopped at a chip shop off Gilmour Street; she gave me the money for their chips. Nobody talked much, and they dropped me on King Street.

Dave Balfour only livened up at one point, when we were waiting at the traffic lights on Old Sneddon Street; a car drew up alongside us, and Balfour did a double-take when he looked over at it. He nudged Christine, and reached down to take something small and black from a door-pocket; something clicked, and he looked anxiously at the back of the small device, glancing up at the traffic lights a couple of times. I thought I could hear a high, whining noise. Christine shook her head and looked away. A little orange light shone on the back of the machine; Balfour held it up against his side window, tapped it against the glass, and sounded his horn. The driver of the car alongside ours looked round.

Balfour waved with his free hand, and was immediately surrounded by a blinding flash of light. I sat trying to blink the harsh reflections away, trying to work out what had happened, as Balfour laughed and sent the car powering away from the lights. 'God, you're so childish sometimes,' Christine breathed. Balfour was still giggling, looking into his rear-view mirror as he drove. 'Give me that flash gun,' Christine said, holding out one hand.

'Sammy Walker,' Balfour said, ignoring her. 'Did you see him? That's the second time I've got him this week!' He shook his head and kept chuckling. Christine looked back at me, raising one eyebrow. I smiled uncertainly.

I walked through the drizzle with the slowly cooling brown packages leaking grease and vinegar onto my jacket, wishing I hadn't agreed to go back to my ma's after closing time. Just what I needed, to go wandering about Paisley all night.

On the way back to the flat I did remember Christine Brice, from my schooldays. She had been fairly good looking even then; one of the well dressed older girls, self-assured, collected, and properly uniformed; very much not a product of Ferguslie Park itself. She'd been in the year above me all right, and I recalled that three years ago, when I still thought my looks could pass for dramatic rather than just horrific, I'd invited her onto the floor at the school's Christmas dance; of course she was older than me and so it was hardly the done thing, but I thought being tall might give me the edge . . .

She'd blushed and shaken her head; her friends had giggled.

I'd crumbled with shame and left the hall and the school. I'd wandered through Paisley – wretched, cold, humiliated – in my tight new shoes and my thin old jacket, waiting until the dance was due to finish, so I wouldn't arrive home before my ma expected me; she'd only have asked embarrassing questions.

When I had got back, I'd told her I'd had a great time.

THREE

They don't seem to have telegrams any more; they have something called telemessages instead; fake telegrams that come with the ordinary mail. One dropped onto the pile of mail behind the small back door of St Jute's vestry six days ago, on a Wednesday. The pile of mail is three years deep; probably enough to fill a couple of postal sacks. It's junk mail mostly, so I ignore it, just go down there every now and again and kick it around a bit, looking for anything remotely interesting. Important mail gets sent to my lawyers; the people who matter to me know that trying to get in touch directly is usually futile.

Rick Tumber ought to know that, but he must have forgotten. The telemessage skidded across the tiled floor when I kicked the pile of mail and I picked it up, wondering whether I should open it or not. This was unexpected, and unexpected things tend to turn out badly, in my experience. What the hell; I opened it.

ARRIVING YOUR PLACE LUNCHTIME SUNDAY 21ST.
IMPORTANT. BE IN. PLEASE. THIS IS GOOD NEWS.
KINDEST REGARDS. RICK T.

Good news. I was instantly wary. Rick Tumber was head of ARC, our record company. When he talked of good news he meant there was lots of money to be made somewhere, somehow. I started making plans to be out of town there and then, though I suspected something would happen to stop me; I wouldn't get round to it.

I put the message back in its envelope and replaced it on the pile, as though pretending I hadn't read it, it hadn't come, nothing was going to change, then I went back up the spiral of stone steps to the choir. I hadn't had any breakfast yet, and what passed for my kitchen and dining room lay in the south transept.

St Jute's, also known as Wykes' Folly, looks exactly like a church, but it isn't. It has what looks just like a graveyard, but it has no graves.

Ambrose Wykes, 1819–1898, was the only son of a successful Dundee jute merchant; he built up the business, turned a small fortune into a large one, and moved to Glasgow to oversee the establishment of another commercial empire in the early 1850s, shipping tobacco from America. He had always been mildly eccentric, dressing his servants as ship's crew – the head butler was the captain, the maids were cabin boys – and equipping his villa in Bearsden with a small lighthouse which attracted the wrath of his neighbours and considerable numbers of migratory birds, but by Victorian standards his oddities were not extreme, and he was a devout Catholic, a responsible husband and a loving father.

At least, he was these things until May 1864, when his wife Mary and their only child were killed in a train crash. The boy was only two weeks old, and unbaptised. Ambrose's grief was deepened by the knowledge that the infant's soul was forever denied entrance to the kingdom of heaven; he began to drink too much, and couldn't sleep; his doctor prescribed laudanum.

Ambrose's mourning went beyond the bounds of good taste; he had the whole of the Bearsden house, and his villa at Hunter's Quay on the Holy Loch, draped in black canvas. The furniture was reupholstered in black, the carpets replaced with black felt, black canvas was placed over all the pictures and portraits, and the servants were suddenly required to dress as undertakers. Most of them left.

Ambrose paid frequent visits to his priest, accompanied by an embarrassed but well paid lawyer, apparently trying to find some loophole in the divine legal code which would let his dead son's soul gain everlasting peace. The priest, his bishop, and several Jesuits all tried to reason with him, but Ambrose refused their comfort. He stopped going to church, he refused to confess.

His business affairs began to deteriorate as he spent increasing

30

amounts of time writing letters to priests, bishops, cardinals, and even the Vatican itself, urging that some sort of special dispensation be found which would allow the soul of his son to rest in peace; he published pamphlets advocating the reinterpretation of certain Biblical verses. Then he began to picket his local chapel; sitting outside the church in an undertaker's carriage he'd purchased, while some of his warehouse workers paraded round with placards urging reform.

These workers, themselves Catholics, were persuaded by their own priests that taking part in such unseemly demonstrations, even at triple time, was bad for their souls, and would do no good for the dead child. So Ambrose hired drunks from the Glasgow slums instead; they swore at the churchgoers, pissed against the church and fought with the police.

Ambrose had ignored the increasingly stern warnings and frosty advice of his few friends, and soon found himself without any at all. By this time his neglected business empire was on the verge of collapse, so he sold out. Injunctions eventually prevented him from picketing effectively, and he withdrew, broken and bitter but still obsessed, a rich but almost powerless man.

His frustration turned to hatred. The pamphlets began to vilify the church on every possible ground, until they too became unsupportably scandalous, and the printers refused to print them. Ambrose bought his own printing company and kept going for a while, until that too was buried under a blizzard of injunctions and prosecutions. He was excommunicated in 1869.

Ambrose remained determined to get back at the church somehow. His solution, after much thought and more brandy, was to make use of one of the few pieces of property he still owned; an empty site on St Vincent Street, between Elmbank Street and Holland Street. He sold almost everything else he owned, paid a great deal of money to an architect who has remained anonymous to this day, and – the rumour goes – an even larger sum to at least one member of the City Council to make sure there were no problems over building permission.

He built his own church. A Gothic design one architectural guidebook calls 'a bastardised blend of truncated Pearsonesque Normandy Gothic and facetious, ill-proportioned Lombardy'. The church was correct in almost every detail: nave, transepts, choir, vestry, crypt, pews, altar; even bells in the tower (Ambrose had them cast cracked so they sounded awful, but another injunction prevented them being rung).

The spare ground at the rear of the plot he turned into a mock graveyard, hiring Protestant stonemasons to turn out gravestones for each of the many enemies he'd made during the previous decade. Each stone gave the correct date of birth, but the following date recorded the death of Ambrose's friendship with whoever the stone purported to commemorate; the time when Ambrose had decided this person wasn't fit to live. His priest, a bishop, two cardinals and a variety of Jesuits seemingly lay beside a collection of lawyers, businessmen, judges, newspaper journalists, city councillors and building contractors, all apparently wiped out in some terrible, class-conscious plague which swept the city from 1865 almost to the end of the century.

The place was known as Wykes' Folly, or – in memory of Ambrose's original business – St Jute's. It became famous, a Glasgow landmark. Guidebooks mentioned it, people wrote to newspapers demanding it be torn down, a small group of free thinkers formed a Friends of St Jute's Society, and various bits of stonework were chipped off – and various insulting words scrawled onto – those parts of the church accessible from the pavement.

Ambrose retaliated by having a madonna and child statue made which showed his own Mary as the Blessed Virgin, and his unchristened son as the baby Jesus.

Ambrose was later to claim – in a pamphlet published privately, long after his death – that his son had indeed been the result of a virgin birth; in attempting to consummate his marriage on his wedding night, Ambrose had suffered a premature ejaculation while just inches from his goal; he retired in confusion, and claimed that he was afterwards too embarrassed to try again. His seed, however, had proved to be made of sterner stuff; it survived its short airborne journey and found what must have been a rather tenuous hold within the flower of Mary's womanhood; just a dewdrop within the heart of the rose, but sufficient to provide one sperm which must have wriggled past Mrs Wykes' maidenhead and connected with an egg. Ambrose thought this little short of a miracle, and it had been one of the reasons he had wanted his

32

child given special treatment in the afterlife . . . but it was also a detail of such an exquisitely personal nature that he had felt unable to mention to the relevant theological authorities.

Ambrose died after his collection of papers, pamphlets and tracts went up in flames on Good Friday 1898, seriously damaging the north transept. Ambrose suffered extensive burns, and despite holding on – and even seemingly improving – in the Royal Infirmary, finally died a few weeks later, on Ascension Day.

Ambrose had left enough money in his will for the folly to be maintained; this money proved sufficient to repair the fabric of the building, though slowly. The ownership of the place was turned over to the still surviving Friends of St Jute's, who used it as a storehouse for atheist publications. They abandoned it in the early 'twenties but couldn't sell it; a term of Ambrose's will had been that the place was not to be demolished or significantly changed from its original plan. I bought St Jute's in 1982, when I decided to make my own retreat from the world at large, and have felt thoroughly at home in it ever since.

The door bell rang about lunchtime, as I was making some ideologically sound Nicaraguan coffee; I don't just have jars of coffee, I have crates of the stuff.

I'd spent the time since breakfast working in the studio in the crypt, just fiddling about with the synthesiser and reading the manual on my new sequencer. I still write tunes; jingles, TV themes, the occasional film score, just to keep my hand in. I don't need the money but it passes the time. The jingles and the themes are two of the reasons I hate watching television or listening to the radio. Haven't been able to stand my own stuff since the band broke up, not once it's out there, public, no longer mine.

I thought it might be Blythswood Betty at the door. Betty is a whore who visits me every couple of days or so, just to keep me from getting too attached to my hand I guess. Nice woman; no nonsense type. I didn't think she was due today, but I lose track easily. I went to see who it was.

Ambrose had had hefty doors and barred windows fitted to his folly, but I have gone one better; closed circuit TV guarding all the entrances. The Holland Street door monitor, heaped in with most of St Jute's other non-musical electronic gear behind the pulpit, showed it was McCann, swaying in the small porch, holding his head and grimacing up at the camera and jabbing a finger at the door. His mouth was working.

I turned on the mike. '. . . pen the fuckin door, eh?'

I pressed the appropriate button and went to meet him.

'Jesus,' I said when I saw the blood, 'McCann, what . . .?'

'Ah, ma heid,' McCann said, stumbling up the steps to the choir, holding a reddened hanky to his forehead. I led him to the bathroom in the bottom of the tower.

'What happened to you?' I put the hanky in the sink and got antiseptic and plasters.

'Wee argument,' he said, sitting heavily on the side of the bath and looking at his hand. He put his head back while I dabbed gingerly at a cut just under his hairline. I've reached that stage where I don't so much have friends as accomplices, and McCann is one of my two closest. He's about fifty, a one-time docker and several times unemployed person; greying now, short but fit, with beetling brows and a collection of lines between those brows which give him the look of one who is perpetually finding much to be unimpressed about, as though the world owes him not so much a living as an apology. This is indeed exactly how McCann feels, so no false signals there.

'You stick the nut on some punter?' I jiggled the TCP bottle a bit too much and some of it ran into one of his eyes.

'Ah! Ya basturt!' He ran to the sink and sloshed water into his eye.

'Sorry,' I said, lamely. I handed him a towel. This is me; Mr Clumsy. I always hurt people. All my life I've been knocking things on top of people, bumping into them, turning round too quickly and bashing them in the eye, treading on their toes; you name it. I'm used to it by now, but then I'm not on the receiving end (apart from the big G, of course).

'Sawright, nevir mind Jimmy.' McCann isn't calling me Jimmy the way he'd call any man Jimmy; he thinks that's my name. I've told him I'm called James Hay. This is actually a joke I've never had the nerve to explain to him; it's Jimmy Hay as in 'Hey, Jimmy!'. Hay is my mother's maiden name. McCann doesn't know who I am; he thinks I'm just the caretaker here.

I tried to unpeel a plaster but it stuck to my fingers; I handed

34

him the packet while I picked the plaster off my hands. He sat down on the bath again.

'What happened?' I repeated.

'Ach, Ah goat intae a wee argument wi some stupit bugger in Brodie's.'

He dried his face, got up and looked in the mirror to put the plaster on. 'What about?' I asked.

'Oh, the usual; poalitics. Some balloon talkin aboot how we needed tae keep nuclear weapons. Ah tolt him he wiz a dupe of the imperialist propaganda machine an the so-called independent nuclear deterrent wiz a farce; we were paying for the Americans' war machine, an that wiz only there to threaten the gains of the workers' states an force the Soviet Union tae devote so much aw their Gross National Proaduct on defence the workers wid question the priorities of the leadership.'

'So he hit you.'

'Naw; he called me a commie an Ah said Ah certainly wiz, an proud of it too.'

'So then he hit you.'

'Naw, he said well then Ah'd want the Russians over here then, wouldn't ah? An Ah said it wiz up to each an every working class to make its own revolution, an the idea that the Soviet Union wantit to invade Western Europe was a load a mince; the last thing they wantit wiz a whole load of Polands and Czechoslovakias oan their hauns, no that they'd get the chance anyway cos if they didnae bomb oot aw the major manufacturing centres in the process, the Yanks wid, an as fur sneak nuclear attacks on anithir country, there was only wan state in history had ever done that, an it wiznae the fuckin Soviet Union.'

'So then he hit you.'

'Naw, then he said it wiz people like me that had wantit to appease Hitler and started the Second World War, so Ah told him it was the communists that had fought against the fascists in Germany, an, far frae helpin them, the Stalinists had cut them adrift just like they cut the Spanish Republicans adrift, an the people who'd done the appeasin were the right wing basturts that thought they an the fascists should be fightin the Soviet Union together, the same ones that had supported the White Russian army an the Imperialist invasion of Russia after the First World

War, an their successors were the ones that still wantit to roll back the revolution noo, usin the threat aw Star Wars or anyhin else they could lay their hauns on, an anybody who couldnae see that wiz a fuckin eedjit.'

I hesitated. 'That was when he hit you?'

'Naw; he said ye couldnae trust a commie an he'd be votin fur the Alliance at the next election. Next thing Ah knew ma heid wiz in his face.'

'You hit *him*?' I said. McCann nodded wearily and rubbed his forehead.

'Ach, Ah didnae really mean tae; it wiz instinct, like. Ah didnae know whit Ah wiz daein. Totally involuntary.' He made a tutting noise. 'See ma heid? It's got a mind of its own sometimes.'

I thought about this. 'I believe this calls for a drink.'

We sat in the nave on pillow-covered pews, drinking bottled Budweiser and shorts of Stolichnaya. 'It's not done these days, you know, McCann. Glasgow's miles better and much nicer; head-butting is out.'

'Oh, Christ, aye, European City of Culture nineteen-ninety, eh? Bloody garden festival . . .' He snorted and drank.

'More hotels.'

'An anuther fuckin exhibition centre. God, this place is goin tae the dogs all right.'

'Aye, but the dogs have left it.'

'Bloody right, son,' McCann said, disgusted. He was still in mourning for Shawfield Stadium, where they'd held the dog racing; its English owners had closed it in October. McCann had had to find other ways of losing money every Saturday. He shook his head. 'Ah wiz doon the docks yesterday; well, where they used tae be. Whit a mess. They're even gettin rid aw the auld fit tunnel, did ye know that?'

'Aye.' The foot tunnel under the Clyde at Finnieston Quay was being filled in.

'There's just yon one big cran left an the rest's aw that bloody exhibition centre.'

'Shug from the Griffin told me they only kept the crane there because they might need it to load tanks in a war.'

'Aye, fuckin typical, isn't it?' McCann shook his head at the general deterioration of everything. 'City of Culture . . . bloody garden exhibitions; just mair excuses fur the businessmen tae make a killin. Fresh paint on the double yellow lines an a bigger subsidy fur the opera.'

'Cynical bastard, so you are, McCann.'

'Ahm no a cynic, Jim; cynicism is fur the rich. Us poor punters are just cautious; cannae afford tae be anythin else. Cautious, an no so stupit.' he drank some beer.

'You banned from Brodie's then?'

'Don't think so. It aw happened in the cludgie; nobody saw.'

'Jesus, you left this guy lying in the toilet?'

'Whit wiz Ah supposed tae dae? Say sorry? Stupit wanker. Hope it knocked sense into him. Ah mean, Christ. Ah coulda been a real bastard and swiped his white stick as well.'

'*What*? He was . . .' I shouted, then saw McCann's grin. He winked.

Glasgow is not, in my experience, a violent city. I do a lot of walking in the city at night, just plodding through the streets, looking, listening, smelling the place, and I've never been bothered. Of course, being six and a half foot and looking like a mutant baboon might have something to do with that. And, okay, so I do carry a shooting stick cum golf umbrella, but that's not just for defence. It rains here, quite a lot sometimes, and I like to have something to sit on, wherever I am. I was stopped a couple of times in the early days by the police, wanting a look at the stick's business end, but they know they can't do me for it.

They seem to be used to seeing me wandering around now; they leave me alone.

The shooting stick has a thick metal plate at the bottom and a stubby two inch spike on the end, and it's not light; a pretty offensive weapon in the right hands (not mine though, I'd probably swing it and crack my own skull. Looks good though; *I* wouldn't mess with somebody carrying one. Mind you, I'm a paranoid coward).

Purely a defensive weapon in other words; a deterrent. McCann, on the other hand, had once told me that when he was younger and running with a gang, one of the little tricks they used was to sew fish hooks behind the lapels of their jackets, so that if anyone grabbed them there to head-butt them they'd get a nasty surprise . . .

Anyway, most of the violence that does take place in Glasgow is between gangs, not against strangers, and usually doesn't happen near the centre. I'd sooner walk through Glasgow alone at night than through London with a bodyguard. For New York, I think I'd want air support; and that's just during the day.

'Diet Irn Bru,' McCann said suddenly, sounding like he was about to cough something up.

'What about it?'

'The very fuckin idea of it, that's whit,' he said. 'God almighty; whit next? Low calorie fuckin whusky?'

'Aren't they working on some new colourless, tasteless whisky to compete with vodka?' I said, sipping some Stolichnaya. In fact this was a total fabrication, to pay back McCann for his blind man in the toilet, but:

'Aye, Ah heard that too,' McCann said. 'Makes ye sick, doesn't it?'

'I don't know,' I said, annoyed. 'Does it?'

'You *sure* your boss doesny mind us drinkin aw this booze Jim?' McCann said, ignoring or ignorant. He held up an empty Bud bottle and inspected one of Ambrose's stained-glass windows through it.

'I've told you.' I told him. And I had told him. McCann always asks that question, and I always tell him it's okay. 'It's okay; he doesn't mind.'

'Positive?'

'Certain; he's given it up. Told me to help myself.'

McCann looked around the crates of drink piled up in the nave amongst all the rest of my Comecon booty, and scratched his chin. 'He should sell aw that stuff if he doesnae want it.'

'Too complicated. Have to pay duty . . . all sorts of things. He can't be bothered.'

'Aye, he must be rich, right enough . . . awright if I . . .?' McCann held up his empty bottle.

'Help yourself,' I told him. McCann went for another bottle.

'Ah've never seen this guy, Jimmy, ye know that? Does he never come round here at all?'

'Last time he was here was . . . must have been a year ago. More, maybe.'

'Whit's his name again?' McCann used the bottle opener tied to the end of the pew, drank from the bottle.

'Weird.'

'Funny name, that.'

'Funny guy.'

'He's no goannae knock this pile doon an build an office block, naw?'

'Can't. The building's got to stay as it is; that's why he got it so cheap.'

'Diddae get a mortgage on it, aye?'

'I don't think so,' I said, not sure whether McCann was taking the piss or not. 'He's rich. Eccentric.'

'Aye,' McCann said ruefully, 'if yer rich yer just eccentric; if yer poor yer a nutcase an they stick ye in the bin.'

'Rank has its privileges.'

'You're tellin me, pal.'

We drank our drinks. McCann looked round at the piles of booze. 'Aye, this stuff's all very well, but Ah fancy a pint of heavy. Cumin up the Griff?'

'Aye; time for lunch.' The Griffin is our local; a decent, unspoiled but lively enough bar with cheap food. I've never shaken off the tastes of my childhood, and still prefer the Griffin's pie, beans and chips to the Albany's five-star steak au poivre with fennel, asparagus, courgettes and new potatoes . . . besides, the Albany would mean dressing up. And a bath too, probably. We got up to go. I took our empty bottles of Bud and chucked them into the shovel of the Russian bulldozer as we passed it on the way to the front doors. I had to get some cash before we went to the Griff.

'An what the fuck's he got all this plant fur?' McCann said, shaking his head at the assembled machinery. I hauled open the small door set into the big main doors – barn-sized; I could get a double decker bus in here no problem – and hauled McCann away from the Polish dump truck (full of vodka bottles).

'They're no his,' I told him. 'The builders left them.'

'Aye, affy funny,' McCann said outside, buttoning up his jacket and staring across the road at the glossy, tinted mirror-shade façade of the Britoil building opposite. When I bought the folly, all that had been there was a hole; the office complex had

39

been completed this year. Just in time for the oil slump and redundancies to be announced. I stopped beside McCann, looking at the distorted reflection of the folly shown on its tiered walls. 'Bloody monstrosity,' McCann said, tutting. 'Ah think ah preferred the hole.'

'You're a reactionary old bastard,' I told him, bounding down the steps to the street.

'Reactionary! Me? Ye big pape.' He hurried down to catch up. 'It's no the likes of me that's reactionary, I'll tell you, pal; nothing reactionary about tryin tae maintain yer heritage, even if it is a hole in the ground; reactionary is yer fuckin entrepreneurs and yer shareholders, attempting tae maintain the capitalist system against the tide of history, an it doesnae matter how ye dress up that sort of . . .'

McCann kept on about progress and regress, action and reaction, and capitalism and communism, all the way to the bank, where I lent him a tenner.

As we walked back to the Griffin, I kept thinking about Rick Tumber's telemessage, wondering what he wanted to talk about, and worrying about his reasons for phrasing it just the way he had.

You get to know how people put things, the way they use words, just where the stresses fall. Trying to recall Rick's rather Midatlantic phrasing style, I couldn't help thinking that if Rick said 'This is good news,' he probably meant '*This* is good news,' contrasting it with something else, that wasn't. Or maybe I was just being paranoid, as usual.

Could something have happened that I didn't know about? Easily; I avoid newspapers, television and radio, for most of the year. I have my Information Binges, but they're few and far between, about every two months or so.

During an Information Binge, I rent a few televisions, buy a radio and order every paper and magazine I can get my hands on. I read everything, I have the radio on constantly and I watch TV; all of it; soaps and adverts and quiz shows and kids' programmes. A good, thorough-going Binge normally lasts about a week; after that I'm usually goggle-eyed with lack of sleep, not to mention sickened at what passes for popular culture . . .

The rest of the time, I still read a lot, but mostly books and magazines, and not even news magazines. So for a large part of the year I'm totally out of touch; they could start the next world war and I wouldn't know anything about it until the streets filled with people pushing carts and prams and sticking tape over their windows . . .

Had I missed something? Was there really that hidden emphasis in Tumber's message?

No; paranoia. Had to be. Rick wasn't consistent enough for anybody to read nuances into his phrasing. His memo style depended entirely on whether he'd just taken a hit of coke, had a heavy lunch or recently fallen in or out of love again. Still, the message worried me.

There was a song once:

> Heard much later that while I sat there
> You were flying back east and home.
> Never read your note at all dear,
> Got the message on my own.
> Threw it into the empty fire-grate,
> Went out, had a good time.
> But as it lay there cold until the daybreak
> – It was burning in my mind.

Nothing startling . . . but I kept hearing the tune in my head, and my old songs have always been bad news, for me or for others. My curse, my jinx; should have called me Jonah at birth and have done with it . . . Mister Mistaken, Captain Clumsy . . .

The doors of the Griffin approached. 'That guy wasn't really blind, was he?' I asked McCann.

'Naw,' McCann said firmly. 'Ah never tangle with blind punters . . .'

'Good.'

'. . . they carry sticks.'

'McCann . . .' I turned to him, but he was grinning at me, and winked.

'Naw,' he said again, as we went through the doors. 'Ye would-nae see me tackle a blind punter.'

41

FOUR

One day in August 1974 I met Jean Webb, walking down Espedair Street, in Paisley.

Jean and I had gone out together, and we'd been almost-lovers, semi-intimate, on the very verge of seriousness, for a while. It had started with the usual, awkward, youthful dates, hiding in the shadows of pubs because we were under-age and fumbling kisses under railway bridges; classic behaviour. I'd been attracted to her originally because she had a nice smile and was five foot nine, reducing the difference in height between heads and mouths by three or four inches compared to the average Ferguslie girl. It had all been rather embarrassing; one or other of us always seemed to be tongue-tied, or just not in a mood to talk, though we got on with each other well enough when we didn't talk.

For some reason, too, I was especially gormless and clumsy in her company; I spilled drinks onto her lap, stepped on her feet, tripped her up accidentally in the street, clouted her head with my elbow when I got up to go to the bar or the gents, got her long brown hair caught in my jacket cuff buttons, bruised her lip with my teeth and once – when we were having a carry-coal-bag fight in the park with another couple – tripped, fell, and threw her over my head into a bush; she was bruised and grazed.

Another time in the same park I was waiting for her, sitting on a bench humming tunes in my head and staring vacantly into space; she came up from the side and was leaning over to say 'Boo!' when I realised she was there; I jumped up to give her a kiss and cracked her on the chin with my head; knocked the poor kid unconscious.

She was all right, a bit dizzy for a few minutes, wouldn't let me take her to hospital, and insisted we went to the disco we'd planned on going to, but she had a bad bruise under her chin, and her father apparently took a lot of calming down and convincing that I hadn't been beating up his wee lassie; he'd been all set to come round to our flat with her two elder brothers, both of whom gave me menacing looks for months afterwards.

I think it was that episode that defined our relationship for me, and – despite what happened later, despite our equivocal consummation – signified the beginning of the end; a combination of your standard adolescent embarrassment and a despair that I just wasn't clumsy-compatible with this particular female.

We persevered. She took the accidental knocks and I put a brave face on the foolishness I felt when I did something stupid. I started to think about being rich and famous not by myself, but with Jean by my side; would she just restrict my freedom, or provide a stable base, somebody to come home to? I wondered what would be best, and also how you could tell when you were in love.

I told her about my dreams. She listened, smiled, did not make fun of them. I gibbered and stuttered away for hours at a time, telling her how famous I was going to be, how much money I was going to make. She kissed me and let me feel her breasts through jumper and blouse and sometimes allowed my hand up her skirt, lying on the floor of her bedroom while the television sounded from the living room. A few times she stroked the bulge in my trousers, but there wasn't much else we could have done even if I had convinced her it was a good idea, not while the telly blared and we waited for the next knock on the door and her mum asking her if we wanted another cup of tea. I told her I'd take her away from all this; London, Paris, New York, Munich . . .

I'd left school and gone to Dinwoodie's, proud of my new status as an earner, but still living at home. She'd stayed on, studying for Art College. She baby-sat for a friend of her mum's sometimes, and I went round there too, a few times. And once, almost, nearly, only just or not quite . . .

On another floor in a darkened room under the flickering blue glow of another television, sound turned down so we'd hear the people coming back, the baby quiet in a room above us; lots of rolling about and bruising deep kisses and heavy breathing, and finally, me thinking *Here we go*! fingers on zips and cotton pulled down and fumbled aside, and the dizzying woman smell of her, pine and ocean, and the stunning heat of her around my hand, while her own fingers closed about me.

Clumsiness and sweat and disjointed adolescent times; you wait for years and then it's over in seconds. And class-inversions. Girls I knew later who'd screw at the drop of a cap but *absolutely not* with the lights on; who'd always risk pregnancy but never suck you off. And odd local fashions, like the Ferguslie schoolgirl who'd been stopped fighting in the playground and wouldn't tell the teacher what terrible thing she'd been called that had started the battle. Eventually persuaded to spell the ghastly insult out through her tears, she said, 'Miss, she called me a fucking C-O-W!'

So when Jean felt that first spasm in her hand, and took me in her mouth, she left me amazed, because on the scoring scale I knew the other lads talked about, this was *way* beyond ten; Jeez, this was an unreal number! It didn't occur to me that maybe she was just trying to keep the carpet clean.

There was too little time after that. Anyway, we didn't have any contraceptives. Sometimes I felt we were the only two responsible teenagers in Paisley, and – in my most frustrated moments – wished we'd just gone ahead anyway, the way everybody else seemed to.

I only found out the next evening, sitting in the pub, that – technically, if you like – I'd deflowered her then. I didn't believe her at first, even though I did recall something giving; I didn't think it was possible like that, with just a hand, a finger, but she was sure, and quite easy with it, and laughed.

But.

Maybe I was embarrassed about it and felt I always would be. Maybe I couldn't understand why she still wanted to wait, why she never again asked me round when she was baby-sitting, or why she wouldn't come to the flat when I moved in there, even when the others were out. I don't know. But I let her slip away.

That spring, she fell while she was helping her mum clean the windows of their flat; she broke an arm and collar bone and cut her head; they were worried about concussion. I'd tried to see her in the hospital that same evening, but they would only let in family; I attempted to explain I was a close friend and I was going away on holiday the next day . . . but got all tongue-tied. I left the hot, chemical-scented corridors of the bright hospital blushing and covered in sweat.

I really was going on holiday the next day; I and a couple of pals had arranged to go camping on Arran. We left, it rained a lot and I had atrocious hangovers for five consecutive days. We came back damp, broke and early, and I felt so bad about not having seen Jean before I'd left it took me three weeks to pluck up the courage to try and see her again . . . only to find that by then her family had gone on holiday.

While she was away I set off in pursuit of a girl called Lindy from Erskine, who was nearly five-eleven, and whose dad ran a bar where bands played sometimes . . . but nothing came of that, either.

When I met her in Espedair Street that summer's day, it felt like I'd never been away from Jean Webb.

God, I was happy that day; I felt like the proverbial million dollars, like I'd won the pools, been granted immortality and swapped bodies with David Bowie all at the same time. President of the World; Emperor of the Universe!

We had a recording contract; an outrageously large advance was lumbering its way northwards even as I walked down Espedair Street; a satisfyingly large whole number for an engine and a string of zeros for carriages, all singing their way up whatever telephone lines Telegraphic Transfers used to get between banks in London and Glasgow.

I saw Jean coming down the street, yelled out, waved my arms over my head, then ran up to her and whirled her round several times without dropping her once. I laughed maniacally, told her I was going to be famous, and gave her no choice whatsoever about coming for a drink to celebrate. She smiled, agreed.

I'd gone along to the band's practice session the night after I saw them at the Union, feeling much more nervous than I'd expected. It was worse than when I'd sat exams, almost as bad as waiting outside the headmaster's room for the belt. Nothing like as bad as it used to be when I was just a kid, though, waiting for my da to get home on a Friday or a Saturday night, in the bad days . . . but that hadn't been nervousness, that had been terror. Slight difference.

117 St Ninian's Terrace was a large detached villa in a street full of them. There were trees between the road and the pavement and no writing on the low walls. The hedges behind the walls looked as though they'd never had a schoolkid pushed through them or a satchel thrown over them. Attached to the side of the house was a double garage about the same size as our flat, and in much better condition. Light edged the long doors and I could hear the Les Paul playing casual phrases. I adjusted the set of my shoulders, checked my adam's apple was still working, walked past a big estate car parked in the gravel drive, and went in through a side door, carrying my ancient, anonymous bass guitar wrapped in a couple of large Woolworth's bags.

They were all there. I was late; one of my small brothers had been using my guitar's lead to tie up another small brother while they were playing Americans Interrogating Vietnamese.

'Oh, hi . . . Weird,' Dave Balfour said. He was sitting on a white iron garden chair, tuning the Les Paul. Christine Brice was sitting on another seat, scribbling away on a sheet of paper. She looked up and nodded. The others were footering around with various leads and amps. The big garage was warm and well lit, and empty save for the band and its gear.

'Hullo,' I said.

'Woolie's guitar, eh?' The Hammond player said, looking at the plastic bags.

'Aye,' I said, resting the bass against a wall. The drummer was holding a joint.

'Smoke?' He said, holding it up. I nodded, took it from him, drew on it lightly. Dope was something I was still a bit unsure about. I was taking very little while I waited to see if my three prod student flatmates – all heavy users – degenerated into giggling basket cases. So far they just seemed to be having a lot more fun than I was. The compensation was that when they were really wrecked it was easier to take money off them at poker. I didn't really want the joint the drummer offered me, but I didn't want to seem churlish. I took a couple of moderate

46

tokes and passed it to Dave Balfour.

'You know the others?' he asked me. I shook my head. 'That's Mickey.' He indicated the drummer, a curly-haired guy with a scrunched up face and glasses, who nodded.

'Weston . . .' This was the Hammond player, a thick-set youth with very long black hair who scowled at Balfour and said, 'Just Wes,' to me.

'. . . and Steve.' The bass player. A little fidgety guy with the making of a beard and very long sideburns.

'This is W . . .'

'Just c-call me Danny,' I said, grinning nervously at each one in turn. Christine Brice looked amused.

I sat comfortably enough for a while, listening to them warm up and practise a few songs; mostly ones they'd played when I'd seen them the previous night, and mostly songs from the second half of the set. Dave Balfour didn't say anything about the criticisms I'd made. He came over as their natural leader; some bands work best when nobody tries to lead, others would work better if somebody does but they all want to be the one, and some, like this one, had somebody who could make the decisions, easily and reasonably, without being autocratic. The others deferred to him happily most of the time, but he listened to and took account of any suggestions. I experienced again a little of that feeling from the previous night; that I wasn't necessary to these people, that I was a foreign body here. But still, all the songs they were rehearsing were other people's.

After an hour or so, I was wondering whether they'd forgotten about me. They were trying to work out chords for a Jack Bruce song, 'The Consul At Sunset', and I was sitting finishing my sixth fag, toying with the idea that they – effectively Dave Balfour – had only invited me along to humiliate me, just because of the things I'd said were wrong with the band and their set. An empty feeling started to form in my belly. My face felt warm and my forehead prickled and itched. I fumbled with the cigarette packet. What was I doing? Why had I come here?

The bastards; the smug middle-class shits with their blond hair and their silk shirts (not that they were wearing those just then). I'd get up and tell them I was popping out for more fags, and never come back. Bugger off back to the flat and leave the self-satisfied wankers to it. The hell with the bass in the Woolie's bag; I'd abandon it; I had my pride. This wouldn't stop me; they wouldn't stop me. It would only make me even more determined to make it one day; let them fart about with other people's material for a year or two, even a record or two . . . when they saw me with my number one album and single on both sides of the Atlantic at the same time, then they'd be the ones who'd feel sick.

'Glad somebody's finding this fun.' Christine Brice sat down on a chair beside mine. 'Can I bum a fag?'

I realised I'd been smiling. I blushed and held the packet out. I lit the cigarette for her; she had to hold my hand because it was shaking, but she didn't say anything. She sat back and watched the others, still huddled round the drums, arguing, tapping out beats, playing snatches of music. 'You remembered me from school yet?' she asked.

I nodded. 'You knocked me b-b-back for a d-dance once,' I blurted.

She looked shocked. 'Did I? When was that?'

'Christmas . . . ssschool dance . . . three years ago, I think.'

She looked thoughtful, then nodded, pulled on the fag. 'Oh, aye; I was dead shy then. Couldn't help thinkin; I'll be staring at his chest.' She laughed, shrugged. 'Sorry, Danny.'

''sall right. C-c-can't blame you. Didn't b-bother me anyway.'

'What about these songs then?'

'Got them here.' I patted my bulging jacket.

'Can I see?' She held out one hand. I hesitated, then gave her the sheaf of papers. She put one boot onto the other needlecorded knee and rested the sheets there, smoothing them out. She looked at them for ten minutes or so, putting the fag out on the sole of her boot. 'Funny chords, Danny.'

'Yeah I know; not my st. . .rong point. Still learning.'

She nodded, flicked through them again, looking thoughtful. 'Hmm,' she said. She got up and went over to the others, talked briefly and came back, holding her guitar. 'They'll be messing about for a while yet. Come on and we'll form a sub-committee. Get your board.'

We went into the house; it was Dave Balfour's parents' place. There was something I now know was a utility room; at first I thought it was a very bare kitchen, with its sink, freezer, automatic washing machine, and tumbledrier.

The kitchen was the size of my ma's living room, but far better furnished. Everything seemed to be wood. As we went through, there was just one small light on, under a long dark line of cupboards, shining down onto a cooker set into the gleaming working surface. It all smelled fresh and somehow expensive, and my head swam for a second.

Beyond that, the house smelled of furniture polish and fresh apples. We went into a huge hall with a wide staircase; Christine stuck her head round a door and talked to somebody inside the dimly lit room, then showed me into a room opposite. The furniture looked too good to sit on. There was an upright piano against one wall. The room was warm; hot air came out of little rectangular grilles set in the floor.

This was 1973, and there were probably hundreds of far grander and more modern houses within a few miles of this one, but to me it was like landing on another planet; I'd only ever seen places like this in films, and somehow hadn't taken them any more seriously than the big-budget film sets that got blown up at the end of James Bond movies. I was out of my depth.

'Okay,' Christine said as she sat down at the piano, guitar over her back. 'Let's get tore into these songs, then.'

It was awkward. I was frightened about her playing the piano too loud and disturbing whoever was in the dimly lit room across the hall from us, and something in me was reluctant to describe just how I wanted the songs to sound, the ideas I'd had on how to arrange them. The whole idea of putting chords to the melodies still tripped me up continually; I was used to whistling tunes and imagining the backing in my head, almost subconsciously. I knew the sound I wanted, but I had no idea how to make it.

Christine could read and write music with a fluency beyond me. She briefly scanned and then offhandedly trashed the chords I had worked and fretted over for days if not weeks, then quickly began scribbling in replacements, testing them on the piano and strumming them on her guitar. I sat beside her on a thin-legged chair I was sure was far too delicate for me and was certain to give way beneath my hulking weight at any moment, and felt quite left out. The bass remained in its plastic bags.

49

Christine got a few comments from me when she first looked at each song, then ignored me for ten, fifteen minutes at a time, only occasionally asking what I meant here, what I thought I was doing here, how I got to there from here, why this went to that instead of the other . . . did you *really* mean this? . . . my spirits sagged slowly as I watched my babies dismembered and then put back together in ways I hardly recognised. The tunes and notes and shapes I had grown used to became just jotted marks on the page; my sight reading simply wasn't up to reconstructing the sound, hearing the chords in my head. I watched the girl work, and felt, as ever, hopelessly alienated, barred; a bum note amongst the harmonies.

'Too many words . . . doesn't scan . . . been done . . . sure I've heard that before . . .' Her muttered comments, spoken – to be fair – as though I wasn't there anyway, were hardly more encouraging.

I wanted to leap up, snatch my songs away from her and run out of the house screaming. My backside got sore, and my legs got sore too, trying to take some of my appalling weight off the creaking, over-stressed legs of the antique chair.

She closed the piano, brought the guitar round and fingered some chords, strumming her right hand over the strings so softly I could hardly hear. She seemed to be playing through a couple of the songs, checking the chords, tutting every once in a while and going back, starting again. After about the fortieth 'tut' and the umpteenth shake of that blonde head, I was starting to wonder what the chances were of sticking in at swarf collection and working my way up through the factory floor towards Dinwoodie's management. Maybe managers lived in houses like this one.

The door opened and Dave Balfour looked in. 'You all right?'

'Yeah.' Christine looked at her watch. 'Ha!' She sat back and stretched. 'We'd better move if you're going to buy us that pint,' she told me. I tried to smile.

We crowded into Balfour senior's Peugeot estate; I half sat, half lay on the back-facing kiddies' bench, under the tailgate. We drove out to a hotel near the Gleniffer Braes. There were Jags and Rovers, Volvos and one Bentley parked outside. Just the place for a cheap drink, I thought.

We sat in the lounge, surrounded by muzak and golfers. The

barman had given me a very long look. Technically I was still under age, though I'd been going into pubs for over a year and a half, but I think it was just my clothes and dirty fingernails he didn't like. I handed over a fiver and very nearly asked him if he was sure when he gave me the change back, but just sighed and took the tray to the table.

I fully expected to trip over somebody and send the whole lot flying, but I didn't. Not everything could go wrong this evening, I thought. Nobody had mentioned anything about my songs on the drive to the hotel, including Christine. I was so fed up I'd gone past being depressed; I just felt resigned, and tired. I distributed the drinks without spilling very much.

'. . . working on the songs, what'd you think?' She was saying to Dave Balfour.

'Aw aye,' he said, looking at me, then back at her. 'So?'

'Play you some later, if you like. Yeah?' She'd brought the sheaf of song scores along and had them on the table in front of her, studying them, blonde hair sweeping over the papers every so often, then being tucked back behind her ears. 'I'll give you a run through a couple of them . . . all right?' She looked up at the others. They looked unimpressed, but she smiled, Balfour shrugged, and that seemed to settle it.

'They any good, though?' Wes of the Hammond said, taking a handful of crisps and washing them down with Export. He munched, staring at me.

'Mmm . . . yeah.' Christine said. I must have looked startled. She pursed her lips, her eyebrows lifted. 'Better than our stuff, anyway.' Dave Balfour and Steve, the bassist, were the ones who looked put out. 'Sorry, fellas,' she told them.

'Ah, well, we'll see,' Balfour said, in a reasonable tone. They spent the rest of the time talking about Monty Python, and which university they were going to go to; Dave Balfour hoped to study medicine at Glasgow, Christine had already started at Strathclyde (doing Physics, I was surprised to learn); Wes wanted to read English, anywhere, and Steve – another surprise – was a music scholar; from what he said he played the violin as well as the bass. Mickey the drummer was the only one who had no such plans; he was older than the rest, a clerk in the local planning office.

Listening to all these academic aspirations, I felt both

inadequate and hopeless. They sounded so sure of themselves, they were all set to head off to do all sorts of professional things. The band was good fun, but it wasn't their great hope in life. They would split up, get together with other friends for a jam session now and again, but it would be a hobby, nothing more. They seemed to be embarrassed about discussing what might happen if they took the music seriously, tried to make a career out of it. It was mentioned once, as a joke. They all laughed.

What am I doing here? I thought once more. They don't need me, no matter how good the songs are. They'll always be heading in different directions, moving in different circles, higher spheres. Jesus, this was life or death to me, my one chance to make the great working class escape. I couldn't play football; what other hope was there to get into the supertax bracket? At this rate the most constructive thing I could do this evening would be to get chatting to Mickey from the planning office and see if he had any contacts in the housing department that could wangle my ma a new flat out of Ferguslie Park.

We had another couple of drinks (paid for by Dave and Christine), then it was back to the Peugeot. 'You go co-pilot,' Balfour said, holding open the passenger's door for me.

I was surprised, and secretly pleased, thinking this was some sort of recognition, a compliment. Wrong. We were doing fifty or sixty on the country road back to Paisley, when Balfour tapped me on the arm and pulled the zip down on his leather bomber jacket, then took both hands off the wheel and said, 'Steer for a second, will you, Danny?' He started taking off the jacket.

I stared at him, then at the headlit road in front, hedges and stone walls rushing past; the camber of the road was slowly angling us into the side. I grabbed the wheel, dry-mouthed, and tried to aim us back into the centre of the road, over-corrected and threw us over to one side. Balfour laughed, dragged the jacket off. 'Dave . . .' Christine said, sounding tired from the back seat. One of the others tutted loudly.

'Fuck's sake,' Wes muttered. I pulled the car back again, over-correcting once more and heading us all towards the wall and the field beyond, our tyres yelping on the road surface.

'I can't drive!' I squeaked, half-closing my eyes.

'Don't worry,' Balfour said, passing the leather jacket back to

Christine, and casually taking the wheel from me, only just in time to prevent us and the car creating an al fresco mural along the wall. 'It doesn't show.' He corrected the estate's headlong charge towards the wall with one effortless flick of the wrist, and we accelerated down the road towards Paisley. I sat back, shaking, palms cold and wet.

'You'll die young, Balfour,' Christine said.

'Just try and die *alone*,' Mickey said. Balfour shook his head, smiling broadly at the lights of Paisley in the distance.

We got back without hitting anything, parked the estate in the drive, trooped into the garage, Christine looked at the songs for a while as we shared a joint (after checking the connecting door to the rest of the house was locked), then, with just the semi-acoustic, and the score propped up on a seat in front of her, she sang 'Another Rainy Day'.

Whereupon, my life changed.

She messed up two chord changes, couldn't quite get down to one note in the chorus each time, and the verses she left out to get it down to approximately single length were the wrong ones, but she sang it like an angel tearing a million miles of silk.

I hadn't imagined it would sound like *that*.

She attacked it. She slammed into the guitar, stamped her foot, and belted the words out through the chords like . . . I thought of machine guns firing through propellers; American marines at the Edinburgh Tattoo, marching past each other twirling flashing bayonettes inches from their noses; a perfect tennis rally; Jimmy Johnstone taking on four defenders and scoring . . . even her phrasing was a revelation. I'd written:

> See those clouds, rain all day,
> But they'll never wash these blues away,
> No I'm afraid they're here to stay, my love

And she sang:

> See those clouds . . . *RAIN* all day
> But they'll ne/ver wash these *BLUES* a-way
> No – *Ah'm* afraid they're *here* to stay . . . mmalove . . .

And it was right! I wanted to jump about the garage doing my

Rex Harrison impression and shouting, 'She's got it! By George she's got it!' Everything else I'd worried about and been depressed by that evening evaporated, just disappeared. I had been right; it was worth it. I was quivering, half-stunned when she finished. I hardly heard the others humming and hahing and David Balfour saying, 'Aye, well, not bad . . .' She held up her hand, launched into 'Blind Again'. She sang it all, and I was close to tears by the end, not because of the lyrics but because it was there, it was real; it had been inside me and now it was born; I saw its faults and knew it should be changed, but I loved it. And somebody else thought it was beautiful too; she must have, to have sung it like that . . .

The last chord faded. I cleared my throat and could only grin inanely at Christine and give her a completely stupid thumbs-up sign. I looked at the others.

'Aye . . . that's all right,' Steve the bassist nodded, looking me up and down. 'I'm sure it reminds me of something, though . . .' Mickey shook his head, I didn't know at what. Wes just stood looking at Christine and chewing on his lower lip.

'Yeah . . . no bad,' Dave Balfour told me. 'Well done, hen,' he said to Christine.

'*Don't* call me "hen",' she told him, putting the guitar in its case. I watched her, and remembered hearing some old saying; Ladies glowed, gentlemen perspired, and horses sweated. Christine was shining, then.

Balfour grinned. 'So, what do you want to do, big man?' He crossed his arms, head to one side as he studied me.

I shrugged. 'Write songs,' I told him.

'What about the guitar?' He nodded at the Woolworthed bass, back standing against the wall.

'What do you m-mean?'

'You wanting to join the band, or what?'

'No. It's just a b-b-bass anyway . . .' (that went down well with Steve) 'I just want to write. I'm not that g-g-g-good on it, aaactually,' (I was trying to reassure the bassist) 'I just wanted a good band to play ma stuff' (Diplomacy).

'Aye.' Dave Balfour shrugged. 'Okay then.' (Success!)

They took half a dozen songs to rehearse with; in three weeks they were ready to launch them on an unsuspecting public, at a Christmas gig in the Strathclyde Union, supporting some briefly successful Glasgow band called Master Samwise. Master Samwise were attracting attention from a couple of record companies, which was the important point.

Frozen Gold were the warm-up band, but the audience was more sympathetic than normal, just because the beautiful Christine was a student there, and had a semi-serious fan club all of her own. It seemed to consist mostly of bespectacled wimps and over-enthusiastic Malaysian students shouting 'Strip! Strip!' at her, but what the hell; it's the thought that counts.

Frozen Gold . . . I *had* tried to get them to change the name, honest.

I gave them a list: French Kiss
                       Lip Service
                       Rocks
                       MIRV
                       Gauche
                       Boulder
                       Sine
                       Spring
                       Espada
                       Z
                       Revs
                       Synch
                       Rolls
                       Trans
                       Escadrille
                       Torch
                       XL
                       Sky
                       Linx/Lynx/Links/Lyncks
                       Flux
                       Braid
                       North
                       Berlin . . . all brilliant names (dammit, at least three of them have been used since by other bands), but they weren't having it. That is, Dave Balfour wasn't having it. It had been his idea. Why not Percy Winterbottom and The Snowballs?

I suggested at one point, though he didn't seem to get the joke. I played what I thought was my trump card and told Balfour that the name sounded too much like Frigid Pink, an American band that had had one hit back in '69 or '70, and hinted that he'd probably just half-remembered that name when he was trying to think of a title for his own band.

No dice. Frozen Gold it was.

So I started trying to think of a way of turning this into an asset. Strategic thinking; when stuck with a disadvantage, remove the 'dis'.

The band played a stormer at the Strathclyde gig.

My songs weren't perfect even yet; they still had a few rough edges, but they went down well (as 'some of our own songs'; I had apparently been granted honorary membership of the band). Frozen Gold had a better reception than Master Samwise. They could have played for another hour but Master Samwise's manager was making threatening signals from the side of the stage.

When I joined the band in the corridor that was passing for a dressing room, I got there at the same time as an enthusiastic young Artistes and Repertoire man from ARC Records called Rick Tumber.

The Waterloo bar, Causeyside Street, August 1974:

'How are you, Jean? Haven't seen you for yyy. . .yonks. You okay, aye?' I set a dark rum and coke down in front of her.

'This a double, Daniel?' She inspected the glass.

'Aye; I told you; we're celebratin.'

'Oh aye?'

'Yeah; come on; no kiddin. I'm serious.'

'You seen the money yet?' She asked, sceptical, drinking.

'I've signed the contract. We've shhh. . .aken hands. It's all set up. Rich and famous; fame and ffffortune. Here we go; yahoo!' I clapped my hands. 'It's g-great; we're away, Jean; we're off; this is it. You want ma autograph now?'

'Ah'll wait till you're on Top Of The Pops.'

'You think I'm jokin, don't you?'

'No, Daniel, Ah'm sure you're serious.'

'We're gonna be famous; honest. Want me tell ye how big the

advance is?' I asked her. She laughed. 'ARC Records,' I told her. 'Heard of them?'

'Aye.'

'They've taken us on; we're gonna make an album; we go to London next month, to a proper studio. Soundproofin; technicians . . . big t-t-tape machines . . . everything.' My imagination failed. 'They're gonna rush it out in time for the Christmas,' I persisted. 'We'll be stars.'

'The next Bay City Rollers, eh?'

'Aw, Jean, come on . . .' I shook my head. 'This is serious stuff; more albums, no singles so much. You wait; just you wait and see.'

'Aye, but will it last, eh?' Jean looked serious. 'What makes you think you'll see any of this money . . . you goantae leave any in the bank for tax, or just spend it all?'

'Jean, ma main problem's goantae be decidin how tae spend it all!' I told her. She looked unconvinced. 'Look,' I said, 'don't you worry; yeah, we might have been ripped off, but one of the guys in the band, the lead guitarist, his dad's an accountant. He's looked at all the contracts and agreements an that, and had his lawyers look at them too; we've probably got a better deal than half the bands you see in the album charts. I'm telling you; we're off tae a brilliant start. An *I'm* going to be the bass player.' I made as though to nudge her elbow, accidentally did nudge her elbow, and spilled some of her dark rum. 'Oh, sorry . . . hell.' She dried her wrist with a hanky. 'Anyway, I'll be on stage; their bass player is leavin to go to music college and . . .'

'Music college?' Jean looked at me oddly.

'Yeah, what about it?'

'Nuthin. Carry on.'

'. . . So I'm gonna be the bass player. I mean, I'm still learnin, but I can do it.'

'Daniel Weir, superstar.'

'Well, no; I don't want t-to be in the limelight, like; really I just want to write the material, but seein as the bass player's leavin, we thought I might as well join, you know? No . . . Ah think I'll be stayin in the background; I'll leave the . . . the sort of figurehead work t-to the t-t-two guit-t-tarists. They're a bit more photogenic. I'll just be sort of . . . *there*, you know? Anyway; I'm writin

57

the songs, well; I'm basically writin the songs, but we've agreed that for this album, seein as I'm needin a lot of help, we'll split the c-credits between me an Dave an Chris – they're the two guitarists; they've been helpin with the arrangements an things. I mean, this is really serious; they're all takin it really seriously; they're all . . . well, apart from the guy that's leavin, and the guy that's a c-clerk with the c-council . . . they're p-p-p-postponin goan tae university, or takin a year off till we see what happens. I mean, they're holdin up their careers while they see how this goes.'

This was all true. Things had moved quickly during the previous eight months. We'd been offered a contract almost immediately by ARC Records, courtesy of Rick Tumber, the A&R man who'd been so impressed by the band's Strathclyde Christmas gig. I'd been all for jumping at it and just arguing about the terms (and having a word in private with this guy Tumber about the need for a new name for the group), but Dave Balfour said no. He told Tumber he didn't think they were ready yet; they wanted more time to practise together. I told Balfour he was crazy.

He wasn't, of course. Middle-class wisdom. Supply and demand. Tumber went away shaking his head and telling us we'd missed a great opportunity, but interest in the band only increased; the gigs improved, the crowds got bigger and the fans more numerous, various A&R people came to watch and listen, producers travelled up from London especially, and a couple of executives from small record companies came backstage after gigs with contracts which only needed our signatures. I looked at the figures and told Balfour he was totally insane and if he didn't sign something soon I'd take my songs somewhere else . . .

. . . Only he wasn't insane, and I'd no intention of going elsewhere.

Apart from anything else, I was starting to get paranoid about the band ripping off my songs; I'd realised that the outside world only had my word for it that these were my creations; I hadn't deposited copies of the manuscripts with a bank or solicitor, nobody could swear that they'd heard these tunes before Frozen Gold did them; if it came to it, it would be their collective word against my single one.

I'd panicked when I first thought of this, photocopied all my songs at enormous expense, and given the envelope full of scores to my mother with strict instructions to give it to Father McNaught, and not to forget to have him note the date he received the package. I prevaricated outrageously when Dave asked if they could have more songs; I said I was working on them. In fact I had about another forty finished – though of course they hadn't had Christine and Dave work on them – and raw material in the form of individual riffs and melodies for another twenty or thirty more. I wanted to see what happened to the ones I'd given them already.

Under great pressure, I eventually gave them another four songs; they now had enough material for an album. This gave them increased credibility in the eyes of the A&R men. The serious offers started to come in in June. After much negotiating, in which I gradually realised that Dave's dad was having at least as big a say as any of the rest of us, ARC won the dubious distinction of signing Frozen Gold for what was then some sort of record sum in the industry. That was what Dave – and his dad – had been waiting for; somebody to put so much money into the band that they couldn't *afford* for us to fail.

The deal was signed, the details worked out. We would make an album, we'd be given all the technical help and session musicians we needed; and a hot-shot producer whose granny had been Scots was assigned to us to get the best out of us and make us feel at home (and they were serious). Publicity had already started.

Dave hadn't got the required exam results to do medicine anyway, Christine had got permission to take a year off from her Physics course, and Wes had decided Eng Lit wasn't so attractive after all; he had his heart set on a Moog synthesiser and, even after trading in the Hammond, there was no way a student grant would pay for that. Mickey gave up his clerical post at the planning office with all the regret of a man wiping dogshit off his shoe.

Only Steve preferred academe to the bright brash world of rock. The others tried to persuade him to stay, and so did I. *I* didn't want to play on stage; the idea terrified me. *I'd* never pranced about a bedroom in front of a mirror miming to Hendrix solos; I wanted to be the power behind the throne, the source. Loads of people could *play* music, it seemed to me, but far fewer could write it. I did do a sort of audition though, and I'm no more immune to flattery than anybody else – less; I have so little experience of being subjected to it – and I gave in. As long as they promised never to shine spotlights on me.

We had three weeks of studio time, and our trio of academics had twelve months to decide whether Frozen Gold was more likely to provide them with liquid assets than a real job. Of course they might have been looking for Fulfilment rather than largesse, but that didn't even occur to me at the time, and I doubt it entered their heads either; 1967 was a long way away, even then.

Dave, his dad, plus Christine and the Balfour family lawyer, had gone down to London to close the deal earlier that week, with written authority from the rest of us to do so. I'd taken a deep breath and made the frightening step of instructing my own lawyer – on Mr Balfour senior's advice. I'd been almost disappointed to discover that the agreement was pretty fair, on the whole. The only possible point of contention was that three-way split on the composition royalties . . . but I had needed the help composing and arranging, Christine and Dave had both done a lot of work, and I wasn't in a position to be too demanding, I thought.

Anyway, I was learning fast; I might not need anybody else's help for the next batch of songs. I made sure the songwriting credits on future material weren't covered by that first agreement; it was a three-album deal (ARC had wanted a five-album deal originally), but there was no clause in the contract that the songs on the second two LPs should also be credited to the band rather than an individual. That was one of the smartest moves I ever made in my whole life. Possibly the only totally intelligent one in fact. Must have been a mistake.

In fact I was being ripped off, but it's all relative. I look on it as the price for having all that wonderful middle-class advice in the first place. Without it I might have had sole credit, but no money. I've met guys in this business who've sold ten, fifteen million records worldwide, and who were, effectively, broke. Jesus, they should have been multi-millionaires even after tax, but the money had all just disappeared, frittered and filtered away through and between contracts and agreements and producers and lawyers and record companies and managers and agents and tax deals.

Thirty-three and a third per cent (an appropriate figure) of a real fortune is worth a hell of a lot more than a hundred per cent of a fake one. A taste for the bottom-line is the most important sense to acquire in this industry.

So there I sat in the Waterloo bar, with Jean Webb, me a man of the world now, set to do great things. Jean had looked cold and a little grey when I swept her off her feet in Espedair Street, but the warmth of the bar brought the colour back to her skin. Her fine brown hair was a little shorter than it had been, but bushy and lustrous. Her face had filled out a little, bringing more curves to her cheek and chin; before her lips had looked a little too full, half-pouting, but now they looked in proportion, and to me – now with a hundred per cent more sexual experience, thanks to a girl I'd met at a party in Dave Balfour's house that May – very kissable. Her breasts, under the ruched bodice of her long dress, looked as graspingly enticing as ever.

'You watch,' I told her. 'The band's called Ffff-rozen Gold; the album'll probably be called *Frozen Gold and Liquid Ice* and the first single'll either be a song c-c-called "Another Rainy Day", or "Frozen Gold".'

She smiled. 'You seem taken with the name.'

'It's a t-terrible name; they wouldn't take any of the names I suggested. But I thought if we have to have that name then what c-can we do to t-turn it into an asset, you know? Something that'll work for us, so I t-took the letters of the t-t-two words, right? F and G, and just tried strumming the two chords, one after the other, and it sounded all right; sounded really good. So they form the start of the song, see? That'll be the first thing you hear on the album; F, G. Our c-c-code, see? Our theme tune, sort of. Not as c-clever as Bach using B, A, C, H, but it's clever, isn't it? It's the sort of thing that gets you publicity, see? Cos it gives people something to write about, or mention on radio programmes; makes people remember the name, too.' My mouth was dry, I was doing so much talking. I gulped at my pint. I was gibbering away at a speed that would normally have had me tripping and stumbling over every word, but I was so excited my stutter, for a change, couldn't keep up with my mouth.

'Well, don't be too clever,' Jean said. 'People don't like folk that're too clever. Nobody likes a show-off.'

'Yes, they do!' I laughed. 'That's what all rock sss. . .tars are!' She didn't look too impressed. 'Aw, don't worry,' I told her. 'I'll not be the one that's showing off. The others can do that. I'm staying in the background, basically. An I don't want to write symphonies or anything show-offy like that; I just want to write songs, stuff you can whistle.'

'Whistle,' Jean said. 'Aye.'

I took another drink. 'Anyway . . . how are you?'

She shrugged, looking into her glass. 'All right. Don't think I'm goantae go tae the art college after all though, but . . .'

I vaguely recalled she'd wanted to do art in Glasgow. 'Oh . . . I'm sorry. How no?'

'Oh . . . you know; various things. Not to worry . . .'

'How's your mum these days?' I'd remembered her mother suffered from arthritis.

'Ah, much the same,' she said. 'They send her away for tests and physiotherapy an that, but there's no really much they can do. Alec's found a job though, down at Inverkip.' I remembered Alec; he was one of the brothers with the come-and-get-yer-arms-broke eyes. 'So;' she looked at me. 'When you off to London?'

'Umm . . . don't know yet. I've handed in ma notice; leave next week. We might go down the week after next; maybe a b-bit later. But the album's to be finished by the end of October. The record company's got a flat near the studio they'll put us up in for free. It's near Oxford Sss. . .treet. You know? Where all the shops are.'

'Aw, aye.' Jean said, nodding. She seemed gloomily amused somehow. I looked at her, and I remembered the times we'd gone out, and cuddling her, and how good her mouth had felt when I hadn't cut her lip or missed it entirely and kissed her nose; I remembered that time in the darkened room, before the blue-bright, silent television; the texture of her skin and the touch of her lips and the hot, sharp scent of her.

This was, after all, the woman I'd promised to take away from here, even if she'd been sure at the time it could never happen and it was all just a pipedream. But I'd spoken a kind of vow, made some form of pledge to her, hadn't I?

Suddenly I wanted to hug her right there; take her by the shoulders and say, 'Come away with me; come to London, come and see me be famous. Be my girlfriend, be mine, or just be a friend, but don't stay here; come away!' I was so fired up with enthusiasm for life in general and my own future in particular that nothing seemed impossible just then; I could do what I wanted, I could make things happen, I could command the world. If I wanted Jean to come with me, I could do it. Difficulties and problems would evaporate before the brilliant force of my decided future. Why not? Why the hell shouldn't I ask her?

I thought about it. Why not, indeed? We liked each other; maybe we'd even loved each other, and we'd been nearly-lovers, or just-lovers. The only reason we'd split up was because I'd been so clumsy in every way with her; but I was getting better at controlling myself now. My stutter had improved, I was tramping on fewer feet and spilling fewer drinks – all right, so I'd spilled a little of Jean's a few minutes ago, but that was nothing compared to what she was used to me doing – and best of all I didn't get so embarrassed any more; I'd never again leave without seeing her, without saying goodbye. But why not make up for leaving without seeing her that time at the hospital? Why not make it so I'd never have to say goodbye again? *Why not?*

There was a quivering, terrifying but incredibly exciting, almost sexually intense feeling in my belly as I thought about asking Jean to come with me. It was like the feeling I used to get playing chess in the school club, when I'd set up some trap, or had seen a brilliant, game-winning move, but it was my opponent's move, and I was sitting there, trying not to tremble or sweat, *praying* that they wouldn't see the danger they were in. The same feeling I used to get in class, knowing I had something to say and trying to pluck up the courage to say it . . .

The words were forming like a song in my mind. But would it be right to speak them?

This was my one big chance. I'd been outrageously lucky so far; I felt like I must have used up the luck of half a dozen normal lifetimes just to get here; there'd never be another opportunity like this. Could I afford to push it even further, try to make that luck stretch to encompass two rather than one? Was it wise or even possible to burden myself with more things to think about, another person to worry over?

I might speak, I might say all I felt and persuade her to come with me, and then screw it up. Even if I was going to screw it up anyway, and her being there would have no effect for good or ill, could I take on the responsibility of messing up her life as well as my own?

And . . . wouldn't it be wiser to wait? See how things worked out. Set out unencumbered for the big bad city and take the risks with only myself to worry about, and then, if I was successful, I could always come back, having prepared the way, and ask Jean to come with me then. Spare her the times of hassle and hard work and nerves, when all was uncertainty and worry. Wouldn't that be better?

And wasn't Jean already part of my past, part of Paisley and school and all that had gone before? That might sound cruel, but how could I ever know the truth of it without getting away from everything I'd known until now, so enabling me to see it all in perspective?

I hesitated, on an edge of indecision.

'Well, look, Daniel, I've got to go.' Jean finished her drink. She looked at her watch. 'Ma mum's expectin me; I'm late already. D'you mind?' She picked up her bag from the seat.

I felt dismayed, let down, but said, 'No, of course not. Hey, I hope I didn't keep you too long.'

She got up, stood by the table. I stood too, feeling awkward, wondering if I should kiss her cheek, or cuddle her, or shake her hand, or what. She just nodded at me, looked me up and down, took a deep breath and said, 'Well, Daniel; just don't forget all your old pals when you're famous.'

I laughed. 'Aw, naw . . . no . . .'

She smiled with one side of her mouth. 'See you, Daniel.'

'Aye . . . yeah, see you, umm, Jean.'

I'd almost called her Chris. I watched her go to the lounge door and out into the sunlight.

I sat down again, feeling suddenly deflated.

There were a couple of old guys over in one corner of the lounge, quietly playing dominoes, nursing their hauf an haufs. Old, grey, hunched, small, I don't think I'd even noticed them when Jean and I had first entered the bar. I shrugged to myself and went back to my drink.

It was only about ten minutes later, finishing my pint, that I realised I'd forgotten to ask Jean how well her arm and collar bone had healed.

FIVE

I woke up in a panic. I didn't even know what was causing it at first, but there was an alarming, erratic whirling and chopping noise filling my bedroom in the folly's tower. I got my eyes open at last and sat up – head pounding after an afternoon, evening and night drinking with McCann – to discover a pigeon fluttering madly about the room. It careened from wall to wall like a fly in a jam jar, scattering feathers behind it and making bewildered, terrified cooing noises. It headed towards the window and thumped against the glass, losing more feathers and leaving a long stream of shit sliding down the glass. It bounced back through the air, circled briefly and then had another go, cracking its head against the glass.

The pigeon repeated this manoeuvre three times while I was still trying to focus properly and untangle myself from the bed-clothes. Each time it missed the opened top section of window – which it must have flown in through – by a few centimetres. I fell out of bed and knocked over the loudspeaker that serves as a bedside table, spilling a glass of water and a silvery container full of some sluggish brown mess all over the sheepskin rug. I lay staring at the debris for a moment or two, wondering what it was, then saw the chunks of meat and the plastic fork sticking out of the glutinously spreading pile of food; I could smell it, too; curry. Must have gone for a take-away last night.

The pigeon slammed against the glass again. 'Cretin!' I shouted, and heaved a pillow at it. The pillow hit the opened top window and wedged in the gap. The bird increased its frantic efforts to smash the glass. I struggled off the floor, dragging most of the bedclothes after me, hauled the pillow out of the top window and started waving my hands about to try and guide the bird through the gap. The main part of the window wasn't designed to open, so there wasn't much else I could do.

It was like trying to catch a small feathered explosion. The bird twittered, crapped on my bed, thumped into a wall and started circling round the light fixture in the centre of the ceiling. It swooped towards me, veered away again, then made for the window once more. I looked at the mess it had left on my bed, and the mess I'd left on the rug. I thought about heaving the loudspeaker through the window so the animal could escape that way, but the window looked onto St Vincent Street and I didn't want to brain a pedestrian. I decided to leave the stupid beast to it. With any luck it would get out on its own, or break its neck. My hangover required attention.

The bird shot over my head and down the tower's spiral staircase the instant I opened the door. I stood breathing heavily, then followed it downstairs.

It was nearly one by the time I felt sufficiently rehydrated to face the outside world. The Griffin was the place to go; if McCann was there he might be able to tell me what I'd done the previous day. My memory entered a sort of grey area sometime round about the middle of the evening, after we left the Griff. We'd gone for a meal then, hadn't we? . . . in fact I thought we'd gone to the Ashoka for a curry, and not a take-away either. I also had a vague recollection of stumbling about in the darkness on a curiously deserted piece of roadway, but that was about all that came back to me. The question was, where had my body picked up all these aches and pains?

I had a shower and inspected myself for signs of damage. I already knew about my grazed hands and barked knuckles, but my knees were bruised and cut too, and there was a big bruise forming on my left hip. My face showed no signs of damage beyond that inflicted by my genes. Looked like I hadn't been in a fight (not that I normally get into fights, but barked knuckles always make you wonder).

My coat was hanging over the large samovar in the choir. The rest of my clothes were missing. A cooing noise came from somewhere overhead, but the pigeon wasn't visible anywhere amongst the plaster scrollwork and dark wood beams of the roof, sixty feet overhead.

The place was cold. I have an industrial space heater which looks like a small jet engine on a large wheelbarrow and runs on paraffin; I lit it and stood twenty feet downwind, keeping warm and drying my hair at the same time, while I dug some new clothes out of an old trunk. I chose a pair of trainers that matched, just for a change.

I felt okay. Coffee, orange juice and most of a bottle of Irn Bru (not the diet version), seemed to have restored my body's fluid level. A handful of paracetamol had blasted the headache, and a couple of seasickness tablets dealt with my queasy stomach. And, no, I was not set for another day's hard drinking; I'm not that stupid, not these days.

McCann wasn't there but Wee Tommy was. Tommy is seventeen or eighteen, tall and thin, and sports a shaved blond head. He is always dressed completely in black. Style; New Austerity. My other occasional accomplice.

Just as McCann is too old to have heard of me in my Weird incarnation, so Tommy is too young. Too young to care if not to know about; to him even Punk is something from the bright and distant past, and anything before that is from some almost mythical age. He regards bands like Frozen Gold as the musical equivalents of multinational corporations; big, efficient, heartless, impersonal, profitable, and with interests and values either irrelevant to his, or opposed. Don't entirely disagree myself. Anyway, he too thinks I'm just the folly's minder, not its owner. He's shown even less interest in Weird than McCann, he just thinks St Jute's is a cool place to hang out, man. (That's almost a direct quote by the way. Don't ask me what's going on; fashions in language have always confused me, too.)

'Drink?'

'Aw, it's yerself Jim . . . Aye, I'll take a wee voddy.'

I got Tommy a large vodka. I was on English shandies; half and half beer and lemonade. 'Aw, Jim,' Tommy said, 'could I have a half a heavy for TB?'

68

'Aye,' I said, looking round. I'd thought Tommy was alone. 'Who?'

'The dug.' Tommy pointed to his feet. Under the table there was a large black dog lying with its massive head resting on its sphinxed legs; looked like a cross between an alsatian and a wolfhound . . . or maybe just a wolf. It lifted its head and growled at me; I growled back and it snorted, lowered its head onto its arm-thick forelegs, probably going back to the contemplation of which of the regulars to gnaw on first.

'In an ashtray, that all right, Jim?'

'What?'

'The heavy; could ye get Bella to put it in an ashtray?'

'Dyae waant a straight ashtray, aye?' The wee wifey behind the bar said as soon as I turned back to order the hound's bevvy.

I admired Bella's toothless smile for a moment and couldn't think of a smart reply. 'Just as it comes, Bella,' I told her.

'That thing yours?' I sat down with Tommy between me and the beast's teeth and watched it lap enthusiastically at the beer-filled ashtray. Damn hound spilled less than I normally do.

'Naw, it's ma uncle's. I'm lookin after it while he's in the hospital.'

'What bit of him did it eat?'

'Na; he's in tae get his piles done.' Tommy grinned. 'He'll only be a few days. You wouldnae bite anybody, would ye, TB?' He reached down and scratched the animal vigorously behind its neck. The dog didn't seem to notice. 'That you on the shandies, big yin?' Tommy looked at my glass.

'Aye. I'm looking for McCann to tell me what we did last night.'

'You up to no good, aye?'

'Probably.' I looked at my barked knuckles.

Drink is bad for you. It's a drug. A poison. Of course I know that; don't we all? It just so happens it's legal and available and accepted and there's a whole tradition of enjoying it and suffering the consequences, even boasting about the consequences, and that tradition is especially strong here in Scotland, and especially in the west, and especially in Glasgow and surrounding areas . . .

I drink too much but I enjoy it, and I've never once woken up needing a *drink*; water, orange juice, something fizzy like lemonade, yes . . . hundreds and hundreds of times, but never the hard stuff. If I ever do I just hope I can catch it there and stop it going any further. All the best alkies start out this way, I'm sure.

But of course I'm different.

Ah, dear God . . . many a good man ruined by drink . . .

The only person I ever saw ruined by drink was my father, and he wasn't a good man in the first place.

'Your YTS scheme finished, or what?' I asked Tommy. He'd been providing cheap labour for a furniture manufacturer over the past few months.

'Aye; finished early. Got ma cards.'

'How come?'

'Ah, Ah was sniffin the glue, ye know? This foreman caught me in the bog wi a plastic bag over ma heid.'

I shook my head. 'You're a mug.' I tried not to sound too much like just another adult.

'Aye, yer right; wiznae even the right glue.'

'What?'

'Water based, or sumthin. Ah'd been there sniffin for about an hour. Ah got sumthin at first like; a sort aw buzz, ye know? But nothin spectacular. Ah'd wondered how that wiz; Ah'd a big enough tin a glue. Smelled horrible too.'

'Water based . . .' I shook my head, and felt too much like an adult. What had I been like at his age?

'Ach, ye've got tae try these things, ye know?' Tommy told me. 'Ye never know.'

'You know/ You never know' . . . no, it wasn't worth mentioning. I marvelled at Tommy's attitude. When I was his age I was paranoically careful. I used my flatmates as guinea pigs, I sought out people who'd been using drugs for years and carried out my own covert psychological examination on them, I even read medical journals to find out what the side effects of the most popular drugs were. Tommy seemed to approach things from exactly the opposite direction; when in doubt, try it out.

I'd survived, but would Tommy? I could just hear him: 'Strychnine? Aye, gie us a wee dod a that . . .' Holy shit. Babes and innocents.

Little dingbat had even tried smack. I'd surprised him when he

70

told me that; I took him by the collar and pushed him up a wall and told him if he touched the stuff again I'd shop him to the polis. Didn't mean a word of it, but it seemed to impress him. 'Aye, okay then big yin, don't get in a fuss. Ah like glue better anyway, apart from the headaches.' (To which my reply was 'Oh, for God's sake . . .')

Oi! These kids today!

But was I just jealous? H was about the only drug I'd never tried; the one substance I was genuinely frightened of, because I knew I had an addictive personality and one taste might be too many. Crazy Davey had tried it and given it up, though not without a struggle, and not without losing Christine for a while, but I didn't think that I'd be able to stop. So, did I envy Tommy his experience? I didn't know.

And what was I supposed to say to him? Don't try all the things I've tried? Stay off grass and cultivate the weed? Holy shit; there's logic for you.

Peddle one of the least harmful drugs humanity's ever discovered, and you get twenty years. Peddle something that kills a hundred thousand a year . . . and you get a knighthood.

Hell no, I don't know what to say to kids like Tommy. It wasn't until I talked to him I even knew what sniffing glue did. You hallucinate, is it, basically. A cheap, nasty, short-lived acid substitute that gives you pounding headaches.

This is progress?

The dog looked up from a dry and empty ashtray, and growled. 'I think he's wantin another one,' Tommy said, digging into one black trouser pocket.

'Nothing for me,' I told him as he got up, taking the ashtray with him. The dog watched him go, then lowered its head onto its paws again. 'When's it his round?' I shouted to Tommy.

'It's his next,' he told me, quite seriously. I looked at him. 'Naw, really; ma uncle gied us a tenner tae buy the dug's drink while I'm looking after him.'

'I bet he leaves before it's his shout.'

Tommy brought the ashtray back full of beer and put it down in front of the dog. It sniffed at the beer then looked up at him silently. 'Hmm,' Tommy said, scratching his head. 'Doesnae seem to want it,'

'Maybe he wanted a clean ashtray.'

'Aye . . . it's a fussy beast sometimes.' He knelt down and risked his right hand again, chuckling the dog under its chin. Its jaws looked like a fur-lined mantrap. 'Yer a fussy beast, aren't ye, TB?'

The door opened and McCann came in, looking a little grey. He looked down at Tommy on his way to the bar. 'Ma Goad, Tommy, Ah've seen ye with some right dugs in here, but that yin takes the biscuit.' He winked at me. 'Aye, big yin, how's yer heid? . . . Mornin, Bella; usual, please.'

'Hi, Mr McCann.' Tommy is strangely deferential to those older than me.

'My head's fine,' I told McCann. 'How's yours?'

'It'll be better by the time I get this down me,' McCann said, bringing a pint of heavy and a whisky to the table. He shifted a canine leg out of the way with his foot as he sat down opposite, and ignored the resulting snarl.

'Hair of the dog?' I suggested.

'Just maintaining an even strain, James; just maintaining an even strain.' He supped his beer. Wee Tommy sat down again. Sounds of lapping came from under the table.

McCann drained half of each drink, then looked under the table. 'That your dug, Toammy?'

'Ma uncle's,' Wee Tommy said. 'It's name's TB.'

'Disnae look ill . . .' McCann said, looking puzzled.

'Whit were you two up tae last night then?' Tommy asked McCann.

'Ho, you no remember, big yin?' McCann winked at me.

'Dancing in the road,' I said. 'And I know we went for a take-away.'

McCann started laughing. 'That aw?' He found this highly amusing. 'Dancing on a "road"! Ho ho ho!' He finished the whisky, shook his head. 'Ho ho ho!'

'It's Santa,' I said to Tommy.

'Ye remember leavin here?' McCann said.

'. . . not exactly.'

'Ye made a date with Bella.' He smiled widely to show us his yellowing teeth and much more healthy-looking falsers.

'Oh,' I said. 'Well, she'll understand.' I looked for her at the bar, but she wasn't there.

'We went to the Ashoka; remember that? But no for a take-away. Dae ye remember sword fightin with the manager?'

'*What?*'

'Ye dinnae, dae ye?' McCann's grin widened to take in his farthest rear molars.

'McCann, if you're making this up . . .' This was serious. The Ashoka was my favourite Indian. A *swordfight?*

'Ah, it wiz only with kebab skewers; Ah think ye'll get back in. Ye were havin a laugh.'

'Yeah, I'll bet I was, but was he?'

'Aw, aye.'

'Thank God for that.'

'Ye remember dancin on the . . . "road", aye?' McCann winked at Tommy.

'Vaguely.'

'D'ye no remember whit bit a road it wiz?'

'Not exactly. Wasn't outside the police station, was it?'

'Naw.' McCann winked at the grinning Tommy again, then took a long, slow drink of heavy. I waited.

'How about doin the striptease?' he asked, stage-whispering.

'. . . Oh dear . . .' I said.

'Ye still no remember?'

'No,' I said miserably. Was that what had happened to my clothes?

'Ye know,' McCann began slowly, leaning forward over the table to me and Tommy, 'the sawn-off flyover?'

Tommy was silent for a second, then sniggered loudly into his vodka and lemonade. I gazed in horror at McCann. I could feel my eyes bulging. McCann's smile threatened to lift the top of his head off.

'Oh *shit,*' I said.

'Yes,' McCann said, rapping the table with one hand.

'Oh, dear God, dear holy shit.' I buried my head in my hands. I brought it out and looked up at McCann. 'How did we get away with . . .? oh no . . . no . . . no . . .' I buried my head in my hands again. McCann laughed; Tommy laughed. I think Bella

73

laughed. I wasn't too sure I couldn't hear the dog laugh.

The M 8 motorway plunges straight through Glasgow; it loops round the northern extent of the city centre and swoops down between the centre and West End, before curving over the Clyde via the Kingston Bridge and completing the bottom half of its S shaped journey through the city by curving west for Paisley and Greenock. It destroyed a great deal, but the city survived nevertheless, and it was left with what's probably the fastest city-centre to airport car journey in Europe.

But there were planning errors, bits where they left slip-roads that don't connect with anything, exits that end in earth banks, forks in the elevated section that only go one way; the other ends in mid air. One of these little motorway follies consists of a third level of roadway, just north of the Sauchiehall Street flyover. The elevated roadway crosses the motorway beneath, but doesn't go anywhere; it's only as long as the motorway is wide, and stuck up in the air all by itself. At some point, the town planners must have thought they could use the stubby relic as a pedestrian footbridge, because there are wide steps at the North Street end. However, these are fenced off, and there are no matching steps at the Newton Street end, so that idea must have fallen through.

This useless flyover is protected from the attentions of children and idiots by sheer concrete legs, overhangs, and those black steel gates across the North Street steps. None of which, it turned out, had stopped me. I'd climbed over the gates and danced on the plant-choked road surface, God knows how far above the motorway traffic. Did a strip. According to McCann I dropped or threw about half my clothes over the edge, trying to hit passing trucks and so distribute my clothing around the country – or even the world – on the tops of containers . . . I just hoped I'd thrown the trainers down and not left them up there; how many people in this city wear one size eleven and one size twelve? At least I knew now why my feet had been so dirty in the shower this morning.

Then a police car had pulled up at the steps, and McCann had shouted to me to get away. I'd dreeped (suspended myself over the drop by my fingers and then let go) into the bushes at the Newton Street end, and run off, dripping and cackling, into the night.

I'm a crazy man. I admit it. I try to act responsibly, but every now and again I totally surprise myself and just go haywire. It's the drink that does it, I swear.

'Who's this guy Tumbler that's comin tae see ye anyhow, eh?' McCann said later, when the three of us were sitting in St Jute's; they were sampling some Hungarian brandy and washing it down with Bud. I was still being good, on orange juice and fizzy spring water. I froze when McCann mentioned – well, more or less mentioned – Tumber's name.

I must have said something about Rick when I was drunk last night. This was something I'd always worried about; getting drunk and giving the whole game away to somebody like McCann; letting them know I was this immensely, disgustingly rich rock star. McCann wouldn't be my friend any more; I have about a million times too much capital to play with. Wee Tommy would resent the fact I'd been the driving force behind one of those glitteringly narcissistic, monolithic seventies' rock groups . . . and both would resent the fact I'd lied to them. I wish I hadn't, but . . . well, it's too late now.

What had I said? I tried to think of something that might fit.

When in doubt, tell something close to the truth. 'He's from the record company that put out your man's songs,' I told McCann. 'Why, what was I saying about him?' I was distracted from McCann by the sight of Wee Tommy's dog loping slowly past the end of the pew carrying something in his mouth that looked like one of my trainers.

'Ye were goantae park the bulldozer on his Porsche.'

Oh, God. I bet I said 'my bulldozer', too. I gave a little laugh. 'Did I say that?' I took a nice long drink of Bud. Tommy belched. Chewing noises came from the north transept. 'Well,' I said, 'he's coming to have a look round, so . . . I'm just hoping he doesn't find anything . . . he doesn't like.'

'What,' Tommy said, 'like five hundred empty Budweiser bottles in the bulldozer?'

'Well . . . no, I was told I could have the drink, but . . . I don't know. I suppose I'm just resentin anybody coming to check up on me . . .' I shrugged, took another long slug. I wondered how I was doing. 'Not to worry. He's not coming until . . . aahm . . . the twenty-first, I think he said.'

'Izzy cumin up for Christmas, like?' Tommy said.

'No, just the day, I think.'

'So he'll no bring his car then?' McCann said.

'Probably fly,' I agreed.

'Take ye a while tae get the 'dozer tae the airport,' McCann said helpfully. 'Better start noo.'

'Forget the bulldozer. No licence for it anyway, and it's left-hand drive. Maybe I'll just clean the place up a bit and make him a cup of tea.'

'Ye'll need tae hire a skip tae clear the empties.'

'Aye, right enough.' I cleared my throat and turned to look in the direction of the north transept, where the chewing noises had ceased, to be replaced by what sounded like canine vomiting. Tommy looked over too, briefly. The dog had bought its round in the Griffin, and kept pace with us for the next hour or so. Bella even let Tommy take it to the gents with him; his uncle had trained it to pee into toilet gutters. We'd all had some food, but the dog had turned its nose up at the plate of pie and beans I'd bought him. 'He's on a high fibre diet these days,' Tommy had explained.

'Beans are high fibre.'

'Aye, but there's too much sugar in the sauce, like.'

'Spoilt brat,' I'd told the dog, then divided the pie and beans up between the three of us. We'd come back to the folly when the dog's money ran out. The hound walked straight but kept stopping at lamp posts, and tried to pick a fight with a great dane on Bath Street. Tommy didn't have a lead for the beast, so it was a matter of forming a defensive wall between the snarling great dane (and its terrified lady owner) and the crouching, quietly growling TB. Suddenly I knew how footballers felt facing a direct free kick. I kept my hands over my crotch.

When we got to St Jute's I suggested the dog might want another drink too. 'Oh.' Tommy shook his head. 'Ah don't know if he's really developed a taste for these continental lagers. Ye don't have any stout at all, dae ye?'

'No.'

'Ach well, try him on the Bud then.'

TB liked Bud. He was drinking it faster than McCann, who's no slowcoach himself. Of course, TB wasn't having to cope with brandy chasers as well. We'd left him in the kitchen, standing over a Tupperware bowl I'd poured three bottles into. I wondered if he'd eaten my trainer.

'So we better no come round on the twenty-first, then, naw?' McCann said. I nodded.

'Better not to. But it'll be all right. I can handle it.'

'Fair enough, pal.' McCann finished another glass of brandy, belched, then lit a fag. I refilled the brandy glasses then went for a pee. On the way back, I passed the hi-fi gear stacked at the front of the pulpit. I'd left a Tom Waites record lying on the turntable: I thought I noticed something on it. I went over to look. It was a pale splatter of pigeon shit. I looked up at the nave roof, thinking about shotguns.

When I got back, Tommy was sitting at the end of the pew, scratching TB behind the ears. The dog was swaying slightly and looking at McCann's cigarette. I wondered if it smoked. Probably didn't like tipped. 'Think we could fix the dug up wi some food?' Tommy asked. 'Ah think it's gettin hungry. Wid that be possible, maybe, aye?'

'Sure. Does it like pigeon? Can it climb?'

'What?' Tommy said, then the hound turned and loped off, heading for the kitchen in the south transept. Tommy just shrugged. 'Aw, never mind then. Cannae be that hungry.' I watched the beast go, and worried about where it would pee. This building was turning into a menagerie, and I don't even like animals.

Well, I don't mind them, but I don't miss them if they're not around. I don't have a pet, and I don't have any plants in the place either. Just not that sort of person, I guess. Inez never did understand me; she had to have plants and animals and people around her all the time. Maybe it was being brought up on a farm that did it, I don't know. She loved animals; she even ended up loving her baby armadillos, which I thought was either saintly or perverse. She got on well with people, she was a natural with animals and she could make any plant flourish. She even had plants that she took on tour with us, to make the dressing rooms feel more human (not that that made sense to me). She had a cat that came with us when we toured the UK, and on the very first date of the European tour, in Amsterdam, she found some scruffy, ragged-eared little black kitten on the way from the hotel to the gig; took it all round Europe for three months and had it

77

quarantined for six months when we came back to Britain. I'd suggested when we first started going together that I might represent a sort of subconscious compromise for her; half-human, half-animal. She'd looked puzzled and said, '*Human?*'

I breathed in the slipstream smoke from McCann's cigarette and thought of Inez. Not because she smoked, but because she was an addiction. I found it hard to give her up. I still think of her. I gave up smoking at the same time, and it tempts me back every so often too. Just one more wouldn't make any difference . . .

'What's this guy Weird like anyway?' Tommy said.

'Eh?' I said. 'Oh . . . quiet. Very quiet. Tall dark silent type. Doesn't have much to say for himself. He's got a bad stutter, which I think is why he doesn't like talking. I mean, I hardly ever see him, but . . . anyway, he pays all right though . . . umm.'

'Izzy weird like, though?'

'Well . . . yeah, a bit.' I pretended to think. 'Like, he only hires people taller than him. He's six-five; sensitive about his height. Only takes people on who make him look small. You should see his chauffeur; he's bigger than me; six-eight. Even his girlfriend's over six foot. You, ah . . . never seen any photies of him?'

I'm always nervous when the conversation gets round to Weird. All Tommy would have to do is go into a record store and pick up that first album and he'd see a photograph of the band on the back, with me staring over the top of the others, big-eyed and grinning. I don't know if I'm recognisable or not; I don't think so, but how can I be sure? Nobody's run up to me in the street wanting my autograph, not for half a decade, but what does that prove?

Thank God for changing hairstyles. I look totally different now (apart from the height, the physique, the wild staring eyes . . .); I used to have a fuzzy bush of long hair, which I wore in something close to an afro style when we were offstage, and had slicked back with old-fashioned hair oil and tied in a blood knot at the back when we were on stage. I had a big bushy beard too; first of all because I still had spots for the first two years of our fame, then because I liked hiding behind it.

And I always wore mirror shades. They became a trade mark. I was hiding behind those too, but they also looked good on stage, and they put photographers off; the flash tended to reflect back into the cameras. I spent a lot of time annoying photographers by not removing the shades, and pissing off interviewers by hamming up my stutter and not having a lot to say anyway. Probably just as well; on one of the few occasions I did give a straight interview, it caused us terrible problems.

On the whole, I communicated best when I didn't say anything. Thanks to Dave and Chris, I got away with this anti-social behaviour. Either one was photogenic enough for an entire band; together they were stunning. They took the heat off me. I'd just have gotten embarrassed, having my big baw-face plastered all over album covers and posters and music papers.

Anyway, I have short hair and I'm clean-shaven now. According to the record company's publicity department, Weird now lives in seclusion on a Caribbean island. Because ARC never say which island, it's a perfect cover story; at least one journalist wasted two months trying to find me, to get an 'up-date on the reclusive life of the mysterious figure behind seventies mega rock band Frozen Gold, the man they called "The Eminence Grease" ' (that was the hair oil. Thank you, NME). ARC and I started another two back-up rumours; the first is that I'm not living on a Caribbean island at all, I'm dead; and the second is that that too is just a ruse, and I'm living in a ruined monastery in Ladakh.

'He's a tax exile, anyway; doesn't come back much,' I told Tommy.

'Ha!' McCann said. 'Ah dinnae ken why he bothers; this fuckin country's practically a tax haven these days.' He drained his Bud bottle disgustedly. He was right, of course; I knew quite a few tax exiles who'd come back to Britain since the Tories dropped the higher tax rates. I didn't say anything.

There was a ragged thumping noise from the stairwell which led to the tower; TB the dog appeared, half-falling, half-running down the steps. He staggered as he hit the tiled floor of the nave, then wobbled upright, and padded off towards the choir, snuffling.

'Parasitic bastard,' McCann said. I thought this was being a little hard on the dog, but then he added, 'Bloody pop stars.'

'Aw well,' Tommy said. 'Ah suppose he was only tryin tae make a bit a cash like.'

' "A bit a cash",' McCann said, scornfully. 'How much is this bastard worth, dae ye know, Jim?'

I shrugged, frowning. I could hear some funny noises coming from the choir. Heavy breathing, it sounded like. What was that animal up to? 'No idea,' I said. 'Millions, probably.'

'There ye are,' McCann said. 'Millions. Probably invested in South Africa and British Telecom and British and American Tobacco and the so-called "Aerospace" and "Defence" industries. Ha!'

Well, Scottish forests and Swedish Government Bonds, actually. Could be a lot worse.

But what do you do? Real soon now I'm going to give it all away to the Labour Party and progressive charities . . . or the ANC or something . . . I don't know. Just as soon as I've decided who's right, just as soon as I think I can give up what I do have . . . I'm as generous as I can be without becoming conspicuous. Specific things for leftish causes, and not a few Glaswegian tramps have been stunned to ask for the price of a cup of tea and be given the price of a bottle of malt whisky. All salves for my own conscience, of course, but it's not always *easy* to be generous, damn it. There was a time, with me and Balfour and a Rolls Royce . . .

'Ye cannae just condemn the man like that,' Tommy said, very reasonably I thought. He seemed to catch the odd noises from the choir too, and looked round. 'What's he supposed tae dae with aw that money?'

'Why make it in the first place?' McCann said indignantly, apparently perfectly serious. 'His own class no good enough for him, eh? If he had any talent at all – an gettin millions a teenagers tae buy yur records is no guarantee whatsoever that the buggir did have any talent, let me tell ye – if he did have any talent, then he should have devoted it to the advancement of his own people.' McCann pointed at Tommy with the neck of his Bud bottle.

'Whit, Paisley people?' Tommy said. Shit, I thought. I didn't know he even knew that much about Weird. How much more?

'Naw naw naw, son,' McCann said exasperatedly, screwing his face up. 'The workers. The working people of the world, the toilers.'

'Aw.' Tommy nodded, standing on the pew and looking down to the choir, where the panting noises had become louder.

McCann's face was stern, severe, decided. The workers; the toilers. Oh, God yes, I wanted to write something that would make a difference to something other than my bank balance and the state of the charts. I tried; there was some socially relevant stuff in there; I even had a couple of Vietnam war songs ready, but the thing ended before we could get them out. I wanted to write anthems for the working class, marching tunes for disaffected youth and oppressed minorities, but . . . I never got round to it.

'Ah . . . Jim . . .' Tommy said. 'I think T B's gettin a bit over-affectionate with your coat.'

I got to my feet. 'What?'

Tommy set off for the choir. 'Naw! T B! Stop that! Bad dug! Get away from that!' He disappeared behind some packing cases.

McCann and I followed him. T B was in the choir, near the still blowing space heater, bent across a chest I'd thrown my old naval greatcoat over. He was trying to mate with it. His rump, supported by two wobbling, tile-skidding legs, was still pumping away enthusiastically at the dark blue mass of the coat when Tommy came up behind him and kicked his backside.

T B dismounted instantly and didn't even stop to growl; he ran off past the pulpit and towards the pile of crates, knocking over a free-standing lamp cluster as he did so; it crashed across my Charles Rennie Mackintosh chair and whacked one of the security monitors, which fell to the tiles and imploded.

'T B!' Tommy yelled, then ran after the beast as it disappeared between unopened cases of Bulgarian sewing machines and boxes of Russian ear-muffs.

McCann and I doubled back and started running, keeping to the east aisle. McCann was laughing as he ran. 'T B!' Tommy shouted again, hidden by crates of Czech televisions. 'Heel, boy. Sit! Sit!'

'Some dug that, eh Jimmy?' McCann panted as we neared the main doors.

'I'll kill it.'

We rounded the corner by the dump truck and skidded to a stop at the same time as Tommy, coming from the opposite direction. 'You see him?' he asked. We shook our heads. Tommy scratched his. 'Shit. I lost him. Sorry about this, Jim. He's not usually like this. I thought he could hold his drink.'

'Never mind,' I said.

'Tell ye what,' McCann said. 'Open one a they big doors and we'll go back tae the pulpit, form a line, and flush him oot. He'll head fur the door when he sees it's open.'

Tommy was indignant. 'He might run away! He might run into the street an get run over!'

I said nothing. McCann snapped his fingers. 'We'll put a big empty packin case just the far side aw the opening, so he'll run into that.'

Maybe I'd had more shandies than I thought, but this sounded like a good idea. We opened one of the St Vincent Street doors by a couple of feet, put an empty tea chest on the top step outside, then ran back to the pulpit. I thought I could hear the sound of running water somewhere inside the piled crates; about level with the boxes of Polish jam. We formed a line with Tommy in the middle and started down the floor of the building, McCann and I taking an aisle each and Tommy clambering over the mountains of cases and boxes. I found the remains of a trainer as we passed the kitchen in the west transept.

'Got him!' Tommy shouted, from somewhere in the middle of the pile. There was the sound of wheezing, scrabbling claws, and glass breaking. Then Tommy said, 'Aw . . .'

'Did ye get him?' McCann shouted from the other aisle.

'Naw, but Ah must have givin him a hell of a fright. Jeez . . . this is honkin. Whit a pong. Sumhin wrong wi that dug's guts . . .'

McCann's quiet laughter echoed from the far aisle. Tommy said, 'Ah really am sorry about all this, big yin. I'll clean all this up after we've caught him, okay?'

'There he is!' McCann shouted. There was a noise of claws skidding on tiles from the far end of the folly, near the doors, and McCann's running feet. I started running too.

I got past the bulldozer in time to see T B's rump and hind legs fly over the packing case we'd positioned outside. McCann tried to follow the dog, but hit the case and sprawled, cursing. Tommy ran up behind me and we pushed the door open to get out.

T B stood at the bottom of the steps, on St Vincent Street,

breathing heavily and looking rather unsteady on his feet. He was staring at us. I helped McCann to his feet; he was rubbing his skinned palms with a grubby hanky. Tommy started down the steps, slowly, holding one hand out to the panting beast. 'Good boy, TB; here boy . . .'

TB stood looking at him, saliva dripping from his mouth, tongue lolling, flanks pulsing, then leaned forward, opened his mouth and threw up onto the pavement and keeled over, flopping sideways onto the sidewalk in front of a young couple walking past. He lay there, flat on the ground, legs straight and eyes closed.

Tommy straightened, stuck his hands in his pockets. 'Aw, shit.'

'Is he all right?' McCann asked, putting his hanky back in the breast pocket of his jacket.

'Aye,' Tommy said, going down to the recumbent hound. 'He's just drunk.' He shook his head. The beast was still breathing. 'Ah suppose Ah'd better get him back to ma maw's. She'll no be very happy.'

'I'm going for my coat now,' I told Tommy. 'If I find anything in the pockets . . .' I pointed at the dog, which had started to snore. I left the phrase hanging and went back into the folly for my greatcoat.

'Is that curry Ah can smell?' McCann said as I kicked the tea chest back through the doors.

Apart from a few hairs, the dog had left nothing on or in the coat. I turned the power off to the smashed TV monitor and closed the door leading to the tower. There was a smell of dogshit in the nave.

Tommy's mother expected him and the dog home for their tea. She lived about quarter of a mile away, on Houldsworth Street. McCann was nursing his grazed hands, and limping. Tommy took TB's front legs, I took the rear. The dog was as limp as a sack of potatoes, but heavier. We tramped through the darkening street, getting the occasional funny remark, but nobody stopped us. McCann sniggered every now and again.

'Must have been the curry,' Tommy said. 'He was obviously hungry or he wouldnae have eaten the wee fork as well.' The dog grunted as though in agreement, then resumed its snoring.

'Aye,' McCann said. 'Some dug that. Can ye rent it oot? Gie it tae people ye dinnae like?'

'Never thought of that, Mr McCann,' Tommy admitted. My shoulders were getting sore. I took a better grip of the animal's legs and looked down distastefully at it; the dog was quietly pissing itself.

The urine was soaking into its belly hair and running down its flanks and round to its back, to drip off there, onto my latest new pair of trainers.

'What does "TB" stand for anyway?' I asked Wee Tommy.

He looked at me as though I was an idiot, and in an almost resentful tone said, 'Total Bastard.'

'Oh, yes,' I said. 'Of course. Obvious really.'

'Ye mean there's nuthin wrong wi its lungs after aw?' McCann said, disgustedly.

'Not compared to its bladder,' I muttered, trying to keep my feet clear of the dribbling canine pee.

'Naw, it's perfectly healthy,' Wee Tommy said. 'It's just . . .' he shrugged, shaking the totally relaxed and snoring hound '. . . it's an animal.'

'Fair enough.' McCann said.

We tramped across the motorway by the St Vincent Street flyover; the rain came on.

We all got wet.

SIX

The weirdness began about the end of '74, after we'd finished the album, before anything had really started happening. We'd worked ten and twelve hour days in the studio, used shifts of technicians, seen virtually nothing of London except the inside of the studio in Ladbroke Grove and the flat off Oxford Street. We still overran by a week, but taking a month to do an album – even with the mixing still to be done – was hardly slow. Some bands take that long for one track.

I got out of the flat exactly once, to wander down Oxford Street and Carnaby Street (it was a relic even then). Bowie clones and skinheads; platform boots and every now and again the confusing sight of people wearing narrow-legged jeans but otherwise look- ing . . . I don't know; up to date, fashionable. There was change in the air: I could almost smell it. I got back to the flat feeling relieved to be out of that bewildering gaggle of styles and sensations.

I still don't understand fashion. Why do people dress up in new styles in the first place if they're only going to act all embarrassed and ashamed about them later? So flares and platform boots look stupid now; just wait till you see how sniggeringly daft spikey hair and torn black T-shirts look in a decade's time. At least flares had the practical advantage of making it possible to change your jeans without taking your boots off. Try that in drainpipes.

I remember thinking it Meant Something that hippies seemed to grow out of the ground and be fuzzy round the edges; the loon pants like stems, the puff-ball hair, the leather fringes and flared, open cuffs; hippies seemed to be part of what was around them; they faded out at the periphery. The harder look inspired by punk (but now very much post-punk) has meant definite boundaries; straight legs, very *assertive* looking footwear, and no-nonsense upperworks; so now everybody looks like para-civilians; streetwise combatants in the battle for jobs.

But that's now and this was then, in the very best age there ever is; when you're young enough not to have lost that head of enthusiasm, and it's still possible to feel *this* is where the wave breaks, with you and your generation; *now* the same old rolling bore breaks up and the frothy fun starts; surf's up!

Well, maybe next time . . .

We were back in Scotland for a month, in a curious limbo. We'd been excited and frightened and nervous making the album. Studios, approached correctly, are just great big toys, and immense fun to play about with, but we were a little intimidated by it all. We'd been living on a sort of continual high for that month – a natural high, apart from the odd spliff in the flat to relax before crashing out, and one occasion when we took some speed to get us through a long session on 'Answer and Question', which we were determined to finish that night.

Once it was over, and we were back in Paisley, it all seemed unreal. I had to tell myself it had really happened, and I think my flatmates thought the whole deal had fallen through, or I'd made it all up. My ma obviously hadn't heard that it was a cliché for the mothers of budding rock stars to lament the fact their sons or daughters didn't have a real job.

I was being careful with the money. Once I'd worked out how much I'd have to save for tax, and how much just living would cost if we had to move to London – which looked likely – my share didn't look all that immense after all. Also, I think I was being superstitious. I felt that if I spent it too showily, I'd be punished. Not God but Fate would turn everything round again; the album would flop. There would be no single, the band would fold, or they'd find somebody else to play bass and write their songs . . . the best tactic was not to have too high a profile. Then Fate wouldn't notice. Intense hubris, tasteless extravagance, would attract some terrible reckoning.

I always meant to look Jean Webb up, to keep in touch, to take her out for a drink or a meal, or just pop round to her mum's to say hello, but I never quite got into the right mood; I always felt there'd be a better time, when my future was more settled, when I had some *really* good news. For whatever reason, I never did get around to it, even though I still thought about her now and again.

So we practised the songs from the album – which we were now heartily sick of – and started on some new tunes. I had worked on these latest songs for much longer by myself, with what I thought was my new-found mastery of compositional technique, before showing them to the others. I wanted these to be mine. Having Dave and Chris rework the first batch of songs, and then, just when I was starting to get used to the material in that form, having it all altered again by Mike Milne, our producer, had been a traumatic experience. This time I wanted to present them all with something more like the finished product (that was how I thought of it. This was before I developed my hatred of the word 'product').

We played some gigs in Glasgow and Edinburgh; my first on stage. To my extreme and delighted surprise, I enjoyed it. I did keep in the background, and though there was a spotlight on me, that was only lit when the rest of the band were spotlighted too; I was never singled out.

I refused to do a bass solo. This was almost unheard of for any band hoping to be classed as anything like 'progressive', but I was adamant. I wore dark clothes on stage, I already had the mirror shades and I'd started growing my beard the day I left Paisley for London and the recording studio.

I was getting my act together, man. The record company wasn't too keen on this at first; they wanted us all to be nice, outgoing kids with bright smiles. Having a six and a half foot semi-scrofulous mutant in the band wasn't really what they wanted at all, but as I did write the songs they couldn't get rid of me, so they must have hoped they could take the rough edges off my strangeness. Some hope. They were confused at first, uncertain whether our youth and the good looks of Dave and Chris meant they ought to try aiming us at the teenybopper market, or Dave's guitar-hero style and my unorthodox but still hummable songs suited us for the progressive charts. Singles or albums? Sensibly, they eventually went for the latter.

Albums were outselling singles by then anyway, and even a record company exec high on coke and his own creative genius knows there's more staying power in a 'serious' rock band than a short-lived teenybopper phenomenon (though of course your teenybopper band will shift a hell of a lot of product very quickly, which means they'll sell all their records while under your contract and not have the time to head for another label offering better royalties).

Mike Milne had had a lot of pressure on him from the company to do his bit in packaging us; they wanted a strong 'credible' album, but they wanted a single too; something smooth and easily marketable, something ideal for Radio One, something they could sell. A cheaper producer would have given them just what they wanted. Milne's time was expensive because he came fully equipped with brains, including the bit people call heart, or the soul.

Somehow, he could immediately sense the weaknesses and strengths in the groups he worked with. While everybody else was still worrying about whether they should change their names and what colour they should all dye their hair, Milne would be working out how to play to those strengths and develop whatever worthwhile qualities he'd found in the band. It was a sixth sense very few people seem to possess; common sense.

In us he seemed to have a strategic view while all around him were looking only at the tactics of marketing us efficiently. He made a virtue out of the necessity of recording the album in a comparatively short time; he kept the sound rough and ready in places, giving it a raw live feel, and he used those of Dave's solos which sounded the most exciting, not the note-perfect, technically impressive but finally rather heartless examples Dave produced when he was trying too hard.

And, thank God, he didn't let us over-indulge in solos. This was the age of the half-hour drum solo; Jesus, I could see the point of a five-minute solo on stage, to give the rest of the band time for a pee or a quick jay – I've known guys who go backstage for a quick blow job off some adoring fan during their drummer's solos – and certainly it keeps the drummer happy (a lot of them get fed up sitting back there, mostly hidden, doing all the hard work), but who the hell actually wanted to listen to thirty minutes, or even fifteen, of mindless look-how-fast-I-can-play drumming (on the other hand, who the hell ever wanted to be spat at, either)?

But quantity was quality then. The bigger your sound system, the faster you could play, the longer your double or triple concept album, the longer your tracks, the longer your solos, the longer your hair, the longer your prick (or your tongue), the wider your loon pants . . . the better you were.

At least it was simple. We had no taste whatsoever but we did have values.

So that first album had ten tracks on it, played for forty-two minutes, and had no drum, bass or vocal solos. The guitar solos, like the songs, were kept short, leaving you wanting more, making you want to play that song, that side, the whole LP again. It was brilliantly but not overly produced, and it had . . . *energy*.

We all went back down to London to give our uneducated opinions and make our usually ignored suggestions during the final week of mixing, and as soon as I heard that first play-through, I knew it was all going to be just fine.

We sat there in silence in front of a mixing board about the size of a squash court – we were only using a fraction of it, but Mike Milne liked to work with the best – and I thought, 'That's it. We've done it', and I didn't even feel terrified at entertaining such a fate-tempting thought. I knew.

I was so certain we were going to be incredibly famous and rich I got depressed about it. It ought not to be this easy. We'd pay. I would, anyway. This wasn't the way I'd imagined it at all. I thought I'd find my band of rough-edged rockers, we'd argue and fight and eventually get a few tunes together, play small gigs in Paisley, then Glasgow, maybe a club or two in London, be dead broke, have vans break down on the M6, borrow money from parents and friends, have a session played on John Peel's show, accept an offer from a tiny shoestring-budget label that'd go bust, play larger pubs, gradually gather a small but fanatical bunch of followers, have continual and confusing changes in line-up, eventually pay for our own single to be pressed and do the label-ling ourselves, be taken on by a sharp manager who'd subtly rip us off but get us on as support band for somebody else's nationwide tour, at last sign with a big company, produce at least one album that did nothing, build up a following in the record-buying public over the next couple of years, have all sorts of legal and contractual wrangles with our management and the record company, play the universities for a while, think about giving up, and *then* bring out an earth-shatteringly good album, or have a brilliant but seemingly non-commercial single that topped the charts for two months . . . that was how I'd imagined it: lots of hard work.

I'd been prepared for that, I'd already accepted all that hassle and effort. It was a profoundly unsettling and disturbing experience when it didn't work out like that at all. Sure, I always thought we'd be accused of selling out, that was only natural . . . but I thought we'd have the chance to be sold in, first.

Our manager was Sam Emery, a big man with thick grey-white hair and an even thicker East London accent who'd have looked tall if he wasn't so wide as well. We'd all taken some convincing that we really needed a manager, but Rick Tumber – now effectively our liaison officer at ARC – explained it all to us, and we accepted we did need something else apart from ARC Records between us and both the rest of the industry and the public. Big Sam came highly recommended, and with a reputation for being straight that had me instantly suspicious; the guy must have worked out some *really* clever scam to have fooled everybody in *this* business, I thought.

Big Sam arrived in time to provide the last push we needed to make success rapid as well as inevitable. It was a simple idea, but the good ones usually are. It was also, again, as commercially good ideas tend to be, rather dubious morally.

The first single was, after all, going to be 'Frozen Gold'. 'Another Rainy Day', ARC decided, was too downbeat for a debut. It was the better song, but just not right for that vital first impression. 'Frozen Gold' it would be then; and that suited my desire for neatness, and my vanity; F, G. My clever idea.

I'd written the song for a male voice; it was for Dave Balfour to sing. Never even occurred to me to do it any other way. When I wrote the words, 'Why do you bite me on the shoulder, why do you scratch me on the back? Why do you always have to make love, like you're making an attack?" I was imagining a couple screwing, missionary position, him on top, her scratching his back, biting him when she came . . . and I stress *imagining*; I was still very much a virgin at the time, but I'd read a lot of my flatmates' *Penthouse*s and *Forum*s, so I reckoned I knew what I was talking about, and of course such physicality was shown to be just a metaphor for a particular relationship, as the song developed (oh, I thought I was *very* clever) . . .

Then Big Sam said keep the backing, but re-record it with Christine singing lead. Dave wasn't sure at first, but Sam said he could lead on the next single, probably 'Another Rainy Day'; he just had a hunch about this one being right for Christine. Rick Tumber didn't think it would make much difference at first, but then became very enthusiastic. ARC's management came round to the idea too. We held up the single for a week, Big Sam got me to re-write the subsequent verses a little, to make the song more personal, less abstract, then Christine spent just one more day in the studio and we released 'Frozen Gold' at the end of September, with Christine singing lead. I still hadn't realised.

The single came out, and I experienced that unreal, dizzying feeling of listening, for the first time, to something I had written being played on the radio. That sense of unreality continued. The publicity had started; there were posters, interviews (though not for me, of course) . . . and not all that many sales. I felt curiously unworried. Something would happen.

ARC got us onto Top Of The Pops. I wasn't sure whether to be appalled or delighted. The same programme as Barry White? Jumping Jesus. But at least my ma and my pals would finally be convinced it was all really happening.

It wasn't until we were rehearsing for the programme that I understood just how smart Big Sam was. Christine's voice had been improving anyway, under Milne's direction, and she'd been loosening up generally, moving better, looking more relaxed and comfortable on the stage, really starting to show that she was enjoying it, but Big Sam had obviously had a word with her, and in that rehearsal I saw what he was up to. I didn't say anything. Then came the recording in the TOTP studio. We got it first time; nobody fluffed their mimes. God knows how; Christine was stunning. I felt *my* eyes staring, I don't know about anybody else.

All it was was that she sang that first verse as though she was living it there and then; it was sex. She started with her hair tied up, in a sort of bun. That was unusual for a start. She wore a black dress with (of course) gold trimmings; Dave wore black flares and a white tuxedo (almost drably low key and tasteful for the time). F, G: F F, E G. We set off.

Christine didn't just sing; she strutted and pouted her way through that first verse, seemed about to kiss the camera, and as she sang 'attack?' she used her free hand to take hold of the collar of the dress and pull. It ripped. Just a little, but it ripped. She threw her head back and marched to the other side of the stage and another camera while we slammed out the middle eight built around F and G. The torn dress flapped a little, exposing her shoulder. She shook her head, spilling long blonde hair out, and sang the rest of the song as though she was just about to either orgasm or kick the next male she saw in the balls. Or both.

The BBC producer was no fool. He made us do it again anyway, even though there was nothing wrong with the first time. The floor manager asked Christine if she'd mind not ripping her dress on this take, and we wasted quarter of an hour while a little old lady from the costume department was located and escorted to the bopper-infested studio. It took her all of thirty seconds to mend Christine's dress.

The second run-through was lacklustre. They broadcast the first one, dress-tearing and all. It had been a close-run thing, we discovered later (there was a reaction against 'permissiveness' at the time and, dammit, it *was* sexy), but they did use it. If they hadn't, we'd still have made it, though perhaps not with that single (the song wasn't all that strong, like I say). But Christine sold it. That dress sold it. Sex did.

I used to have a video of that programme, and it all looks fairly tame now, but only relatively. This was pre-punk, remember, and even though one shoulder was hardly in the same league as Jim Morrison's dick, we are talking about a family show here. But even watching it five or six years later I remember I still felt my hair rise a little and a slight sweat prickle on my skin. There was energy there; Christine exuded it, and Milne had captured it on the record. Energy; excitement. You know it when you see it, and when kids see it, when they hear it, they go out and buy records.

All well and good. Yahoo for us. But we started out with a gesture of exploitation, of sex and violence, and of male-against-female violence at that; we took some stick from the women's movement, and I didn't blame them. Some bands earn their fame; we bought ours.

God, there were letters to the papers, there were headlines *in* the papers, people wrote in and phoned to the BBC, we must have come fairly close to having questions asked in the House of Commons. And a couple of million adolescent boys wanked to the memory of Christine that night, and then went out and bought the single on the following day. Well . . . not two million, not buying it, but a lot. We made number two, which around Christmas means a lot more copies sold than the majority of number ones throughout the rest of the year. The album suddenly became Eagerly Awaited the morning after the programme was shown, and when *Frozen Gold and Liquid Ice* did hit the shops, it sold out. Even most of the critics liked it, which really was extraordinary. Pressing plants went onto three shifts. Christine turned down vast sums to appear nude for the sort of magazines my flatmates used to buy and I used to borrow from them.

All those young boys had come, but we had arrived. It was Fame City, and we'd been given the key.

Weirdness. Years later I'd look at old papers, or at Mickey's scrapbook, and I'd see photos of us at some party or celebration, with *really* famous people; other musicians, popular comedians, politicians, minor royalty, and there they'd be, and there I'd be, in the background, *and I couldn't remember anything about it at all*. Nothing. Nada. Total blank. If you asked me, Have you met these people? I'd swear blind I hadn't. No memory of it whatsoever.

The whole next year after that first hit passed in a daze. It was exactly like getting steaming drunk and waking up the next morning not knowing what the hell you'd done, only this lasted for a year, not a night. I look back on it now and I wonder how the hell I didn't walk in front of a truck, or sign away the world rights to all future compositions, or say something outrageously slanderous, or just drink myself to death or start on heroin; I was on the same automatic pilot that somehow (usually) sees utter drunkards through their binges, stops them from falling out of windows or off kerbs or picking fights with entire gangs.

'Another Rainy Day' (sung by Dave, but if you watch the TOTP programme we played it on, the camera spends more time on Christine than it does on Dave) got to number three in February '75. Dave, who'd insisted as being credited as 'Davey' on the album, and was becoming known as that, was disappointed we hadn't had a number one single yet, but the album had been number one album for five weeks, so it wasn't too hard to bear. It was probably only because so many people had the song on the album that they didn't bother buying the single, even though they were different versions of the song.

I think the main reason Dave was worried was that he wanted to be the band's usual lead singer, and was worried ARC would favour Christine over him because the single she'd fronted had done better. And I'd thought he'd just wanted to be a guitar hero.

Two things: one; shortly after that first TV appearance, I mentioned to Dave how much better Christine's singing was; not so much technically, but in the way it came across, and how much looser she seemed to be, moving about the stage, confident, in control. She had seemed almost prim when I first saw the band at Paisley Tech, and now she was, well, I don't think I actually used the word 'raunchy', but that was what I was getting at. I put it down to the influences of Mike Milne and Big Sam, and just the fact of being in the big time now. Dave grinned and said, 'Na, all she needed was a good fuck,' winked at me and walked off.

Now, I'd always assumed they'd been at it constantly since long before I knew them (over a year previously by then), and apart from that . . . shit, I just objected to the whole idea, and not solely because I was jealous. *Asshole*, I remember thinking.

Two: middle-class planning again. A few years ago I asked Rick Tumber why even when we had a perfectly good mix on an album, ARC always re-mixed the songs before issuing them as singles. Rick grinned the way people do before they put a Royal Running Flush down on top of your three aces. 'For the singles album, Danny boy,' he told me, 'your real fans'll buy everything you've ever released, but even some real fans never buy 45s; they wouldn't buy a singles album either, if they already had all the material on the albums they've already bought, so we make all the mixes different and then they have to buy the singles album too and so you and I make even more money than we would have made anyway because they've bought seven albums not six, or eight not seven or whatever it is or however you count it, but what the hell; we sell more albums even though it's all the same material and it's cost the same amount of studio time and so on, not that that accounts for much of the unit cost but you know what I mean, and . . . .' This explanation lasted another ten minutes. Never guess he'd just filled his nose with Columbian Ajax, would you?

But do you see the point? Jesus, *I'd* never have thought of that. They were looking at least four or five albums and maybe the same number of years ahead; that's real forward planning. That's middle-class thinking. That's looking ahead. The middle classes are brought up like that. They get salaries they make last all month, they'll take out Life Assurance *without* getting the hard sell, they'll invest in the future, they'll buy a wee stupid car so their kids can go to a good private school (and it makes good sense anyway; so economical). They can keep drink in the house without having to drink it all. Not like your working class at all. If you've got it, spend it; if it's there, drink it. Hence the weekly wage and the local off licence.

But there are common denominators everywhere. I can remember when it was a matter of real importance to know of a group more obscure than those your friends knew about; not just any old group, but a band playing *progressive* music. If that band then went on to become really famous (even though that would be regarded as selling out), then your status as a person of immense good taste was assured. It's called gambling, or investing. Looking for a horse they've been shoeing with lead until now, or a stock quoted low but about to rise. Everybody plays the same game; it's just some people make more money out of their version.

Then came *All Wine Tastes Sour*. From that, 'Old Budapest' (the song about the note lying in the grate) only made number eight, but 'You'd Never Believe' hit number one, and stayed there for three weeks. Davey sang that. He was very pleased. It was only knocked off the top spot by Rod Stewart's 'Sailing'; so, no disgrace.

The first album went gold the same week the second got to number one. The songs on *All Wine . . .* were credited to me. Dave and Christine shared a twenty per cent arrangement fee. That had led to some tension, but I felt I was in a position of power; nobody else in the band had written anything worth recording on anything other than a cassette machine. If what I said didn't go, I would. Take it or I'll leave.

Dear God, such arrogance shames me now.

UK tour; breaking in the States so over there for a two-week whistle-stop promo tour, answering the same questions and waking in Holiday or Ramada Inns and staring at the ceiling and wondering, Where the hell is *this*?, then back into the studio to record *Gauche*, and then, thank God, a rest.

Why do I remember these *pastorals*?

We'd recorded *Gauche* at Manorfield Studios, in Herefordshire; Lord Bodenham, socialite and photographer, had put us up at his little place while we were working. This wasn't just sixties style Hey-look-how-hip-I-am; he was a major shareholder in ARC. Took the snap on the back of the first album, even though everybody remembers the photo on the front; a solid tear of 24-carat gold caught with very fast film as it smashed into blue-stained water with a thin covering of ice (publicity made a lot of the fact that it was real gold and the tear-shaped blob weighed sixty pounds and there were three security guards in the studio when the shot was taken . . . all my idea, I am half-ashamed and half-proud to admit).

October again already, my goodness. Lord Bod had pissed off to Antibes, but he'd encouraged us to stay, so we did. We'd used backing singers on the UK tour, and kept them on for *Gauche*. One of the three girls was a lady called Inez Rose Walker. Tall, raven and ravishing, statuesque and stately, always well-spoken and occasionally foul-mouthed, Inez had impressed me no end. I suspected she'd impressed the good lord rather a lot as well, but nothing seemed to come of that.

Set the scene. The Sex Pistols were still in captivity, a year away from bringing the language of every street corner to a single television studio. Malcolm McClaren was presumably still fine-tuning the neat concept of turning the turntables on the big record companies; instead of a band selling lots of records and them not getting any money, he had the Sex Pistols act so unpleasantly that although they didn't sell any records the companies gave them lots and lots of money just to go away. Springsteen had just released 'Born To Run' in the States; the shock waves had yet to rock Britain. And Led Zeppelin were still selling very well indeed, thank you.

Mind you, so was James Last. Oh, and Disco was big.

Party time. ARC were saying 'Thank you' because *Gauche* had entered the album charts at number one, on advance orders alone. The fact that we had now completed our three album deal and could now go wherever the hell we wanted for as much money as possible had, of course, absolutely nothing to do with such conspicuous extravagance.

ARC brought a small circus to Lord Bod's. Lions and tigers and elephants too. Fire eaters and jugglers and trapeze artistes, multitudinous chimps and a human cannonball, not to mention three alcoholic clowns with real red noses.

I'd never seen a lady trapeze artiste in the flesh before, and immediately fell in love with the one that turned up. God, those muscles. It was only thanks to Inez that I got over her; I fell for Inez instead. As well. Both. Oh, Christ, I don't know. There was no safety net, I'll tell you that.

'You don't know what you want to do, do you?'

I looked aghast at her. We were walking up a narrow road in the place called Golden Valley, between a village called Vowchurch and another village called Turnastone. It was a bright autumn day, blue sky and fresh wind. The leaves were just starting to fall off the trees and we were walking up a clefted road between the two villages, high banks of earth and trees to either side, red, brown and yellow leaves beneath our feet.

'What?' I said. 'Of course I do. I know exactly what I want.'

'What then?'

'Well . . .'

'Ha! See?'

'No; come on . . . be fair. I'm thinking.'

'Oh, dear; you think *that's* an excuse?'

'Hey! Stop giving me such a hard t-time here . . .'

'Oh well, I'm sorry . . .'

'. . . I know exactly what I want to do. I want to . . . change the world!'

'Oh, I see. For the better?'

I laughed. 'Of course!' (I never could see when I was having the piss taken out of me.)

'Oh, well, good. That'll make a change.' Inez nodded, stared ahead up the slope of the steeply banked road.

'I'm not just in it for the mmm-money, you know. I know what it's like to be p-poor. I mean . . . "European" and "No Lesson For Us";' – she'd sung on both – 'they've both got mmm-messages. I don't know if you could call them protest songs, but they're . . .'

'Commercial. They're commercial songs. Bits off an album. Don't kid yourself.'

'Jee-zuz! You're really so cynical, aren't you?' I was amazed. Inez walked beside me, arms crossed, marching up that slope through the scattering of golden leaves.

'*I'm* cynical!' She laughed.

The sun broke through the clouds then, and at the same time a wind blew up from behind us, stirring and swirling the golden-brown leaves around our feet, lifting her hair and mine and combing our faces with it, and belling out her long dress. The wind settled and strengthened, the leaves started to move, and as we walked up that short hill between the dry banks, the breeze filled, and it shifted the tumbling leaves along with us, moving them slowly uphill like a strange stream backing up against the pull of gravity, spreading them and rolling them slowly up the slope at the same speed as we were walking, so that for a long and dizzying moment we seemed to walk and stand quite still together, travelling islands caught within that bright, chaotic flow, our ankles tickled by the brittle flood, our eyes tricked by the relative movement of those charging, rolling, whispering leaves.

The effect lasted for only a few seconds before the wind blew stronger and the leaves outdistanced us, but for that brief time it was magical, and something so powerful and odd I could never express it. It remained something we shared, alone. Never could give it to anybody else, no matter how hard I tried.

I remember taking rather a lot of drugs that autumn, staying in that grand, impressive house. Once I climbed a tree and reclined on a long oak bough, quite at my ease, head buzzing, while watching a juggler on the gravel path beneath me. I lay there, elbow on branch, head in hand, looking down at the circus juggler, and watched the Indian clubs whirling up towards me and then back down, and thought that there was something quite profound and remarkable about watching juggling from above, especially when the juggler was too intent on his skill to notice the observer. It was one of those perfect metaphors one only ever experiences under the simplicities of a drug; at the time it is both obviously unique and impregnably apt, and – afterwards – utterly unfathomable.

And several times, in those balmy autumn days, I thought, *This is the life*.

Do you blame me?

By *Gauche* I was no longer trying to prove anything about what a wonderful song writer I was. My own name wasn't actually mentioned once on the writing credits on that album; instead I used a variety of rather silly aliases. The songs were variously credited to O'More, Sutton, Sundry, Thistle and Hlasgow; only I knew these were Justin O'More, Oliver Sutton, Alan Sundry, Patrick Thistle and Gerald Hlasgow (the Scotsman). Ah, good Lord preserve us from our own in-jokes.

One joke fell thoroughly flat in a privately embarrassing way; I'd called the company which published the songs 'Full Ashet Music'. People at ARC had looked puzzled, but didn't raise any objections. I'd thought my little pun was at least mildly amusing, but I hadn't realised that an ashet was now only a *Scottish* word for a serving platter, and not one recognised any more by English people, let alone Americans. As I was trying to fool myself that I was a nonchalant, debonair and sophisticated man of the world at the time – a real international citizen and discreetly famous person – I found this accidental parochialism a terrible loss of face, even if nobody else ever brought up the *faux pas*.

I hadn't realised how much of my speech marked me down as from north of the border; not just the obvious accent, but the words and phrases I used, too. I didn't know people in London didn't say 'neither it is' or 'back the way' or 'see what like it is' or 'see the likes of me?'; I didn't know English people didn't call shopping 'messages', or little fingers 'pinkies'; and I didn't realise that knowing all those other words would, to some people, make me seem ignorant.

I knew I wasn't. I knew I was a clever big bastard. I also knew I would never be quite as clever as I'd once thought I was, but I was content, and happy with myself in a way which at the time seemed not to come with a time-limit attached. I'd set out to do something and succeeded, if not beyond my wildest dreams – no seriously ambitious person ever does – then certainly not far away from them. Nothing was so tough. Nothing was impossible if you put your mind to it. The world could be tamed. I knew it all. And there was more to come; this was just the start. Just watch me now.

I recall vaguely considering whether to adopt a higher profile in the band; perhaps even do a Bowie, and change image and/or name for each different album, but Captain Captivity, Walter Ego and Eddie Currents never did get further than the planning stage. Just as well too.

We had gone back to Paisley together only once, on the Scottish leg of the UK tour, though the others had been back individually a few times. I went to see my ma; she was still living in the flat in Ferguslie. I'd tried to persuade her to move out and let me buy her a place, but she wouldn't let me. What she had done was fill the flat with gaudy junk. Whole walls were covered with Woolworth's repro paintings; dusky maidens with flowers in their hair, white horses galloping through moonlit surf, moon-faced waifs leaking crystal tears . . . all on a background of red flock wallpaper.

There was a lot more stuff like that, but I didn't hang around to do an inventory.

We threw a party at a local hotel for our old pals; I think we all worried about it being an embarrassing failure. Would they think we were being patronising? Would some of my mates, and maybe Mickey's, break the whole thing up? Would people just not turn up? Would they mix at all if they did attend?

We were right to worry. If we hadn't worried, we might have been too complacent and, just by our attitude, put people off. Instead we worked hard at making it work; persuading people to come, making the arrangements, having a local band play music but having a couple of new songs worked out so that – if we were pressed – we could do some acoustic stuff by ourselves late on. Not to mention providing free beer and three minibuses to shuttle people back to their homes after it was over (there were jokes about an armoured car to make the run to Ferguslie, but as far as I know minibus and driver both survived).

It worked. The party was a great success. We said we'd do it again next year, we were so enthusiastic and enjoyed ourselves so much, but we didn't; we were on the European tour then and just didn't have the time. We always meant to make the time, sometime, but other things kept cropping up, and after a while – after a surprising number of years had slipped by, almost without us noticing – we were slightly ashamed at ourselves for not having kept our promise, and there was, I think, an unspoken agreement that it would be easier all round not to repeat the party, and to pretend we hadn't broken our word.

Jean Webb came to the party, with a boyfriend.

I hadn't seen Jean for nearly a year, and hadn't thought of her for months, I suppose, and I was partly surprised and partly annoyed with myself for feeling jealous when she turned up at the party with a tall young gas fitter called Gerald, who wore glasses. The truth was, I'd either forgotten how bonny she was, and how nice, or she'd become a lot more of both during the time I'd been away.

I wondered what she might have said, and what might have happened, if I had asked her to come away to the big bad city with me, a year before. It was a fleeting feeling though, and I slipped easily into the role of local-boy-made-good-but-not-bragging-about-it when I talked to Jean and Gerald.

She was working as a secretary with the gas board. She had all our records. Her mother was still bad with the arthritis. Her father was out of work, but the brother at Inverkip was still bringing in some money; her other brother was going to business school to study accountancy. No, she wouldn't be going to art school. They were a good crowd at the gas office.

Gerald wasn't one of our fans – he was more of a Soul man – but he thought it was good to see local people doing so well, and liked Dave's guitar playing.

At one point, when he'd gone for the drinks, Jean, her hair a red-brown halo of curls, and her fuller, less girlish face peeking out from that tangled mane, smiled at me and said, 'You're lookin well. Are ye happy, Daniel?'

I think I must have shown my surprise. Before I could reply, she laughed and squeezed my hand, briefly. 'Daft question, eh?'

I shrugged, unsure what to say. 'It's . . . everything's hhh-happened hell of a fast, but . . . yeah, I'm pretty happy, I suppose. Ask me again in a year or t-two, when I've caught up with myself.'

Jean nodded, smiling, looking from one of my eyes to the other. 'Aye, we've missed you, Daniel. Old place isn't the same without ye.'

Stumped again, but for longer this time, all I could manage was a great show of humble embarrassment, and, 'Aw, gee, shucks . . .' said in a silly voice, before Gerald came back with the drinks.

Intervals. Brief frozen disconnected moments, time passed on other worlds.

From the fairytale setting of that great, ancient house in the soft, undulating English countryside, my whole life took on a curiously foreshortened and rosy look, and even Ferguslie Park assumed a hazy aura of nostalgia. Going back there blew a hole in that particular fog bank, but it closed up again pathetically quickly; a month after visiting my ma and her collection of mass-produced crap, I was thinking about how *cosy* the place had been, and what a fine crucible for forming my precocious but not yet fully-plumbed talent.

Well, I was still young.

How do you work out when you were most happy? Dunno myself but, however you measure it, I was happy then. It was a more relaxed, fulfilled happiness than that I'd felt just after the contract was signed, or after I'd heard my song on the radio for the first time, and, of course, part of it – I still don't know how much – was due to Inez.

My first real lover; my first proper (improper) relationship.

Inez with her dancer's body and her wild tempers and her rough-house, rowdy, roguish sexuality; holy shit, the trapeze artiste could not have been more athletic. What did I excite in her? She must have seen something, and she can't have cared for the money (I said 'Mmm-marry me' and she said 'Nnn-nope'), so what was it kept her with me, fairly faithful and unfairly jealous, for those years? I never did work it out. I asked her, direct, often enough what she saw in me, but all she ever did was frown deeply and tell me it was absolutely none of my business.

The breathtaking nerve of that floored me, every time. Fair enough, I thought, unbloody but bowed. A couple of times she insulted me in front of people, and once Davey said afterwards I was stupid to let her talk to me like that. I can't remember what it was she said; I can't remember what it was I said in reply to Davey. But I didn't do anything.

Inez and I slept curled up together, her front against my back, and often I would wake during the night, feeling her breath against me in the darkness, warm and fragrant, and find that she had, very lightly, I think always unconsciously, cupped her hand around my balls, so that my scrotum lay in her fingers and palm, like a nest within the bowl of a tree. She never hurt me, and I don't think she ever woke up like that – she'd always have changed position later on in the night – but I must have woken up to find myself held gently like that dozens and dozens of times.

It seemed to me then a sweet and endearing gesture.

But it was a magical time anyway, in that old house.

Once when I'd gone back indoors to fetch a cardigan for Inez, and have a pee (oh, ye gods, during a game of croquet, would you believe?), I stood in the second-floor bathroom washing my hands and looking out through an open window.

Before me were the grounds; a strip of parkland backed by a low hill strung with tall young trees; birch and maple and elm. To one side I could see an edge of the circus tent, pitched on the deeply shadowed park, its pennants fluttering in the wind. It was late in the afternoon; the circus' band was playing on the far side of the house, on the terrace. Music drifted on the breeze like smoke.

The wooded hill opposite me was bright in the autumn sunshine, and people were walking on paths within the wood, their clothes picked out by the gloaming light. As I watched, another strong gust of wind came and shook the trees, and leaves dropped from their branches like rain from a sunlit cloud; glorious and glittering in the warm air. My mouth dropped open, and I watched, quite overcome, as the fluttering shower of golden leaves burst down upon the walking people, like confetti for the wedding of some unseen woodland spirits.

SEVEN

'There's a funny smell in here, so there is, Jim.'

Well, yes. Pigeon crap and dogshit, dog vomit, dog pee, and curry. Apart from that. . .

I spent a deeply unfulfilling couple of hours yesterday evening, sniffing and searching and mopping and scraping and washing and cleaning. The pigeon is still at large; I can hear the little bastard cooing sadly every now and again, somewhere up in the roof. I have put my umbrella up over the turntable to protect it from further aerial bombardment and, if I remember, I'll take a wander down to one of the specialist hi-fi shops to look for a new turntable cover. I used to have one but Wee Tommy and I broke it one drunken night, testing the point at which more-or-less regularly shaped objects with cavities underneath stopped behaving like frisbees.

Plates; yes. Most hats; yes. Perspex turntable covers; not really.

I threw out both the curried rug and the sheet the pigeon shat on (luckily, I have several cases of Rumanian bedclothes). I could have washed them instead, but my greatcoat had finally become so dirty – following my adventure on the motorway flyover and TB's hairy attempt at copulation – that even my fairly robust sensibilities were becoming offended. So I stuffed the coat into my heavy-duty industrial Czech washing machine and left the pair of them to fight it out.

I didn't have another coat, or even a warm jacket to wear while my coat was in the wash, but I took a look at the weather and decided it wasn't a day for going out anyway. It was a cold, grey day; showers of sleet and hail blew hard over the city, swirling like clouds of frozen white buckshot. A day for staying in.

Besides, I was expecting somebody. No pigeon today; this morning the visitor to my bedroom was an altogether more acceptable one.

I lay on my side, head on hand, watching Betty smoke.

Ah, the following-fornication fag, the post-coital cigarette, the aprés-orgasm gasper. That's the one I miss most of all. Every time Betty lights up I think . . . just one. Just one, now, for old time's sake. It's allowed; your conscience would understand . . . but then I think about how I'd feel later. The big G again, rearing its siren head and wanting to be fed.

'Yeah, I spilled some curry yesterday,' I said, economising with the truth.

Betty tutted. 'Cannae stand curries. See ma Jack? He'd eat them fur breakfast dinner an tea, so he wid. Basturt used tae smell like a take-away when he didnae smell like a distillery.' She sucked in smoke and held it, obviously enjoying her cigarette. I felt my mouth start to water, but I ignored it. The sheets had slipped off her breasts as she filled her chest, and I was smiling at her rosy nipples. She saw me looking, pulled the sheet back up and said, 'Hi, you,' in a disapproving tone.

Betty is curiously prim in some ways. She won't undress in front of me, and she always pulls the sheets up to cover her chest when she sits up in bed. I find this amusing, almost quaint, but she gets annoyed if I say anything, so I don't. She's been climbing up this tower to this room for the past two and a half years now; two or three times a week as a rule. Keeps me sane, keeps my libido ticking but not boiling over. I really feel quite an affection for her, even if her heart is, as I slightly suspect, pure brass.

Betty is about forty, I think. She won't say. She is petite, she has scrunched up wee toes from far too many pointed shoes, legs she is proud of, and a pale, allowing body. Dyed blonde hair; naturally brown. It's only over the last few months she's told me anything about herself. That wasn't what I was paying for, and none of my business. I think she maintains this rule still with the rest of her clients, but maybe not; we'd all like to think we're special, even when we're just paying for attention.

Maybe it's only because she's been seeing me so long she feels she can talk. I must be boring to her now; we are more like old friends than whore and john. I'm sure at first she was terrified of me; a huge weird-looking guy living in a big church. Nutcase; maybe dangerous. I've always wondered whether she expected my prick to be in proportion to the rest of my body (it isn't, but what a bastard that the one average thing I do have is not the sort of thing you can point to in public and say, 'Look, see? I'm normal! I'm just like you guys!'). I meant to ask her about that, but . . . I never did get around to it.

She seems to enjoy sex; tells me I'm the only one that makes her come. Somehow, the way she says it, I believe her . . . but I still half-suspect she says that to all the marks. Maybe I'm just a bad and cynical man, though.

'Have you heard anything from him?'

'That bastard? Not a peep. He can rot.' Betty draws on the fag again. A steely smile crosses her face. 'Ah hope he's missin his curries. They dinnae serve too many a them in the Bar-L.'

Betty's husband is six years into a ten year sentence for assault and armed robbery. He was part of a gang who split a trucker's skull and nicked forty tons of fags from a transport café's trailer park. He'd be due out soon if he didn't keep hitting his fellow inmates. Probably after their snout; old habits die hard.

Betty's eyes narrowed. 'Aye, Ah bet there's somethin else the basturt's missin as weel.' She put the fag out in a saucer balanced on her sheet-covered tummy. 'He liked his nookie, did that man. No much good at it, but he liked it. Couldnae go two days withoot it. Wonder whit he's daein aboot that in the jile?' Her face held an unkind smirk. 'Wee chap too; a right hard ticket, but just wee . . . an he had dead smooth skin, no much hair . . . Ah've oftin wondered whit aw they big hard men thought aboot when they saw him take his kegs aff fur the shoors.'

She smiled widely at one of the twin peaks her knees made under the bedclothes, plainly imagining her husband stripping in front of twenty large, scarred, sex-starved lifers. I looked away.

He used to knock her about; broke her arm once. I already know all this. He was one of those men – they can't be unique to Glasgow – who know in their hearts that for all their edgy, belligerent hardness they are just unhappy kids, emotional retards.

They can drink and they can fight, but even they know that's not enough, and the only other way they have to prove they're men is by knocking as many weans out of their wives as possible. Betty has an amusing story of being chased round the flat by her Jack; he was after the packet of pills he'd discovered and she'd snatched away from him. He caught her eventually, and threw them on the fire.

Her best story, the one that makes me most angry, but one that she tells with a sort of baleful irony, is of the time she was sent down for three months for soliciting, by a judge who'd been one of her clients.

I was incensed; I'd always regarded the law on prostitution to be almost as stupid, almost as guaranteed to bring law in general into contempt, as the law on drugs (with the laws they still have on homosexuality running a distant third), but to discover an act of such gross, such focused hypocrisy being perpetrated on somebody I knew and liked made the arrant nonsensicality of our supposedly shared values far clearer for me than they ever had been before. I wanted to get that judge's name and expose him; get him, somehow.

Betty couldn't understand why I was so angry. She told me to stop being daft. Occupational hazard. She'd met worse bastards than that. I think she decided then not to risk telling me about some of the *really* bad experiences she's had, in case I took off after some violent client with an axe.

Anyway, I'm glad she could tell me about that, even if there are all those things she won't talk about. I think she has at least one kid, but she won't talk about that either. Maybe in another few years.

Betty and I have a very simple and satisfactory relationship; we screw, and I pay her. I remember that I used to think that any man who had to pay for it was a rather pathetic creature, and could not understand that quite a few of the rich, not unattractive men that I knew did just that. I think I understand now. The physical need is dealt with, but emotional commitment never even arises. Just a transaction. Easy to get along with. Clean and simple.

It's only recently I've started to worry about exactly why I'm doing this. Betty might be a mother figure to me. She doesn't look very similar, but there is a vague similarity. Worse, there's her man and my da.

Because he too was in the Bar-L. For most of my childhood, in fact.

You want to hear a sad wee story? I was five years old, having my birthday party in the flat in Ferguslie Park; my ma and four or five of my brothers and sisters. My ma had made a special effort for me, buying a cake and putting candles on it. I had a present, we all had paper hats, there were lots of bottles of skoosh to drink and that cake to eat, once I'd blown the candles out.

Only I never got a chance to, because my da came home after being down the pub, and he'd heard a rumour – I don't know; probably just somebody making a joke or some thoughtless remark – that my ma had been seeing some other man. He practically kicked the door in, stormed through to the kitchen, and picked my ma out of the seat. Us kids just sat and watched, amazed, frightened.

He held her by the chin, swiped her across the face with his other hand. I can still see her hair flying out, still hear the noise her head made as it cracked against the kitchen cabinet, smashing glass, sending cups and saucers flying. She fell, he picked her up and hit her again, shouting and swearing. She tried to beat him off, but he was too strong. He threw her down and started kicking her.

We were all just young. We sat on our seats and screamed, tears streaming down our faces, howling. Steven, a year older than me, jumped off his seat and went to help ma; he was battered across the face and fell back against the formica table, spilling our lemonade. My da stood over ma, kicking her and shouting and throwing mugs and cups and plates down at her; she was crumpled against the cupboard under the sink, sobbing, arms over her head, all curled up like a baby, blood flowing from her head. My da kicked her a few more times, then heaved the kettle out through the window. He turned the table over, skelped me and the others he could reach round the ear, then walked out.

We clustered round ma eventually, going down to where she lay on the lino, in that same position, and all of us were crying, close to hysterical.

Happy fifth birthday.

And I never did get to blow out my candles.

My da reappeared three nights later, with some flowers he'd stolen from a garden, brimming with contrition and tears. He hugged my ma and swore he'd never raise his hand to her again . . . but then he always did that.

I must have taken it bad. I went to school that autumn, and did all right except that I wouldn't say or write or use the number five. For me, the numbers went; one, two, three, four, (blank), six, and so on. I wouldn't say the word, I wouldn't use the figure. It was a blank space, something I didn't want to think about.

Took a school psychiatrist two years and a lot of patience (and tea and biscuits) to worm that out of me. I wouldn't think about it. I couldn't remember anything anywhere near my fifth birthday. I had terrible nightmares, about being chased by a lion or a bear or a tiger, and being beaten and mauled before I died/woke up, but I wouldn't remember anything about that birthday.

By the time I was persuaded to dig up that memory, my da was safely in Barlinnie prison. Killed a man. Nobody in particular; just a guy who annoyed him one night in a bar, and who happened to have a thin skull. Hard luck really. He'd been a regular visitor to the local nicks since before I was born; for stealing, assault; always when he was drunk. Not really a violent man, just a stupid one, a weak one. He knew he became belligerent when he drank, but he always thought that next time it would be different and he'd stay in control. So he kept on getting drunk and he kept on getting violent and he kept on getting into fights and he kept on getting sent to jail.

Here's my joke about my da. It so happens that he really did despise education; thought all students were wasters and poofs. He used to boast that he'd been to the University of Life (no, honestly; he really used to say that). Well my joke is; my da went to the University of Life . . . but he kept getting sent down.

Funny, eh?

He was eventually transferred to Peterhead prison, before Betty's husband went to Barlinnie, so they could never have met, which I think is a pity. He got out ten years ago. My ma took him back; by that time he was a wee, grey, broken man, and now he sits in their new house in Kilbarchan and stares at the telly all day. He won't touch drink or go out, and he goes to bed when my ma tells him. I don't know what they did to him to make him like that, but in my less charitable moments I can't help feeling it was no more than he deserved.

But maybe I'm just a callous bastard.

'Yer a bit pale yerself.'

'Hmm, what?' Betty rescued me from my memories. 'Pale?'

'Aye; ye look like ye've been in the jile yersel, so ye dae. An what's this?' Betty picked up one of my knuckle-skinned hands, inspecting it briefly then letting it fall back to the sheets. 'Didnae think you were a fighter. Whit ye been daein?'

'Nothing.' I looked at the grazes on my fingers, and flexed them.

'Aye ye have. Ah know whit fighter's hauns look like. Ye've been fightin, haven't ye? Whit wiz it aboot?'

'I haven't been fighting. I was climbing something and I grazed my knuckles.' (But I'm starting to wonder; did McCann tell the truth? Did I hit somebody? What about after McCann left me; I went to get a take-away curry somewhere after we split up. What happened after that? Was I in a fight? I suppose I could have been . . . But no; I don't know how to fight. A street-wise twelve year old could probably take me, even when I was sober. I'd remember something as traumatic as . . . as a fight . . . wouldn't I?)

'Aye, ye fell doon the stairs. Pull the other wan; it's got bells on it.'

I laughed. 'I didn't fall; I was climbing.'

'Were ye trying tae break in somewhere?'

'No; it was just . . . I was drunk. Just climbing. I wasn't trying to nick anything.' I put my hands under the sheets and lay on my back.

I lay, she sat, silent for a while. I stared up at the high ceiling of the tower bedroom for a while. I was thinking. 'You know,' I said eventually, 'I've never stolen anything in my life.' I looked at her. 'Isn't that extraordinary?'

'Bloody amazin,' Betty said, dark eyebrows lifting briefly. She leant down, subtracted another fag from the packet. 'Ye sure?'

'I think so.' I nodded. How on earth did I get through my childhood and youth without nicking anything? All my friends did. Almost everybody I knew did. I didn't; I was frightened. I always imagined what it would be like getting caught; the guilt, the awful feeling of knowing you'd been told not to do something, having done it and then being caught and punished. The appalling sequentiality of it, as though it was all pre-ordained, already set up. I couldn't bear that. Fear stopped me. Fear of guilt. Fear of the sheer *embarrassment*. Fear of what my mother would say.

So instead I ended up feeling guilty about not joining in with my friends.

Betty lit another cigarette. I lay there thinking.

I didn't think I'd even stolen any hearts. Not with my looks. I had my fans when I was Weird, and sure some of them were female, but that was different. It's a very dubious proposition indeed that fans actually love their idols; they worship them but they don't, can't, love them. It might feel like love, but have kids, adolescents, suddenly learned how to tell what is and isn't love? Jesus, I didn't know when I was that age. I don't even know very much more about it all now, and I've been trying to work it out for half my life.

But even if you can call the glorification of the average star 'love', I wasn't even a normal idol. I think I was chosen by some kids as a sort of anti-hero figure, proof that you didn't have to be pretty to be in rock, but there was also a sort of adult-baiting perversity about making me an object of adulation. Kids stuck posters of me up on their walls to shock their parents. Weird leered down, mirror-shaded, wild-haired, scowl-mouthed, from thousands of bedroom walls, something menacing but contained; a safe cheap thrill and a kind of token totem of glossy threat. I displaced the prettier stars so that kids could make a point; as though, in its own small, modest way, my elevation to honorary stardom prefigured the half-sincere, half-pretended disgustrionics of punk.

Or maybe I was a different sort of threat, and kids encountering parental resistance to their latest choice of clothes or decoration used me for comparison; you think *this* is bad; think yourself lucky I don't look like *him*. Could be even simpler of course; maybe they just found my big stupid face funny.

No, I don't think I broke or stole any hearts. I didn't steal Inez'; that was safely under lock and key, somewhere deep inside her. It had been stolen once before, and she'd had to pay a lot – in exactly what currency of the heart, I never did find out – to get it back, battered and torn. It would never escape or be stolen again. She was in control from the start. We lived on her terms.

Christine . . . no, she loved me for a while, or said she did, but it was as a friend, I think . . . Maybe even as a pet. That was the way I felt with her; like a big stupid clumsy dog; likeable and loveable, but too keen to please, too liable to jump up and slobber all over your face, and slap ornaments off tables with a wagging tail.

There were others: Anthea, Rebecca, Sian, Sally, Sally-Ann, Cindy, Jas, Naomi . . . but I don't think they really lost their hearts to me either, and I don't think I wanted them to, really. Too much responsibility. I wanted to be *liked*, not loved. Love was dangerous. Love could cripple, love could kill.

But I never wrote songs like that. My songs, when they were about love, were fairly conventional, if a little more enlightened than the standard of the time (and one hell of a lot more enlightened and unobjectionable than what you'll find in the contemporary rump of rock, heavy metal). The most I ever did was write sarcastically about love *songs* ('Love in Transit'; 'Well when the seas freeze, and the air leaves, will you really still be loving? Will you behave, past the grave? And are the ghosts of dead lovers still coming?'), which is better than nothing, but not vastly so.

I was too conventional altogether. I ought to have spread my wings, flexed my muscles; all that shit. I could have written different songs, I could have been more radical, more adventurous, more daring. Instead I just kept on churning out the same old stuff. Oh it changed a little as we went on, but not that much. Why did I keep doing that? It wasn't the money; after the first couple of albums, and finding the number of cover versions being done, I knew I could live quite comfortably for the rest of my life without writing another note, and that was really all that concerned me. So what was it? Why did I produce all those nice hummable songs?

Because it was easy. Because it was expected of me. Because it was what people seemed to want. Because they always seemed to see more in what I was doing than I did, and the tunes I thought all very standard and conventional were praised as stretching the limits of the popular song, and creating a fusion of rock and classical styles. (What? My knowledge of classical music began and ended with the fact I didn't like it. I thought you fused rock and classical music by putting strings on a backing track . . . and we only ever used strings twice in about sixty songs . . . But if that's what people say, who am I to argue?)

But I should have made the effort. I ought to have experimented more. I was writing the sort of songs I wanted to write, but I should have wanted to write different sorts of songs. I know me; it wouldn't have been difficult to interest myself in something a bit more challenging and original. If I'd done that, if I'd listened to different types of music, I'd have thought, 'Hey, I quite like this. This is okay . . . but I could do it better,' and at least have made the attempt. But I never got round to it.

Betty's exhaled smoke made a grey-brown cloud across the tall window on the far side of the bright, warm room. Smoke rolled slowly against grey cloud. A few seagulls crossed the sky.

There was a little more noise than usual from St Vincent Street; they were ceremonially opening the wonderful new Britoil building across the road, and the area was thick with police and security men.

I had, reluctantly, allowed a policeman into the folly that morning, to check the roof of the tower for snipers. I don't think he liked the look of me any more than I liked the look of him, but at least I hadn't had a police marksman stationed on my roof.

Betty sighed and stubbed her fag out in the saucer, exhaling smoke and lying back. Her breasts were slipping out again. The very tops of her aureoles were exposed above the sheet. She licked her lips, gazing vacantly at the far wall. She stretched, still not looking at me, put one of her arms back behind her, between her head and the white plaster wall; blonde hair spilled over her smooth forearm, gold on white. I lay there, thinking about what her mouth was going to taste like; faint disgust and extreme nostalgia combining.

Maybe I could ask her not to smoke when she's with me; I'm the client after all. But I couldn't. That would put a barrier between us, make everything less natural. I'd no sooner ask her to do that than ask her to do some of the 'special' things some of her other clients requested.

But I guessed I was a fool to pretend that my relationship with Betty was anything other than a commercial transaction. Can't buy me friendship. Well, I'd settle for sex and a chat. Even if the sex was rubberised (Betty is – very responsibly – worried about AIDS) and the chat only reminds me of things I'd rather forget.

'Ah suppose you're gettin randy again?' Betty looked at me disapprovingly. I was surprised.

'How did you guess?'

'Two fags.' Betty put the saucer/ashtray down on the bare wooden floor and lay down, turning to me. 'You alwiz want it again aftir two fags.'

I laughed, but uncertainly. Am I really so predictable? Betty put out one hand to me, rolled on her back.

'Men,' she said, through a sigh. I kissed her.

Her mouth tasted of smoke, her hair smelled of cheap perfume. A curiously comforting combination.

'There's still a funny smell in here,' she said, unrolling a Durex down my dick.

'You get to like it eventually,' I told her.

She wrinkled her nose up, lay back again. 'You're weird,' she said. Then: 'Whit's so funny?'

EIGHT

There is no such thing as too much money. Anybody who has more money than they know what to do with has no imagination. You can always find new things to spend money on; houses, estates, cars, aircraft, boats, clothes, expensive paintings . . . Most really rich people usually find thoroughly appropriate ways of getting rid of some of their funds; they take up ocean-going yacht racing, they collect a string of racehorses, they buy newspapers and television stations or car companies, they fund prizes and scholarships or give their money and their names to hospital wings or new bits of art galleries. Purchasing a chain of hotels is a popular option; gives you places to stay all over the world, and you don't lose any time buying the hotel when you want to sack the manager.

God almighty, offer me any sum of money from one pound to total control of the entire world economy and I could tell you just what I'd do with it, without even having to think very much.

But only in an advisory capacity. Only theoretically. Don't expect me actually to do the things I'd say I'd do. I know now that, regardless of how much money I have, I'll stay much as I am. I had my fill of trying to be somebody else, of fulfilling my own fantasies and making them up for other people; tried that, been there.

Mine turned bad on me, mine turned lethal, eventually.

But I did my bit. I played my part in the great commercial dance; I accepted all that money and I spent it on all sorts of daft, stupid, useless, wasteful things, and quite a lot of drugs too. I had my flash car (even if I couldn't drive it) and I had my big house and my estate in the Highlands.

The house was made up of equal parts of draughts and damp, and the estate was ten thousand acres of bog and scrappy heather. The only things I left planted there were wellington boots, sucked off by the clinging peat. There were deer on those there hills and fish in them there burns, but I didn't want to kill any of them, which made the whole enterprise a bit of a waste of time. I sold it eventually, to people who drained the ground and planted trees. I made on the deal, of course. I bought my ma a house in Kilbarchan, and I put up half the money for the Community Rehearsal and Recording Suite we donated to Paisley Council.

I even owned an island for a while; an inner Hebridean island I picked up ridiculously cheap at an auction in London. I had all sorts of wonderful plans for it, but the crofters resented me even though I meant well, and when I thought about it I guessed I'd have felt the same way if I'd been one of them; who did this lowlander, this Glesga Keelie, this youth of a 'pop' star think he was? Why, I didn't even have the Gaelic (I was going to learn the goddamn language, but I never got . . . oh never mind).

They'd seen too many grand schemes come to nothing, too many promises disappear into the mists, and too many owners spend all their time somewhere else more comfortable and sunny. They were a surly and unfriendly bunch, but they had a point; I sold the island to them as soon as my accountants had worked out a way of writing it off against tax. Lost a bit on that one, but you can't win them all.

So I've done all that, and I got fed up with it. My dreams came true, and I discovered that once they did, they were no longer dreams, just new ways of living, with their own problems and difficulties. Maybe if I'd been working on new dreams while the old ones were coming true I could have kept going, heading for even greener hillsides, even newer pastures, but I guess I just ran out of material, or I used it all up in the songs.

That might be it. Maybe I used up all my dreams in my songs so that I had none left for myself. That would be ironic, almost tragic, because at the time I thought I had perfect control; I thought I was being clever, using my songs, using my dreams, to

117

find out more about myself . . . a shame, really, that what I found out just wasn't worth the finding.

I think I hoped to find myself in my fantasies, to see the shape of who I really was in the pattern of my realised dreams, and when it all happened, and I did, I just wasn't very impressed with what I found there. It wasn't that I actively disliked myself, just that I wasn't as interesting and fine and noble a person as I'd thought I was. I used to think that all I needed was the opportunity, and I'd blossom, I'd flower, I'd spread my wings and fly . . . but discovered in the end that I was a weed, and that some buds just never open, and that some caterpillars were only ever worms with an identity crisis.

So I became a hermit crab instead, and look at the big shell I found! Well, I'm no shortarse. I need the headroom.

St Jute's and I are suited.

'Wes, you're not serious.'

'Hey, of course I'm serious.'

'No, I . . . no, not even you. You c-can't be serious. You can't mean it. Come on; it's a joke.'

'It's not a joke, man. One day everybody'll live like that. This is the future and you'd better get used to it.'

'Jesus, you are serious.'

'I already told you that.'

'You're mad.' I turned to Inez. 'Tell him he's mad.'

Inez looked up from her magazine. 'You're mad.'

'See?' I said to him. 'Even Inez agrees.'

Wes just shook his head and looked out of the car window at the passing Cornish scenery. 'It's the future, man. Might as well get used to it now.'

The Panther de Ville swept down the high-banked Cornish lanes, between the rainswept golden fields of summer. Clouds moved like bright ships, alternately battleship grey and the colour of the sun. The air was warm and a little humid outside and we had the air conditioning on. I refilled Inez' tumbler with champagne. She, Wes and I were on our way down from London to Wes' house, for that weekend's party.

The big car braked suddenly as we came round a bend and found a tractor backing a trailer into a field from the road. I tutted, shook my hand and reached for a napkin. 'Hey, Jas,' I said, 'we're not in a hurry.' Jasmine stopped the car to wait for the tractor to unblock the road. She looked round from the driver's seat and pushed her cap back, showing the shaved sides of her head. She'd rather taken to the punk look over the last month. I'd preferred it when she had long blonde hair, but I wasn't going to say anything.

'Spill your champers, did I?'

'Yeah.' I filled Wes' glass too, then my own.

'Never mind, love; carpet's champagne coloured, innit?'

'Jas, the bodywork is champagne coloured, but that doesn't mean I'm going to wash it with Moët.'

Jas looked at my full tumbler. (Flutes are impractical when you're travelling. Especially when Jas is driving.) 'Give us a glass, Dan,' she said.

'Wait till we get to the house,' I told her. She looked peeved.

'Give us some coke, then,' she suggested.

'What?' I shouted. 'Are you kidding? Last time I gave you that stuff we ended up doing a hundred and forty down the M6! Never again!'

This was all true, by the way; no exaggeration. After that incident, I'd decided the de Ville was maybe a bit too highly powered for Jasmine; she'd only passed her test that spring, after all, and the twelve cylinder Jaguar engine was tuned-up to lay about four hundred horsepower on the road, if you kicked the beast hard enough.

I'd rung up Panther and asked if there was any way of sort of shutting off half the cylinders or something, but the dealer said no, there wasn't, in a voice that seemed to want to ask me whether I was certain I was really fit to own such a fine motor.

I'd have switched to another car but I didn't want to let the de Ville out of my sight; I'd mislaid five grand's worth of coke in the upholstery somewhere when I'd been drunk, and I was still looking for it.

I remembered stashing the drug, but not exactly where; as well as being drunk and stoned I'd been in a severe paranoid fugue, not simply because I was carrying the stuff but because we were in the middle of Hyde Park at lunchtime, and Jasmine had the Panther doing fifty miles an hour over the grass, scattering

119

sunbathers like startled grouse and accounting for at least two brace of deckchairs.

We'd had an argument about sex; Jasmine wanted some and I had prioritised getting to the record company office for a Rolling Stone photo session above finding the nearest drive-through car wash and parking in it while Jas climbed into the back with me and took off her uniform. She calmed down eventually and somehow we got out of the park without being arrested, but in all the excitement I forgot I'd planted the coke in a Safe Place and didn't remember until a week later when we were starting to run out of the stuff. I knew I hadn't thrown it out of a door or window because Jas had found a way of locking them all so I couldn't jump out. Anyway, I was still looking for the cocaine and when I did find it Jasmine wasn't getting any, not when she was driving, not after that last time on the M6.

'Thought it was speed, didn't I?' Jasmine giggled roguishly.

'Oh, very funny, Jas.' The tractor had cleared the road. I nodded forward. 'Road's clear, Jasmine.'

'Go on,' she said, winking at me. 'Just one glass.'

Inez put her magazine down. 'Jasmine,' she said tiredly.

'I . . .' Jas began. Then a fusillade of car horns sounded from behind us. Jas looked unconcernedly over our shoulders through the rear window, then put both elbows on the back of her seat. 'Come on,' she said. 'I drive better smashed.'

'I wish she wouldn't use that word,' Wes muttered, shaking his head and looking at the earth bank opposite. The honking noises behind us increased.

'Jas,' I said, pointing forward again, 'just drive.' I pressed the button that elevated the glass screen between us, and Jasmine's elbows were slowly lifted up; her face assumed a look of annoyance, and as the glass hissed up into place she was turning round to look furiously at a small red Mini, squeezing past us from behind. She lowered her window and started shouting inaudibly at the car and giving it the finger. I listened in via the intercom.

'—unt!' Jas' tinny voice shouted. 'Ever been fist fucked? Wanna start?' I turned the intercom off again. The car leapt away, spilling more champagne. I rocked back in my seat. The Panther was accelerating hard, the grassy banks and hedgerows blurring past. The rear of the red Mini was rapidly coming closer.

120

I stabbed at the intercom button again.

'And don't you *dare* run that car off the road, you bitch! Just slow down! You know what happened the last time! I'm warning you!' Jas stamped on the brakes, looked round glaring at me, then threw her champagne-coloured chauffeuse's cap down into the footwell. She settled down to thirty miles an hour and thereafter drove hunched up over the wheel with her epauletted shoulders set in their 'I do *not* want to talk about it' position. I dried my hands again and sat back in the seat.

'She's got to go,' Inez said, turning a page in her *Cosmopolitan*.

'She's right; it's you or her,' Wes told me. I shook my head.

'I'll keep her on till I learn to drive myself,' I told them. Inez guffawed. Wes looked away at the fields again, shaking his head.

'Wes,' Inez said, putting the magazine down and looking at him seriously.

'Yeah?'

'*Are* you serious about this . . . bugging?'

'Sure.' He nodded. He took the silver cigarette case from the rosewood table set between Inez and me and took out a joint. 'Yeah; of course.' He used the cigar lighter, sat back, looking at Inez and me in turn. Inez pursed her lips.

'Well, I'm not staying in your house then, Weston. I'll find a hotel in Newquay. How about you?' She asked me. I shrugged, took one of the spliffs as well.

Beautifully rolled. This was the other reason I kept Jas on.

That and the fact that her father was a gangster from the East End and she'd threatened to tell him I'd raped her if I didn't keep her near me. I didn't fancy a radical penisectomy just then so I agreed. Jas wanted me to screw her but I was half-terrified that if I ever did she'd develop an even closer attachment and I'd never get rid of her (elephantiasis of the ego is endemic amongst rock stars, never forget), and also half-reluctant not to have her around. She was a pet, a conversation piece. She had character. It was all bad, but she had it.

'Well?' Inez said, pointedly. I sighed. I still wanted to stay at Wes' place; it would be something different. But Inez probably expected me to come with her.

'Yeah, all right,' I said. 'Hotel.' I gestured with the flats of my hands to Wes. 'Sorry,' I told him.

'Hey, that's all right, man.' Wes stared out over a low hedge at the sloping fields and towards the distant line of surf breaking on the rocks of the north Cornish coast. 'Still a free country,' he muttered, then sighed and said, 'hey; let's put on some sounds. Too quiet in here.'

Jasmine eventually passed the red Mini on a straight stretch of A class road. She cut in sharply and the Mini flashed its lights at her, but at least she didn't spill any champagne.

Ah, Jesus, big houses, fast cars and sleek women. Fame and fortune; nothing wrong with it as long as you're young enough to enjoy it and old enough to control it.

The others didn't make as much as I did, but they all made a lot. We hit the industry at a good time, when albums were selling well. We peaked in the UK in '78, the same year the greatest number of records were sold, and by then we were big in the States too; big worldwide, in fact. Far too much has been written already about what we represented, where we fitted in and what we stood for, but I suppose there's some truth in it all somewhere, and I guess I would go along with the idea we were a sort of half-step towards punk; just different enough to be novel, not quite mad enough to be a threat.

We fell between two stools and made our piles, if you want the gist of it. We were claimed as being all sorts of things; we had a foot in more camps than we had feet to put them in. We were the band that made your brain think and your foot tap at the same time (not a trick everybody can manage, mind you; there are some real thickets around). We had – dare I say it – class.

And we were the band whose gimmick was . . . music. Oh, yes, we had that reputation, God knows how. I was immensely proud of it at the time but it all seems meaningless now. We put our songs together differently, we used different patterns of musical development, unusual chords, unlikely but convincing layers of sound. Hell, all I was trying to do was sound *just the same* as everybody else; those were my attempts to be *normal*, for God's sake. I just kept getting it wrong, that was all.

But when anyone asked how we did it, how we'd got where we had, I used to tell them that it was just the tunes. That was it. In the end it's the music that sells. Tunes people can remember and hum and whistle and plunk out on their own guitars.

All the rest, from the chords, the arrangement, the instrumental virtuosity, to the image, the marketing, the pyrotechnic stage shows . . . all of it's just window dressing. In the end there's only the music. In my case, literally the tunes; my lyrics are rarely more than competent, and not even always that. Music is the stuff; comparatively few people have sold lots of records on the strength of just the lyrics. And music travels better, too.

Of course, fashion sells, a beat can sell, a particular style or technique or skill or just artist can sell, and increasingly what the industry tries to package and sell is *image*, but none of those are as reliable or as durable as a good tune.

Image is easier to manipulate corporately, though, and the big companies feel it's something they control rather than the artist, so they like it for that reason alone. We just happened to be what people wanted at the time; we were lucky. But ever since Elvis Presley – possibly ever since Frank Sinatra – the companies have been trying to take the luck out of it and *design* the images of the bands and singers they push. They've been trying it for years and they're getting very adept, and now – ironically – the whole idea of an *image* is so much taken for granted as an important – often vital – part of what makes a group successful that the kids have started doing it themselves; they work on their image as much as the songs, before they ever get as far as the A & R men! Strange days indeed.

Oh, well, what the hell. Wasn't like this in my young days though. Well, not as far as I know . . .

We toured the UK, Europe and Scandinavia, and the US; we made *Night Shines Darkly* and got ready to tour the world. We'd stayed with ARC, but we'd negotiated another three album deal so reasonable and fair that to this day Rick Tumber winces whenever it's mentioned.

We'd had plans to form our own record company, put out our own stuff, have more control, but . . . we never got around to it. It took all our time and effort touring and recording; setting up a record company and making it work would have needed too much time. I was disappointed and relieved at the same time. I'd had all sorts of crazy plans (and bad titles) ready. I'd wanted to call it the Obscure Record Label, but that was shouted down as soon as I mentioned it, and I think I lost interest after that. We stayed with the big boys and they gave us lots of sweeties; tons and tons of candy.

As Frozen Gold, the five of us were probably outgrossing the GNP of some small third world countries, but most of us had no fixed abode. I had to ring up my accountants to find out where I lived. We'd all bought places of some sort in Britain; I had my Scottish estate, Davey had a mansion in Kent, Wes had his house in Cornwall, Christine owned a small block of flats in Kensington, Mickey had installed his parents in a house near Drymen, overlooking Loch Lomond, but none of us were domiciled in the UK.

Tax reasons, of course. We weren't allowed to spend more than three months in Britain, but for three years running we didn't even manage that amount. We spent so much time out of the country touring there was no point in being registered for tax in Britain (and I didn't think Sunny Jim Callaghan's watered-down-rosé government deserved my money anyway . . . what a joke that seems now). I think, technically, we lived in LA for the second half of the seventies. But it might have been the Cayman Islands.

Made no difference to us. We stayed in hotels in major cities, we stayed in apartments and houses connected to recording studios in Paris or Florida or Jamaica, we stayed with friends and famous people and sometimes we spent a week or two in our places in the UK, and occasionally visited our parents.

Just living out the dream . . . or our separate dreams.

Davey's was to be the guitar hero incarnate, but I think he knew even then that their heyday had been and gone. He got there just too late, in time to hit the wave as it started to collapse. He didn't play any worse because he wasn't getting the adulation he thought he ought to get; he may even have played better, trying harder, but I don't think he ever thought he'd fulfilled his dreams.

He didn't just want to be mentioned in the same breath as Hendrix or Clapton or Jimmy Page; he wanted them to be mentioned in the same breath as *him*. But the time to construct such legends had passed. He'd never quite be on the same level, even if he was as good (and he believed he was). So there was always something left for him to aim for.

At the time, I didn't envy him.

Perhaps it was some unfulfilled part of Davey's extemporising talent that sublimated itself in practical jokes and hair-raising stunts. He'd gone from being David Balfour, esquire, to Dave Balfour, to Davey Balfour to Crazy Davey Balfour. That was what they ended up calling him in the papers. For once, they were just about right.

Davey started doing things to hotels. He'd taken up climbing, and would occasionally swarm up the outside of the hotel rather than use the elevators. There's a hotel in Hamburg where they still talk about the time the mad Schottlander decided to set up a record for getting from lobby to roof, up the stairs, by motorbike. He did almost kill himself with that one; came down in the lift with the motor idling, and arrived back in the lobby half-stupefied with carbon monoxide poisoning.

On stage, for one UK tour, Crazy Davey had been Mad Man. This had been his own idea, not mine. What happened was that Davey would go offstage for ten minutes or so, and then reappear in a blaze of lights and dry ice through (if it was available) a hole in the stage.

He had a power saw strapped to each arm, screaming away with the trigger throttles taped on maximum revs; lit welding torches were tied to his knees and flaming blowtorches to his ankles. On his head he had a light crash helmet like the ones canoeists wear, with a couple of electric drills bolted to the top and running. Dozens of lights and sequenced flash units completed the immediate effect. He'd just stand there for a few moments, while the crowd, most of whom had heard of the stunt and had been waiting for Mad Man to appear, went wild.

Then stage hands would come up with bits of brick, steel, wood and plastic, and hold them up to Davey; who stretched out an arm, or flexed a leg, or just nodded; sparks flew and metal tore; dust rose and bricks disintegrated; sawdust showered and boards snapped; plastic burned. All the time, Davey was singing ('After-burn') . . . or trying to. The noise was bedlam, actually, full of interference, but it was effective.

It was an insanely dangerous stunt, and we had some problems with fire regulations, but what really killed the act were two things. First, Davey nicked a little finger on a drill at the Glasgow Apollo gig and had to have it bandaged; it was his right hand, so it didn't matter too much, though he still felt he was only playing at about ninety per cent; but nobody would insure his fingers while he was doing the act, and that did worry him. The other thing that killed it was Big Sam; the stunt wasn't right for us, he said; too violent, just not the right image.

The rest of us agreed, and Davey seemed happy just to have done it.

Then there were the practical jokes. There was one American tour when he took to sabotaging my hotel room every second or third night. It started out with unscrewing the door handle from the inside, so that it came away in my hand, but escalated to the stage that the guy must have been putting more effort and thought into how to surprise me that night than he was into playing for a stadium full of customers.

I'd almost got used to coming back to my room to find everything in it had been turned upside down, or that it was utterly bare, stripped even of the carpets and light fittings, when one evening Davey surprised me with a better trick; he lowered himself on a rope into my room, hung the television out of the window held only by a rope tied to the inside door handle, then took all the screws out of the door hinges.

I came back to my room, put the key in the lock and turned it, then watched the door go flying across the room to smash through the window and follow the TV down the six floors to the flowerbeds. The edge of the swiftly retreating key took a chunk out of my thumb, which I did not find funny.

Another time I couldn't get my door to open at all; I was getting wary by then, so I had the night porter come up and remove the door. When we got the door off eventually, we were faced with a blank, off-white wall, like solidified fog, except it was *warm*. Davey had filled the entire room with expanded polystyrene; he'd got a couple of big drums of the two fluids required, brought them in through the window with him, and just let them slosh out all over the carpet. What looked like a huge mutant mushroom of foam had extruded itself from my window.

Hotel managers hated Davey, but he always paid for all the damages, and he treated it as such a joke it was difficult to get really annoyed with him. Even the time with the foam-filled room, he'd booked me a replacement and moved most of my gear into it before carrying out the prank.

How they gave him a pilot's licence I'll never know, but they did. Davey bought a light plane, made sure his mansion in Kent came equipped with a grass strip and a hangar, and even went to the length of having a simulator installed to help him with his technique. I suspected he bribed somebody for the licence, but everybody I've talked to says that isn't possible. Maybe giving Davey a pilot's licence was the CAA's idea of a practical joke.

Mickey Watson seemed fairly normal compared to the rest of us; he turned up, drummed, went away again. He'd got married to a girl he'd known since primary school (a whirlwind romance nevertheless, on one of our sporadic returns to Scotland), and they were starting a family – that was why he wouldn't be at Wes' party that weekend; his wife had just gone into hospital to have their first kid. Mickey was always there when he was supposed to be; in the studio, at the rehearsal suite, on tour . . . but at the same time he seemed to be living on a different plane from the rest of us. To him, despite all the money and the fripperies, it was still just a job.

We took it seriously, in our own ways. We worked at being Rock Stars; not musicians, not even Personalities or ordinary Stars, but Rock Stars. It was a way of life, like a religion, like becoming a totally different person. We *believed*; we had an obligation to our public to behave like Rock Stars, off-stage as well as on, and we did our best, dammit.

Mickey took a different view. Occupation: drummer. End of story.

He's a farmer now, in Ayrshire, raising potatoes and wheat and big healthy children.

Christine was Christine. She achieved by accident what Davey was continually planning and striving for but never quite managing; they compared the others to her. Her voice had developed in range and power, but that was the least of it; what got them bouncing off the seats was the sheer guts she put into her performance. She growled and breathed and screamed her way through songs; always in control, still note-perfect, but bending and twisting her voice and the words and the tune into shapes and sounds I'd certainly never thought of. Took my breath away, and

I heard it every night on tour; God knows what effect it had on anybody else, hearing it for the first time. Must have been like crawling out of the desert and being hosed down with iced champagne.

I think Christine could have sung a toothpaste jingle and made it sound quiveringly erotic, tearfully tragic or side-splittingly funny, just depending on how she felt that night; in her mouth, my words sounded like poetry, even to me. Just by changing her phrasing and the tone of her voice she could switch from making you think of a koala bear in tears to a wolverine on heat. Stunning. That was the only word that fitted. And she never lost it; even after the End, the Fall, when the band broke up, she just kept on going, formed her own band and more or less never stopped touring; singing and singing and singing.

Wes MacKinnon, one-time Hammond king, had taken, when on stage, to surrounding himself with vast numbers of synthesisers and organs and electric pianos and assorted other keyboards; banks of them, whole staircases of white and black keyed machines with coloured switches and blinking lights and LEDs. I sometimes wondered if Wes might have been happier as a drummer; he seemed to want to hide himself from the audience behind these ramparts of electronics (Mickey was heading in the other direction. He'd switched to transparent drums so the audience could see him better).

Wes didn't restrict his technophilia to the stage; he had a fetish, I think, about buttons and Light Emitting Diodes. He owned a succession of scientific calculators which offered longer and longer lists of functions Wes couldn't even pronounce let alone use, and a whole string of home computers, each one faster and more capacious and cheaper than the previous one; he had to have the latest, so as a rule he'd only just finished learning how to use one machine when he threw that out and bought a newer one.

He had an obsession with sound purity too (he now runs his own CD manufacturing plant and I think he's already got a prototype DAT cassette machine, smuggled out of Sony by a well-paid mole). Putting on a record was a small ritual for Wes. At home, he wore white gloves when he handled an album.

He finally brought his computer fetish and his mania for perfect sound together when he got hold of a used IBM mainframe and had recording-studio tapes transferred directly onto disc-packs; he could then programme an entire evening's listening from his computer terminal. No scratches, no rumble, no tracking errors. Cost him well into six figures just for the hardware, and he was temporarily sickened when CD came out, but it kept him happy for a few years.

The IBM machine was installed in his house on the north Cornish coast, along with frightening amounts of surveillance equipment and some very powerful all-weather strobe lights . . .

'We need a bigger sound system, man.'

I breathed in hard through both nostrils and faced into the darkness. My nose was numb, the back of my throat felt thick. I felt faster than a speeding innuendo and sharper than a rad-fem's tongue.

Both barrels. Here it comes. Columbian nirvana. I felt like the top of my head had been blown off and replaced with a diamond. 'What?' I said instantly, glaring at Wes. '*Bigger*? You want a bigger sound system than we've got already? Are you crazy? We could knock small buildings down with the one we've got. Get anything more powerful and it'll be covered by the SALT agreement. We're registering as low-yield underground weapon tests already. Right now we use more electricity than some African countries generate; what are you trying to do; cause blackouts? You cornered the market in candles or hurricane lanterns or something? Christ almighty, have you seen the size of our speaker stacks? They're like office blocks; people live in them. There's a ten-person squat going on in the stage-left bass stack, didn't you know? Been there for two years and the roadies only noticed because the squatters applied to put in main drainage. What . . .'

'Calm down, man. Stop exaggerating.'

'You want to saddle us with fifty thousand law suits from people with no eardrums and you accuse *me* of exaggerating? Shee-it.'

We were standing on the long front porch of the house along the coast from Newquay. Wes didn't have a name for it yet. He was still thinking about it. I'd suggested 'The Plumbers' because the place overlooked Watergate Bay, but Wes didn't seem to think much of this idea, and I'm not even sure he'd heard of

Watergate, at the time or since. 'Dunbuggin' might have been another name for the place, except that it could not have been less appropriate.

It was long after midnight and Wes' party was just starting to hit the plateau phase. Music thumped out from the big drawing room on the far side of the house. It was a dark, close night; no sign of stars or moon. The air smelled sweet and fresh, alternately scented by the land and by the sea, which could be heard but not seen, beating and crashing against the rocks a hundred feet or so from the house.

We stood looking out into the Atlantic darkness and shared a joint. Wes sat down at a garden table and fiddled about with the six-inch reflector telescope standing on the porch. God knows what he expected to see.

He'd been quiet for all of two seconds. I couldn't bear it.

'You want a bigger sound system?' I said, just to check.

'Well.' Wes looked thoughtful. 'Not necessarily *bigger* . . . just *louder*.'

'You're mad.'

'Maybe, Weird, maybe . . . but we're not loud enough. We need more decibels, man.'

'Hearing aids,' I decided. 'You've cornered the market in hearing aids and you're trying to drum up trade, or organ up trade. Well, it won't work. You'll have the Monopolies Commission and the anti trust people onto you. Not to mention the British Medical Association and the Food And Drug Administration. My advice to you is, forget it.'

'Do you know if any other bands are using electrostatic speakers?' Wes said thoughtfully. He looked through the telescope's eyepiece into the pitch-black overcast.

'Jesus, now he wants to electrocute us. You're a sick man, MacKinnon. There's something wrong with your filters; the white noise is coming through. Your brain's envelope is torn. Return To Zenda. Who is number one?'

'Give me that jay, Weird; you're gibbering.'

'God, I feel good. Could we go swimming? I feel like going swimming. Think anybody else would feel like swimming? Where's Inez; have you seen her? You want to come swimming?'

'Na, man. Don't do it anyway, like. You'd probably imagine you could swim to New York and we'd never see you again.'

'A length? No; I was only going to do a couple of widths. Want me to bring back some Guinness from Dublin?' I was jumping up and down by that stage, swinging my arms around in swimming motions.

'Na,' Wes said. He got bored with the telescope and turned to an FM radio lying on the table. He turned it on and it relayed the sounds of the party to us, muffled. He changed the frequency, then stopped when he found some panting noises. 'Hey man; listen. People humpin. Hey!' He looked up at me. I was still jumping up and down.

'You're sick. I told you. You are a sick and crazy man. That must be illegal. You'll get the jile.'

'No, man . . .' Weston grinned happily, listening to the sounds of a bed creaking and two people breathing heavily. I moved a little closer and stopped jumping up and down. I wondered if I could recognise the heavy breathing. It was getting quicker. 'That's beautiful, man.' He turned the frequency control again. I felt slightly disappointed. My arms and legs were sore but I started jumping up and down again. The radio relayed what sounded like people screwing again.

'Hot damn,' I said between jumps. 'There's a lot of it about tonight.' 'HOT DAMN. THERE'S A LOT OF IT ABOUT TONIGHT.' My own voice bellowed back from the radio and turned into a feedback howl. Wes chortled and switched the radio off again.

'That was you,' Wes grinned. 'There's a mike over the door, just behind you.'

I turned round and looked for it but I couldn't see it. 'You're still a deeply sick and disturbed man, Weston.'

'No, I'm just ahead of my time, Weird.'

'Bull. . .shit.'

'Suit yourself.'

Weston had bugged his own house. Every room. Totally wired for sound and broadcasting on all channels. He had bugs everywhere; from the old kitchen pantry to the new double garage. No bedroom or bathroom was spared. He'd even bugged the loft. Anybody with a good FM radio could pick up every sound in the house so long as they were within about two hundred feet. We all thought Wes was crazy, but Wes thought it was a great hoot.

'It's the future, man,' he'd tell you. 'In the future everything's going to be bugged. Telephones and offices and televisions and radios and everything, man. There'll be no way to stop it. They can fit bugs anywhere already. You know they can bug a room by shining a laser at the windows now? It's true, man. You'd better believe it. This is the future and you might as well get used to it now. Anyway; what's so wrong about hearing people fuck or crap? Everybody does it; there's nothing shameful about it, man; what does it matter? Why be shy of things most people do every day? It's crazy, man. They just want you to be that way so they can control you; they're getting inside your head, installing censorship circuits, and you're helping them. Just let it all hang out, man.'

Wes, you'll gather, felt he'd been born too late. He was a mid-to-late-sixties man really. Most people had moved on but Wes used his money to move both back to the past and forward to the future at the same time; anything other than stay in the present. *Now* I knew why his keyboard runs usually went in opposite directions at the same time.

Wes wasn't stopping at audio intrusion only. He had ordered camera equipment, he'd told me. First sound, then vision. Soon he'd have closed circuit TV in every room. Twenty channels in full colour, from cellar to rooftop view.

I sat down heavily on the top step of the porch. Wes handed me back the jay. I looked out into the darkness. The waves crashed beneath us. 'We need more light here,' I said suddenly. 'There's just too much darkness here. More light is required.'

'You want more light?' Wes said, in a strange tone of voice that made me look round suspiciously at him. 'I think we can fix that.' He sniffed in the sea salt smell, lifting his head and seeming to scent the air and listen to the beating waves for a moment, then he was out of the seat and marching down the lawn. 'Follow me, Weird.'

I followed him down to one edge of the lawn, almost out of range of the house lights. He pointed to a low wall which divided lawn from rocks. 'Sit there,' he said. 'Look down there.' I could hardly see where he was pointing, but it seemed to be down to the rocks.

'I'll just be a minute. Okay?' he said.

'Okay.' I sat and watched his shadowy form move back towards the house. I looked out to sea, straining to see anything other than darkness. After a while, using the edges of my eyes, I could just about make out the white surf falling through the night to the rocks, rolling on the unseen ocean.

Then there was a buzz, and the rocks lit up, flashing blue white.

The surf incandesced, brilliantly white. It happened again and again; a machine-gun fire of stuttering light bursting from large film-studio light stands, topped with strobes. They picked out the surging billows of the surf and chopped them up into single frames, staccato images of utter clarity punctuated with a darkness you could almost hear.

Waves rolled in, in stop motion, detonating against the ragged edge of rocks in freeze-frame sequences, spray falling back and the next roller coming in pinpoint percussions of light.

'Oh . . . *wow*!' I said, mouth hanging open. I looked to one side of the display, to see how much of the rest of the bay the strobes illuminated, and saw Davey Balfour, almost out of the range of the lights, and almost back into his jeans, which he was pulling on, running away along the rocks and into shadow.

In that shadow, for one instant of light, before she ducked back into the darkness, I saw Inez' face, neck and shoulders.

I shook my head. 'Hell, you could have *said* something,' I muttered to myself. The light show went on. The joint burned down and singed my fingers. Wes came down the slopes of grass towards me, face appropriately beaming.

'What d'you think, man?'

'Impressive,' I said, getting off the wall and walking up to him. 'Very impressive indeed.' I flicked the roach away into the darkness; it flickered under the strobes like something seen in an acid trip. 'Seen Jasmine?'

NINE

I sniffed my fingers; they still smelled of rubber, or lubricant, or whatever the hell it is makes condoms smell the way they do. Betty hadn't always been so doubly cautious; it was only during the last year – as stories about AIDS multiplied faster than even the disease – that she'd started using the damned things. I'd washed my hands at least once since last night, but they still smelled. I wondered if anybody else would be able to smell it.

I lay in bed. It was raining; another rainy Saturday in Glasgow. Hail and snow mixed in with the rain, and a ragged-clouded sky between the showers. Rick Tumber was due to arrive tomorrow. I thought about getting out of the city again, but couldn't think where to go.

Edinburgh? I hadn't been there for a year or so and I'd always liked the place. Or maybe I could get a booking at one of the hotels in Aviemore and have a terribly festive and maybe even snowy Christmas there. But I didn't feel like it. I have a very old-fashioned attitude to Christmas; I try to ignore it. This is an old-fashioned Scottish attitude, of course, not an English one.

It's changed here too now, largely thanks to TV and a combination of very expensive toys, saturation advertising and the tyranny of a child's tears, but even I can remember when most people would work Christmas day to get an extra day at Hogmanay. All changed. But I still hate Christmas. Bah and humbug and all that.

I didn't want to stay and see Rick Tumber, but I couldn't be bothered getting up and going. Even the fact it was raining was enough to put me off. Anyway; McCann and I usually investigated a few pubs on a Saturday night, and I hadn't said I was thinking about going away. It would be bad manners to pull out now.

I sniffed my fingers again, thinking about Betty and wondering whether I felt like heading down to the crypt to guddle about in the studio. There were a few jingles and potential themes I could work on, but I didn't really feel very enthusiastic. Rain beat against the windows of the tower bedroom. I turned on the TV monitor and looked at the dull grey views of the various doors and walls. God, it looked depressing.

Wes did eventually rig his house for vision as well as sound. People stopped coming to see him after a while; maybe that was what he had in mind all the time. I did screw Jasmine, and we both found it a thoroughly disappointing experience. We tried a few more times but we just didn't match. She took the chauffeuse uniform with her when she went off to front a punk band; I counted myself lucky she hadn't taken the car as well. Last I heard she was married to a car dealer, had two kids and lived in Ilford.

I peered closely at the monitor when I switched to the Elmbank Street camera. There was an anorak-covered figure struggling through the rain with an overloaded shopping trolley out there, and it looked suspiciously like Wee Tommy.

The shopping trolley was loaded with white cylinders.

I got down to the door just as he rang the bell.

'Aw, hi there, Jim; ye all right, aye?'

'Fine. Come in.' He came in, dripping rain from anorak and trolley. 'Tommy, why have you brought a shopping trolley full of' – I looked closer – 'whipped cream containers?'

Tommy had about a hundred of the pressurised cans all jumbled in the trolley. He had enough whipped cream there to cover a small building with the stuff. Tommy hung his anorak up and stood looking down at the rain-spotted white cans. 'Laughin gas,' he said, in a conspiratorial tone. I shook my head.

'This is whipped cream, Tommy. You wanted a dentist's, not the dairy section of Tesco's.'

'Na, na,' he said, picking one of the containers up. 'There's gas inside here too; the stuff that pushes the cream out. It's laughing gas; nitric oxide.'

I took a can from the pile in the trolley and inspected it. 'What? You sure?' I found the ingredients label; sure enough, the propellant was nitrous oxide. Inez, Dave, Christine and I had had some laughing gas once, in Madrid I think it was. Very odd stuff.

'Aye, I'm sure. One of ma mates said his brother read about it in *Scientific American*.'

'Good grief.'

'Want tae try some, eh?'

'Mm, not particularly, but don't let me stop you. Come on into the body of the kirk.'

The space heater was on at full blast, filling the folly with its booming white noise. I'd put on some Gregorian Chants to compete with the sound. Tommy and I sat in a couple of the CRM chairs, just far enough downwind from the space heater not to overheat. Tommy had taken his black socks and black jumper off to let them dry; he draped them over the shopping trolley we'd brought up the steps from the vestry. He selected a can of foam. 'Ah'm really sorry about the dug the other day, Jim,' he told me, shaking his head and compressing his lips. 'That dug was right out of order, so it was. Ah'd a skelped it, but it wouldnae have done any good.'

He didn't add that it would probably have eaten him if he had.

'It's all right,' I said. 'I cleaned everything up. Don't worry about it.'

'Well, it's back with ma uncle now, so Ah reckon we're safe from it now. Unless his piles act up again, of course.'

'Well, of course.'

'Sure you don't want one of these?' Tommy offered me a whipped-cream container. I shook my head.

'I'm trying to give them up. Do you want a drink?'

Tommy thought about this. 'Aye; Ah'll take a wee voddy, if that's all right, Jim.'

I brought a bottle of Stolichnaya and two glasses. There had been a brief hiss while my back was turned. When I got back to the seat, Tommy was pressing down the top of the cream can and frowning. 'Get anything?' I asked. He shook his head.

'No much.' He put that canister on the floor and took another one, raising it to one nostril and then pressing the nozzle button. He jerked back as a small blob of foam squirted up his nose. 'Ah, ya bastard!' I tried not to laugh as he leant forward, blowing his nose.

'Try bumping the base a bit first,' I suggested.

Tommy tried that with the next one, and avoided getting a nostril full of foam. The hiss of gas was still very short, though. He smiled ruefully and reached for another container.

'Where did you get all these, anyway?' I asked him.

'I've got a pal works in Presto's; he's been stashing the odd can from the boxes as they come through, ye know? Got them out tae me today cos of the Christmas rush, 'nat.' He snorted from another can, then put it down too. He giggled, experimentally, then looked at me as though waiting for a reaction. I shrugged.

'Anything?' I asked.

'Nup. Don't think so.' Tommy started taking the containers out two at a time, bashing them on the carpet-covered stone floor and snorting from both at once. He went through about twelve of the cans that way, then sat back, breathing hard and looking a little odd. He tried giggling again.

'Now?' I asked him.

'Bit light-headed,' he said.

'Oxygen high,' I told him.

'Is that what ye get from them?' Tommy looked at another can. 'Well, Ah dinnae feel smashed.'

'No, you still look glazed.'

Tommy looked at me, then giggled again, then started laughing. I sat back with my vodka for a moment or two, decided it hadn't been that funny and reached for a couple of the cans.

The truth is, I don't know if the damn cans worked or not. Wee Tommy and I sat there, telling each other jokes and laughing and giggling, but for all I know it was just suggestion, and the minuscule amounts of gas in the canisters had little or no effect. We laughed because we thought we ought to.

I've seen people fooled into thinking Capstan Full Strength cigarettes were joints, accept speed and paracetamol as cocaine, and not notice that their drinks have been watered down until they're practically alcohol-free. It all depends what you're expecting, what you've been told to believe in.

Tommy left to go and sign on, leaving me with a shopping

trolley full of dud whipped-cream cans. I guess the folly, with its bulky stacks of Comecon produce, seemed like an appropriate resting place for the massed containers. Full of 'product'. That's what the cans say. They're full of whipped 'product'. Not 'cream' or 'milk-derived froth', or even 'tacky white gunge bearing a vague resemblance to something that might actually have come from a cow', but 'product'.

Product. Jeez, the buzzword of the century. Everything's 'product'. Music is 'product'; product produced by producers for the industry to sell to the consumers. I don't think anyone has quite had the nerve yet to refer to paintings as 'product' yet (except as a put-down, perhaps), but it must be on the way. They'll quote the works of dead painters on the stock exchange. Picasso's blue-chip period. Gilt-edged frames. We put a value on what we treasure, and so cheapen it.

I felt like sitting there, amongst all my Eastern Bloc goods, feet up on my CRM chair, the space heater filling the folly with throaty white noise and the comforting trace-smell of paraffin, and finishing off the bottle of Stolichnaya by myself . . . but instead I went down to the crypt and footered about with some of my appallingly expensive musical equipment, tinkering with ideas that would probably end up as advertising jingles, or themes to movies that were never quite as good as their trailers promised.

I met McCann in the Griffin. We always meet there on a Saturday night; we Go Out, we Do The Town. We even dress up; I have been known to wear a tie, and what would pass for a suit. For some reason, I wore just those things on this occasion.

I had no idea this would lead to disaster.

'You're lookin smart, Jimmy.'

'Appearances can be deceptive,' I told McCann.

'Whit dae ye want?'

'A half and a half,' I said, and suddenly wondered why a half-pint of heavy and a whisky isn't just called a 'One', or a 'Whole'. Maybe they are, somewhere. McCann returned through the crowd with the drinks; the Griffin was busy and noisy. I brushed some sleet and snowflakes off my coat.

'This you gettin yerself tarted up fur this man comin ta morrow?'

I looked at McCann over my beer glass. I had almost forgotten that Rick Tumber was coming tomorrow; working on music for any length of time has that sort of effect on me. I shook my head. 'No,' I said.

'Oh. Where are we goin tae go then?'

I thought. McCann looked moderately presentable himself. I was in a sort of restless, challenging mood that made me want to do something I wouldn't normally do, go somewhere I wouldn't normally go. 'Somewhere different.'

McCann looked thoughtful. 'Ma boay,' he said, referring to his son, who is about twenty and has earned his father's undying scorn by joining the army, 'wiz tellin me aboot one of they fancy nightclubs, last time he wiz here. Place called Monty's. Just aff Buchanan Street.' McCann looked at my battered but still echoingly stylish handmade Italian boots, and my newly cleaned greatcoat, then pulled one slightly frayed shirt-cuff down from under his jacket sleeve. 'They might let us in.'

'A nightclub?' I said, grimacing. I've never liked these places; they're better up here than they are down in London, where they tend to be full of noisy, mannered, ill-mannered, over-privileged people I'd normally pay a great deal of money just to avoid, but even in Glasgow I object to paying outrageous amounts of money to drink suspiciously bland cocktails in the sort of place where people go to be seen.

'Just fur a look,' McCann said. 'The boay wiz sayin that wan o the wa's is glass; like an aquarium; there's a big tank full a fush behind it, an a mermaid swims aroon inside.'

'Oh, good grief.'

'Or we could do the clockwork orange pub crawl.'

'What?' I glared at McCann. The Glasgow underground runs in a circle. The trains used to be red and have leather upholstery and wooden interiors; they creaked a lot and had a smell you never forgot; nowadays they're wee plastic-looking bright orange things, and they've been nicknamed the clockwork orange. The associated pub crawl involves travelling right round the tube circuit, stopping at each of the fifteen stations and walking to the nearest pub for a pint and a whisky (or a half and a half, if you're some sort of cissy). McCann and I have been going to do this for at least a year, but we haven't got around to it yet. 'This is hardly the weather for it,' I said.

'You decide then,' McCann said, shrugging.

The mermaid in the room-sized tank looked vaguely familiar, but if I had ever seen the girl before, I couldn't place her.

A young blond waiter brought our drinks. This was a relief; I'd been afraid that the mermaid in the wall-tank would be just the beginning, and the whole club would be planned around some agonisingly literally worked-out theme based on mermaids and mermen, or the sea, or something equally awful.

It wasn't; it was just a posh bar with an atmosphere somewhere between a private library and a lively gentlemen's club; shelves full of books, a deep carpet, rather nice wooden tables with leather tops, and a surprisingly young clientele (or maybe I'm just getting old). The ceiling fans, whirling gently under a black roof, were something of an affectation, especially in December, but I'd seen a lot worse.

Not a laser or a fog-bank of dry ice or a flashing light in sight. The drinks were only breathtakingly expensive, not coronary-inducingly dear, and McCann seemed pleased we had a table where we could see the mermaid, who had long black hair and large breasts. The aquarium filled most of one wall of the club, and teemed with bright fish swimming between pillars of rock and coral; tall green fronds waved above a floor of golden sand.

'That's a bonny lassie,' McCann said, watching the tank avidly.

'I hope she's not the only reason you wanted to come here,' I said, drinking what certainly tasted like a full-strength Manhattan. McCann had been going to ask for A Long Sloe Comfortable Screw Up Against The Wall, but changed his mind when he saw we were getting a waiter rather than a waitress, and got a Killer Zombie instead.

'Not at all.' McCann looked disgusted with me. 'Ye don't think Ah wanted tae come here just tae ogle some poor exploitit lassie forced tae dress up like half a fush tae earn a crust, dae ye?'

'Hmm,' I said. 'No, I suppose not.' In fact I wasn't sure about this at all, but I couldn't be bothered arguing. Apart from anything else, the mermaid looked quite happy in her job. She didn't look cold, none of the fish in there with her appeared hungry, and she was smiling in a non-air-stewardesslike way when she dived down from the unseen surface, waving at people at nearby tables. Also, she wasn't likely to be molested by the customers unless they'd brought along a frogman's outfit, or a sufficiently large explosive charge to breach the tank's glass. As for being exploited . . . who wasn't? Would McCann have been happier if she'd been working at a supermarket checkout, or clattering away at a typewriter in some office?

I've known people who dressed in Savile Row suits and Gucci shoes and were still complete bastards, so what in hell's wrong with looking like half a fish? Dammit, *we*'d dressed up to come here; McCann and I had had to conform to some sort of code, to have any chance of getting into a place with bouncers on the door.

Even when I was Weird, when I was The Man In The Black Coat With The Greased Back Hair And The Beard And The Mirror-Shades, I was dressing up; that was still a sort of uniform, because it became expected of me, and that's what makes the difference, that's what makes a uniform a uniform, not official rules and regulations . . . Jeez, the number of kids I've seen dressed exactly the same as each other who've said they dress the way they do to be 'different'.

Ho ho.

'Ma roon, want anothir wan?' McCann said suddenly. I looked at my glass. My God, that had gone down quickly. I was comfortably settled in a large leatherish easy chair. We'd agreed just to call in here for one drink and then go somewhere else, but it was cold and sleety outside, and . . . what the hell. I had enough cash. I could always lend McCann some if he ran short. Probably end up going for a curry later, I shouldn't be surprised.

'Aye' I said. 'Same again. Easy on the ice.'

We had a few more drinks. McCann became convinced the mermaid was looking at him when she smiled and waved, but then just as he was talking himself into going up to the glass and waving back – maybe holding up his address or a note asking what the girl was doing after work when she'd found her land-legs again, or asking her if she needed help out of those wet things – the mermaid left the pool; McCann watched with dismay as her scaly blue plastic tail disappeared through the mirror surface of the pool.

'She's gone,' he said.

'She can't,' I told him, 'stand being apart from you any longer and she's gone to get dressed to come round and ask you what a nice Marxist like you's doing in a capitalist clip-joint like this.'

'Aw, shit,' McCann said, ignoring me and dipping his head down to the table top to look up through the glass to the surface of the pool.

'Still after a piece of tail,' I said, shaking my head.

'Aw, come back, hen,' McCann groaned from the table top.

Hen? I thought. From fish to fowl in less than a minute. God, that was fast evolution. I looked round the busy bar. Actually, I knew how McCann felt. There were some good-looking women in the place, and I was lusting after several of them at once. One, standing at the bar, one foot on the brass rail, reminded me a lot of Inez. The same hair, roguishly tangled and perfectly kempt at once; the same long back and easy stance; definitely the same backside. The woman at the bar was wearing light-brown trousers. Inez wore jeans and trousers a lot, too. There was nothing wrong with her legs (though she thought there was), but her bum was just fabulous.

I signalled to one of the waitresses, stared at the woman at the bar, and thought about Inez. Ah Jayzuz, Inez, Inez; my bitch in britches, my *salop* in salopettes. I think she was the only one who ever really hurt me, just because I eventually did believe that it might last. It never crossed my mind, before or after, that a relationship I might have with a woman would prove permanent; I always assumed they were either taking pity on me, were merely satisfying their curiosity, or had made some uncharacteristic mistake in a moment of weakness.

I saw myself as the sort of guy who gets women on the rebound, if he happens to be in the right place at the right time; it was close to inconceivable that I might form a relationship entirely on my own merits. Even when sheer weight of numbers seemed to disprove this theory, I just assumed that a proportion of the women who'd thrown themselves at me, or hadn't run off screaming when I threw myself at them, were only doing it because I was famous, a Rock Star. So I never did expect too much, and thus was never grossly disappointed. Maybe I was trying not to get into something that might remind me of my parents' God-awful running-battle of a marriage, but if so, it wasn't deliberate. I just always assumed that I was an unattractive git who'd be picked only once all the nice guys had been spoken for.

But Inez slipped in under my guard. I don't know if she had her own assumptions – about permanence and making a home, maybe – and these assumptions were somehow stronger than my rather casual, unfounded premises, so that I absorbed hers, and was slowly, osmotically, virally, taken over . . . but however the hell it worked, however she became part of me, it hurt when she tore herself away.

Hell, I didn't really mind that she'd been screwing Davey (but was that why I later went with Christine, to avenge myself?); what annoyed me was that they'd been doing it so long and hidden it so carefully. And it stopped, after that night when they were caught in the strobe lights. That was, crazily enough, even more worrying.

I wouldn't have minded having a good excuse to diversify myself a little bit, with Inez there to come back to, and I'd have been equally happy for her to have the same freedom. Ah, those wonderful days when the worst you had to worry about was VD, or, in my case, a paternity suit. Inez and Davey could have gone on if they liked; I wouldn't have sulked. I could have handled it, I swear. But instead they both vowed never to do it again, and I was left with a nagging sense that it shouldn't have mattered that much in the first place.

Actually, to this day I think we were largely right about relationships, and I *still* think there's far too much of a fuss made about both sex itself and any fidelity associated with it . . . but these are not the times to shout about that too much, I guess.

'Same again?' I nudged McCann. He drained his glass, nodding. I looked around for the waitress I'd signalled earlier. I couldn't see her. I caught the eye of a waiter cruising nearby, and ordered a double round. This seemed like a wise precaution if the waiting staff were becoming as lackadaisical as the continuing absence of the waitress suggested. I considered whether perhaps she'd thought we'd had enough to drink already and had deliberately avoided us, but this was quite out of the question as we were both still fairly sober.

'Ah'm away fur a pee,' McCann told me. I nodded. He seemed

to have a little difficulty standing up, but he does have a bad leg from an accident in the yards when he was an apprentice, so that wasn't really surprising. I went back to contemplating the girl with the fabulous bum. She really was like Inez. I'd seen her face by now, which was quite different from Inez', but everything else about her was right.

Maybe I should go up and see if she'd ever been a fan of Frozen Gold; she was talking to a couple of guys, but neither of them seemed to be all that close to her; I might – what was I thinking of? I put my glass down, frowning at it. Perhaps I had had quite a lot to drink. I usually only started thinking about accosting women and telling them I had been a famous rock star right at the end of an evening, mercifully shortly before the stage of total oblivion.

Dammit, I felt pretty good. It wasn't fair of God or evolution or whatever to make drink so pleasant when it does you so much harm. I decided to slow down a bit; cocktails can be misleading.

McCann came back to find me staring, mystified, at six large glasses full of drink. 'Did ye get some fur me too?' he said, sitting.

'Ordered twice,' I explained.

'Ah know that; ye ordered two roons; but ye've got three.'

I scratched my head. 'Waitress,' I said. Apparently I *had* ordered another round from that waitress, after all. I couldn't remember this, but it was the same waitress, and the right drinks, and she insisted I had ordered it, so . . .

'Ye daft bugger,' McCann said, and attacked the first of the waiting triad of Killer Zombies. I shrugged and sighed, then launched into a Manhattan, vaguely wondering whether some cider ought to be included in the recipe, to make the connection with the Big Apple more obvious.

Maybe not.

The woman I'd seen at the bar was still there. Other foot on the brass rail now. Bum still glorious. Soft curvings. Peaches and apples and buns and bums, I thought, wandering. God almighty, women look so good. How do they *do* that?

I stood in a bathroom in Jamaica once, naked, doing body-builder poses in front of the mirror for a laugh while Inez took off her make-up. I sucked in my belly and clasped my hands under my ribcage in that sort of over-and-under grip body-builders use, then swivelled on the ball of one foot and put one leg out to the rear, flexing the muscles on my arms. Inez sloshed water over her apricot scrub. I held my pose for a few seconds, looking at my patchy brown–white nakedness, then relaxed, and stood facing the mirror and shaking my head at my reflection. I looked myself up and down.

'You know,' I said to Inez. 'When I look at the male body – naked, especially – I wonder how on earth women can take men seriously.'

Inez looked up for an instant, and made a snorting noise. 'What makes you think we do?' she said.

I hope I looked suitably hurt.

'Doan't you fuckin give me that shit, sonny!' McCann shouted.

I was jerked out of my reminiscences. My eyes were still focused on the bit of the bar where the woman with the wonderful rear-end had been, but she'd gone. McCann was turned away from me, arguing with somebody sitting to our right. I was sober enough even then to think *oh-oh*.

I looked over. McCann was face-to-face with a young man wearing glasses. 'Ah, away home, ye old fool! Don't . . .'

'Less aw this "old", ye wee basturt! Don't you fuckin call me "old"!'

The young man with the glasses turned to his mates, nodding back towards McCann. 'Fuckin calls me "sonny" then tells me not to call him "old"!' His two pals shook their heads. I could tell McCann was seething. I glanced around; a few people were looking at us, but so far the whole place hadn't started going quiet – always a bad sign – and the horizon was still clear of bouncers. The place was crowded and noisy enough to cover a minor verbal skirmish. Still time to get McCann away quietly.

He sat forward, wagging one finger at the guy with the glasses. 'It's that sort of stupit, defeatist attitude like yours that plays right intae the hands of that fascist bitch!'

I tugged at McCann's sleeve, but he ignored me, and with his other hand wiped his mouth free of some spittle. 'Aye, an dinnae you smile like that an look at yer mates either, laddie; Ah know whit Ah'm talkin aboot, which is mair than you do, Ah'll tell ye! Fuckin coalition . . . *coalition*?; just anuthir fuckin disaster fur the wurkin class . . .'

'Ach, away ye go . . . .' The young guy waved his hand dismissively at McCann. I tried to pull him round to look at me.

'McCann . . .' I said. McCann fended me off with his elbow; I still had a grip of his sleeve, and the shrugging motion he made pulled one side of his jacket off, showing his shirted shoulder beneath.

So it was my own fault, I guess. Because (a) it must have looked to the young guy as if McCann was taking off his jacket for a fight, and (b) I pulled back at McCann's sleeve again (and noticed that the place was now going quiet, and that there was a large person in a dinner jacket making full speed through the parting sea of heads and shoulders towards us), and when McCann shrugged and pulled again, and looked half-round towards me, I was distracted by the bouncer steaming at full tilt towards us – with another now in his wake – and slackened my grip on McCann's sleeve.

His arm, released, shot forward, and his fist connected with the face of the guy with the glasses. Hardly a punch at all; barely enough weight behind it to knock the guy's glasses off. In a less fraught situation we might have dealt with it, explained it, apologised, bought the bloke a drink, had a more sensible and measured discussion about the merits or otherwise of coalition governments . . .

But no; instead, pandemonium.

The bloke with the glasses reeled back a bit, more surprised than hurt; his two pals stood up and the nearest one reached over and swung at McCann, landing a smack on the man's head which lost some effect because it was at maximum range. McCann reared up and leaned forward, bringing the man who'd hit him well within reach; a left hook floored him; or at least tabled him; he went flying onto a table full of drink and rolled onto the laps of some shrieking girls.

The man with the glasses was down on the floor, looking for them. I grabbed McCann from behind, under the oxters. This was partly to stop him hitting anybody else, and partly to drag him out of the way of the second pal of the bloke still scrabbling around on the floor; this guy – bearded, red haired – threw their table out of the way and charged at McCann.

The table he threw caught the second bouncer right in the

146

balls. I thought these guys all wore cricket boxes, but this one certainly didn't. He folded. The first bouncer was right in front of McCann; I hadn't seen him. I was still holding McCann under the shoulders, pulling him back so hard I was starting to fall over; I could feel the chair behind me starting to tip and slide, but there was nothing I could do about it.

The bouncer put his hands out towards McCann's lapels. I had a sudden image of McCann having reverted to his old habits without telling me, and of the bouncer burying fish hooks in his fingers . . . but he didn't get the chance; McCann, arms trapped, used his legs as we fell back; one foot came up and cracked the bouncer under the jaw. He fell, we fell, and the guy who'd cracked the other bouncer in the goolies dived straight through the gap between us, right into the heavy wooden back of another chair.

I rolled over on the floor as McCann wriggled free and jumped up. People were shouting and screaming and grabbing coats and drinks; some were leaving. The bearded guy was on his feet again and squaring up to McCann, while the guy with the glasses was getting ready to punch him from behind. I kicked a fallen table over at him, which distracted him. One of the bouncers was making weak moves to get at McCann and the other man. The guy with the glasses threw himself at me.

Things were getting out of hand.

I fended the guy off with one hand, deflecting him across an area of clear floor; he rolled across the carpet and skittled a couple of men over. I looked round to see McCann holding a chair over his head, back to the glass wall of the mermaid pool. The guy with the beard had found a fire extinguisher from somewhere; he heaved it at McCann, but it missed and slammed into the glass behind him.

I half-expected the wall of glass to smash and fill the whole place with water, but it didn't happen. McCann retaliated with his own heavy artillery, chucking the chair back, catching the bearded man across one arm. Another bouncer made a flying rugby tackle at McCann, but hadn't allowed for the reaction from throwing the chair; as McCann went back against the glass, the bouncer shot across his bows and rammed a table with his face.

Somebody crashed into me from behind; I fell over one of the bouncers. A foot caught me in the ribs and something landed on the side of my face; I jumped up, swinging wildly with both fists as people piled out of the place around me and bottles, glasses and chairs flew about; one glass went spinning up to disintegrate against a ceiling fan, showering the place with splinters.

McCann was in the centre of the room again, trading punches with a bouncer at least a foot taller than him. Somebody bowled into me and I ended up on the floor once more; a table crashed down, narrowly missing my head; I punched a guy swinging at me with a champagne bottle – those things are *heavy*, let me tell you – and struggled up again.

One of the ceiling fans – the one hit by the glass, I think – took a direct hit from a bar stool and fell; it dropped almost to the floor then jerked to a stop on its flex, bringing a shower of black and white plaster flakes crashing down. Incredibly, it was still slowly spinning, and the blades scraped rhythmically over the arm of a chair and the shard-covered surface of a table.

McCann leapt up and butted his bouncer, flooring him. I ducked as somebody threw a glass at me from an emergency exit.

There weren't very many of us left now; everybody seemed to have left. The bodies on the floor outnumbered those of us left standing. I saw four or five black-suited figures gathering behind the bar, and turned to McCann – dishevelled, and bleeding badly from the side of his head – to tell him to get out, but saw the man with the beard coming up from behind, a broken glass in his hand.

There wasn't time to shout, but McCann must have seen the look on my face; he turned and caught the guy's hand, punched him in the belly, sending him back against the glass of the tank, cracking his head against it, then went to butt him.

Maybe the blood from McCann's cut forehead had got into his eyes, I don't know. He didn't seem to see the bearded man slide unconscious down the glass and onto the carpet; McCann's head went swiping forward and crunched into the plate-glass wall of the pool.

It cracked. There was a noise like a rifle shot, and I thought for an instant that it was the sound of McCann's skull splitting, then a line flicked up the glass wall, from top to bottom, and a thin, hissing spray of water leapt out at McCann's legs and torso.

He swayed, dazed, and his legs started to go.

I ran up to him, grabbed him as he slumped and got one of his arms over my shoulder. I half-knelt, then lifted and straightened, pulling McCann up again. I turned for the nearest exit.

The four or five bouncers at the bar had become six, including a small, very angry looking guy who I suspected was the manager.

They weren't behind the bar any longer; they were standing in a rough semi-circle in front of us, and three of them were holding pickaxe handles. A fourth one held what looked like the long lead weight out of a sash window. Number five slid a knuckleduster onto his large right fist.

The manager was armed only with a cigar and a look of quivering, apoplectic fury.

I wanted to swallow, but my throat had gone dry. McCann stirred, drew himself upright and wiped some blood from his face. The hiss of escaping water filled the bright space behind us with white noise. The still-spinning ceiling fan scraped laboriously across table and seat arm, grating on fragments of glass and highlighting the silence in the empty club with a hesitant beat like brushes on a snare drum.

The manager looked at us. McCann took his arm from over my shoulder. A frightened-looking waiter closed an opened emergency exit. The bouncers moved just a little closer. Another got up from the floor, coughing. The manager looked round at him, then back at us. The backs of my legs were wet; either I'd pissed myself or the leak from the pool was soaking my trousers. McCann stooped suddenly and came back up brandishing a lager bottle. 'Never mind, Jim,' he whispered throatily, 'we'll sell ourselves dearly.'

'Oh, Jesus,' somebody moaned.

I think it was me.

'Youse,' the manager said, pointing at me and McCann with his cigar just in case we thought he was talking to the bouncers, and seeming to have some difficulty controlling his voice, 'are goan tae regret this.'

I wondered if they'd let us go if we told them we already did.

The bouncers took a step forward. McCann snarled and without taking his eyes off them, flicked his arm back, smashing the lager bottle against the glass of the pool. The hissing sound didn't alter.

I was listening desperately for the sounds of approaching sirens, but there weren't any, just that hiss from behind, and the scraping of the dangling, lopsided fan, like the noise of a non-automatic record-arm at the end of a record.

McCann brought the jagged-ended bottle back round in front of him and brandished it at the bouncers. They just smiled. The three with the pickaxe handles hefted them. The manager turned away. McCann's hand holding the broken bottle was shaking.

'Wait!' I shouted, and reached inside my coat with my right hand.

Everybody froze.

It took me a second or two – as I fumbled inside my jacket pocket – to work out that they thought I might have a gun.

It crossed my mind to try and carry on the bluff, but I knew it wouldn't work; they'd have to see a gun, and I didn't have one. I found what I was looking for and pulled them out.

Charge cards.

I flourished them at the manager. He shook his head once and turned away. The bouncers looked angry and started forward. 'No!' I screamed. 'Look; this is a platinum Amex card! I can pay!'

The bouncers hesitated; the manager looked round again, then came forward. 'Whit?' he said, then grimaced. 'What?' He said, more carefully. I gulped, waved the bits of plastic fiercely.

'Platinum! I swear! And the Diner's Club; they'll confirm . . . just call them up. I promise; just ask. There's a number you can call, isn't there? Just ask them! Please! This wasn't our fault, honestly, but I'll pay for it! All of it! Just call up! A couple of minutes; if they don't say it's all right you can let these guys do anything you like to us, but just ask, just *call up*!'

The manager looked unimpressed. He looked around the deserted, shattered club. 'Do you realise how much this is goan tae cost?'

'I can afford it! I swear to God!' I tried not to shriek too much. McCann was taking no notice. He was trying to stare down three of the bouncers at once, and growling every now and again.

'See that windae, on that pool?' The manager said, nodding behind us. I didn't take my eyes off him, but I nodded. 'That windae alone cost twenty grand.'

'Call it thirty!' I shouted, and gave a sort of anguished, hysterical cackle. 'Say fifty for the lot!'

The man looked as though he was about to spit at us, or just shake his head and walk away and leave us to the bouncers, but I took a very tentative step forward, and with one hand outstretched, offered him the cards. He peered at them, then did shake his head, snatched the plastics from my grasp and headed for the bar. 'Don't let them move,' he muttered. The bouncers relaxed fractionally and just stood looking at us. I suddenly knew how a dying wildebeeste feels, surrounded by vultures.

'There's no point in this,' McCann whispered hoarsely from out of the side of his mouth. 'Might as well get it over with now as later.' He rocked forward on the balls of his feet. I heard myself whimper; I grabbed him by one shoulder, still not taking my eyes off the bouncers, who were looking very alert again.

'Oh God, please don't do anything, McCann,' I pleaded. 'Just wait a minute, will you? Please?'

McCann shook his head and growled, but didn't do anything else. I could hear the manager talking somewhere behind the bar.

The next couple of minutes passed with a glutinous slowness. The hiss of escaping water behind us didn't change, and the slow four-beat scrape of the wrecked fan seemed to drag time out like entrails from some sacrificial victim. The carpet under our feet slowly soaked with water from the pool behind us. The bouncers were starting to look impatient.

The manager came back.

My heart beat in time to the fallen fan, shaking my whole body. Felt like you could have heard it in London. The manager looked ill. Pale. I looked down at his hands. He was holding my cards, and an Amex voucher.

A wave of relief swept through me with the intensity of an orgasm. 'Mr Weir?' the manager said, clearing his throat on the words. I nodded. 'Will you and your . . . friend come with me , please?'

My knees almost gave way. I felt like crying. McCann started, and looked at me disbelievingly. One of the bouncers stared at the manager. The little man with the cigar shrugged, nodding at me and holding up the Amex card. 'Yer man here could buy the whole fuckin club . . .' he said. He sounded tired, almost sad. 'With either card.'

McCann dropped the broken bottle and stared at me, open-mouthed.

'What did we say? Fifty thousand?'

The manager bit on his cigar, seemed to hesitate. 'Plus V A T,' he said, as though swearing. I thought about quibbling, but didn't. The bouncer who'd got the table in the balls right at the start of the fracas had recovered and was leaning beside me on the bar as I filled out the Amex voucher (I checked the figures carefully; Jesus, even I hadn't filled one out for this much before).

'That's amazin,' the bouncer said, dabbing at a small cut on his forehead with a napkin. 'Ah've got all your albums, know that?'

I re-checked the voucher, nodded. 'Oh, aye?'

'Aye; Ah went tae all yer concerts at the Apollo; an that wan at Barrowlands, remember?' I nodded. 'An the two in the Usher Hall; seventy-nine, that wiz, aye?'

'Eighty, I think,' I said.

The big guy nodded happily. 'Aye; Ah used tae think you guys wiz great. An you were really brilliant; you used to write the songs, didn't ye?'

'Some,' I said, finally signing away fifty-seven and a half grand. I glanced over at where McCann was sitting on a bar stool, one of the waitresses sticking a plaster onto his head. He was looking at me with an expression I couldn't read.

'Na; you wrote them all, didn't ye?' The bouncer by my side insisted. 'Aw those other names were just fur a laugh, were they no?'

'Well,' I said, noncommittally, and left it at that.

'Oh, here, wait a minute,' the bouncer said, with the look and tone of somebody who's just had a really good idea; he disappeared round the side of the bar. The manager was inspecting the voucher I'd signed. He'd already had me confirm the name and address of my lawyers, which the Amex people had given him as the place they sent my statements to, but he was still suspicious.

The bouncer who'd been a fan came back with an album. One of ours. Well, in a way; it was *Nuggets*, the God-awful-titled collection of album off-cuts and not-quite-good-enough attempts at singles that ARC put out after we'd split up. It was a poor album; the best thing on it was a high-speed punk version of 'Long-Haired Lover From Liverpool' we'd done as a joke one very drunken night in Paris. I'd disowned the LP when they brought it out, and still had arguments with Rick Tumber about it (and especially about that title; *Nuggets*, I ask you).

'Hey, Mr Weird, would ye sign this, aye?' The bouncer looked enthusiastic, grinning happily.

I sighed. 'Sure.'

McCann had had the nerve to order another drink; he slurped noisily at a lager and scowled at me. My earlier euphoria at not being turned into a mewling heap of pulped flesh and broken bones had evaporated. The bouncer with the album looked at my picture on the cover, looked at me, and grinned boyishly. 'Aye, ye can see it's you. That's amazin. You just back here visitin, aye?'

'Aye,' I said, getting off the bar stool and handing the manager back his pen. He took it and put it in his inside jacket pocket, along with the carefully folded Amex voucher.

'Hey,' the bouncer said, looking serious all of a sudden, 'Mr Weird, I was really sorry, ye know? Tae hear about . . .'

'Yeah,' I said, quickly. 'I know. I don't like talking about it . . . sorry.' I shrugged, looked down. He patted me on the shoulder.

'Aye, 'sokay, Mr Weird.' He sounded sincere. *Jesus*, I thought. *Six years; six years ago it happened and people still talk about it like it happened last week*.

I gave the guy a weak smile and walked over to McCann. 'You okay?' I asked him. 'Ready to go?'

McCann nodded. He finished his lager. We made our apologies again, shook hands with the bouncers (they were getting five hundred each; there were no really serious injuries, so they were happy enough), then we left.

We walked in silence through the smirring rain and sleet to West Nile Street, where I hailed a taxi.

'You really who they said?' McCann asked, standing outside the taxi as I held the door open for him. His wee, grey eyes stared into mine. There was still some dried blood on his face.

'Aye.' I looked down at the dark, glistening road, then back to his eyes. 'Yes, I am.'

McCann nodded, then turned on his heel and walked away.

I stood there, still holding on to the cold handle of the opened taxi door, and watched him go. Sleet curled on gusts before the slabs of light from shops. Headlights and rear lights moved above the rain-bright roads, and the streetlights seemed to wear little flowing capes of rain and snow, swirling cones under the orange lamps.

'Haw, Jimmy!' the driver shouted. 'Sgettin cold in here; you gettin in or no?'

I looked at him, a white face in the darkness.

'Aye.' I climbed in and closed the door.

TEN

You can't even give the stuff away. Crazy Davey once tried to give away his Rolls Royce, just to prove a point.

It was the eve of the Three Chimneys tour (not that I knew that at the time). We were driving through the leafy lanes of Kent, just off the motorway, heading for Davey's mansion near Maidstone. It was . . . summer of '80, I think. We were leaving for the States on the first leg of our new world tour the following week. Davey and I had been up in the East End of London, at a rented warehouse in Stepney where a frighteningly large number of roadies and technicians had been putting the finishing touches to the stage set we'd be using on the tour, including the Great Contra-Flow Smoke Curtain.

We'd had a final test of the whole rig the previous night, and it all worked; the Curtain itself, the lights and lasers and magnesium charges and smoke bombs . . . everything. We'd even bought a new sound system, perversely enough to keep Wes quiet. I told people the old one was bought by a quarry company in Aberdeen; they just pointed it at a granite rock face and played some Sex Pistols at maximum volume; much cheaper than dynamite.

If you ever saw that set, Smoke Curtain and all, you won't need me to tell you how good it was. If you didn't, well, tough; you never will. It was dismantled and never used again after one hot and humid night in Miami, just a month later.

'What do you want to do?' Davey said, shaking his head. He lit a cigarette, put the cigar lighter back in the dash. He was driving appallingly fast; he made Jasmine look *safe* for Christ's sake. I was just glad that he'd chosen the Roller for the trip up to London. It wasn't as fast or as flimsy as the 'only slightly rusty' Daytona he'd bought himself for Christmas.

Davey had started collecting cars. The Rolls hadn't been his first choice of limo; he'd wanted a Russian Zil ('You know; one of those big black bastards the Politburo boys hang out in'), but hadn't yet got his hands on one.

I took up all the tension I could on the seat belt and told myself Rollers were solidly enough built to let you crash in comfort. 'I mean,' Davey said, waving the cigarette round vaguely in my direction. 'So we've got some money; okay; a hell of a lot, as far as what we might have thought we'd ever get, yeah?'

'Yeah,' I said quickly, wondering if agreeing quickly would make Davey put both hands on the wheel again.

'But it's nothing really, I mean not compared to what some people have, like . . . Getty, or the Sultan of Brunei, or the . . . ah . . . the Saudis; you know, the royals. Even our royals have more, and, like, companies have even more. I B M· ΓTT; Exxon . . . I mean, what they've got makes our . . . our money look like petty cash, am I right?' He looked round at me.

I nodded as quickly as possible, hoping he'd look back at the road. I certainly did. 'And countries,' Davey went on. 'Look what the States or the Russians spend on weapons, billions, isn't it?'

'Sure,' I said, watching the thirty-mile-an-hour limit signs of a village approach rapidly with a feeling of cautious relief. 'But that doesn't mean we couldn't do something.'

'What, though?' Davey said, braking as we passed the speed limit signs, so that we were only doing about fifty-five. 'I mean, we already donated that studio in Paisley. Probably the best thing we could have done, but what else could we do?'

The no-limit signs flashed by and the Roller lifted its snout as we accelerated again. I wondered again why the hell I'd agreed to let Davey drive me down to his place. Wanted to show me his new plane.

Jesus, what was I doing? Stay out of the plane, I told myself. I couldn't forget that trip down the Corinth canal in the unmarked plane. What would he try here? Flying through the Dartford Tunnel? Stay out of the plane.

I clutched the edges of my seat, considering whether it would be more or less terrifying if I closed my eyes. 'I don't know,' I said (my voice still sounded normal, don't ask me how). 'Maybe just . . . give it to the Labour Party, or something like that.'

Davey looked at me as though I was crazy, an opinion I was starting to share. I looked away and concentrated on the appallingly narrow road ahead, hoping he might take the hint and do the same thing. 'We *do* contribute,' he said. 'We're all fucking members. You made us all join when you won that forfeit game of Diplomacy in Geneva, remember?'

I remembered. I already gave lots of money to the Labour Party; I even gave lots of money to the Communist Party, even though I hadn't dared join (they still asked you about having been a member on the US visa application).

'Yeah,' I said, 'but I mean give a *lot* to them, like . . . I don't know; ninety per cent; just keep back what we need to . . .'

'NINETY PER CENT?' Davey screamed. 'Are you *insane?*'

'Well, I don't know; that was just a f-figure off the . . .'

'You must be crazy, Dan; I mean, why the hell bother with all this if you're going to give it all away? I mean, okay, we get well paid; we know that. Sure; we get paid more than a nurse or a doctor and people, and sure that's a bit crazy, but we do work, for Christ's sake; we put in the hours, we sweat, man . . . and how long's it going to last, eh? You know what it's like; we've been flavour of the month for a few years, but how many people get that? Fuck all; that's how many. Very damn few indeed.' Davey took both hands off the wheel to gesture Italianately. I closed my eyes. 'Us; The Stones, Led Zep . . . the Who, I guess . . . but how long's it going to last?' I dared to look; Davey had both hands on the wheel again. 'There aren't any guarantees, you know that. We could be nobodies . . . next month. Next year, anyway. No money . . . or bugger all money coming in, and with all our overheads, and tax to pay to . . . to wherever we're supposed to be living these days.' Davey shrugged. Another village swung into sight round a bend and Davey eased the brakes on again; hey, only fifty this time. We zipped past parked cars and bunches of kids leaving school.

'Oh, come on,' I said. 'Even if we didn't make another penny, none of us would be p-poor, ever. We might have to sell a house or two; you might have to get rid of the plane, but . . .'

'Yeah, exactly,' Davey said. 'So why not enjoy it now, while we can?'

'We could still have a damn good time on a hell of a lot less.'

'Yeah, and we could lose whatever the hell it is we've got that puts bums on seats and . . . and albums on turntables, because we'd know ninety per cent of everything we did was for somebody else.'

This struck me as an almost sensible comment. I looked, mildly surprised, at Davey as we cleared the speed limit and powered off again.

'Some people do it,' I said. 'They play for the love of it and they don't need all the money they make. They put it back.'

'That's them. We're us. I'm a middle-class kiddy, Danny boy. It would go against the grain. You do it; don't let me stop you. But don't be too surprised if you get no thanks. It isn't as easy to give money away as you think.'

'Hmm,' I said, in a sceptical tone of voice.

'You don't believe me, do you?' Balfour grinned. 'Okay; next village we get to, we'll try and give some away.'

'Davey,' I shook my head. 'Don't . . .'

'No; I'm serious. We'll try and give some away. We'll see who'll take it.'

'That's not what I meant; that isn't the sort of thing I . . .'

'It's the same principle.' Davey slowed the car again as a small village appeared over the summit of a small hill. 'Here; we'll try this place.' The Roller dropped below forty for about the first time since London. 'I know;' Davey said, grinning. 'I'll try and give the car away; that's putting my money where my mouth is, isn't it? Must be worth thirty K, minimum. I'll try to get rid of it.'

'Davey,' I said, tiredly.

'No, no.' He held up one hand, and put the cigarette out, blowing grey smoke at the windscreen. 'I insist.'

So we stopped in this little village somewhere north-west of Maidstone and got out – me still protesting: Jeez, you'd have thought it was my car – and Davey took the keys out of the ignition and went up to a man cutting his hedge in front of a smallish terrace house. 'Excuse me!' he said breezily. He brandished the keys with the RR tag and pointed at the car, standing at the kerb, door open. The man was about fifty, greying, heavily bespectacled; a soft, gentle-looking guy.

'Yes?'

'Would you like that car?' Davey said, pointing. The man looked surprised at first, then smiled.

'Oh,' he said slowly, looking at the Roller. 'Yes. It's very nice.'

'Would you like one of those?' Davey said.

'Oh, I suppose, yes, I would, but I don't know I could aff. . .'

'It's yours,' Balfour said, thrusting the keys at the chap. The man looked down at the keys. He laughed, shook his head, but didn't seem to know what to say. 'Go on,' Davey said. 'I'm serious; you can have it; I'm trying to give it away. Take them; we can complete the formalities later. Go on!' He pushed his hand with the palm-held keys spread on it towards the man, who actually backed off a little. The old guy smiled uncertainly and looked around; at me, at the car, up and down the road, at the nearby houses, including his own.

I leaned against the car, elbow on the warm bonnet. It was a mild summer evening, slightly hazy, and with the smell of woodsmoke on the gentlest of warm, lazy breezes. I heard the hooter of a train, in the far distance, and a dog barked. Balfour went on trying to get the guy to take the keys, but he wouldn't. He kept smiling and shaking his head and looking round. I wondered if he was looking for his wife or somebody, or just feeling embarrassed and hoping his neighbours weren't watching.

Finally, he said, 'You're from that programme, aren't you?' He laughed nervously and looked up and down the road again, shading his eyes at one point. He smiled at Davey. 'You are, aren't you? That . . . what d'you call it? Aren't you?' Davey looked back at me. I shrugged.

'You found us out, sir,' Davey said, smiling insincerely and taking out his wallet. He handed the guy a twenty-pound note. 'Thank you for taking part, though.'

We left the guy looking puzzled and holding the twenty-quid note up to the light, shears still in one hand.

'A draw,' I said. 'You did get him to take some money; twenty notes, to be precise. And it was a rotten example anyway. Totally irrelevant.'

Davey was still beaming as we swung off the public road and into a poplar-lined gravel drive which led to a large house in the distance, past a small airstrip and a new concrete and steel hangar. 'Bullshit, Danny. He turned down thirty grand. Even if he had taken it, you think he wouldn't have stayed suspicious? I mean even after he'd got the log book in his name? Or if he did believe I'd done it, know what he'd think of me? Know what he'd think of the guy who'd been so kind and generous? He'd think "What a stupid bastard," that's what he'd think. Believe me.'

I toyed with the idea of making some remark on the lines of, If the guy with the hedge clippers hadn't believed him, why should I? but we were doing eighty up that narrow gravel drive, and there was a nasty-looking corner coming up Balfour had already braced himself for, so I just shut my eyes and dug my fingers into the leather under my thighs instead and waited for the sickening lurch of the four-wheel drift I knew was coming.

Musical beds, and starting to feel . . . not old, but that events in the lives of those I knew and used to know, were gathering pace . . . starting to feel no longer young, I suppose.

Davey and Christine had gone to the Greek islands that spring, after the European tour ended. Inez and I joined them on Naxos for the second two weeks. We stayed at a villa on one of the less-frequented lengths of coast; the house belonged to the promoter of the tour we'd just finished and had a jacuzzi and all the luxuries but, best of all, it didn't have a telephone.

The villa came complete with its own fast cruiser, but that wasn't good enough for our Davey; he'd got his pilot's licence just the year before, and he'd always thought the ideal way to tour the islands – apart from taking a year or two and going by yacht – was to have a nice villa somewhere fairly central, and a seaplane.

Which was exactly what we had. Davey had hired a six-seat seaplane which we used to visit a different island every couple of days. This seemed like a rather frantic pace to me; I'd thought the whole idea of coming here was to get away from the pressure of tight schedules and being somewhere different every second night, but Davey didn't seem to see it that way.

So we flew as far afield as Crete, Rhodes, Thásos, and even, one day, Levkás, which is on the far side of the Greek mainland from

Naxos, and a good couple of hours flying time away. I think the main reason Davey wanted to go there was so he'd have an excuse to fly down the Corinth canal (*under* the bridges, of course: 'You mad bastard; *that's* why you painted the registration number out this morning,' 'Don't worry; it's only emulsion; it'll wash off.').

Then one lunchtime, on Naxos, I got drunk and Inez didn't, and I fell asleep, and when I woke up there was nobody else about. I found a note on the kitchen table, in Inez' hand: *Gone to Piraeus for fresh (cows) milk. Back for dinner.*

I shook my head at the lack of an inverted comma, threw the note away and took a slice of melon from the fridge. I wandered through the dining room, dripping and scattering little black seeds. Luxury to be so messy without Inez there to shout at me. I sat on the terrace with my feet up on the rails and looked out over a small olive grove and the villa's cove of beach towards the bright blue sea; a haze was just starting to form. Tiny white specks, wavering on the uncertain surface, were ferries. It was at least six hours by ship to Piraeus, but the seaplane could be there and back in two.

It wasn't too terrible to be alone; in fact I thought it might be quite pleasant, just for a change. I went for a walk, to a little village on a hill, and sat drinking a cold beer or two under the shade of an ancient, gnarled tree, mirror shades gazing out to sea over the brilliant white jumble of buildings. In certain directions, all I could see was either white or blue; whitewashed stone or the sea–sky vault. Donkeys clopped and clattered up from the lower village, loaded with bottles and giant tin cans. A cat came and sat looking up at me; I ordered a little pastry for it.

The cat ate the pastry; I drank my beer and watched the donkeys pass, wondering what it must be like to live in a village like this . . . One of those places where nothing changes much, where time must seem like a standing wave, not something always at your back, the breaking surf, the breathtaking one-way ride to the dry, dead beach, Goodbye . . .

I'd heard that one of my prod flatmates had been killed in a car crash, last time I'd gone back to Paisley. I'd looked up one of my other flatmates, and we'd met for a drink. That was when he told me; it had happened two years ago. And I'd bumped into one of Jean Webb's aunts, in a Glasgow coffee shop where my ma and I were taking a time-out during a shopping expedition. The old woman came over to chat with my ma, and mentioned that Jean was married now; she and Gerald had a wee girl (I didn't catch the name); just toddling now; och, a bonnie wee thing.

Sitting there, mildly bored, listening to my ma and the other woman talk, I thought again about Jean Webb, and experienced a strange sense of loss, regret. Married; a mother. I'd have liked to have seen her again. But it had been a long time ago, and . . . I wasn't sure what it was; I felt a sense of something like incompleteness when I thought about her. It was as though she was somebody I should have known fully, perfectly, and then parted from, older and wiser, still good friends . . . instead, somehow, we had never got that far. I'd messed it up as usual, clumsy to the very core of my being. Would Gerald mind me looking them up? Did he think I was a first love, know I'd been a sort-of first lover? And was I jealous of him because of the child?

Ah . . . better not to. Leave it. Leave them alone. As long as she was happy . . . I hoped she was happy.

Steamy Glasgow coffee shop on a rainy October weekday, wedged in with shopping bags; glare-white and azure view from a village on a hilltop, across the Cyclades in late spring.

You pays your money and toddles off home in both places.

I had a shower when I got back, then lay naked on a lounger on the terrace, drying in the sun and waiting for the drone of the seaplane's engine when it returned. I was reading *Sense and Sensibility* and thinking about mixing myself something long and cool and alcoholic, when Christine appeared out of the lounge.

'Oh,' she said.

I jumped a little, then put the opened book down across my groin.

'Sorry, I thought . . .' Or something very similar was what we both started to say.

'I didn't hear you come back' I said. Christine hesitated at the door, looking a little bleary-eyed, dishevelled, and confused and amused as well. She gave what might have been a shrug, then sat down on a hanging basket-chair, throwing me the towel that had been on its seat.

'Back from where?' she said, yawning and rubbing her eyes. 'I haven't been anywhere.'

'Didn't you go to Piraeus? I found a note.' I picked the towel off my legs and repositioned it modestly. 'About going for milk; Inez must have decided she needed cows' milk for something . . . I suppose just she and Davey must have gone. You been asleep?'

'Oh, it shows?' Christine smiled, and stretched, arching her back and neck and putting her arms out in front and above her. She was wearing a long white T-shirt. It rode up over her thighs; I found myself looking furtively at her blonde pubic hair. She pulled the T-shirt down, and I saw her looking at me. She cleared her throat while I blushed. 'God,' she said, laughing. 'We're all at it. Want a drink?' She got up.

I nodded. 'Anything. Beer.'

'Two beers,' Christine said, disappearing.

Oh, well, I thought, what with all this topless sunbathing and all, I guess I've seen more or less every bit of our Christine. I wondered what Jane Austen would have made of it all.

Christine came back, bikini bottom on too now, and we drank our beers, and waited for the seaplane, and gazed out into the hazy blue.

She closed her eyes at one point, and put her head back on the lounger. I studied her face, thinking she looked older than my usual mental image of her. There were little lines at the corners of her eyes, and between her dark eyebrows.

She opened her eyes, looking at me.

'Can't seem to stay awake,' she said, though she didn't sound drowsy.

'I have that effect on most people,' I said grinning.

'No, I'm just tired. Very, very tired.' She stared at her empty beer bottle and turned it this way and that in her hand.

'It was a tough tour,' I said. She just nodded her head after a while, then brought the bottle up to her lips and blew across the hole, producing a low, faltering note.

The plane didn't come back that afternoon. We drank a few more beers, played some tapes we'd brought with us, had a couple of games of cards.

The evening came on, and it started to get dark. If the plane didn't come in the next half hour or so, it wouldn't come at all; even Davey had drawn the line at night landings on the water. We waited, while the sun's glow faded and Venus, and then the stars, slowly brightened . . . but; no plane.

'Think they've flown back to Britain for pasteurised?' I said. Christine had an angora jumper on now, though her long brown legs were still bare. She shook her head slowly.

'Probably a break-down.'

'We should have had a radio we could call them up on,' I said.

'Hmm,' Christine said. She got up. 'Let's eat. Want to walk to that little place we were in the first night you were here? Along the coast? You know; Thingy-os or whatever. It's a bit of a walk, but . . .'

Stuffed peppers, red mullet; bitter coffee and incredibly sticky sweets. The gods were smiling on us that night; not a single noisy German youth in earshot. The restaurant had champagne, too. We ate our fill, and wandered back along the shore path and across the beaches, clutching a last bottle of champagne and talking and belching.

Christine yawned, stood on the beach and looked up at the clear sky. I stopped too. She took a slow drink from the bottle, then handed it to me. 'What's that?' she said, pointing.

'What's what?' I looked.

'That; there; beside those stars. Across from the moon and down a bit. Moving. Is that a plane? A UFO? What is it?'

I saw what she meant eventually, after she'd got me to kneel down and she'd crouched behind me, arm over my shoulder, so I could follow the line of her arm. 'Oh, that,' I said. 'It'll be a satellite.'

'Really? I didn't know you could see them. Are you kidding me on?'

'No; it's a satellite.'

'Hmm.' Christine shook her head. 'Never knew that . . .' She took the bottle back, yawned and drank. 'So fucking tired, Weird.'

'Come on,' I said, holding out my hand. 'We'll get you back to your bed.'

She shook her head, sat down heavily on the sand. She looked towards the quietly breaking waves. 'Do you know what we've been doing the past two weeks, Weird?' she said. I squatted beside her.

164

'Just relaxing?' I suggested.

Christine took a deep breath. 'Trying to get Davey off smack, finally, for good . . . at last . . . one last . . .' She looked round at me. 'Did you know he'd been taking it?'

'There's a lot of things I don't know,' I said; one of the stock, off-the-peg answers it helps to carry around with you if you're as naturally conversationally clumsy and awkward as me. In fact, I'd guessed Davey was on something, but I hadn't been sure. Like I still wasn't sure whether Christine knew about what had happened between Davey and Inez. Inez and Davey had both been vague on that point.

So it all came out then, sitting on that dark beach, on golden sand and before a blue sea, both of which had lost their colours till the dawn; all the hurt and tension and the fear poured out of Christine, and I sat there and just listened.

How he'd started, how he'd controlled it at first; the talk of only weak people really needing it but he was living on a high all the time anyway; H just intensified it, and how he got his greatest kicks out of playing on stage; nothing could match that, and how for the past few months, including during the tour, she'd been trying to get him to stop, and thought he had, then found he hadn't, and discovered things about herself and about him she hadn't known; that she felt responsible for him, that he could, nevertheless, infuriate her to the point of hate and rage; that he could use the drug to hurt her; taking it to spite her when she annoyed him; and encountering the user's duplicity and illogic; I've given it up; I've virtually given it up; I'll give it up tomorrow; hey look I went a day without any so I deserve some as a reward . . .

She'd talked and shouted and screamed, she'd hit him, threatened to break his fingers, shop him to the police, she'd searched all his clothes and possessions and thrown the stuff out when she found any; finally, she just hadn't let him out of her sight for the last couple of weeks of the tour (I had noticed they'd seemed very close in one way and very distant with each other in another way, towards the close of the tour), and the same for the first two weeks here, on Naxos.

And so she was tired, not just because Davey was one of those people who didn't seem to need very much sleep, and she didn't

165

dare go to sleep before him, but because of the tension, the concentration . . . And so, also, she'd needed to tell it all to somebody.

We sat there and drank most of the champagne, and watched another few satellites drift slowly overhead; and there were a couple of shooting stars too, thin bright silent lines that disappeared before you had a chance to look at them.

'Anyway . . .' Christine said, 'I think he's over it.' She looked at the brushing line of white where the waves hit the beach. 'I hope he's over it.'

I couldn't think of anything to say. I put my arm around her, patted her shoulder. 'Weird,' she said, closing one eye and looking at me from very close range, 'I'm going for a swim.'

'Oh?' I said, as she peeled off her jeans and jumper.

'Coming in?' she asked. She took off a T-shirt under the jumper, snagging it round her head for a moment and giving me a chance to ogle her breasts in the moonlight and think, *Oh God, I'd love to screw you, Christine.* 'Oh, fuck,' she grunted, finally hauling the T-shirt off. She stood in her bikini bottom, looking down at me. 'Well?'

'I don't have any Ys on,' I told her.

'Weird, I've already . . . oh, suit yourself.' She padded down the sand to the water. 'It's still quite warm,' she said. 'Come on in.'

I shook my head. She waded in a little further until the small waves were breaking around her knees, then stopped, turned round to me and stepped out of the bikini bottom. She threw it up the beach to me. 'Does *that* make you feel any better?' she said, then turned and ran and dived forward.

I stood up, watching the splashes of her easy-looking crawl draw slowly away. I stripped too, and laid both lots of clothes neatly on the beach.

My crawl is spectacular but inefficient; Christine swam rings round me. I had my feet tickled and my bum pinched, water splashed at me, and I lost the race back to shore.

We lay there, side by side on the sand and breathing hard. I lay looking up at the stars and the chip of moon, and shivered a little. I wanted to turn over and kiss Christine, but I knew I wouldn't. These things don't happen that way with me. Besides, I tried to tell myself; it would be too tidy, and too much like a deliberate revenge, to form the fourth side of this eternal square on another beach, before another line of surf, under the high-tech lights of passing spy satellites . . .

Forget about it.

I wondered where Davey and Inez were: in bed, in Athens, or an island between here and there? Or had they really given up their little affair, and were they chastely apart, separate rooms while the plane was repaired?

Jesus, I thought, for all I know they're both at the bottom of the Aegean. But that didn't bear thinking about.

Christine gave a big, sort of whistling sigh at my side. I tipped my head a little, to see her staring up at the stars again. I let my gaze wander down her body, over nipples and belly and mons and thighs and knees, and I thought what a damn shame it was that it seemed so important that I be the woman's friend, and be thought trustworthy and kind and somebody she could talk to, when what I really wanted to do was throw myself on top of her and cover her in kisses and be covered in hers and pull her legs apart and have her pull me inside her and . . . oh, dear God; that didn't bear thinking about either.

I looked back up into the sky again. The stars in the north were gone; cloud must be moving in.

'You pointing out any particular star, Weird?' Christine asked lazily.

'What?' I said, mystified. My arms were both down at my sides; what was she talking about?

Christine showed me. Her hand was wet, warm/cold. She propped herself up on her other elbow and said, 'Well . . . what are we going to do with you, Weird?'

'Do you' – I cleared my throat – 'want a suggestion?'

She brought her head down to mine, but as I reached up with my hands and opened my mouth, she kissed me briefly on the nose and pulled away again. I opened my eyes to see her holding the champagne bottle. She sloshed what was left of it around in the bottom of the bottle, stroking me gently with her other hand. 'You ever had a champagne head-job, Weird?'

'A champagne hedgehog?' I said, mishearing.

'Head job . . . I mean, blow job,' she said, laughing. I shook

167

my head. She put the bottle to her lips and threw her head back. Her cheeks bulged as she put the empty bottle down, held up one finger and said, 'Mmm mm m-mmm mm.' Which I think was meant to be, 'Don't go away now.' Then she lowered her head.

'Ka-*pow*!' was my considered comment, I seem to recall.

Then we screwed on the beach, and a couple of times back at the villa.

A storm passed over late in the night, coming from the north: thunder crashed and lightning flashed. She moved half-waking, made a small whimpering noise, and I held her still salty body close to me as the storm which had kept Davey and Inez in Piraeus moved above us.

'You want to call the next album *what*?'

'I want to call it "We'll Build You A New One, Mrs McNulty",' I told Davey. I looked at him briefly, then quickly looked back to the racetrack; Balfour had almost lapped me. I tried speeding up, but came off at a bend I'd misjudged twice already; the little plastic Scalextric car flew off the black track and flopped into the pile of three cars underneath; two of mine and one of Davey's. I reached for another car and slotted it into the track as Davey cackled (another half-lap gained).

'Mad,' Balfour told me, as his car swept past where we sat. 'You're mad. That is a crazy title. ARC'll never let us call an album that.'

I shrugged. 'I'll talk them round to it.'

We were sitting in tall chairs which were perched on top of a large table at one end of what had been the mansion's dining room; it was a good fifty feet long, and Davey's model racing set filled most of it. He must have had about a hundred yards of track spaghettied throughout the room, and at least a dozen booster transformers connected to distant parts of the track, all controlled through the handsets via a small computer. The roadway swooped and zoomed amongst packing cases and stacks of ancient books and piles of old curtains and bedding.

Davey had positioned mirrors at various points throughout the room, so you could see places where the track disappeared from view, but it was tricky driving. When a car came off – which happened fairly often – you just pulled another one from a pile of boxes behind where you sat (on a very broad table) and slotted it into the system where the tracks passed directly in front of you.

The winner was the first person to notch up ten circuits on the automatic lap counter. I hadn't wanted to play – I knew Davey would win – but it was so damn impressive when you first walked into the room that it would have seemed churlish to decline the challenge. I loved it, actually; I kept rocking this way and that in the high-backed chairs we were sitting in, and nearly fell off the table several times.

'Ten,' Davey said, and let his car cruise to a stop in front of me, just beyond the lap counter. I was concentrating on the hill-climb section of the course, a good forty feet away in one corner of the room. Davey leaned forward in his seat to look at the lap counter. 'Yep,' he said. 'Ten.' He looked at me. 'You've got six.'

'Will you back me up with Tumber for that album title?' I asked him.

'No.'

'Aw, go on.' I got the car to the top of the sheet- and curtain-draped pile of packing cases and tea chests, despite a couple of places where I wagged the tail a bit, and started down the far side, slowing fractionally.

'No, it's a stupid title.'

'It's a great title. It'll intrigue people.'

'It's a stupid title and people'll just go "What?", and they'll forget it and they'll be too embarrassed to go into a record shop and ask for it.'

'Rubbish.'

'That's exactly what it is.'

I took the car over a series of sinuous chicanes held up by strips of Meccano over an old iron and enamel bath full of water. I'd already lost two cars into the bath in hopelessly one-sided confrontations with Davey in the chicanes.

'We have to be adventurous. We need to keep surprising people.'

'Not with a title like that.'

'Look, just back me up with Tumber. I've already spoken to Chris; she'll go along with you. Wes doesn't care and Mickey won't argue.'

Davey packed some grass into a small pipe, and watched me

169

bring the car over a succession of humpbacks it was all too easy to go into mid-air from. The trick seemed to be to let the car take off, but land and re-slot before the next bend. I took it slowly, determined to get this car back. 'Tell you what,' Davey said. My heart sank. I knew that tone. I should have said, Never mind, there and then, but I didn't. 'Let's race for it. If you win, I'll be right there. I promise. I'll be even more enthusiastic than you for . . . Mrs McNaughty or whatever the fuck it is.'

'McNulty; the name's McNulty. Don't pretend you've forgotten it. And no; you'll win the race. You've been practising; this is my first time.'

'I'll give you a start. Four laps. That what you lost by this time, and you're improving already, so it'll be fair.' As though to confirm this, I brought my car in, bringing my lap total to seven. I stopped the car on the starting grid in front of us. Davey lit the pipe, and said between sucks, 'Four laps; that's fair.'

'Make it five.'

He handed me the pipe, shaking his head. 'Drive a hard bargain,' he gasped. 'Okay.'

I sucked the smoke in, scalding my throat. I didn't like the way Balfour had agreed so readily. 'What,' I said, then coughed, 'what if you win?'

Davey shrugged, positioned his car and mine exactly on the starting grid. 'You come for a ride in the plane.'

'What, now?' We'd had a couple of bottles of wine with the meal Davey had slung together (he had a sort of cook/butler/general gofer who usually lived in the house, but he'd given the guy the week off), and we'd drunk a few Glenmorangies and smoked a few pipes too.

I'd been trying to put off going for a flight until tomorrow, after being reminded of the way Davey drove. I hoped it would be foggy tomorrow, or it would rain torrentially, or there'd be some unseasonal snow (unlikely in Kent in August, but I was clutching at straws). I certainly wasn't going up after Davey had been drinking and smoking.

'Yeah; now.' Balfour said.

I shook my head. 'No way.' I handed him back the pipe. We finished that, then he brought out a small leather case from his jacket, hanging over the back of the chair. Inside, there was a mirror, a razor blade, and a little snuff box. I regarded this lot dubiously.

Ten minutes later: 'Ah, what the hell; okay. Let's race!'

'Bastard!'

'Ten–eight. My race, I believe.'

'Bastard! You weren't even trying the first time!'

'Not really. Ha ha.'

'I'm still not going up in that plane with you. I'm too tall to die.'

'Na; I've gone off that idea myself. Let's get drunk instead.'

'Now that,' I said, crossing my arms, 'is more like it.'

It was late at night and we'd almost finished the bottle of Glenmorangie. I think it was still the first bottle but I wasn't sure. We were in a room that had been converted into a small private cinema, where Davey had been watching some stunningly taste-less Swedish porno movies and I'd been listening to the Pretenders on the headphones and building joints for something to keep my hands busy. After a while I realised I was dropping more dope into the darkness than I was managing to get into the numbers, so I stopped rolling and started smoking, blowing grey-blue clouds into the path of the projector beam until Davey told me to stop and handed me a can of strong lager.

I remember drinking that, and then the room went dark; Davey dragged me, still smoking I think, and definitely giggling, from the seat. The mansion seemed very bright after the cinema; I grabbed a pith helmet from a bust in an alcove at the top of the stairs and pulled the hat down over my eyes as we marched arm in arm down the stairs. I stumbled about at the bottom, bumping into things I couldn't see and laughing, then Davey pulled me out into the fragrant air of a summer's night.

'Now what?' I said, craning my head back and trying to see out of the bottom of the pith helmet.

'Drive around the estate,' Davey said, shoving me into the back of the Roller. 'The three chimneys tour. I've only done it twice and I want to see if I can improve my time.'

'Three chi. . . oh hell, whatever,' I breathed, collapsing back in the seat and staring out the rear window at the darkness. 'Wake me up when we get back.'

The Roller purred, and we set off. I lay looking at the ceiling for a while, and must have been dozing at least when we stopped. I looked over the back of the front seat to see we were parked on grass in front of a large dark building, and Balfour was preparing a couple of very hefty lines of coke on a mirror balanced on the tray of the Roller's opened glove box. I pushed the helmet back, ogled the lines of white crystals and said, 'That it? We done it yet?'

'Not yet,' Davey said, snorting one line through a section of plastic straw and then handing me the straw and mirror as he sat sniffing and snorting and breathing hard, staring at the tall building in front of us. 'And don't spill it, he said.

Unnecessarily; I'd already disposed of the stuff, though I'd done the lot up one nostril and was feeling oddly imbalanced as a result. I lay back down again to wait for the effect, but Balfour dragged me out of the car and we stumbled across the grass to open a large door and then crash around a bit inside the unlit building, our only illumination coming from a torch Balfour held. I cracked my head on something and was very glad of the pith helmet.

'Careful!' Balfour said, and opened a door; I clambered up into what felt like a car interior, still too stupefied to work out what was going on. I lay back across a couple of seats and closed my eyes.

The realisation hit at exactly the same time as the coke, and at the same time as a powerful engine – much louder than the Roller's whispering motor – burst into life. I clawed and fought my way upright as we bumped across the grass; I slipped on something and fell to a thrumming floor, my helmet coming off and rolling away in the darkness. I felt for it, retrieved it, jammed it back on and headed forward to where I could dimly see Davey strapping himself in, lit by the lights from the dials and controls on the dash in front of him.

'We are!' I howled, hardly able to believe it was really happening, that even Balfour would be so insane. 'You – We – This really is . . .' I spluttered, then was thrown back as we accelerated. Balfour clicked lights on, and I saw the airstrip in front of us. 'No!' I shouted.

'Shut up and sit down,' Davey said calmly, peering at some dials. We leapt forward again, heading down the field. I looked for a door handle.

'You're mad,' I told him. 'Stop this! You bastard! Let me out!'

'Will you stop shouting?' Davey said, and pressed a stop-watch into my shaking hands. 'How can I concentrate when you're shouting like that?' The plane powered down the grass, bucking and heaving on the uneven ground.

I gave up looking for a handle in the darkness – I could never find the door handles in cars, so I knew I'd no chance in a plane – and threw myself over the seat at Balfour. I managed to get one hand to his throat. 'Let me out, you mad son of a bitch! I'll kill you! I'm not kidding; I'll kill you now; I'm not letting you take me up in this thing!'

'Look, stop being melodramatic, will you?' Davey said reasonably, and detached my hand from his neck without looking at me. 'I'm about to take off; you're distracting me, know what I mean?'

'Take *off*?' I screamed, and threw myself back into what I imagined was the comparative safety of the rear seats. I lay there quivering, backside stuck in the air, hands over the pith helmet, but the plane didn't tip back and soar; it slowed, and made a sudden turn which pressed me (still whimpering) hard against one side. Then the engine roared, I was thrown against the backs of the seats, and the bucking and heaving increased dramatically in both frequency and amplification. 'What . . . what happened?' I shrieked over the racket.

'Oh, I wasn't really taking off before; I was just taxiing to the end of the field,' Davey explained in a reasonable voice.

'Bastard!' I scrambled to my feet and threw myself forward again, grabbing at the back of Balfour's head and just missing.

I saw him flinch and duck and heard him say, '*Now* I'm taking off.'

'Aargh!' I shouted. The aircraft's nose reared up; a line of lights beneath us fell away, the blurred ground disappeared, some trees flicked into and out of sight just like that, and I was thrown back again as we climbed.

I froze. I went into some sort of temporary catatonic state, my hands clawed round the back of the seat beside the pilot, my eyes fixed staring straight ahead, my body – even my heart, it seemed – stopped, fixed, stalled.

'Hey, you dropped the watch; here.' Balfour reached over to me and pressed the watch into my stiffened fingers. I was staring into the starless dark beyond the steeply tipped windscreen, my teeth vibrating in time to the labouring engine. Davey adjusted some controls. 'Sit down, Danny. You'll be more comfortable.'

I found my way into the co-pilot's seat. I got the harness on somehow. I could see lines of light beneath us; the sodium yellow of streets in towns and villages, and the tiny white spears and dim rubies of a motorway. I stared, transfixed. Then I looked over at Balfour. He was smiling, looking quite relaxed and happy. If I could have made it out over the engine, I bet I'd have heard him humming to himself.

He'd had less than I had, I told myself. He wasn't drinking as much as me and he had less dope and it doesn't affect your reaction time so much anyway and besides the coke should counteract it a bit . . . shouldn't it? I stared at the stop-watch in my hand as we swept out across a stretch of darkness I suspected was water, heading for an isolated bunch of bright lights in the distance.

'You all right?' Davey asked me.

'Ha ha! Fine!' I said. I looked at the stop-watch again. Then I dropped it and put both hands round Balfour's throat. He looked mildly surprised but didn't take his hands off the controls in front of him. 'Take us down. I may still kill you, but take us down right now; hear?'

Davey tutted. 'Look, you've dropped the watch again. I'll need you to work it in a few minutes. Will you behave yourself? You're getting excited; I knew I shouldn't have given you so much cocaine.' He shook his head; I could feel his neck move in my hands.

I realised I was dealing with a complete madman impervious to any reasoning or threats, and let go of his neck. I resigned myself to my death and picked up the stop-watch again. 'Fair enough. Just say when.'

'That's more like it.'

'But if we ever do get down intact, I'm still going to kill you.'

'There you go again,' he told me, settling himself in his seat and staring forward. 'Just calm down. Get that watch ready.' I stared forward as well.

We were approaching what looked like a huge factory of some sort; a gigantic building lit from inside, its many outbuildings blazing yellow under sodium lights; from the centre of the building a huge chimney rose, hundreds of feet high and lined with levels of red lights like vast necklaces of LEDs. We were flying just under the level of its summit. Smoke twisted lazily from it, and ghostly white steam drifted from bits of the brightly lit buildings beneath. We were flying straight at the chimney stack.

'What the hell,' I breathed, 'is *that*?'

'Kingsnorth power station,' Davey said, still aiming us straight for the vast concrete tower. 'Ready with the watch?'

I watched the chimney get closer and closer. We weren't climbing over it; we were at least fifty feet beneath the summit, and on a collision course. I pressed back in my seat, eyes goggling. 'I said, ready with the *watch*?' Davey said, annoyed.

'Yes,' I croaked weakly. I closed my eyes as the chimney, almost filling the screen in front of me now, came up to smash us like a midgie against a flyswat.

'Now!' Davey yelled. I felt my thumb press down on the watch; the plane flipped on one side, I was forced hard down into my seat and the engine roared. When my eyes opened again we were back on an even keel and the power station was behind us. We were heading across darkness for another distant set of lights and another red-speckled tower. The light-bright field and flickering flares of a big oil refinery glittered away to one side. I couldn't swallow and my eyes were stuck. Everything had dried up.

'One down,' Davey said happily, and nudged me, grinning. 'Watch going all right?' I nodded dumbly and stared with appalled fascination at the next power station, as it drifted slowly closer.

We rounded that chimney too, then another. I found my eyes kept closing of their own accord whenever those massive concrete barrels filled my sight. Each time we banked, I was pressed into my seat, and we passed the smoke stack. I had no idea just how close we were coming each time, but I swear I heard our engine echoing off the concrete on the third pass.

We headed back for Kingsnorth and finally swung round it again; I clicked the watch off as we dropped suddenly, sickeningly towards the dark waters of the Medway.

'Got to do a bit of low-level stuff now,' Davey explained. 'Just in case we've been spotted on anybody's radar; don't want them to know where we land, do we?'

I closed my eyes. We rose, fell, my stomach going light then becoming very heavy in turns. I felt sick. We banked left, right, left again, then kept on doing that, and rising and falling as well.

I waited to die; I waited for a gasp or a shout from Balfour, for a shudder as we clipped trees and then nose-dived; for the bright flash of pain and flame, for oblivion, and as I waited I tried to tell myself it wasn't really happening and I was just having the most awful nightmare of my life, in bed, in our hotel in London, beside Inez, or Christine, or better yet between the two of them . . . any second now I'd wake and I'd be all right. I told myself even Balfour wasn't this crazy, not to really do this, not really . . .

Unless he'd taken my brief liaison with Christine harder than I'd thought; shit, I hadn't thought of that! Was that it? Was he going to nose-dive now and kill us both, or throw me out over a sewage farm, or did he just not care whether we crashed or not? Jesus; I'd thought it was all settled; Davey and Christine were back together, Davey had stopped the smack, Inez and I were going out again, even if things weren't totally back to normal yet . . . He couldn't have been lying about not being angry, could he?

Meanwhile I was pulled this way and that; left and right and down and up, as if I was being tipped forward, thrown back, and stood on one side and then the other . . .

I opened my eyes, looked out. What could I see?

Just lights.

What could I feel? Like I was being tipped one way and the other, like I was being thrown forward and angled back.

Suddenly I remembered what Balfour had bought along with the plane to help him learn how to fly. I leaned over to him with my fists clenched and screamed, 'You son of a bitch!' at him. I unclipped the harness and got shakily to my feet as we flew along a light-lined valley. I moved to the door, trying to keep my feet as

176

the cabin rolled and dipped. 'You total bastard!' I shouted. 'You can stop that now; turn it off! I've worked it out, *asshole*!' Balfour was twisting in his seat to look at me every few seconds or so, his face puzzled and worried. He shouted something to me but I couldn't hear for the noise of the 'engine'.

I found the door handle eventually. I waited for Davey to turn round again and then gave him the finger. 'Bastard!' I yelled again. 'You can stop it now; I know. Very convincing, and I was suitably scared, but I know it's a goddamn . . .' I pulled on the handle and yanked the door open.

I didn't get to say 'simulator' because next thing I knew I was hanging half out of the plane holding precariously on to the door handle with one hand and staring down through a hard bellowing wash of air at dark fields tearing by a hundred feet below. Something white fell out of the door and went fluttering and tumbling away, falling behind us and then disappearing in a stand of trees. I didn't even have the breath to shout or scream. The plane tipped on one side and I fell back into the cabin again, hauling the door closed behind me. I lay across the seats once more, quivering with aftershocks of utter, mortal terror.

'Danny,' Balfour said in an exasperated voice. 'That was silly, and you just lost my log book, for Christ's sake. I'll have to start a new one now. I mean, what if somebody finds it and connects it with the Three Chimneys tour? I could be in serious trouble, Daniel . . . Jesus, man, you're more trouble than I thought. Just sit there and don't move until we land, okay?' He sounded quite upset. He belched, and I heard him muttering to himself.

I lay across the seats, paralysed and dumb and quietly pissing my pants.

Balfour must have seen the funny side of it all as he came in to land, because he was laughing so much as we taxied in he missed the hangar and crashed the aircraft into the Roller, breaking the prop, decapitating the silver lady and severely denting the motor's bonnet.

'Oh, shitbags,' he said, as the engine died and splinters of the propellor fell back and thumped on the roof of the plane's cabin.

I might have laughed then, but I was hanging out the door again by that time, and laughing as you throw up is as technically difficult as it is respiratorially unwise.

*　　*　　*

I'd dropped the stop-watch out the door when I opened it in mid-air, too, so Davey never did find out if he'd beaten his own record for the power station circuit.

It was the last time he made that journey.

Five weeks later, involuntarily true to my word, in Miami, I really did kill him.

ELEVEN

'Dani-elle, ma man! How the devil are you?' Richard Tumber bounded up the steps from the hired Ferrari parked at the kerb; he stood on tiptoe and put one arm round me. 'Heyyyyyy . . . good to see ya again . . .' He punched me on the shoulder. 'Weird!'

I looked up and down the street, hoping not too many people were witnessing this. They weren't; it was a cold and showery Sunday and respectable folk were at their dinner. 'Rick,' I said. 'Hi. Come in; how are you?'

'Magic, me boy; magic.' He stepped in through the main doors and looked round the folly. 'Still living in the mausoleum, eh?' He clapped his kid-gloved hands together and rubbed them, nodding and clicking his tongue as he inspected the interior of St Jute's. The pigeon chose that moment to flutter briefly from one high rafter to another, cooing in the slightly panic-stricken manner of a bird that hasn't seen a proper meal in three days. 'Hey.' Tumber grinned, seeing the animal. 'You got a pet!'

'Sort of,' I agreed, and helped him off with his fur coat. Underneath, there was a very baggy suit that looked sloppily made but which I didn't doubt had cost him a laughable amount of money. Silk shirt, natch. Bow tie. He carried a very slim leather briefcase (when I first knew him, his briefcase was aluminium) and he wore graded Porsche glasses. I'd have staked money on the briefcase containing a Filofax, up until a few months ago at least, when I heard they were starting to be regarded as . . . well, *Out*, dear (Jeez-uz).

179

'You okay?' he asked, frowning at me.

'Fine,' I lied.

'You look . . . peaky. What was it you used to call it? "Peely-wally", yeah?'

'Yeah.' I shrugged, put a hanger inside the fur coat and hung it on a clothes' rack of cellophane-wrapped Bulgarian suits. 'Just a hangover.'

'You been getting . . . "steaming", eh?' He grinned, punching me on the other shoulder.

I nodded. Rick has the approach to professional and personal acquaintances of one of those magazinettes that come with credit card statements and colour supplements; he likes to personalise things, as standard. Three Gold-Tooled Initials . . . Your Name Here . . . so whenever he meets me I'm treated to a barrage of West-Coast Scottishisms in spoken inverted commas, for at least as long as it takes for him to think he's put me at my ease.

We sat in my best chairs, near the sound system and the electronic gear at the back of the pulpit, far enough downwind from the space heater to be able to talk without raising our voices, but still within its draught of warm, paraffin-scented air. Tumber took off his jacket and put his feet up on a loudspeaker. He'd accepted a small glass of Stolichnaya. He lit up a black and gold Sobranie and looked serious. I waited for him to say something. He nodded once, gave a sort of half-smile with one side of his mouth, pursed his lips.

I fiddled with my glass, wondering what was going on.

'Damn,' he said, taking his feet off the speaker and sitting forward on the edge of his seat, staring down at the tiled floor through the clear liquid in his glass. 'I don't know what to say, Dan.' He looked up at me, and took his Porsche glasses off, rubbing the bridge of his nose as though he was tired. He seemed oddly naked and vulnerable without the glasses. He put them back on again. 'I'm . . . sorry, I know how much you meant to each other, even if you hadn't . . . well, no; look . . .' He held up one hand as I opened my mouth to speak. '. . . I guess there isn't anything we can say, either of us, but, well, I want you to know . . . well, I guess I felt the same way you did.' He looked away, shaking his head.

I had the oddest feeling of *déjà vu*. What year was this, for

God's sake? This was what he'd said after Miami, after Davey died. What sort of weird time-warp was I – or he – in? Had something else happened? I didn't know what to say. I wanted to ask, What the hell are you talking about? but there was a silence between us now I didn't feel able to fill, a confusion in me I didn't want to admit to.

I was still trying to cope with last night, with the combined effects of a bad hangover, bruised ribs and the awful feeling that I'd lost a friend. I'd been to the Griffin when it opened, leaving a note on the door of St Jute's for Tumber, but McCann hadn't appeared for his usual Sunday drink. I'd waited an hour, drinking fruit juices, then left a message for McCann with the barman and come back to wait for Rick. So I had enough to think about, and I didn't even want to ask if some new catastrophe had befallen anybody I knew.

Nevertheless, I had to say something. I was still wondering what it should be when Rick knocked back his vodka and reached for the leather briefcase.

'Life goes on,' he said briskly, with the air of somebody deliberately putting a brave face on the hardly-bearable. 'I brought some incredibly pure coke with me. You still indulge?'

I shrugged, feeling weakened, suggestible, vacuous in every sense.

'You know I used to be able to fuck twice within the space of one side of an album?' Tumber said. We were playing table tennis on the slightly dusty table right at the back of the choir under windows depicting hares chewing the cud, the two fathers of Joseph, God showing his rear parts to Moses . . . that sort of thing. Playing table tennis coked up had seemed like a good idea at the time but, as usual when it came to games, I was losing, and in this case I seemed to spend most of my time chasing the ball around under the table and across the floor. I had no idea how we suddenly started talking about sex.

'Really?' I said.

'Yeah,' Tumber served again. 'Twice in twenty minutes.'

I missed a topspin slam completely and had to follow the bouncing ball across the tiles again.

'Wow,' I said.

181

'Yeah.' Rick got ready to serve, and I crouched, feeling tiger-tense and twice as fearsome, and staring at the point on the table where I expected the ball to bounce. Then Rick straightened again, rubbed his chin and looked up to the roof. I looked on, aghast. 'I mean, it was a while ago. The record was *Let It Be* . . .' He frowned, crossed his arms, seemed to say more to himself than to me, 'Now who's flat were we using? I always thought it was that one in Argyll Street, but . . .'

'Serve!' I shouted at him. He started as though he'd just noticed me, and crouched to serve again, the ball held in his left palm like some strange plastic offering.

'Sorry,' he said. 'Will I serve now?'

'Yes!' I screamed.

He served.

'Aah!' I yelped, returning.

'Well anyway; you should have seen this girl, Dan. What a body. I swear her tits didn't change shape when she lay down. That usually means silicon, but she was one hundred per cent natural, believe me. We'd done it once and then we just started doing it again, and, well, fucking zap-pow, man . . . anyway we were still lying there panting and quivering when the side finished and the turntable switched itself off, and I got up, dripping everywhere, and turned the album over, and then went back to bed, and . . .'

'And turned her over . . .' I laughed, which gained me a point when Tumber laughed, and missed the ball. My turn to serve.

'You asshole, Weird,' Tumber said.

We played a short rally which I lost, of course. Rick served again. 'So I'd come twice in twenty minutes, and I thought, "Hey, that's pretty good; you must be some sort of sexual athlete there, Ricky boy." '

'I wonder if they have *heats* for sexual athletics,' I pondered aloud.

'And I started,' Rick went on, 'timing myself like that, with sounds. Doing that deliberately, just to see, you know? I wanted to keep a check on my performance.'

'Uh-huh,' I said. I lost another point.

'Yeah,' Tumber said, serving again. 'I only stopped doing it with Judy . . . you remember Judy? When I was in love?'

'I remember. You seemed almost human for a while. It was disconcerting.'

'Thanks. Anyway I stopped doing it with Judy cos it felt wrong, and even after we split up I didn't do it because I'd sort of forgotten about it, and then a couple of months ago I was screwing these two gorgeous black chicks, and I'd just put *Brothers In Arms* on, and I humped one then the other, and it finished and I realised I'd done it again; twice within one side, and, like, I was completely exhausted, but I was so fucking pleased I'd done it, and then I realised . . .'

'What?' I said, missing the ball again and going after it. It bumped up against a box full of Rumanian plum jam.

'It was a fucking compact disc, man,' Tumber said, disgustedly. 'I'd taken about fifty fucking minutes and I felt twice as knackered.' He shook his head. 'Jeez, was I pissed off.'

'My heart bleeds for you,' I told him. 'My bladder leaks for you; my pituitary secretes for you. What were you doing in bed with these two women, anyway?'

'What do you think I was doing?'

'Asking them, was it good for you two?'

'Wrong. In fact, they're a double act. I'm thinking of signing them.'

'I didn't know you'd formalised your relationships to quite that extent,' I said, and actually won a point. Tumber tossed the ball back to me.

'My relationships are changing a lot, Danny. I'm getting careful in my old age.' Rick stood up suddenly from the crouched position he'd assumed to receive my serve, put his hands on his hips and said, frowning with annoyance, 'Christ, isn't it a fucking bore wearing those goddamn willy wellies?'

I didn't move, but looked up from my serving stance and said, 'Yes.'

'Never mind,' Tumber said, crouching again and winning off the return. 'I'm laughing; I used the profit on my Telecom shares to buy into London International.'

'Asshole,' I told him.

'That's about the size of it.' he grinned.

We sat in the restaurant of the Albany hotel, Rick's usual base on the rare occasions when he visits me.

We finished our game of table-tennis. He'd won, of course, though I did score a couple of points, which I always regard as a moral victory. We'd had some more coke, talked for an hour or so about The Business, bad-mouthing everybody we could think of, then we drove the couple of hundred yards to the Albany in Rick's hired GTS (though only after he'd complained about the car-hire people at the airport not having a black Porsche to match his glasses; a red Ferrari was all very well, but it *clashed*).

When I'd woken up that morning I'd put on what I'd been wearing the night before, so I was just about respectable enough to be allowed into the Albany, once I'd put my tie on.

The meal was all right, though Rick made a fuss over the wine, and I'd insisted on tomato sauce with my Chateaubriand, just to be awkward. We sat back, belching and slurping brandy; Rick sucked on a Havana cigar. While we'd talked, I'd felt several times that Rick had steered clear of something, a subject that he didn't want to raise, but I hadn't tried to find out what it was. There were, anyway, two things perhaps; what he'd come to talk about, and whatever disaster he'd awkwarded his way round earlier. I was trying not to think about anything too deeply. I just sat with the man and pretended it was like old times.

'. . . God, yes, I remember that party.' Rick laughed. 'Amanda caught me screwing Judy in the flowerbeds; bitch tried to run me through with a rake, or a hoe, or something agricultural like that.'

'Horticultural,' I said. 'And rake would have been appropriate,' I said, drying my eyes.

We'd been reminiscing about the parties Davey had given at the mansion in Kent, and Rick had been telling me about the time Davey had lost control of his traction engine during a tug of war with Wes' Range Rover, a local farmer's tractor and his own Daytona (with Christine at the controls). He'd won, but – accidentally he claimed – drove the machine into the main marquee, through the bar and over several tables, scattering shrieking guests like hens before a car. He hit one of the two main tent supports, demolished half the marquee and set fire to the rest; it must have been one of the few fires that year put out with a combination of water transmitted from an ornamental pool by an ice-bucket line, and champagne. I'd missed that particular soirée, but the ones I'd been to had been only marginally less interesting.

Rick and I had reached that stage where neither of us could think of any more appropriate stories, so just sat there for a few moments, shaking our heads and sniffing and drying our eyes.

I took a deep breath. 'So, what brings you up here anyway?' I asked him.

He sat back, swirled brandy. 'How do you feel about making another album?'

'Terrible. The answer's no.'

'Well, have you really thought about it? People in the business are asking me about you, without me having to ask; they all want to know if you're going to do anything again. We get letters from fans asking where you are and if you're working on some new project; the interest is there, Dan. I mean, with *Personal Effects* doing so well, and after all this time; you'd be crazy not to think about it.'

'Is it doing well?' I said. 'I didn't know.' *Personal Effects* was the album I'd released as a solo effort – though with lots of session people, of course – in '82, a couple of years after the band broke up. I'd been all fired up and enthusiastic about it at the time – I'd taken a year and a half off after Miami and I was missing recording and playing – but when it came out . . . I don't know. I'd lost interest.

Happened even before it came out, come to think of it; I remember sitting at a mixing console one day, talking over the right balance for some track or other, and I just suddenly felt, *What the hell? What does any of this really matter?*, and I could never summon up the enthusiasm again, after that. Not for any length of time. The album didn't do very well, anyway. Not by Frozen Gold standards. *Personal Effects* was my second choice for a title; I'd wanted to call it *Looks Like Shit To Me*, but ARC – Rick, in other words, because he was boss by that time – had vetoed that.

'What?' Rick looked amazed. 'Don't you read the music press at *all*? Listen to the radio? It's been in the forty for the past six months; a bit of publicity and you'd be in the twenty at least. Make a come-back and I'd guarantee top ten. God damn it, Dan, don't you check your royalty statements?'

'No.'

Rick shook his head. 'You're an exasperating man, Daniel. Don't you get any thrill from . . . from playing music? don't you miss the applause, the lights? The people?'

'I keep my hand in,' I said defensively.

'What?' Tumber snorted derisively. 'Jingles for adverts and TV series? Big deal.'

'And film scores.'

'Ha; you've done one. So the music was the best part of it; so what?'

'There were two, and there's another couple in production,' I said. I didn't like having to defend myself like this, but I couldn't let Rick twist the truth that way without setting him straight.

'So there were two. And as for the two in production; I've talked to those people; to Salmetti, and Grosse; they like the music all right but they don't like the way you work; they're both thinking about paying you off and getting somebody else. You expect them to write the films around the music, not the other way round. That's crazy. They expect you to take scenes and write stuff specially for those bits, not just send completed tapes and scores and expect them to cut what they've got to suit. The most they'll do is use your stuff as themes up front, but even that's unlikely. And don't bother telling me you didn't know any of this, Danny boy, because I know you didn't; that's another thing they're not very happy about; even film people expect letters to get answered *eventually*. Besides all of which, the big money in film music these days isn't the sort of stuff you're writing at all; they want rock bands singing three-minute singles. You're out of date.' Tumber sat back, drank his brandy.

This was Rick talking tough. I nodded thoughtfully.

'Well, I don't care. I don't need the money.'

'I know you don't need the money; I *do* look at your royalty cheques. But what about *you*, Danny? Don't you need to know who the hell you are? Don't you need something else besides sitting around in that fucking . . . tomb up there feeling sorry for yourself and emptying crates of commie booze? Christ, man, you're an artist. You're a fucking piss artist at the moment, but you're still a clever man; you could be doing things, you could be making a difference, you could be taking part. That's what you should be doing; *taking part*, showing some of these spotty fucking brats how it's done, for Christ's sake.' Rick sat back, then leant forward again, jabbing the cigar towards me. 'You're just the guy to do it, too. People have only half-forgotten about you; you're a legend now, the whole band is, even more so now that . . . what? What is it? I say something funny? What?'

'Legend,' I said, shaking my head. 'Bullshit.'

Rick reached over and touched my arm. 'It's been four years, Danny boy. You forget what industry you're a part of. You make a small fortune in a couple of months in this business; you make enough to last you all your life in a year, and you're yesterday's newspaper in eighteen months. Show me Adam Ant now.' He sat back, shaking his head, apparently thinking he'd proved his point. 'Four years is just right to become a legend; long enough so a lot's happened, not long enough for people to forget about you. All that stuff about you living on a Caribbean island, or in a monastery in the Himalayas, or being dead . . . that's just perfect. You'd be crazy not to make a come-back. You've got the material; you've told me so yourself. Jesus Christ, Danny; you're thirty years old . . .'

'Thirty-one; you forgot my birthday again.'

'Oh well, pardon me . . .' Tumber shook his head, looked pained. 'Aw, come on, Dan; you're still a young man; you going to vegetate up here for the rest of your life? Drink yourself to death? Fucking hell; forget about the money; give it all to Geldof for all I care . . .'

'What, your share too?'

Rick looked wounded, as though this was an unfair departure from decent negotiating behaviour. He sighed heavily, burped lightly. 'I'd sooner do a no-profit deal with you than none at all, Danny. I'm not saying I'd be happy, but I'd rather you just . . . *worked*, even if it doesn't do anything to improve our year-end figures. I don't like to see waste, Dan. I don't like to see people just throwing away what they've got. There are enough people in this country who'll never even get a chance to work, who can't make anything of themselves, who can't use whatever kinda gifts they've got. But you could if you wanted to; you've got the choice. You're just . . . I don't know; lazy, too sorry for yourself. We've all been hurt by what happened to Christine; it's a tragedy, we all know that; a tragedy . . . but . . .'

He talked on for a bit, and a couple of times, when he waited for answers, I nodded, or grunted, or shrugged, and did whatever was appropriate, but I didn't hear what he said.

My eyes filled, briefly, at one point, but I blew my nose in the stiff napkin, and sniffed, and I don't think he noticed. I stared at his face without seeing him, listened – apparently avidly – without hearing him.

So it was her.

It was Christine. Oh, Christ Jesus, what had happened? I didn't want to think about it and I couldn't stop thinking about it. What had they done to her? Was she dead? Was it that bad, was it the worst? I thought back to the way Rick had talked when he first arrived that afternoon, the things he had said, the tone he had used, the way he had sat . . . and I couldn't tell. It might be something less than that, but I didn't think it was. She might have been pregnant and lost a baby, or been hurt in an accident, or . . . my imagination failed.

Most of the things I could think of were either just not severe enough for Tumber to have acted the way he did towards me, or things he might have followed up on, like if she'd been badly injured he'd have said something about me going to visit her or sending something. No, I couldn't think what it might be . . . prison? I latched on to that, like a drowning man. She'd been done for drugs in the States in some place with crazy penalties and locked up for a couple of years . . . but he would still have said something about going to see her, writing to her . . . Oh, Jesus, Jesus, Jesus . . .

'. . . Dan? You all right?' Rick Tumber looked more concerned than I could ever remember him looking. I sniffed, nodded.

'I, ah . . . I'm sorry. I was thinking about Christine.'

'Oh,' he said. 'Yeah.' He looked away, and slowly brushed some crumbs off the tablecloth.

God forgive me; this was terrible, but even now, even now I was trying to cover up, trying to not let on how little I knew; even now I was pretending I knew something, even if not all; 'What . . . exactly happened?'

Rick's brow flickered, as though he disapproved of my

ignorance. I shrugged. 'I only . . . heard,' I told him. 'No details. Can you tell me?'

Tumber cleared his throat, took a slightly shaky breath. We both watched his right hand stub out the stump of the fat cigar.

'It seems . . .' he said, after a pause, and a sigh, '. . . the guy was . . . some moral majority freak . . . I dunno; one of these fundamentalists or . . . some fucking nutcase; I didn't hear what church . . , sect or whatever . . .' Tumber shook his head again, still addressing the hand delicately tapping out the cigar. 'He just turned up at the hotel, in Cleveland, with a Saturday Night Special. He'd travelled up from Alabama, apparently, specially. Ah . . . like, they'd had tighter security in the South when they were playing there, just because they had all the demonstrations and such, and death threats, but I guess they didn't think Cleveland was so much of a threat. Anyway; he was waiting in the lobby, and when she came out the lift, he . . . he shot her. Got her bodyguard, too; blew the guy's brains out. Wounded Chris in the side and head; she got as far as the sidewalk outside, screaming for help, but the guy just followed her and put another two shots into her, on the ground, before a hotel guard shot him.

'She died on the way to hospital. The guy's trial probably won't be till the summer. They can't decide whether he's mad or not; usual story. Said God had told him to do it, because of . . . the act; you know; the guitar, at the beginning . . .'

Rick's voice altered suddenly, and he said, in a sorry, pained voice, 'Jesus, man, I didn't want to be the one to tell you all that. I really didn't. I'm sorry. I can't tell you how sorry. I don't know what more to say, Dan.'

'Yeah . . . excuse me.'

'Sure, man.'

I went to the toilet to cry.

Rick came and got me twenty minutes later, after the management became worried and sent people in to ask if I was all right. So they all say; I don't remember. I just sat in the cubicle, silent, hearing nothing, until Rick's voice brought me back. The funny thing was, I didn't even cry. I got up from the table, where my tears had been welling, and on the walk from the table to the gents my eyes went dry, like there was some terrible sucking emptiness inside me, drawing it all back in, soaking down into some strange, awful pit inside me.

I was led from the toilets like a zombie. Rick wanted to get a doctor but I said I'd be all right.

He walked me back to the folly.

'You sure you'll be okay, Dan?'

'Yeah; I'll be fine. Really; fine. It's just, I hadn't heard. Thanks for telling me.'

'That's okay. Look; why not come back to the hotel; we'll get you a room. You don't want to sleep in this big old place by yourself.'

'I'm better here. I'll be okay.'

'You sure?'

'Yeah, positive.'

'Well, I'll see you for breakfast, at the hotel, all right? You promised. I don't leave until after eleven. Breakfast, okay? About nine.'

'Nine. Yeah.'

'Okay then; you sure you'll be all right?'

'Yeah. Fine. See you for breakfast.'

'Okay; good night, Dan.'

'Good night.'

TWELVE

Yes, it is like sex. Performance; the show, the live act.

We had never been bad at it, and by now we were very good. I always thought I was the weak link, standing there just playing non-virtuoso bass and occasionally tapping my foot, but according to some people I was the base, too; something the others could build on; a rock, a foundation. Well, so they say. I think too many things are over-analysed, and a lot of the effort's wasted, just unnecessary. We were popular; end of story and so what?

But it is like sex. Of course. Getting out there and doing it, under the bright darkness of the hiding lights, in the bowl or beneath the arch, after the build-up of tension and the slow engorging of the venue where the people sit and stand together, sharing that warmth and sweat and scent, sharing the same obsession, the same fixation and anticipation. Oh, you enter into it, you become part of it; secreted beneath, preparing nervously in some distant dressing room, you can usually hear, you can always sense; you can *taste* it.

And there, suddenly appearing, in the blaze and smoke and the crashing chords, or just drifting in, like we did once, pretending to be road crew, fiddling with the gear, then starting to play, one at a time, almost casually, so that people only realised slowly, and the roar grew slowly, swelling and filling the place around us . . . the initial nerves evaporating, the beat setting in, taking over, governing. And the greater rhythm, the light and shade of slower songs and faster songs and the few spoken intervals, when either Davey or Christine could just stop, listening and gauging and feeling, and mumble or shout or scream or just talk reasonably, make a joke; whatever fitted the mood, whatever moved us on, whatever kept that unstated game-plan on course and sent us all forward again.

To the climax, to the big finish that was one of many, to the stamping, chanting, swaying recalls, the encores, and the anticipated fetishes of old favourites, the old textures everybody knew and could join in with and be part of. Finally, sweating, betowelled, the lights back on, a last, quieting, basically acoustic, two-person finale, to smooth the raw exhausted edges of that ecstatic energy away; a last scene of touch and tenderness, like a breathed post-coital stroking, like a hug, before the people go, drained, fulfilled, buzzing into the dark streets and home.

Sometimes you thought you could go on forever and never stop, sometimes you just wanted it all never to end; there were ten times like that for every one of the few when you just weren't in the mood and it was done – though professionally, and to the insensitive, just as excitingly – mechanically, by rote.

But when it did seem you could keep going forever, time went odd, and it was as though it had stopped, or vastly extended, stretching out . . . yet when it was all over, when it had all gone and you were thinking about it, back in normality, everything within that singularity, everything about that unutterably different period of time seemed to have taken up only one single instant. Sometimes, whole tours were like that, as though it had all happened to somebody else and you were another person entirely and had only heard about it, second hand, third hand, at any number of removes.

You played, and you were part of it as it was part of you; you were no less you – in fact, you felt *more* alive, more alert and capable and . . . coherent – but, at the same time, though continually conscious of that differentiation, you were integrated too, a part not apart; a component in something that was the product, not the sum, of its constituents.

A sort of ecstasy, all right; a charging, pulsing sense of shared *joy*; a bodily delight felt as much in the brain as in the guts and skin and the beating heart.

Ah, to go on and on like that, you thought; to be at that level forever . . . Well, it was impossible, of course. It was light and

192

shade again, the sheer contrast of the mundane and the fabulous; the dull grey weight of the endless workaday days, and the bright, startling burst of light in the darkness, as though the five or more of us on stage before those thousands, even tens of thousands, were a concentration of excitement, glamour, life; the very pinpoint place where all those ordinary lives somehow focused, and ignited.

I never did work out who took energy from whom, who was really exploited, who was, if you like, on top. Sure they paid, so that act might be called prostitution, but, like a lot of bands, we actually lost out on some tours. Playing live, we gave them their money's worth, sometimes more. The albums were where we coined it in, not the tours. You paid your pounds or your dollars or your yen for the particular wavy pattern of gouged, printed vinyl, for the hidden noise a diamond could bring out, or for a certain rearrangement of magnetic particles on a thin length of tape, and that was us making a living, thank you very much. Me especially, me more than the rest, even though we'd come to an agreement where the others got between five and ten per cent of the composition rights, as an arrangement fee (well, it was only fair).

But playing, touring, going up there and doing never quite the same thing each night, or every second night; that was the buzz, those were the times that made you feel you were really doing something different from everybody else, something worthwhile. God knows it got to me, and I always did stay in the background. What it was like for Davey or Christine, the binary stars of that focal point, standing at the ground zero of our self-created storm, I can't even imagine.

And it was addictive. You always thought you could give it up, but you always found you wanted more, and it was worth a lot of time and effort and expense to make sure you did. The applause, the screams, the shouts and yells, the stamping feet, the crowds and the ingenious, mad or pathetic attempts to make it through our layers of defence to get to see us individually, one-to-one, just to look, or to hug, or to gibber, or to pass on a tape and entreat.

For Davey and Christine, at the epicentre of it all, it meant more than it did to me, and, because they were different people from me, because they felt almost like a different species sometimes, they lapped it up, they revelled in it, they drank it deep. I tried, even with just the pale version of the fame that was my share, but I couldn't take to it naturally, the way they did.

It frightened me. For a long time it wasn't too bad anyway, and then for a longer time after that it was new, different and interesting and exciting, but then, after the first few tours, it started to get to me . . .

The crowds, the sheer weight and press of them. The invisible, besieging hordes out there in the darkness, baying and bellowing and stamping their feet. The way it took so many of them so long to recognise a track . . .

Jesus, if I even half-know a band's work I can spot a song within a bar; the first few notes of the introduction and I know it; but we'd play an intro, just the way it was on the album, and it would take . . . seconds, bars and bars for our fans to spot which favourite it was, and start trying to drown us out . . . I thought maybe it was just the time delay, sound taking that long to get from them to us, but I worked it out, and it wasn't; it was just people being *slow*.

But I'm not a natural crowd person; I don't pretend to understand or to relate to any of that sort of behaviour. I've never felt like part of a mass of people, not even at a football match. In a crowd of any sort, at a game, a concert, in a cinema or wherever, I never get totally carried away with whatever's going on. Part of me is always detached, observing, watching the other people around me; reacting to how they react, not to what they're reacting to.

There was a lot more I found worrying; like the people who wanted to know what sort of toothpaste we used and what our lucky number was, and what we wore in bed; like the backwoods geeks that were convinced to the point of inanity and insanity that they were The One for Davey, or Christine, or – God help them – both.

Then there were the Christians. Oh, jumping Jesus, the fundamentalists, the people who made old Ambrose Wykes and his folly look positively sensible and sane, and necessary.

Largely my fault. I'd said the wrong things.

It had happened on our first big tour in the States. I'd always been happy for Davey and Christine to do all the talking; they were the beautiful ones, after all, whereas I looked like a hench-man in a Bond movie; hardly ideal prime time or front cover material. But in New York a lovely, intelligent, serious girl had requested an interview specifically with me, for a college magazine. I'd said I'd do it, but I'd been determined to put on my dumb and stuttering act the instant she asked me what my favourite colour was or how did I feel about being a rich and famous rock star?

Instead she asked sensible, reasonable questions, several of which actually had me thinking about them – suddenly seeing things in a new light – before answering; usually we all just re-gurgitated the same old answers to the same old questions. She was sweet and witty and nobody's fool, and I even made a date with her, after the tour was over, after failing to convince her she should join us for the post-concert party. Jeez, I wasn't heavy, I wasn't pawing her, I didn't even flirt with her; I acted the gentleman and I just said I'd enjoyed talking to her and could we meet again?

Bitch sold the interview to the *National Enquirer*. About two per cent of that interview was about religion, another three per cent about politics, another five about sex; in the paper, that's all we talked about. *I* talked about.

According to that article I was a communist atheist who'd screw anything in skirts and was anyway bisexual (I'd admitted I'd slept with a guy once, just to see what it was like; it was nothing special and I kept having to think of women to keep a hard-on, and I made the point that I'd avoided sodomy from either end, so to speak and, while the whole experience wasn't totally unpleasant, I'd no intention of repeating it; *and, damn it, I'd said it was off the record*!). I was also trying to corrupt and pervert the minds of all decent, patriotic, mom- and dad-loving American children with my vicious, drug, Marx, anti-Christ and semen-sodden song lyrics.

Oh, did we have some albums burned south of the Mason–Dixon line.

Suddenly it was noticed that the instrumental on the first side of *Liquid Ice* was called 'Route 666'. The number of the beast! Oh God, oh Jesus, lock up your nuns! This was a joke, of course; I'd originally called the song '25/68', naming it according to the opus-numbering system I'd used when the only places my songs existed were in an old school exercise jotter, a low-fidelity, high-hiss C-60 cassette, and between my ears. '25/68' sounded too much like '25 or 6 to 4', by Chicago, so I renamed it after about ten seconds' thought, in the studio just after we'd recorded it.

Meant nothing. But suddenly it was a Sign that I was a Devil Worshipper. All the other lyrics were put under the microscope as well then; professors of colleges in the South where the level of learning was such they thought evolution was a blasphemy started writing learned articles proving that everything I wrote was directed at destroying the American Family, Flag and Way of Life.

Holy shit; *I* should have been so lucky!

Ah, what the hell; we didn't lose out. We must have sold another three or four extra albums for every one thrown onto flaming pyres, just because of all the publicity. And having maniacal fundamentalist Christians turn up shrieking and waving banners where we were playing eventually became part of the show; they were as much part of the entourage as the groupies.

But there were death threats. I started to get paranoid, worrying about car bombs, people breaking into my hotel room . . . worst of all – because you could always protect yourself from that sort of threat, with enough security, sufficient money – I worried about somebody with a rifle in the auditorium. It might have been crazy, because of course there were always police and security men outside and inside the venues, but maybe not that crazy. If somebody was determined, they could get in, they could smuggle a rifle in beforehand and then buy a ticket; they could even get a job in the place, long before we arrived – tours are set up long enough in advance – and take a gun and a telescopic sight in any time they wanted. A spotlight operator would be the ideal person; those were the people that scared me most, I don't know why . . . the man with the Super Trooper and the Winchester M/70 Magnum . . .

I know it's crazy, but I started wearing a bullet-proof vest on stage. It made me feel like a looney, but it was the only thing that let me play; the worry about being out there, naked and exposed under the lights, picked out with the others, a tall, broad, stationary target, was starting to affect my playing. Sticky fingers; almost stage fright, a couple of times.

The vest was embarrassing – I kept it a secret from the others for months – but it calmed me; it worked. I could face the unseen mob and play them their music, and afterwards, as the police shoved people back from our limo and we crawled past clutching hands and anguished faces mouthing God knows what, secure within our thick green glass windows and armoured steel, on our way to secure hotel suites and whole floors patrolled by large men with bulging armpits, I could look into the night-time craziness of the people who wanted to tear us apart because they loved us and the people who wanted to tear us apart because they hated us, and feel less crazy: a sensible madman in a world where only paranoia prepared you for reality.

The Great Contra-Flow Smoke Curtain, the idea conceived that day in the English countryside outside Winchester, when Inez and I made a cloud and I danced in the ashes, the total bastard of an idea it took several months and a hundred grand to get just right, was produced by using lots of dry ice, fans, heaters, smoke machines, and lights, both laser and ordinary.

It consisted of fan-driven dry-ice machines, positioned above the front of the stage, and smoke machines – also fitted with fans, plus powerful electric heating elements – which were set at the edge of the stage beneath, directly under the line of ice machines, but staggered, so that each two-metre wide nozzle pointed at the space between the equally large ice-smoke outlets above, where giant intakes sucked the warm smoke away to outside vents; similar intakes between the smoke machines sucked the dry-ice fumes away as well, to avoid filling the whole auditorium with freezing fog.

There were lights positioned inside both smoke and ice machines, shining straight up and straight down respectively, as well as batteries of lasers and spots and strobes set up to illuminate the Curtain itself from various angles and directions. The Curtain was created by the opposing, interspersed streams of vapour, alternately boiling up and fuming down.

We had twenty-four of those units, though the number we actually used on any given night varied according to the size and shape of the venue's stage. It looked impressive as hell once it was all working, but getting the streams set just right, so that the currents didn't get all mixed up, and making sure the intakes didn't suck the ice fumes or smoke from the machines right alongside them, proved to be extremely tricky; we needed a Curtain check before the gig that was longer than the lighting and sound checks combined; and the Curtain had to be fine-tuned for each different auditorium. We were never entirely sure it was going to work.

We couldn't just leave it at that, of course, even with all the fabulous lights; we set up a massive battery of fans and what I guess were de-tuned concussion grenades or claymore mines or something, so that, instead of just switching the Curtain off, we could blast a gigantic hole out through it, revealing the band in one vast, backlit explosion of smoke and sound and light. And we had big booms and moving platforms built too, and wire harnesses set up, so that we could just suddenly appear through the Curtain, more or less anywhere.

We played a few gigs in Britain, without the Curtain, getting ourselves together, trading freshness for tightness, I guess, then we were ready to head across the pond for the American part of a world tour that was intended to take us through South America, Japan, Australia, and even – firsts for us – India and Nigeria before heading back through Europe (East and West) and Scandinavia, for a final set of British dates.

We'd just brought out *Nifedge*, the vastly complicated double album we'd been working on since '78. Symphonic, lyricless, frighteningly expensive (not to mention twice as long as it had been supposed to be), we'd recorded it in '78 and '79, and spent a year trying to mix the bastard. Recording and releasing *And So The Spell Is Ended* (not intended to be a prophetic title, but apt as it turned out) in late '79, was quick and simple by comparison, even though it was still the most musically complicated and studio-time guzzling album we'd recorded, apart from *Nifedge*.

Even the songs on *Ended* were starting to sound too contrived to me; we'd taken twice as long to record single songs for that album as we had to lay down the whole of *Liquid Ice*. We were getting to be obsessive, losing sight of the music in the beguiling mathematical filigree of production and mixing possibilities. Wes, ever the perfectionist, was the instigator of all this, but we were all affected. We were becoming . . . I don't know; choked; decadent, even.

Looking back, I'm surprised we avoided it as long as we did, given that we were hardly bursting with street cred to start with.

And So The Spell Is Ended went platinum in what seemed like about a nanosecond; it outsold anything else we'd done. It was a muscle-bound, over-developed, strangled album; a collection of fairly reasonable songs held together with tourniquets, but it sold. Topped the American charts for weeks; they were rationing it in some stores, selling it straight out the back of trucks in other places. I'd suggested a special flammable edition with some kind of compressed, flattened fireworks worked into the vinyl and the cover, for the mental fundamentalists to burn, but this sensitive and caring idea was cruelly rejected by ARC, by now, of course, headed by Mr Rick Tumber himself.

It was my turn to receive the platinum album; it was presented to me at a ceremony in New York where I got very drunk later on and slightly disgraced myself. I thought I'd lost the damn thing then, but a couple of years ago, unpacking some cases in the folly, I found it again. I prised it out of its glass case and tried playing it, just for a laugh.

It was a James Last record.

Jesus, we're not even on the same label.

You want it in a nutshell?

Phht. Dribble. Crack. Whee. Crash, Splash. Zzt. Beeeeep.

The 'Beeeeep' was Davey dying, Davey dead. It happened like this.

We'd done Boston, New York, Philly, Washington, and Atlanta; everything was working, the tickets had sold out within hours, punters were going bananas for us, and even the fundamentalists seemed to have gotten tired and largely given up on us, partly, perhaps, because by that time Davey and Christine were back together again and talking about getting married and having a family. Mickey Watson's exemplary bourgeois and stable family life was also made the subject of several exclusive illustrated articles. Also, Big Sam had made sure I hadn't been allowed to do any more interviews, and had put out rumours that I'd just been kidding some poor gullible cub reporter when I'd said all those horrible things. So the moral majority mob and the people who thought the universe was six thousand years old had mostly drifted off.

We'd had fairly stiff security in Atlanta, all the same, but it hadn't been needed, not for axe-wielding Bible-thumpers, anyway. The Official Souvenir Programme wielders/thumpers were another matter, and probably no less lethal if they'd come within range. We arranged similarly tight minding for Miami too, even though we knew it probably wasn't necessary; Florida is Florida, not Dixie.

Our convoy of trucks was delayed getting to Miami; one of the Macks was involved in a crash on the freeway. Nothing too serious, but the driver and his load were held up by the local sheriff. We'd hired a 737 (painted gold, but of course) for the American part of the tour, so we got there in plenty of time, but setting up all the equipment in time for the show proved a frenetic and slightly chaotic experience for the road crew.

The auditorium we were playing was one of the smaller ones on the tour, though the stage was wide enough to use twenty of the smoke/ice units. We'd sold out, they told us. Could have filled the place twice over, easy. There'd been some confusion over the number of tickets for sale at the door, but otherwise everything was looking good.

It was a hot, sticky, muggy day, followed by a hot, sticky, muggy evening; the air conditioning in the dressing room was noisy and dripped water, the champagne was not vintage, the bread for our sandwiches was rye, not wholegrain, and Christine's Chablis hadn't been chilled properly . . . but you learn to live with these hardships when you're on the road.

I was learning to put up with something else; not having Inez around. Things had never been completely right between us after Naxos – though, looking back from far enough away, maybe they'd been going wrong since Wes' party at the house overlooking Watergate Bay . . . hard to tell. Ah hell, it's all a long story, and there's doubtless still a lot of it I don't know, but what happened in the end was Inez married Lord Bod. Remember him? Photographer and socialite and one-time ARC shareholder (not any more, or I'd have left the label). They'd been conducting a discreet on–off relationship ever since they'd met, ever since Inez and I'd met, at Manorfield Studios and Lord Bod's house, where the leaves blew and fell and I watched a juggler from up a tree.

Lady Bodenham. Hot damn; did she have her sights on that all along? Did that strategic, middle-class planning get me again? God knows; *I*'m not going to ask her.

So Inez had pulled out of the tour with two weeks' notice and we'd had to find a third backing singer in the middle of the usual last-minute organisational panic just before a major tour; could have sued her under the contract we had, but we didn't have the heart.

I tried not to think about her; I involved myself in the logistics of the tour and spent all my spare time writing new songs. And despite missing Inez, at first it felt good to be back on the road again.

Back on the road . . . with no idea we were about to crash, that night.

The set we were playing included a quarter – twenty minutes – of *Nifedge*. We had had plans to perform the whole thing, making it the second half of a three-hour-plus concert, but there were too many problems. The main problem was we didn't have the nerve to do it, but that's just a personal opinion. Big Sam and ARC both thought it was a potentially disastrous and fan-losing departure to perform a lyricless piece of music as long as a movie to entire stadia of people who'd probably come to hear us recreate our singles. Probably correct, but pretty gutless. If you did *nothing* but give people what they already like, there'd be no new sounds at all (a state it's possible to feel we are already fast approaching if you listen to some radio stations).

Anyway. We were doing the song 'And So The Spell Is Ended' (itself a good twelve minutes long, just on the album), and the first side of *Nifedge*. Plus all the favourites, to keep the unadventurous happy.

We'd been delayed getting to the auditorium, held up while we waited for a helicopter to fly us in; the crowds and traffic outside the place were too dense to get a limo through. We started about half an hour late, in an atmosphere of sweat and heat. The air conditioning in the main hall had broken down and the place must have been sweltering even before they let twenty thousand excited, often dancing, mostly smoking humans inside it. Once they were in place it became like a sort of vast communal sauna.

201

We'd decided to start slow, so began with 'Balance', where everything's black dark (saving the Curtain for later; people had already heard about it, so we didn't always start with it working), and first the drums, then one, then two guitars, then vocals and finally bass and synth together gradually join in and build up, each lit as they slot in, but (the clever bit) all at about half-volume. We played a different, quieter, more wistful version of the song for concerts anyway, using harmonising backing vocals where on the album version there's just the band playing raw and a purposeful, eventually driving, beat, and the lulling effect on a keyed-up audience was always – assuming we played it with conviction – dramatic.

After the last line of 'Balance' faded away ('. . . as the balance . . . of your mind . . . was disturbed . . .'), Wise William, our mixing wizard, wound the volume up to near maximum, we fired all lights and slammed into 'Oh Cimmaron'.

Audience reaction: Wild.

We played another twenty, twenty-five minutes of well-known stuff, then let the stage go dark, and kept it that way while the Curtain was switched on. Lights, music; on into 'And So The Spell Is Ended'.

Our first on-the-night hitch with the Curtain; one of the dry-ice machines had packed up. The fan had fused, motor burned out. After a couple of minutes a few wisps of dry-ice vapour leaked over the unit, but otherwise there was nothing; just a vertical column of clear air where there should have been a soft waterfall of cold mist, just left of stage centre, about where Davey usually stood.

We carried on anyway, as we'd agreed if something like that went wrong. It would take too long to fix, and the effect was still impressive. Spots spotted, lasers lased, and the Burst (when the whole centre of the Curtain was blown out by small explosive charges), all worked fine.

We started side one of *Nifedge*.

I was sweating. I felt thirsty already, and the noise was intense; I didn't know whether we had the monitors turned up too high, the crowd were just exceptionally rowdy, or there was just some sort of weird resonance with the main speakers and the shape of the auditorium, but the noise sounded deafening to me; an inter-

202

nal feedback. I had programmed myself well enough by that time (translation; I was professional enough) not to be unduly put off, so I still did my bit, played my part and my music, but I felt . . . strange.

Perhaps, I remember thinking, we've hit that point in a tour when you've lost the initial impetus of enthusiasm, have yet to work up the momentum of routine, and cannot yet tap the energy of knowing it will all be over soon. Happens that way sometimes, I told myself.

We played. They listened. A few must have heard the album on import, or got their newly released copies very early (or been incredibly avid fans) because some of them seemed to recognise a few of the tunes, and even sang along with one or two of Christine's lyricless voice parts.

The Curtain had gone through its paces, firing all up, then all down, then sweeping through a whole slow staccato sequence of firings, flowing left–right, right–left across the stage. The still-misfiring unit near centre stage made the whole display less than perfect, but you could tell just from the noises the punters were making the overall effect still impressed.

We got to the end of our twenty-minute (nearer twenty-five minutes, on stage) excerpt of *Nifedge*. That side, that movement (if you like), ends with one vast sustaining chord, punched out by every voice and instrument on stage, plus a synth key-triggered echo and reverberation sequence looping the resulting noise through a pre-figured programme for a digital analyser/sequencer which, at the time, was state of the art.

A stunning, sublimely furious noise, with the sound system at a hundred per cent plus whatever reverberations the venue could provide.

In Miami, the noise sounded like the crack of doom, like the whiplash of a galactic arm snapping, like an earthquake wave riding a major power line; we hit our individual assemblage of notes all at once, in a single blasting moment of impacted noise.

And brought a small section of the house down.

Ho ho, ha ha.

And killed Davey.

Because the dry-ice unit above him had blown a fuse, and the fan didn't work. Because the unit had been put up wrong; in the rush to construct the set, they'd put some part on upside down, and excess vapour and liquid couldn't drain away. Because the air in the hall was very humid, and the moisture in the air, the natural heat of that steamy city, and the collected body-breath of all those worshipping people, had collected around the great unused lump of granulated dry ice sitting way above the stage there. Because a bolt had been tightened up with a monkey wrench, not a torque wrench. Because this was before the days of radio mikes and leadless guitars, so we were all connected up, linked to the machinery.

So the whole lot snapped and crashed and fell. Missed Davey by a good few feet, but spilled its load of collected water all over him and his guitar and, in seconds, while we were still trying to work out what the hell had happened, and the audience were still applauding the spectacular effect (that burgeoning bursting bow-wave of water had happened to be caught in an accidentally delightful pattern of lights and lasers), the water rushed and/or seeped into some errant wire, some badly connected part of an amplifier, and promptly electrocuted our Davey.

Lasted . . . maybe two seconds, maybe five. Seemed like about three hours, but you could probably find some ghoulish bastard with a bootleg tape who could give you it down to the nearest tenth of a second.

Before we ran for him, before he fell, before that ghastly, jerking, stiff parody of a guitarist dropped from rigidity to slackness across the stage, before Wise William and his cohorts finally realised the circuit breakers – also too hastily installed, we found out later – weren't working, and cut the power manually.

And we gathered him up, and we took him to the stage exit. He was blue, silent, heart still beating weakly, but breathing only with the assistance of us all; taking turns at first until the paramedics in the ambulance took over. The medics and the ambulance were there according to the contract, but they only let Davey die slower. A chopper was ordered, but would take too long to get there.

We went with the ambulance, but it got us, effectively, nowhere.

The crowds were too great.

There were just too many people. We got him into the

204

ambulance, we surrounded him with our own bodies, we did all we could, but none of it was enough, because there had been a mix-up with the tickets, especially with the number for sale at the door, and so there were even more people milling, ticketless and frustrated outside the auditorium than there were inside.

And we just couldn't get through the crowds.

I stood on the ambulance roof at one point. Stood there with its lights flashing round my ankles and its exhaust smoke rising around me, like some tiny image of our stage show, me the star at last, and howled at those people, looking down a crowded alley of them to a crowded street of them, and fists clenched, head back, I screamed with all my might, 'Get oot the fuckin WAY!'

. . . but did nothing, accomplished nothing, communicated . . . nothing.

The swarming chanting tides close round the ambulance and its quiet, unminding cargo, like antibodies round an infection.

We all thought that he would somehow live, that he of all people would find a way to pull through; another crazy death-defying stunt . . .

But, he didn't; a last practical joke.

DOA.

Davey Balfour. 1955–1980.

RIP

And that, folks, was very much the end of that.

    end of (a) story

    roll up that circuit diagram

    finished with engines

    shantih

THIRTEEN

'Good morning. Mr Daniel Weir?'

I looked at the two young, clean-shaven men on the grey screen. Coats, suits, ties. I said, 'Yes.'

The one who was speaking held a card in a little plastic wallet up to the camera. 'I'm Detective Constable Jordan, this is Detective Constable McInnes. Could we have a word with you, Mr Weir?'

I think I was silent for a moment or two. Then I said, 'Of course,' and let them in. I thought it must be something to do with the club called Monty's, and that broken aquarium. What had happened? Another death? Another chance catastrophe? Had one of the bouncers turned out to have a thin skull, or suddenly collapsed with a fatal blood clot in the brain? Had the cracked glass given way without warning and crushed or sliced in half some glazier or plumber? Nothing seemed too bizarre or outrageous.

I'd spent the first part of the night curled up on the floor of the bedroom, foetally tight, occasionally shivering, then climbed up to the tower's highest room, which is quite bare, just a couple of seats, and sat there, looking out over the city for a while. Then, still unable to sleep, still thinking about Christine, about Davey and about my own Jonah of a life, I went down to the crypt and tried to distract myself with music, composition, messing about with old tunes and new tunes, until I gave that up too and went for a cold, quiet walk through the mostly sleeping city, aimlessly wandering, growing cold and tired and coming back, and still not able to cry, and deciding that there really was very little left for me, that I had been responsible for both of their deaths and, if there was a God, then it was either a sadistic bastard, or didn't give a damn. And, if there wasn't, then the patterns and currents of cause and effect we dignify with the name 'fate' sure as shit seemed to be trying to tell me something.

I came back to the folly at last, decided that I just didn't want to live any more. I climbed to the top of my high, blasphemous tower and looked down at the street, but knew I couldn't do it that way.

What else? The only deadly drug I had was booze, and I suppose I could have tried drinking a couple of bottles of vodka, but my stomach has always protected me from the worst effects of alcoholic poisoning, acting as a safety valve and simply chucking back out the offending liquid before it has time to inflict maximum damage, so I didn't think that would work.

I lay, unsleeping and dry-eyed on my bed, and put on the radio, hoping to hear a human voice.

White noise; static.

It filled the darkened room, filled me, and I thought it might send me to sleep, but it didn't. The bright, meaningless sound washed and broke over me, and I let it, surrendering to its enfolding, random signal, closing my eyes.

And I knew then how I'd kill myself.

I switched the radio off again, as the chilly, watery dawn slowly heaved itself out of the cloudy eastern skies.

I had breakfast with Rick Tumber at the Albany, before he caught the shuttle back to London. We talked. I said I'd think about making a come-back. He seemed relieved, apparently believing I hadn't taken the news of Christine's death too hard. But then he didn't know how much of it had been my idea.

He checked out, paid his bill, and set off for the airport in the GTS. I walked back through a sudden, thin sunlit shower of sleet to St Jute's. The policemen came half an hour later.

Tommy was in custody; they'd gone to his parents' address to question him about the theft of a quantity of whipped-cream containers; he'd assaulted a police officer and resisted arrest.

Detective Constable Jordan took my statement. I said I hadn't known the cans were stolen, but that I had let Tommy snort the gas; how this fitted in with Tommy's own story, I had no idea. DC Jordan cautioned me and told me that charges might be brought against me at some point in the future. They'd be in touch.

I think they might have searched an ordinary house for drugs, but St Jute's must have looked a little daunting.

'Is this place used as a warehouse, Mr Weir?' Jordan asked, eyeing the chaos of crates and boxes and assorted plant and vehicles.

'Not really,' I said. 'This is my home.' The policemen looked at me sceptically. 'I used to be in the music business,' I explained. 'The record company sold a lot of records in the Communist Bloc, but they don't like to part with hard currency over there; we came to an agreement we'd take goods in lieu of royalties. This stuff is what we couldn't sell.' The two detectives exchanged glances. 'My lawyers have the appropriate bills of lading and import documentation; Macrae, Fietch and Warren. Contact them if you want to check.'

They took a desultory look round the place, perhaps wishing that the assembled merchandise really had been stolen, but they left with only the shopping trolley full of whipped-cream cans.

I watched them go, put my coat on again, turned off the space heater, the gas and the electricity, stood in the centre of the choir for a while, looking round (I listened for the pigeon, but couldn't hear anything), then I left by the Elmbank Street door, certain I would never see the place again.

Because I'd killed Christine, too. Me and my clever, stupid, blasphemous, believer-baiting ideas.

It went way back, the way these things usually did, rooted ineradicably deep in the past, tangled in with all the times you thought you'd done the right thing, made the correct decision. So you thought anyway, but always, in there, hidden away, was the thing that made you pay, the one wayward idea, the garbled but effective message, like a cancer, single-cell but growing, spreading, filling; killing.

After the first US tour, when I'd made my ill-advised remarks, and we'd had a little trouble with the fundamentalists, I'd been stunned that people like that still existed today – my sheltered upbringing, I suppose – and then angry that such idiocy could have that effect and be given the credence it was in schools and textbooks and people's lives. That anger surfaced once when I was with Christine, producing a bad germ of an idea.

Lying together in bed, in the Year of Our Lord 1978, I believe, in one of the cavernously cold rooms of Morasbeg. I'd bought the place the year before, in a misguided fit of acquisitive enthusiasm, taken with the idea of being a Highland landowner (I hadn't bought the island yet; that came later).

We'd been talking about the fortnight's touring holiday we'd just taken, on Mull and Skye and the Hebrides. Christine had driven. We hadn't been able to come back from Lewis on the day we wanted because it was a Sunday, and so we'd been stuck in Stornaway for a day, twiddling our thumbs and watching all the good folk going to the kirk. Remembering that had got me onto religion generally, and the Christian fundamentalists I'd offended in the States in particular.

'You know what we should do?' I said, sitting up and taking the binoculars from the bedside table.

'What?' Christine rolled over in bed, propping her head up with one honey-coloured arm (it had been a sunny second week on the Isles.

The bed in the main bedroom was situated within a huge, magnificent but heat-leaking bay window on the second floor, looking out across acres and acres of hummocky heather and marshy grass, with a glimpse of the sparkling sea to one side. I fiddled with the focus on the binoculars, searching for deer.

'We should make those Neanderthals *really* sick; I mean, they keep accusing us of trying to corrupt youth and all that shit, and taking the name of Christ in vain; well, we ought to *think up* something deliberately, that would upset them.'

Christine was silent for a moment or two. 'How about calling the next album "Fuck God"?' she suggested.

'Too subtle,' I said. 'Needs to be more obvious. We're dealing with genuine rednecks here.'

'Uh-huh,' Christine said. I scanned the wind-blown waste of Ardnamurchan while Christine stroked my hairy back.

209

'Re-enact the crucifixion,' I said thoughtfully, my eyes screwing up as I pointed the binoculars towards the glittering sliver of sea to the south-west. 'But use a *black man*!'

'Too tasteful. Besides, they might *like* seeing a black guy getting nailed to a cross.'

'Hmm. You're right.' I looked into the burning golden glare of the distant sea, fuming light over silhouetted dunes and waving grass. For a second I thought a shadow against the brassy reflections off the sea looked like a deer, but as I juggled with the focus it disappeared.

I remembered the previous week, when we'd been together and alone on a beach on Iona, looking west to the sunset; the Atlantic rollers came crashing in long lines of surf and spray, and for a few moments the two of us, watching the head of what we thought must be a seal, suddenly saw its whole sleek-fat, suspended body within the green cliff face of the next up-rearing wave; outlined, upright, as though standing inside the wave, silhouetted by the sunlight falling from behind.

'Got it,' I said, putting the binoculars down.

'What?'

'Your name.'

'Christine? Brice? All of it?'

'Part of it; part of Christine.'

Christine looked quizzical. 'Forget the I, N, E,' I said. 'What's left? "Christ"!'

Christine gazed at me levelly, blue eyes, honey skin, long blonde hair all tangled. 'Wow,' she said.

'We play on that; we have *you* crucified on stage!'

'Oh, thanks.' She nodded.

'I know!' I laughed. 'We have you on a giant guitar; you lie on the neck, and it has a sort of cross-brace . . . no, there are two ordinary sized guitars forming the cross-piece of the cross. That's it! You start out on that, lying down on it, in the dark, and then you're levered up to vertical, as the lights come up, and you're hanging there on the cross, crucified, then you jump down, taking one of the cross-piece guitars with you, and you launch into the first song!'

Christine snorted, threw herself down on her back, hands behind her head, staring up at the brightly grey plaster of the long, high-ceilinged room. 'Yeah, that would offend a few people,' she agreed. 'Still a bit subtle, all the same.'

I shrugged. 'Images stick. It would work. I'd suggest we actually try it, but they'd lynch us.' I came down beside her, put my arms round her, cradled her.

'Well, they might lynch me,' Christine said. She arched her back; my fingers fell into the muscular hollow her spine left as she flexed herself towards me.

'Aye, well; we cannae be havin that noo, can we, lassie?' I laughed. Still cradling her, I shook her, carefully, always fearful of hurting her.

'No, indeed.' She brought her arms up to my neck. Her entangled blonde hair slid across the white pillow like gold chains over snow (and for a fleeting instant, I thought *Suzanne takes you down* . . .), before we kissed.

She got in touch, four years later, to ask me whether I'd mind her using the idea in her stage act; she was in the process of forming her own band, La Rif, and was getting ideas for the stage show together too. I told her she was welcome to use it. I wish I could say I also told her to be careful, to think twice, that it was a silly idea, not serious . . . but I didn't. I was chuffed; I thought how wonderful it was to have such extensive influence, to have old throwaway ideas fall on fertile ground and bring forth fruit. And I was gleeful, thinking how it would outrage those I despised.

At the time Christine got in touch, Davey had been dead for a couple of years; I had only just started work again, on my own album, after nearly eighteen months of doing not very much of anything at all; it never crossed my mind that Christine would be in any real danger from the stage act. I don't know why, because it should have; maybe Davey's death was still too fresh and I just didn't want to think about anything like that. So I encouraged her.

The reaction was pretty much what you'd expect. Incredible publicity, of course, but mouth-foaming vilification from the moral majority and the megabuck TV evangelists; some southern states wouldn't let Christine appear at all, others would only let her play if she didn't do the guitar–Christ act. Death threats, too, of course.

211

So who's a guilty boy, then?

Ah, bugger it aw; Ah'm awa tae dae awa wi masel.

Jesus, what else was there for me? I'd been saddled with my great, hulking, graceless body and a face fit for pantomime, I'd been born poor and clumsy and too nice or too weak to be a businessman or a successful crook, so that I could have been forgiven for giving in then, and accepting the type-cast role life seemed to have waiting for me; local freak, somebody people threatened their children with; I could have done my best in a proper job and spent the rest of my days getting nowhere but being a great help to my mates and being called the Big Yin and never scowling when people asked me, What was the weather like up there? or, What cathedral had I fallen off? and maybe I'd have found somebody who loved me and I could love or maybe not, and fathered lots of little ugly kids, but I didn't.

I'd tried to do something more *impressive*, more *memorable*, and for a good few years there I thought I'd been doing all right. I'd clawed my way out of being an ugly nonentity and established myself as an unhandsome star; I'd made money, I'd been places and done things and amazed people and pleased them, and I'd scandalised a few too. I could do good things, I could be something else than what seemed to be inevitable. I could create grace, I could *compose* grace, even if I couldn't be graceful myself.

But every time I thought I'd proved that, something happened to wipe it all out, and I was left in the wreckage, surrounded by the dead and broken dreams, and staring, appalled and confounded, at the proof of my own infectious, terminal, clumsiness. I was the ghost at the feast, the angel of destruction, the kiss of extinction. Marked out for bad luck, like some poisonous insect which advertises its lethal chemistry to potential predators with bright, outrageous colours. I'd cheated; I'd made my own good luck, overpowered that natural signal, ignored that uniform . . . and unknowingly had shifted the bad luck on to others, so that they suffered in my place.

I walked through the city to Great Western Road, and took a bus there for Old Kilpatrick. It seemed important to walk, or catch buses, or try to hitch a lift; I didn't want to take a train or hire a taxi; I wanted to start then and there, walking, and just keep going, my journey unplanned but determined, only my destination set and definite.

Maybe it was just a sort of hopeless nostalgia, remembering the time, in my early teens, when a gang of us from Ferguslie had bussed and hitched this way, heading for . . . Crianlarich, Oban, Mull; however far we could get before our money ran out. We ended up camped on the banks of Loch Lomond, shivering in the rain with our good shoes caked with mud, wondering if there was a hotel bar nearby which wouldn't throw us out.

Whatever. The wet pavements, the north wind, the palely gleaming buildings and the bright, busy sky took me to the great broad road which led over the hills and down the banks of the river and far away. I sat on the bus, not really thinking, but feeling frozen, stuck, rusted up inside.

I watched the faces of the people in the bus, and I listened to their talk. They seemed like real, proper, normal folk and I was the weird one all right, I was the freak. Their lives, with all their diversity and complexities, for all their sudden changes and surprising additions and omissions, must have been of the ordinary stuff, the standard fare.

Mine seemed then to have been even more grotesque and deformed than I'd feared in my darkest moments. The world belonged to these people. I had had colossal effrontery contaminating it with my presence for this long; now was time to pay, now it was time to admit life had been right and I'd been wrong all the time, and dispose of this mutant frame, put to rest this twisted, alien monstrosity.

I felt tired, as the bus moved through the suburbs and the people got on and got off and the day moved from fair to showery and back again. At Old Kilpatrick I must have been dozing; the bus stopped, jerking me awake, and I found myself there, almost in the thin shadow of the Erskine Bridge, by the side of the river. There were low hills and trees on the south bank, and higher steps of grass and stone scarps beyond the houses of the town and the road I was heading for, on the north side.

Hitch-hiking has a lot in common with fishing. I'd forgotten just how brain-numbing hitching could be; any other time I might have been exasperated. Right then, the very zombifying tediousness of it came as a relief. I stood, I watched the cars and vans and trucks join the boulevard heading west; I kept my arm out and thumb up, and tried to look as sane, unmenacing and non-homicidal as I could. So I must have amused a fair few drivers even if, over the course of a couple of hours, none of them stopped.

I left the roadside for the leaky cover of a tree when a shower came on, shivering a little in my great dark coat and thinking in a vague, distant sort of way how ironic it was, to be sheltering from a little drizzle, when I was intending to drown myself in the sea just as soon as I got there. The shower passed, the traffic went on, the cloud-tangled sun fell gradually across the sky towards the firth and the mountains of Argyll.

I thought of Christine, then tried not to. I thought of Davey and could hardly remember him as he had been; I kept seeing his photograph, recalling his guitar and his voice from individual songs, remembering what he looked like in videos. I thought of McCann and Wee Tommy and Betty and Rick Tumber and – God help the brutes – I even thought of TB and that stupid bloody pigeon, and like the past twelve years the past one week seemed all jumbled and fragmented and confused, as though I was incapable of holding even that brief amount of time in my head and keeping it coherent.

The rain came on again but I stayed out in it, though people rarely ever stop when you're dripping wet. Grim, unmoving, slowly soaking, I watched the cars and trucks hiss and rumble past, wipers waving, lights shining.

The rain ceased.

It was three o'clock before anybody stopped; a garage mechanic in a Land-Rover pick-up. He could only take me as far as Dumbarton, a few miles down the road. I stood by a roundabout he recommended, in what I reckoned was probably the same shower of rain that had soaked me earlier and moved on.

I got the next hitch within five minutes, just as it was starting to get dark.

'Where ye headin, big fella?'

'Iona,' I said.

'Aw aye. The island?'

'Aye, off Mull.'

214

'Aw aye. Ye smoke?'

The man who'd stopped for me was seventyish, crouched over the wheel of his Hillman Avenger. Bald; wisps of grey hair. An old, greasy-looking deerstalker lay on the back seat of the car with some parcels and a Frasers bag. Baggy suit and thick glasses. He was going to Arrochar, so he could drop me at Tarbet, about two thirds of the way up the west side of the loch. He held out a packet of Carlton. I was about to refuse, automatically, but then said, 'Yes, thanks.'

I took a cigarette. The old guy leaned over the dash and pushed in a cigar lighter. 'The name's John McCandless, whit's yours, big fella?'

'Dan. Daniel Weir.'

'Bit dreich for hitch-hiking the day, Dan,' Mr McCandless said, giving a sort of laughing cough as we headed up the dual carriageway towards the southern end of the loch. The lighter clicked out and we lit our cigarettes.

'Aye, it is that,' I agreed.

'And whit takes ye away tae Iona, Dan?'

'I've got some friends there. Spending Christmas with them.'

'Very nice.' He looked round at me for a moment. 'Ye no got a bag or somethin with ye, son?'

'No,' I said, pulling on the cigarette. The tobacco-hit was making me feel dizzy. 'I've got some gear out there, left it with them the last time I was there.'

'Aw, aye.'

The cigarette tasted bitter and harsh and reeked of the past. I drank it in, listening to the wipers hum back and forth and the engine roar monotonously; water trickled down the back of my neck, coldly inquiring, sinuously intimate, raising goosebumps. For a dizzying moment of *déjà vu* I shivered, and remembered standing in the grey rain of Ferguslie Park, thirteen years ago, setting out with my songs crumpled in my pocket and my hopes none too high, to see a band called Frozen Gold playing at Paisley Tech.

I smoked, watched the rain drops fall and spatter, then smear away under the tired flaying of the wipers. I ought to have asked Mr McCandless what he'd been buying, what he'd done before he retired, if he'd always lived in Arrochar, what his kids were doing, what age the grandchildren were . . . any number of polite, decent, small-talking things, just to be human and show some interest and a little gratitude at having been picked up on a rainy evening. But I couldn't.

Partly it was selfishness; the same what-the-hell attitude that made me take the fag, even though I'd finally given up smoking five or six years earlier; this was my last evening on earth (not my last day; I'd never get to Iona, or probably even anywhere near the sea, in one go now) so I thought I deserved a little indulgence. But also I didn't feel capable of pretending to be interested; I wasn't, and I couldn't act it. I wasn't really part of other people's world any more.

'Ye in work, Dan?'

'No,' I said. 'Had some once, but . . . not any more.'

'Aye, bad times.' Mr McCandless shook his head, still staring ahead.

I thought: *Here come the thirties; here comes the depression*, but Mr McCandless surprised me, and didn't make the usual connection. He just shook his head again and repeated, 'Aye, bad times.'

I smoked my cigarette and watched the rain come down.

When he left me at Tarbet it was almost fully dark and still raining. I stood on the road heading north, thumb out for a while, but nobody stopped. I ignored the big old hotel at the road junction and walked on down the road until the pavement disappeared. As I stood looking into the darkness down the winding loch-side road, the rain came down heavier. There was a small hotel a hundred yards back, its sign lit. I turned back to it.

'Yes?' The man looked me up and down. He looked like the owner.

What did he see? A tall, gangling, brutish man with straggly black hair and a shadow of stubble; hook nose, staring eyes, shoddy long coat, dripping wet.

'I'd like a room, please. Just for one night. I won't be . . .'

'Sorry, we're full. Christmas, you see.'

'Just a room,' I said. I took out a handful of notes from one pocket. 'I won't be needing breakfast or anything.' I counted out five tenners. 'I can pay in advance; I'll be leaving early.'

The man – a plump English guy, wavy brown hair that looked

dyed, and nervous eyes – made a papping noise with his lips, looking down at the money in my hands. 'Ahm . . . we might have had a cancellation. I'll have to ask my wife.' He disappeared through to the public bar, sending a wave of warmth and noise out behind him.

His wife was plump too; she looked into my eyes and smiled in a friendly way. 'I'm sorry, Mr . . .?'

'Daniel Weir.'

'I'm very sorry, Mr Weir; we are fully booked up at the moment.'

'Your husband thought you might have had a cancellation,' I said, slowly folding up the tenners.

'Well, no; we've a couple who haven't confirmed or arrived yet, but' – she glanced at a wall clock – 'we couldn't really give you their room yet. Another four hours or so, and if they haven't arrived . . . perhaps then.'

'I see. Thanks anyway. Good night.' I turned back for the doors.

'Good night. I'm sure you can find somewhere else. Which way . . .?' But by then I was back out in the rain.

Trucks swept past. The dark, lapping waters of the loch were only a few yards from the road, once it ran beyond the village. The multi-axled trailers on the big trucks went spraying by, massive tyres rumbling. I stood on the damp pavement, wondering why I was bothering to go to Iona. Why not do it here?

I couldn't. Even in my death, in that one thing we all share, I wanted to be different; throwing myself into this picturesque but rather tame old freshwater loch, or mangling myself under some truckload of tin cans or treetrunks, seemed too normal, too close to society. I wanted the wilderness and the waters of the world-ocean. It wasn't ego, even now I don't think it was that; it was . . . taste. Appropriateness.

No room at the inn; I sighed and walked back to the big hotel at the road junction, ready for another rejection. They let me in without a murmur, a wee lassie getting me to fill out the Access voucher there and then; it was a double room and she talked me into having not only breakfast ('Oh, you might as well, Mr Weir; it's inclusive'), but dinner too.

I agreed to dinner because I'd stopped feeling tired and started feeling hungry, and it was still not half-past four. Long winter

217

nights. I hadn't allowed for any of this. I was shown to my room. I observed its anonymity for a while, wondering how many hotel rooms I'd been in in my life. I had a shower and dried my clothes over radiators. I dried my hair and watched some kids' television for a little, then turned it off. I dressed, went to the bar, had a few drinks, bought a packet of cigarettes and smoked half of them, had dinner, then went back to the room.

All that time, I was waiting.

Waiting to feel something, waiting to suddenly burst out crying, or to suddenly feel all right again, better once more, or go hysterical and take a running jump out of the nearest high window . . . but none of that happened.

It was as though some autopilot had taken over, as if a temporary government was running things, some skeleton crew of the mind; the king is dead, long live the regent . . .

On Iona it might be possible to know again; that was where I was heading and everything had stopped while I got myself there. Once I'd arrived, when I was facing those blue-green waves; then I'd start thinking again; then, when I was finally faced with it, the reality of killing myself and just not being any more; opting out of this insane, tasteless, murderous circus where the freaks are too often wiser – but also more despised – than the thronging marks.

I was still convinced I'd do it. I was almost looking forward to it. I'd heard that old people could accept death and there was some sort of meta-tiredness which had nothing to do with the quick sleep of night; a lulling, draining, glacial sapping of life's own life over the years, winding up, powering down . . . I'd thought it was just some sort of excuse, a lie the old told to convince themselves they wouldn't mind dying and so draw the sting of fear. But now . . . now I wasn't so sure. I thought I understood that tiredness.

I lay down fully clothed on the bed with the lights on, staring at the ceiling, waiting for something to happen.

I must have fallen asleep.

When I woke up I didn't know what time it was. It was still dark and there was music playing in the room next to mine. There was no clock in the room. I turned on the television but there was only white noise on all the channels. I rubbed my face and yawned, then took off my clothes (and thought: For the last time.

218

I'll go in fully clothed tomorrow; quicker, less ridiculous, somehow). I climbed into the wide, cold bed, put the lights out.

The music was too loud. It was going to keep me awake, I knew it, too, which would make it even harder to ignore. It was . . .

. . . us.

I hadn't recognised it at first; music always sounds different through walls, but it was Frozen Gold all right; *MIRV*. It was side one; 'The Good Soldier' faded, and was replaced by '2000 AM'. So I'd slept through 'Oh Cimmaron'. Next 'Single Track' and then 'Slider', and then, very likely as this was probably a tape played on a ghetto-blaster, side two as well.

Too loud. Loud enough for me to be able to make out Christine's voice, Davey's guitar. I lay there, listening, unable to stop it, paralysed and transfixed and frozen.

And at first I laughed, because there is another song, on *Personal Effects*, which contains the lyrics,

> Just an old rock star in a cheap hotel,
> He's sung too many songs about love.
> Kept awake all night in his en-suite hell,
> By his old hit played too loud above.

And it was a low, despairing sort of laugh, the laugh of bitter appreciation that life could always kick you when you were down, just to make sure you were still watching the show, and with that laughter came an odd, half-appalled revelation: there was no real division between tragedy and comedy, they were just tags we'd stuck on our hooligan consequences as we stumbled and stampeded through the world's definitive grotesqueries, just a set of different ways of looking at things, from person to person and time to time, and a set of different moods to see them in . . .

And Davey sang 'Single Track':

> Ash blonde criminals abound in my mind
> And you snow-princess were the worst I could find

And Christine sang 'Whisper':

> But this is only what you say,
> One single way in all the ways.
> I hear the flood within the drought,
> I hear the whisper in the shout.

And Davey sang 'Apocalypso':

> 'The dam has just gone,' said the cripple we passed
> 'But we shall live on,' he said, breathing his last.
> 'Oh please allow me,' said the young cardinal
> But the wafer, we've heard, tastes a little too real

And Christine sang 'The Way It goes':

> Well I suppose this is the feeling,
> That pretends to true love's wonder,
> Finds you standing, finds you kneeling,
> Never fails to push you under . . .

And together they sang 'Across From The Moon And Down':

> You put your shell-like ear to a shell,
> Just to know what the bone will tell.
> You hear no roaring ocean's flood,
> Just the sweet, salt sea of your blood.

And I listened, and my laughs died away, and I just sat there, my heart thumping, and my breath coming quick and shallow, and gradually – only lightly at first – the tears came.

And that was when I grieved for Christine, and finally fell asleep on my damp, salty pillow, to wake the next morning at the sound of a passing train, at once relieved and disappointed, and reluctantly resigned to my life.

FOURTEEN

There's this sloth in the jungle walking from one tree to another, and it's mugged by a gang of snails, and when the police ask the sloth if it could identify any of its attackers, it says, 'I don't know; it all happened so quickly . . .'

And that's the way I feel. Everything seems to take about the right amount of time *at* the time, but later . . . Jeez, where did it all go? You look back, and sometimes you think, Did I really do all that?, and other times you think, Is that all there is? Is that all I managed to get done?

We are never satisfied. Don't even know the meaning of the word.

My ma finally decided to give up the flat in Ferguslie, and I went back there in . . . summer of '81, it must have been, to help her look for a house and arrange the money. I don't think my arguments had convinced her; I think she hadn't been getting on with her neighbours so well, though whose fault that was I never knew.

We found the house at Kilbarchan. Ma, ignoring my hints and suggestions, had it redecorated in red flock and moved the stock of Woolies' repros in. She set out a room that was to be my room. I'm only half-ashamed to admit I've never spent a night there.

Almost without my noticing it all my brothers and sisters had grown up. A couple married, one at Uni (wee Malcolm, though God knew how, I remember thinking at the time, unless they did degrees in Kung Fu), two – amazingly enough – in work, and one in the RAF.

My da came out of prison that year and went to stay with my ma. I told her she was a fool to take him back, but she did. I wouldn't even meet him for a couple of years. When I did, after Ma persuaded me, it was like meeting a stranger. A quiet, insignificant stranger with eyes that never seemed to look directly at anybody.

I'd spent the year after Davey died doing not very much of anything (once we'd got the horrendous legal problems caused by abandoning the tour out the way). I'd travelled a bit, aimlessly. I'd sold Morasbeg, and started looking for somewhere else to live, to settle down in the UK now that the Tories had made it so cheap for us rich people to live there. This nest-quest for a wee hoose ended when I found St Jute's, so whether you count it a success or a failure rather depends.

I'd spent quite a few months, on and off, half-heartedly learning to play an analyser/synthesiser/sequencer (the sequencer part let me correct the bum notes my thick, clumsy fingers made), with vague intentions of doing a solo album, and maybe some film work. I'd sold the Panther long ago. I started having driving lessons once, but I gave them up.

One day, with nothing to do in Paisley, I thought I'd look up a few of my old pals, see if anybody was still where I remembered them, or could be traced. This made a change, as I'd spent a large part of the previous year avoiding those who knew me – or had known me – well. I had withdrawn, I had turned my friends away, though I'd known they'd only wanted to offer sympathy and comfort.

So perhaps the pain was dying, the memory healing a little, at the end of that year, though I confess that perhaps I was just getting restless. I was, after all, starting to have a few ideas for songs again, after so many fallow months I had begun to think – not without some relief – that the ideas had dried up.

Whatever; I went looking for people.

I called on Jean Webb's parents, only to discover that cancer had killed Mr Webb the year before and Mrs Webb was in a wheelchair, looked after by her retired older sister, who'd never married; another of Jean's aunts. We had tea. Mrs Webb's twisted fingers could barely hold the cup.

I asked her how she managed with the stairs up to her flat. She said she could struggle up and down with a stick and her sister's help; anyway, she was near the top of the council list to be moved to disabled accommodation. She explained all this as though it wasn't important, and as though having to explain it was slightly annoying.

We talked mostly about her children. The son who'd gone to business school was a trainee accountant in London; the one who'd worked at Inverkip was in the army. Jean and Gerald were living in Aberdeen; Gerald had a job in the oil industry. Jean had lost her second child, born prematurely. They'd been advised not to try for any more. The daughter, Dawn, was three years old; very forward, and bright for her age. Jean came home quite often; I'd only missed her by a day.

The rest was inconsequential. All of it was depressing. I only remember one thing she said, apart from the news of her family. Somehow we'd got on to the subject of advice; what you told your children, how you tried to help them grow up.

Mrs Webb sat in her wheelchair, the cup and saucer on an adjustable table her sister had wheeled in front of her. She looked out the window to the flats on the other side of the street, looking away from me as the light failed.

'Ach, son,' she said, slowly shaking her head. 'Ye try to bring your kids up right, and give them advice an that, but they dinnae listen. Ah God, it hurts ye at the time, but who's tae say they're wrong? Ah listened, Dan,' she looked at me, then glanced at her sister, sitting crocheting on the couch across the room. 'Ah listened tae ma mum, did Ah no, Marie?'

Marie nodded slowly, without raising her eyes from her work. 'Aye, you listened, hen.'

'Ah listened tae ma mum,' Mrs Webb continued, gazing out the window again, 'because she'd had a hard life an Ah thought she knew what she was talkin about. Well, maybe she did. Ye know what she told me?' Mrs Webb glanced briefly at me. I raised my eyebrows. 'She told me tae keep the heid,' Mrs Webb smiled at the quiet street outside. ' "Keep the heid, Jessie," she'd tell me; "Just take it easy"; that's whit she'd say. Whit she meant was, Ah wiznae tae dive straight intae things; Ah wiznae tae breenge about the way Ah always did – cos Ah was a right wee tearaway when Ah wiz a wean' – another quick glance at me – 'or Ah'd regret it later.'

'Well, me and Bob always took things easy; we were careful wi our money an we didnae get anythin on credit.'

Mrs Webb's sister shook her head at her crocheting and said, 'No,' in an approving, confirmatory way.

'We saved when we were able, an we never took any risks. We tried tae give the weans a decent start in life, an we tried tae set things up for our old age.'

She was quiet for a few moments. Her sister's needles clicked in the background. I wondered whether I ought to say something. She went on, 'But Ah don't know if ma mum was right. She might have been right for her, cos Ah know now she'd done things in haste an been sorry for them all her life, but . . . Ah don't know, son; if Ah had ma time tae live again Ah think Ah'd be a wee bit less cautious. Ah'd live a bit more for today an no tomorrow, an Ah'd tell the weans the same, though God knows Ah'd probably end up regrettin that too.'

She turned away from the window to look at me again and the sad, solemn expression on her face changed, became a smile. 'Aye,' she said, 'it's a sair fecht, is it no?' But with the smile, and what may have been a shrug, and with the slow, delicate picking up of a teacup, made the statement seem merely ironic.

A sair fecht.

A sore fight, indeed, Mrs Webb.

I left the flat depressed but, as I walked down Espedair Street, back into town under a glorious sunset of red and gold, slowly a feeling of contentment, intensifying almost to elation, filled me. I couldn't say why; it felt like more than having gone through a period of mourning and come out the other side, and more than just having reassessed my own woes and decided they were slight compared to what some people had to bear; it felt like faith, like revelation: that things went on, that life ground on regardless, and mindless, and produced pain and pleasure and hope and fear and joy and despair, and you dodged some of it and you sought some of it and sometimes you were lucky and sometimes you weren't, and sometimes you could plan your way ahead and that would be the right thing to have done, but other times all you could do was forget about plans and just be ready to *react*, and sometimes the obvious was true and sometimes it wasn't, and sometimes experience helped but not always, and it was all luck, fate, in the end; you lived, and you waited to see what happened, and you would rarely ever be sure that what you had done was really the right thing or the wrong thing, because things can always be better, and things can always be worse.

Then, being me, I felt guilty about starting to feel better, and thought, *So, you've heard a little bit of home-crocheted philosophy, and seen somebody worse off than yourself; is this all it takes? Your revelations come cheap, Daniel Weir; and your soul is shallow . . .* but even that was part of the experience, and so explained, and expiated, by it, and under that startlingly gaudy sky – like something from one of my ma's Woolworths' paintings – I walked, and felt I could be happy again.

FIFTEEN

In the hall now, at Arisaig, watching the little kid on the trike, trailing coloured streamers, round and round.

A train woke me, just as the dawn was seeping from the sky above the dark hotel. I dozed, rang reception to order a taxi to Glasgow, had my breakfast, then went back to the city, taking a newspaper with me and sitting in the back of the cab, partly to avoid small-talk with the driver. A young Arrochar lad, he was content to listen to the radio while I tried to find out what else had been happening in the world recently.

I went straight to Wee Tommy's ma's, but there was nobody in. Next came St Jute's and then the Griffin, to see if McCann had replied to my note. There was nothing fresh on the pile of junk-mail inside the folly's door, and no sign of or message from McCann at the Griff.

I went back to Tommy's folks' house and put a note through the door telling them to get in touch with my lawyers. Then I went to see them.

Mr Douglas, senior partner at Macrae, Fietch and Warren, said he would contact a firm specialising in criminal work, and a good advocate, and would have the former find out where Tommy was and whether any other lawyer had received instructions to defend him. He was sure they could come to an arrangement. I signed a letter authorising him to make all necessary disbursements to deal with Wee Tommy's case, as soon as his family got in touch.

Macrae, Fietch and Warren's offices are on Union Street. I left them, buzzing with energy, wanting to do something. I marched up the road to the side entrance to Central Station, found a phone and rang the Griffin. Bella answered.

'Aye?'

'Bella; it's . . . ah . . . Jimmy Hay,' I said, my mood of busy happiness evaporating instantly as I realised I didn't even know what name to use now.

Bella wheezed. 'Aw aye; that Jimmy Hay the Dan Weir?' She laughed bronchially. I was left, stunned and dismayed, unable to tell whether it really was all a big joke to her or she was being deliberately unkind.

'That's right,' I admitted quietly, as Bella's cackles subsided.

'Okay then, Jimmy; ye'll be wantin that boyfriend of mine Ah suppose, aye?'

'Eh?'

'Ma *boay*friend.' Bella wheezed and laughed at the same time. 'Haw, heid-the-baw,' I heard her say to somebody else, 'it's that big ugly guy wi the funny hoose.' I closed my eyes, wanted the ground to swallow me up. 'He's just cummin,' Bella said. 'Here he is noo.'

'Aye?' It was McCann.

'McCann?' I said, fearfully.

'Ah, it's yersel, is it?' McCann said.

'Yes,' I said, feeling foolish now, not knowing what to say. Ah; what the hell. 'Are you still talking to me?'

'Ah'm talkin tae ye noo, am Ah no?'

'I know, but are you still talking to me? You know what I mean. Are you mad at me? I mean angry?'

'Course Ah'm angry, but that doesnae mean Ah'm no talkin tae ye.'

'I'm not a real capitalist, McCann; I don't own any shares . . .'

'Aye, aye. Look; dinnae apologise to me, son; life's too short. Buy us a drink an Ah'll tell ye what a lyin basturt ye are.'

'Right! Stay there!' I said.

'No the noo,' McCann said, exasperated. 'Ah've got tae go fur ma check-up at the infirmary; Ah only came in fur a quick hauf on ma way; Ah wiz pittin on ma coat when ye rang.'

'When'll you be free?'

'Ach, they take ages; might be oors. Ah'll get back when Ah can, but probably no before five.'

'Okay, I'll see you then.'

'Right ye are, then.'

'Oh!' I said. 'McCann; do you know anything about Wee Tommy? I've put a note through his mum's door and told her to use my lawyer; I'll pay.' I wanted to bite my tongue.

McCann tutted. 'Aye, money talks, eh?' He sighed. 'Naw; I havnae heard anythin more. Ah heard the polis came tae see you, that right, aye?'

'Aye. Look, can you think of any other way of getting in touch with his mum and dad?'

'They might be at his auntie's. Ah'll call in; it's on ma way.'

'What, now?'

'Aye, if ye'll let me aff this fuckin phone . . .'

('Hi you; swear box!' Bella shouted in the background.)

('Aw, shut up, wumin,' McCann muttered.)

'That'd be great . . . or I could phone them,' I suggested.

'They're no *oan* the phone,' McCann said loudly. 'Noo will ye let me go? Ah'll have tae run if Ah'm tae see them an get tae ma appointment. Goodbye.'

'Take a taxi!' I yelled. 'I'll p. . .'

But he'd rung off.

I stood for a moment, holding the phone and remembering something about names . . . (The first time I'd met Wee Tommy, in the Griffin, I'd leaned to McCann and muttered, 'He's nearly the size of me; why's he called "Wee"?' and McCann had muttered back, 'His da was called Tommy, tae.' I must have looked puzzled. 'Couldn't they,' I said, 'have called him "Tam" instead?' McCann had just looked at me.)

Names; Wee Tommy . . . Jumping Jesus, he must have known all the time!

The policemen had asked for me by name. 'Daniel Weir?' they'd asked. That was what they'd said, and it didn't seem to mean anything special to them, I'd have known. But they knew my name, and the only people they seemed to have talked to had been Wee Tommy, his pal at the supermarket, and Wee Tommy's mum. So Wee Tommy must have told them. He'd known, or guessed, who I was.

I left the phone and wandered across the station concourse, grinning. I didn't know what to do next.

The big black electronic noticeboard flashed yellow with changing orders of departures. Intercities to London and Bristol, a slow train to Edinburgh (I didn't even *know* about that; I thought all the Edinburgh trains left from Queen Street), trains to Stranraer and Ayr and Largs and Wemyss Bay and Gourock . . . passing through Paisley.

The next Paisley train was at platform thirteen. It left in five minutes, according to the station clock. They operate something called the Open Station system here now; no ticket checkers at the barrier, you just walk onto a train, and pay the guard when he comes round if you haven't got a ticket.

Fifteen minutes later I was in Paisley, heading for Espedair Street.

Paisley had and hadn't changed. Busier with cars, maybe not quite so busy with people. Newer, brighter, sometimes different shops. A few higher buildings. I walked through the angled sunshine of a December's day, experiencing a strange mixture of elation and . . . I don't know what to call it; exalted bitterness seems closest. I sang to myself, inside my head, the songs I had heard the previous night, in the hotel, through the wall and through the years, remembering Christine's voice and the taste of her lips, the way she moved on stage and the touch of her body.

I walked and remembered, and I found I was humming a new tune, to the beat of my steps, and heard new words combine to fit the tune. And the words said:

> I thought this must be the end
> And never again we'd meet
> It's just I hadn't reckoned on
> Espedair Street
>
> It's the wrong side of the wrong side of the tracks
> The dead end just off Lonely Street
> It's where you go, after Desperation Row
> Espedair Street

And thought: Ha ha! As I walked to Espedair Street.

Which was a real disappointment, to be honest. They seemed to have knocked a few bits of it down, but I couldn't be sure which bits. It looked less homogeneous than I remembered, more mixed up and unsure of itself. There was a new pizza place just at

229

the Causeyside end; it looked out of place to me, something bright and plasticky from another age, another planet.

Across the other side of Causeyside Street was the Waterloo Bar, where Jean Webb and I had sat that day, twelve years before. It didn't seem to have changed much. I thought of going in for a drink, just for old times' sake, but didn't. I walked down Espedair Street instead, trying to remember which flat had been the Webbs'.

Just an ordinary street; low tenements, more modern low flats (I couldn't even remember if they had been here the last time; the street looked different), semis and detached houses, an old, derelict school, and a new snooker club in an old factory building. I turned around at the far end and started back, oddly deflated.

I tried to recapture the feeling of anticipatory joy I'd experienced that day I'd met Jean, or the sensation of sublimely resigned bliss I'd experienced, seven years later, after visiting her mother, walking down the same street under that stunning sky. Of course no echo of emotion sounded from either occasion.

I walked, humming my new tune, while the words said.

> You thought those times would never stop
> The glass would always be refilled
> You used to be right over the top
> But now you're just over the hill

I stood at the traffic lights on Canal Street. There was a man waiting on the other side, looking curiously at me. Suit, coat, briefcase; not the sort of person I'm used to having stare at me. It had been years since somebody recognised me in the street and let me know; an intensely embarrassing experience.

This man looked like he wanted to talk. I considered walking away down Canal Street, so I wouldn't pass him . . . but what the hell. The lights changed. We met in the middle of the road; he put one arm out, as though to stop me, put his head to one side and squinted with one eye. 'Dan Weir?' he said.

'Yes?' I said. He smiled broadly and put out his hand, shaking mine. 'Glen Webb; remember me?'

Jean's brother; the one who'd been in the army, if I was right. I nodded. 'Yes, of course.'

He glanced at his watch. 'You got time for a drink?' He half-turned, to head along with me. He seemed honestly pleased to see me.

I shrugged. 'Well, why not?'

We went to a new, overly plush bar called Corkers; subdued lighting and plump green upholstery. A fan on the ceiling; is this the new insignia of yuppie hangouts in Scotland? Isn't a place proper without a prop? I had a pint of export, ignoring the attractions of inferior British copies of anyway awful American lagers. Glen Webb had a non-alcoholic lager.

'Thought it was you. Hope you don't mind me accostin you in the street like that.'

'No, that's all right.' I said. 'Doesn't happen very often these days.'

'You retired now, aye?'

'Aye, sort of,' I said. I'd never thought of it like that, but he was right. 'What about you? You look prosperous.'

'Oh, I'm doin all right for myself. I'm working for a firm in Glasgow now; just on my way to do somebody's books.' He laughed, and I thought: wrong brother. This was the accountant who'd been in England. 'Well, this is a right surprise. I was just talkin to Jean about you the other day.'

'How is she?'

'Fine. A lot happier now she's settled down again.' He took a sip of his gassy lager. 'You knew she'd got divorced?'

'No,' I said, surprised. And, right there and then, before the words were fully out of his mouth, something inside me seemed to leap.

'Did you know Gerald? Her husband, did you?' Glen asked. I shook my head. 'Ah, well, he wasn't a bad guy really, but I think they just . . . drifted apart, you know? And then she found out he was seein this other woman . . .' He shrugged. 'All sorted out now. You knew they had a wee girl?'

'Dawn,' I said, pleased to be able to remember.

'Aye. Well, Jean and her live in . . .' He frowned. 'Damn me, I can never remember the name of the place . . .' And I was sure he was going to say 'Bahrain', or 'Adelaide' or something, but he didn't. 'Arsey? Harris-egg . . . something like that. I've got the address somewhere . . .' He reached down to his briefcase. 'Near Fort William; on the Road to the Isles.' He searched the briefcase for a few moments, then shook his head. 'Must have left it at the office. Never mind.'

'Arisaig?' I suggested. He snapped his fingers.

'The very place. Anyway; the two of them seem to be happy enough there. What about you? This you makin a sentimental journey, or what?'

'Yeah, I suppose I am,' I admitted.

'Aye, I always come up this way myself, just to look at my mum's old flat. Daft, isn't it? Doesn't even look the same since they were all renovated.'

'Aye, I know.' I supped my beer meditatively. 'Yeah, it is a bit daft.' We sat in silence for a moment. 'How's your mum?'

This time, I was sure the answer would be 'Dead', but I was wrong again. 'Ah, she's no too bad. She's in a wheelchair now; my aunt Marie looks after her.'

'Aye, she was in the wheelchair last time I saw her.'

'Of course, aye; she told me about that. Thinks you're wonderful.'

'What? Who does?'

'My mum. Oh God, aye; she thought it was great, you calling in like that. Her with a famous rock star in her wee flat, taking tea.' Glen laughed. I shook my head, looked down. This has been my Modesty Act for so long it's no longer an act. I felt the way I had when I'd just left her flat that time, the way I had at the far end of Espedair Street quarter of an hour earlier; saddened.

'Whereabouts you livin these days?'

'Oh, I . . . move around a lot. I'm in Glasgow, just now,' I said, lying, and wondering why I lied.

'Ah, well, if you're ever moving around in the Highlands, you should drop in and see Jean. She'd appreciate it. Still talks about you a lot. You've got a couple of fans there, her and wee Dawn.'

'Really?' I tried to make it sound self-deprecating without making it sound insulting to them. I busied myself with my glass. My heart was misbehaving. This was absurd.

'Aw, aye,' Glen said, smiling. 'Great to be famous, eh?'

I agreed it was, most of the time. We spent another five or ten minutes talking about other old friends we had in common, and people we'd gone to school with, until Glen looked at his watch and started draining his lager. I finished my pint. 'I've got to go,'

Glen said, taking up his briefcase. 'Here;' he handed me his card. 'Give us a ring if you want Jean's address . . . or my mum's; you're always sure of a cup of tea there.'

'Thanks.' We went to the door. A light shower had started outside, and we stood on the pavement, under an awning, while Glen dug into his briefcase for a small umbrella. I looked up and down the street.

'Aye, you'll see a few changes in the old town, I suppose.'

There were actually fairly few in sight from where we stood, but I knew what he meant. I nodded. 'Aye. There weren't any places like this here then,' I looked back at the bar we'd just left. 'The Waterloo doesn't seem to have changed much, though . . . not from the outside, anyway.'

Glen Webb unsheathed the little Knirps and fiddled with it. 'That your old watering hole, was it?'

'No,' I said. '. . . I think the only time I was in there was once with Jean; I was celebrating because we'd got our first advance. Practically kidnapped her to get her to have a drink with me.'

'Oh, God.' Glen grinned, opening the umbrella. 'You wouldn't have needed to kidnap that lassie.' He nudged me with one elbow. 'If that was the time she told me about, she was nearly asking you to take her with you.'

Did I stare? I don't know. I looked at the man, and listened to the traffic roar. 'Aye,' Glen chuckled, 'you'd a narrow escape there.' He held his hand out again. We shook hands. 'See you again, sometime, Dan. Give us a ring. Take care now.'

'You t-too . . . goodbye.' I said.

Glen Webb walked off into the bright drizzle. I stood, brows furled, thinking furiously.

I walked back to Gilmour Street, over glistening pavements, under slowly darkening skies, wondering if I was stupid enough to do what I was thinking of doing.

McCann was sitting with a half and a half in front of him when I strode through the doors of the Griffin. 'Oh fuck, it's Bill Haley. Ye want a drink?' McCann stood up.

'A pint of heavy,' I said. I rolled my eyes. 'Bill Haley,' I snorted.

'A pint of your finest heavy beer for Zippy Stardust here,

Bella,' McCann said. I didn't bother to ask whether it was a deliberate mistake. 'Well you're lookin pleased wi yersel,' he told me. McCann's forehead was not a pretty sight, but I'd seen him with worse damage.

'Come and sit with me a minute, McCann,' I said. McCann looked at me oddly.

'Your check-up all right?' I asked once we'd sat down.

'Right as rain. They asked me aboot this, mind.' McCann pointed to his bruised, cut head.

'What did you tell them?'

'Ah said the wife fell down the stairs.'

'The *wife* fell down the stairs?' (Apart from anything else, McCann is a widower.)

'Aye; on top of me.' McCann winked.

I shook my head. 'What about Wee Tommy?'

'Ah found his maw and paw; they were at his auntie's right enough. In a right state. Ah gave them that number, of yur lawyers. They were very grateful. Wee Tommy's in court Thursday; Ah called in again on the way back from the hospital an his dad wiz back an sayin according tae yur lawyers they think they can get him oot on bail. That okay?'

'Perfect. I'd come along on Thursday, but I might not be here. I'm leaving; probably just a holiday, but I'm going tonight. Or tomorrow morning, anyway.'

McCann didn't look surprised. 'Aw aye? Where aboots ye goin?'

I took a deep breath. 'Arisaig.'

There are times when you can't do the sensible thing, when you can't act like a responsible adult at all; you just have to do whatever insane thing comes into your head. When bad people do it they end up murderers, when good people do it they end up heroes, and when the rest of us do it we end up looking like total idiots. But when's that ever stopped us?

I'd got the train back to Glasgow Central, couldn't see the shuttle bus for Queen Street, judged it would take ten minutes for me to get to the front of the taxi queue, so walked the quarter mile. There were only two trains a day to Arisaig on a Tuesday, and I'd just missed the last one – the 1650 to Mallaig – by five minutes. I'd stared down at the empty tracks, fuming.

Then I calmed down and tried to think rationally – however inappropriate that might have been, given my current state of mind. I was crazy doing this anyway, but I was totally mad to think about going right now. I had to see McCann; I'd agreed to meet him, and I still didn't know what was happening about Wee Tommy. There were a couple of other things I had to do as well.

I went to see when the next train was and picked up a time-table. 0550 tomorrow; ten to six in the morning, for God's sake; a sleeper from London. I bought a ticket and booked a seat (first class; old habits die hard). Due in to Arisaig at 1118. I got myself a cheapo digital watch in the station and set the alarm for 5 a.m. It seemed like a long time to wait. I had a horrible feeling I'd talk myself out of it by then.

Oh heck, might as well go the whole hog . . .

I ran to Macrae, Fietch and Warren's again, had the reception-ist ring the Griff to say I'd be there in half an hour, and caught Mr Douglas before he left the office.

'I *beg* your pardon, Mr Weir?' he said when I told him what I wanted to do. He'd gone a bit pale.

'It's perfectly simple,' I told him, still breathing hard from the run. 'Let's get my Will out and we can have it drawn up from that in five minutes.'

It took twenty, and Mr Douglas frowned when we took out the bit about being of sound mind, but it was done.

'I cannot believe, Mr Weir,' old Douglas said, adding weight to his words by the slow removal of his half-moon glasses, 'that you are not going to regret this . . . hasty decision.'

'I'm sure I shall,' I agreed, feeling pompous. 'But it has to be done.'

Mr Douglas just sighed. He'd refused to do it at all (referring to my 'excited and agitated state') at first; we compromised by dat-ing it for the following day, to give me time to change my mind. I signed it and caught a taxi to the Griff.

'*Whit?*' McCann said.

I jangled the keys under his nose. 'It's yours. Take them. I've kept the Holland Street key because I'm going to stay there the night. As of tomorrow; all yours.' (Technically a lie, but what the hell.)

'You fuckin crazy?' McCann had never looked so puzzled, or so worried (not even in Monty's).

'McCann, I've been crazy for years; you know that. Will you take the goddamn keys?'

McCann drank from his beer glass, looking sideways at the keys in my hand. He shook his head. 'Naw; Ah want tae know whit's goan on.'

'McCann,' I said, despairing, 'it's perfectly simple; I've had some very bad and . . . maybe, some very good news, over the last couple of days. I came close to killing myself . . . or I think I came close . . . But even then I was,' I waved my hands in the air, jangling the keys, 'I was of sound mind. I still am, and I'm going to go over the hills and far away, to see an old friend who may or may well not be pleased to see me but I've got to see her . . . and, anyway, I need to make a break, I need to get away from myself. I've seen my lawyer and what's going to happen is it's going to be as if I had died; I've signed a document which more or less has the same effect as my Will; all the money goes.

'You get the folly and everything in it. Do whatever you want with it. At the moment everything in the folly includes a pigeon, and you've got to make sure it gets out somehow, also there may be some tapes and stuff like that, and a few personal things, but otherwise it's all yours. Also, I want you to see a woman called Betty gets in touch with my lawyers too. She'll turn up at the folly; you'll know her.

'I'm getting the early train tomorrow and for all I know I might be on the next one back, in which case I'll see you in here tomorrow and we'll both go to court on Thursday; or I might be away longer. It depends. All I'm asking you to do is keep in touch with my lawyers to check out what happens with Wee Tommy, and take the keys of the folly.'

I held the keys out again. McCann glared suspiciously at me. 'Please, McCann,' I said. 'Don't do this to me. I know I don't deserve it; I lied to you and I'm sorry . . . but please, please take the keys. It's important to me.'

McCann put his glass down. He looked at the keys in my hand, then into my eyes. He took the keys from me, eyes narrowing.

'If this is a joke, Ah'll break your fuckin neck, pal.'

I sat back laughing, but with a niggling worry in the pit of my belly, thinking about Glen Webb, and wondering at what might be my own absurd gullibility. 'If this is a joke,' I told McCann, thinking of the wild coasts beyond Arisaig, 'you probably won't need to.'

And so I sat in the Griffin bar with my friend McCann, and after a few drinks it was almost as it always had been, and we talked and laughed and I told him a little about my previous life, and I don't think he believed me when I told him how much money there was, or where it was going (but he approved, in theory), and I reassured him I wasn't going to be broke, even though the future royalties from all the old stuff would be distributed as well. A gentleman called Mr Richard Tumber was going to get a phone-call in a day or two which would delight and amaze him. I'd make a new record, but I was starting from nothing again; I needed an advance.

We left, and McCann went home and I went back to St Jute's and tried to sleep but couldn't, so sat up, in my high tower, on a vigil in which I looked out over part of the city and part of my life, remembering and regretting and re-living and sometimes smiling to myself, and realised that there were an awful lot of things in my life I hadn't got round to, and killing myself was just another one of them, and knew that I was doing a foolish thing, but that sometimes only foolish things worked.

In fact I was doing two foolish things, which is exactly one more than you're ever allowed to get away with at the same time . . . but that couldn't be helped, because both giving it all away, and going off on an absurd, naïve, immaturely romantic and probably doomed quest for an old love were *required*; they were the only possible things I could think of which might get me out of the rut, the inwardly spiralling groove I seemed to have been in for the past few years. So I had burned my bridges and I was leaping before I'd looked and I was already anticipating repenting at leisure. What am I doing? I asked myself.

Espedair Street. I worked on the song through the night, verse and chorus, not using a guitar or the keyboards but just singing it to myself in my head and gradually working it out. I wrote the words down on the back of Glen Webb's card, in tiny, tiny writing.

It wasn't really Espedair Street or Ferguslie Park or anywhere you could point to on a map; it was somewhere of a different sort, an amalgam of places and feelings and times, and a place only I knew about. The song was finished before it was time for me to go.

I left a saucer of milk and some crumbled bread and biscuits out for the pigeon, then went down to the crypt and gathered up the back-up master tape of all the songs and music I'd been working on over the past year or so. I should really have told McCann I might want to come back and use the studio for a wee while, but I'd forgotten. Maybe I could rent the place from him for a few weeks. Whatever. Not to worry.

I trimmed my beard and cut my hair. I stopped and thought for a minute, then found an old canvas bag and stuffed a few spare clothes into it. Taking the shooting stick/umbrella seemed like a good idea, too; I'd carry that. A bottle of blue Stolichnaya nestled into the clothes in the canvas bag, looking quite at home. Emergency rations.

I took a last look round the old place, feeling happy and sad and full of hope and dread all at once, then left by the Holland Street door and put the key back through the letterbox. It was a fresh, cold, dark morning and I walked quickly to Queen Street to catch the train.

The train left on time, its diesel loco chugging into the tunnel heading north out of Queen Street. We moved through the dark city, past housing schemes and old factories and stagnant canals to the suburbs, curving west towards the north bank of the river, which we neared after the city dropped behind. I saw the lights of the Erskine Bridge, near where I'd stood hitching in the rain, two days earlier. The lights of cars moved on the motorway on the Clyde's far bank.

The carriages were old; the train used steam heating, and the smell of it, damply warm and enveloping, filled me with an odd mixture of longing and contentment.

Between Dumbarton and Helensburgh, with the lights of Greenock glittering on the far side of the river, I looked back and saw the first hint of dawn in the clear skies over Glasgow.

The train climbed into the hills; Loch Long was dark, its mountains tree-lined. Navigation lights winked as the young day went from grey to steely-blue. We crossed over to the shores of Loch Lomond between Arrochar and Tarbet. The train laboured out of Arrochar & Tarbet station, percussive voice echoing in the hills, and we rumbled past the hotel I'd stayed in the night before. It was this train, twenty-four hours earlier, that had woken me.

The loch was blue, smooth, quiet under the line of mountains.

I passed a while singing 'Girl On A Train', and humming 'Chattanooga Choo-Choo' and 'Sentimental Journey', trying to remember the words.

Rannoch Moor was a desert of snow. The train startled a herd of forty or more deer, brown–black shapes leaping and running across the white. I went to the buffet, where the smell of steam was even stronger, and ate a bacon sandwich and drank a can of beer. Back at my seat I nibbled at a chocolate biscuit and watched as frozen Loch Trieg appeared way below us; the train slowly descended the mountainside to meet it. The sky was clouding over.

Ben Nevis stood lumplike, still mostly visible, over Fort William. I got out while the train waited in the town's station, ate a pie in the station buffet and bought a newspaper.

The train set out again, heading out the way it had come in, before swinging left for Mallaig. It crossed the Caledonian canal, then swept and wound its way along lochsides and through the hills and the tunnels and over viaducts and bridges, until – suddenly – there was a sea loch, shores matted with weed, waters diced and parcelled with the floating structures of a fish farm.

The line wiggled and twisted through a neck of land, then, in the midst of tumbled rock and tall, crowding trees set in dark flowerless masses of rhododendron bushes, the sea appeared, its horizon bordered by far masses of cliffs and mountains. I felt ashamed that I couldn't tell whether I was looking at islands in the distance, or parts of the mainland.

Then Arisaig at last, under high grey clouds and a fresh north wind. I'd been humming the new song to myself for parts of the journey, but now it suddenly changed and I found myself humming 'Cry About You':

Must have been the cold north wind
Blew some rain into my eyes,
Must have been an old smoke ring,
Won't you ever realise?
– You ought to know
– I'd never go
And cry about you

Superstition. Rabbits' feet, blue blankets; a rosary. Something
to hold onto and make you feel you weren't completely alone after
all. So my song was my comfort and my heart was knocking at the
door of my ribs like it wanted to get out, and I found a phonebox
in the village and rang Glen Webb's office in Glasgow to get his
sister's address, only to find he wasn't in that day and they didn't
know where to get in touch with him.

I went to the nearest hotel and sat in the public bar, wondering
what to do next. I asked the barman if he knew Jean Webb, but
he didn't. This was a small village and I found it ominous. What
if Glen Webb had got the name wrong? Why hadn't I waited,
done some checking, for God's sake?

According to the timetable I'd picked up in Glasgow, there was
a train – the same one, turned round, I guessed – leaving Mallaig
at twenty-past twelve. It'd be here eighteen minutes later . . . but
it would only take me as far as Fort William. Shit.

I ought to get on it anyway. This wasn't working out. I was a
crazy man. I shouldn't be here; I'd done an insane thing and
given everything I ever owned away, and I should get the hell
down to London *now* and tell Tumber I was going to make
another album and could I have lots of money *immediately*?

But maybe it was just fear. I knew I wanted to see her. Even if
it was only for an hour, just a few minutes, I had to see her, just to
say . . . oh God, what? I nearly asked you to come away with me a
dozen years ago? I'm a lunatic who at the moment is totally
penniless apart from what I've got in my pockets and some plastic
money I can't afford to use and don't qualify for any more, so
please let me stay with you, I'm very good with children, honest?

Insane, insane, insane. And how likely was it she was . . .
unattached? Just her and an eight year old who'd probably take
one look at me and run screaming. It didn't seem likely. She must

240

have come here for a reason; some huge, quiet, kind Highland man with a soft voice and hard hands . . . Jesus, I could almost see him now . . .

But I still wanted to see her. I'd come here; I couldn't just turn back. Besides, she might hear I was here, after all; they can't get many six-six monsters stopping off in Arisaig in the middle of winter. And how would she feel if she knew I'd been here and not come to see her, if Glen was right about her being pleased to see me? But I knew it wasn't going to work; you just can't do things like this and get away with it. So why not leave now, with the dream at least still intact, so that you'll never know whether it might just have worked? Wouldn't that be salvaging something? Isn't that where the smart money would go? God, impossible to know what to do. I reached into the coat pocket where my change was. My fingers closed round a coin.

I thought, *If it's heads, I'll stay here and look for her. If it's tails, I'll get up now and go to the station. Train to Fort William then train tomorrow – or even taxi if they'll take me that far – to Glasgow; London and Rick before teatime.*

Heads I stay, tails I go.

I brought the coin out; it was a fifty pence piece. And it was tails.

I put it back in my pocket, in with the rest of the change. I finished my drink and took up my bag and took the glass back to the bar.

One thing about not knowing what to do, and tossing a coin to decide, having made up your mind you'll definitely do whatever the coin says: it sure as hell lets you know what you really want to do, if it says the wrong thing.

I left the bag with the barman, booked a room for the night and I went to the local post office, to ask where Jean Webb lived.

'Och aye; Mrs Keiller, aye, she said her maiden name was Webb.' The old lady in the post office seemed to be quite used to having hulking, brutish strangers ask after local women. 'She has the one wee lassie, that's right.'

'Yes, Dawn,' I said, still desperate to prove I knew them and I wasn't some homicidal sex maniac come to rape and murder them both. The old lady didn't seem bothered in the least.

'Aye, that's her name. They've a house at Back of Keppoch.'

'Is that far?'

'Och, no; just over the headland. A mile, perhaps.' The old lady looked at the clock above the counter. 'Of course, she'll be at work right now.'

'Oh.' What had I been thinking of? It hadn't occurred to me she'd be working. Idiot.

'Aye, Mrs Keiller works in the office at the fish farm, at Lochailort. Do you know where that is? You'll have passed it on your way.'

'Um, yes . . .'

'Here, I'll show you on the map.'

I bought the map in the end. Mrs Gray – Elsie – said if I wanted I could phone the fish farm from there, if it was urgent. I declined the offer. I'd go to Jean's when she got back from work.

I sat in the bar, gazing out to the rocky confines of the sea loch beyond the roofs of Arisaig, sipping export shandies, because the last thing I wanted to be, when I saw Jean, was drunk.

I am a sentimental man, a weak man, a pliable man, and nobody is better at twisting me round their little finger than I am.

I am totally selfish, even when I'm being selfless. I give everything away, I come up here on a hopeful, hopeless mission of the heart, seeming to give all for love, but I'm not really. I've come here for, at the very least, absolution. I want Jean to confess me, to say that it's all all right, that I'm not really a bad man, that the last twelve, thirteen years haven't been wasted; oh God, she's not going to say, Stay with me and be my love, but she might put her hands on my poor fevered brow, she might let me kiss the ring. Absolution; forgiveness, hail Jean, full of grace . . .

We are all selfish. Sell up and go to the slums of Calcutta, work with lepers in the jungle . . . at my most cynical I ask whether even such things are not selfish, because it is easier for you to live with yourself having done that, knowing you have done all you could, rather than suffer the cramps of conscience. Throw yourself on the grenade; you do so knowing you are the hero, and there will be no more times when the terror of death might make you turn and flee.

But maybe I'm just a bad, cynical man.

So, Weird goes looking for his old love. Surrender. It looks like adventure but really it's hiding. Ah, Jayzuz, the ways we invent to get away from our responsibilities.

The only thinking animal on the goddamn planet, and what do we spend most of our time trying not to do?

Correct.

We join armies, we enter monasteries or nunneries, we adopt the party line, we believe what we read in ancient books or shit newspapers or what we're told by plastic politicians, and all we're ever trying to do is give somebody else the responsibility for thinking. Let us enter this order, obey that one; never mind we end up being told to massacre or torture or simply believe the most absurd thing we've ever heard; at least it's not all our fault.

Nothing to do with us, John; we just did what we was told . . .

And Love; isn't that just another route to the same thing?

I did it for the wife and kids. That's what it's all about isn't it, I mean? Sacrifice; work hard . . .

Ah, God, it's better than outright selfishness, spending all the money, beating the wife and terrorising the weans, but amn't I just using something similar to get away from my own responsibilities? Simulating my own financial death through a legal trick, going off on this ridiculous adventure . . . playing, just playing. Looking for a way out, a way back to the cradle and the milk-wet breast.

Who am I trying to kid?

(Answers on a postcard, please, to . . .)

The winter afternoon darkened.

I ate in the hotel, studying my newly bought map, humming my new tune and playing around with it. The map showed there was a walk round the coast from Arisaig to Back of Keppoch. I thought about taking that route to the address Mrs Gray had given me, but it was getting dark and I'd probably break my neck falling over some cliff. That would be ironic; putting my Will into effect while still alive and then dying the next day.

I'd take the main road and risk getting run over by a car instead.

I got to Jean's house just after four. It was new, a bungalow, one of about half a dozen under a group of pines, looking out over a curved beach and a rocky bay to the Sound of Sleat and the distant mountains of Skye.

The house was dark. I sat down on a wall, to wait. I hoped

there was nobody else in any of the other houses, a couple of which had lights on, who'd look out and see me sitting there . . . then felt annoyed with myself, for being so easily embarrassed, so prone to guilt. I put my chin in my hand and tried to ponder the links between guilt and embarrassment.

I decided I wasn't smart enough to figure it out, not right now, anyway. But is there a song in it? That was the question. Never mind was there any truth in it; was there a song?

No idea. I sat on the wall and I sang silent songs to myself.

A car came along the road, lights bright in the gloaming. It stopped outside the house. Faces looked towards me. Somebody got out on the far side. I heard people talking, in the car. The person on the far side was talking to the driver and somebody else inside. I heard a young, female voice say, 'Wait a minute, then.'

A young girl walked round the car. Slim, dark, short haired; schoolbag, uniform. She walked right up to me, lifted her face to mine (I'd slid off the wall). 'Excuse me, are you Mr Weir?'

'Ah . . . I . . . yes.' Surprise. How did she know? It took a second or two for me to realise this must be Dawn. 'Are you . . .'

'Dawn. Pleased to meet you.' She put out her hand. I shook it; it felt tiny and fragile and warm. Dawn; her grandmother had described her as 'bright'. I smiled, remembering. She turned back to the car. 'It is; it's a friend of my mum's.'

'Right you are, Dawn. See you tomorrow.'

'Aye. Thank you; good night,' the girl said.

The car drove off. Dawn turned back to me. 'Would you like a cup of tea, Mr Weir?'

'Call me Daniel, please,' I said, inside the house. Dawn had made tea. She poked at the banked-up coal fire.

'All right. Would you excuse me a minute?' She went back through the kitchen. I sat, holding my cup of tea. The living room was a little bare, but warm. The house still smelled new; paint, new carpets. TV and video and hi-fi; a home computer on a shelf beside the TV. I saw these things with a sense of relief; they didn't seem too badly off, even though the room did have that vague air of containing only half the contents of another room, in another house, somewhere else.

Dawn came back struggling with a huge wicker basket full of

chopped logs. I managed to put my teacup down without spilling any and jumped up to help her, far too late, as usual. 'Oh, thanks,' she said, as I helped her lower the basket to the hearth-side. She chucked a couple of logs on to the fire. 'Mum should be back in a wee while. How's your tea?'

'It's fine,' I said, sitting down again. Dawn sat down too, straight-backed, in a seat. She was thinner than I'd expected, especially about the face. I tried to remember what her father had looked like but had only the vaguest impression, and even that somehow included a pair of overalls, whereas the one time I'd met him he'd been wearing a suit.

Dawn was looking at me. There was an uncanny sense of calm, almost serenity about her. It made me uncomfortable.

'How did you know it was me?' I asked her, breaking a silence only I seemed to find awkward.

'Mum described you,' she said. 'She's got all your records,' she added. 'You haven't made any recently, have you?'

'No, not for a while.'

'Why's that?'

I opened my mouth to speak, then couldn't. I closed it again. I put my cup down, suddenly consumed by a ridiculous urge to cry. I coughed and cleared my throat. 'That's a very good question,' I said. 'I think it was because I was . . . fed up. Fed up with . . . recording, with music.' The urge to cry vanished as quickly as it had appeared. I sat there, looking at this calm, self-possessed kid, and felt about three years old. I shrugged. 'I don't know,' I admitted.

'Oh,' she said, politely, and sipped her tea. A car engine sounded outside: Dawn got up and left the room. Lights swung over the closed curtains of the living room. My heart started misbehaving again, thumping madly. Great; I was going to have a heart attack just sitting here. That should make for interesting legal complications if anybody contested the Will.

I heard the outside door open. I stood up, smoothed back my hair. Footsteps. Then, 'Hello, honey . . .'

'Mum . . .'

'Mmwah' (the pronounced noise of a quick kiss). 'Look, can you put that lasagne in the microwave? I said I'd help decorate the hall; I've got to . . . What is it? What? Through . . . ?'

I cleared my throat. Jean came through the door into the room, looking puzzled, and a little concerned. I smiled, gave an awkward sort of wave with both hands, jerking them out from my body once, then back again. 'Hello . . . Jean.'

'Daniel . . .' She put her scarf and bag down on a chair, came up to me. 'Hello.' She laughed, hugged me. I hugged her back, smelling the perfume of her dark coat and her short, still wildly curly brown hair; a few tiny threads of silver in it now. She drew back, still holding my arms. Her face was a little fuller than I remembered, but it seemed to have matured, rather than aged. 'What are *you* doing here?'

Dawn sidled in through the door, looking bashful.

'I was nearby . . . I thought I'd drop in . . .' I said, and felt a quiet moment of despair, that the first thing I'd said to her was a lie.

She laughed, shaking her head, brought a handkerchief out of one jumper cuff, put it to her nose. 'Sorry.' She sneezed. 'I've a cold.' She looked up, eyes bright, shook her head again and said, 'Oh, this is good; it's so good to see you again. How are you? What have you been doing? Have you eaten yet? I've got to dash out . . . or you could . . .' She turned round to look at Dawn, leaning her back against the far wall, looking and not looking at us. 'Has Dawn . . .?'

'Dawn's given me some tea,' I said. 'I . . . I heard you say something about . . .'

'The hall.' Jean turned back to me. 'We're putting up the decorations tonight, for the dance tomorrow. Why don't you come along?' She patted me in the ribs with the back of her hand. 'You're just the height to reach up into the corners.' Before I could reply, she turned to Dawn. 'You want to come, love?'

Dawn shook her head, smiling shyly, and looked down. 'Homework,' she said. 'My turn to go to Alison's.'

So we dropped Dawn at another house and headed towards the local community hall, in the village, in Jean's car. 'I thought you must have a car. You're not travelling by train, are you?'

'Um . . . yes, yes, I am.'

'What, just you? I thought you'd have managers and minders and groupies and hangers-on and . . .'

'No, just me.'

'Well, it's great to see you again. Are you going to stay? We've got a spare room.'

'Umm . . . well, I thought I might. I did ask them to book me a room at the hotel.'

'What?' She sounded slightly shocked, almost insulted and thoroughly amused, all at the one time. 'Oh, we can't have that. If you don't stay with us people'll think we don't wash the sheets or something.'

'Well, I thought people might . . .'

But then we were there, and the car was parked. The sunset was really over, but a thunderously deep stain of red still lay across the furthest limit of the western sky. I looked out to it for a moment. Skye was somewhere out there, more felt than seen.

'Bonny place, isn't it?'

'Aye, it is that.' I looked at her. 'What brought you out here?'

'Friends,' she said, 'I know people here. What brought you?'

'Oh . . . I wanted to see you.'

She was silent for a moment. 'Very good,' she said, and I could almost smell her nodding more than I could see her. 'Good. Right; come on in to the body of the kirk.'

We walked towards the village hall. 'Hope people don't mind me showing up . . .' I said.

'Why should they?' she said.

'I don't know. I worry about just . . . turning up.'

'Thank God you have. I'm a terrible blether, Daniel. I told people I knew you and I think they've been waiting for you to appear for about a year now. I was getting ready to explain that I only knew this famous rock star *fairly* well.' She squeezed my arm briefly as we went up the steps into the hall. 'And don't worry about staying with us; I've been trying to cultivate a reputation as a wicked woman and you're the first real chance I've had.'

I didn't get a chance to catch her expression as she said this, or say anything else, because then we were in the hall, bright with lights and full of people standing on tables and chairs, and full of tables and chairs anyway, and people were trailing coloured streamers and long unconcertinaed lengths of glittering decorations and pinning up puffballs of Santa Clauses and snowmen and twirling pointed stars, and there was a wee boy on a trike who was pedalling furiously round the place, in the open spaces of the wooden floor, tearing past people and ducking under tables and skidding round chairs, and people were laughing and shouting and throwing packets of drawing pins and reels of sticky tape about and music was playing.

I was introduced to a variety of people whose names I instantly forgot, and told where to hold up decorations. I did as I was told and then couldn't find anything else to do, as all the high decorations were put up, and so I just stood, I suppose, looking a little confused, in the midst of all this work and effort and hilarity and the wee boy whizzing round on his bike.

'Here; sit down out the way , Daniel,' Jean said, pointing me at a chair. 'You look confused.'

'It's funny; I come out here to the wilds and the wilderness, and I'm surrounded with all these *people*.' I laughed.

'Not put off, I hope?' She stood, arms crossed, looking down at me; indulgent, amused . . . and I don't know what else.

I rested one arm on a table by my side. 'No; not put off.'

'Can we tempt you to stay over Christmas . . . maybe even Hogmanay?' Her voice was a little lower, a little more measured than it had been.

I looked up at her. 'Oh . . . yes. Of course; Christmas . . . New Year . . .' I nodded. 'Yes. That would be . . . if you don't . . .'

'We'd love to have you. How long can you stay?'

I shook my head. 'Well . . . I don't know. I'll . . . Look, just . . . I mean . . . as soon as . . . I mean I might . . .' I couldn't even think what it was I wanted to say, let alone start trying to say it. 'Oh,' I said, leaning back on the table, temporarily exhausted by the effort of it all. 'Kick me out when you want.'

'Daniel,' she said, smiling very seriously and shaking her head, 'I wouldn't kick you out of anything.' Then she went back to help with the decorations.

I leant my elbow on the table again, and felt it tip. I looked down at one of the legs. I patted my pockets, looking for a wedge. I found a piece of plastic, cracked it in half and slid it underneath the leg, steadying it.

It was only after I'd sat up again and done a double-take and looked down that I realised what I'd used was my platinum Amex card . . . I swear.

*　　*　　*

248

I look up again, laughing quietly to myself. The wean on the trike races past.

They've tied great long lengths of different coloured paper streamers to the back of the wee boy's bicycle. He's still speeding round and round the hall, past people and between sets of chairs, head down and pedalling as hard as he can, but now he's got a long, swirling train of colour streaming after him.

On the tape machine somebody is playing the Northumbrian Pipes, and in the midst of that simple, tootling, jigging music, I'm sitting back, rubbing my bristly chin and feeling happy again, and wondering if it'll last, and watching the bairn on the trike, the streamers flowing behind him like a rainbow wake, whizzing round and round and round.

Futura now offers an exciting range of quality fiction
and non-fiction by both established and new authors.
All of the books in this series are available from good
bookshops, or can be ordered from the following
address:

Futura Books
Cash Sales Department
P.O. Box 11
Falmouth
Cornwall TR10 9EN.

Please send cheque or postal order (no currency), and
allow 60p for postage and packing for the first book plus
25p for the second book and 15p for each additional
book ordered up to a maximum charge of £1.50 in U.K.

B.F.P.O. customers please allow 60p for the first book,
25p for the second book plus 15p per copy for the next
7 books, thereafter 9p per book.

Overseas customers including Eire please allow £1.25
for postage and packing for the first book, 75p for the
second book and 28p for each subsequent title ordered.

Futura